PARISH!

"Originally, the format was that we'd have these groups, but from there, you'd go out and do other things, parish things," said Johanna Cavallaro, a member of the same group as Kennedy. Cavallaro gives her time to a variety of parish ministries, especially helping the elderly, and the groups have nurtured a similar sense of mission in other members as well. "People have gotten more involved in whatever interests them," Cavallaro said.

Patterson, a member of another group, created and spends long hours running the Ministry of Winter Grace, which provides for the needs of the elderly—such as food shopping, telephone calls to check on their well-being, and help in preparing Medicaid forms. Her membership in the small Christian community, she said, has enriched that commitment because of the group's constant reflection on the Gospel. "I really feel for me, personally, it's what Jesus is calling me to in my life."

That group, which meets twice a month at Agnes Kickham's home, has helped Patterson with Winter Grace, and they provide service in other ways. "I have witnessed in this group enough response to need to know that if any need came up in the parish, we would be the first to do it," said one member, Deacon Bill Byrne.

Sensing that willingness to help, people outside the group call to ask for the group's prayers. "It's getting around that we do have this sense of mission," Kickham said. "We're touching other people's lives."

With Patterson and Mary Kennedy as coordinators, the groups that resulted from Halligan's work are still using the formats that she developed for reflection on Scripture. Kennedy would like to see those groups growing, but she understands why they are not. "I really think that at St. Brigid's there are just too many things for people to be involved in," she said. "There's not enough time."

—☗—

Though the groups that specifically call themselves small Christian communities may not be growing, other small groups keep developing—such as the young mothers' prayer groups, a men's group that started from an in-home retreat led by Gaeta, and a new group that grew from the family life ministry committee.

Each month, the family life ministry committee meets to plan the family mass and other liturgies. "We found that in discussing liturgy that we needed more time to spiritualize the experience and to discuss the Gospels," said Estelle Peck, the director of liturgy and family life. "We never had the time in the format of that meeting."

Then some of the women from the committee experienced an in-home retreat, led by Gaeta. "Out of that flowed this very natural desire to continue to pray together," said one committee member, Maggie McCartin. So they decided to meet regularly as a prayer group.

One month, the group met at the home of Meg Nix. Early in the evening, she had to leave the room to take a phone call. Nix and her husband, Chris, were adopting a baby from China. The phone call was from another prospective adoptive parent, who was about to travel to China with them. The news from the adoption agency was bad: The process had ground to a halt. Nix returned to the prayer group, stricken. "I could barely even talk," she recalled.

"She was so distressed that the most natural thing in the world was to lift this to God," McCartin said. So they spent the rest of the evening praying for Nix and her husband. "The most wonderful feeling came out of it, because we sat and held each other's hands and prayed out loud together," Nix said. "The Spirit was here with us, for sure."

Not long after that, the bureaucratic snarls ended. On Good Friday, the Nixes left for China. "Father Frank sent us off," Nix said. "He just had the entire congregation praying over us." On June 2, 1996, at the family mass, Gaeta baptized Grayce Marie Nix and marched through the church, holding her up proudly to present her to the community.

Once the Nixes had adopted Grayce Marie, the other women in the prayer group felt a real sense of participation. "It's a very beautiful spiritual bond that we share," said McCartin, who was in the sanctuary with the Nixes at the baptism.

McCartin's husband, John Castellano, became part of a men's prayer group in much the same way as his wife did: after an in-home retreat that Gaeta led. "Seven or eight people felt, let's continue," Castellano said. The group meets every other week. Castellano can't make every meeting, but Lou Marchesi, Peter Haarmann, Eliot Freedman, and Jose Renter are the group's constant backbone.

"We talk about the Scriptures," Castellano said. "What are they saying to us, and probably more importantly, what has our experience been since we last met? Has God been present, or has God been absent, or some combination?"

Men often find sharing about personal issues off-putting. But Castellano said the men in his group freely discuss such problems as aging relatives, struggles with children, and stresses in the marriage and at work. "It's bringing us to our world in a more grounded fashion," Castellano said.

—ᙏ—

Another small-group effort in the parish has been the Renew program, which has produced many small communities in other areas. Renew is a spiritual renewal process, divided into five six-week seasons, each with a theme for reflection.

The Renew movement places strong emphasis on small community development. "I've believed in small communities for fifty years now, since I was a kid," said Monsignor Thomas Kleissler, who launched the movement in 1978 in the Archdiocese of Newark and is now director of Renew International. "The reason it made sense is it got religion out into everyday life."

As the national study seems to show, people who have been through Renew often remain in permanent small communities. "By far, the greatest number in the country have come from Renew," Kleissler said. But at St. Brigid's, which finished its fifth Renew season in 1996, it is too early to tell. Some Renew groups showed signs of becoming permanent. Others did not.

The program drew people from all over Long Island, which posed geographical obstacles to continuity. And it focused on young adults, whose lives are by definition in flux. "Every season, you had to get used to a whole new group of people," said Jennifer Gallagher, who runs the parish's youth ministries and led one of the Renew groups. "That kind of prevented any kind of long-term group relationship from happening" in her group.

One member of another Renew group, Joe Corvi, is a case in point. Like many others, Corvi discovered the Renew process at St. Brigid's, even though he lives outside the parish, in Bayside. "I was praying for about a year and a half to find a prayer group," Corvi said. A friend told him about Renew at St. Brigid's.

Corvi has not become part of a permanent group. "I've been in all different groups and had all different people," Corvi said. Still, Renew has worked on other levels. "My best friends are now from St. Brigid's," he said. "I've seen a lot of great things happen through it. I really feel the Holy Spirit works there."

Corvi's experience is typical of the yearning for the support of a small community that lies behind the whole movement. In his book *Small Christian Communities: A Vision of Hope*, Monsignor Kleissler described a 1986 Vatican study of new religious sects. The document said that a search for a sense of community was one of the primary reasons for the rise of sects. In response, bishops around the world recommended a rethinking of the traditional parish community and greater reliance on "basic ecclesial communities."

That is what is happening at St. Brigid's. "I just think the need is there for another experience of church," Gaeta said. "I don't think the large group experience is able to fulfill everybody's needs."

In these groups, people fill their greatest need: finding God's presence in one another. That is why Julia Waszkiewicz has decided not to move to Florida and leave behind her prayer group. "I won't go," she said, "because I would miss all these wonderful friends who have really been God to me."

A children's choir from the Hispanic community sings on the feast of Our Lady of Guadalupe.

At the school, Kathryn Abdale invited her grandmother, Edna Veth of the Bronx, for the "Special Persons Day."

A young mothers' prayer group prays at Maura Goodwin's home.

Visiting a Spanish-speaking family, Sister Judy Mannix, the director of parish outreach, speaks with the county social services agency on their behalf.

Stephanie Ann Vivona and Michael Rafanelli, one of the engaged couples who experienced the parish's Pre-Cana marriage preparation program.

LEFT: During the presentation of the gifts at the family mass, Msgr. Francis X. Gaeta accepts the hosts from a child and, in a typical gesture, offers an embrace.

BELOW: Guitarist Guillermo Roman and children practice for the Thanksgiving Day multicultural mass.

The band at the weekly rock mass, The Six.

During the monthly Jesus Evening, a healing mass, Father Michael Maffeo and other parishioners pray over those who come up to the altar.

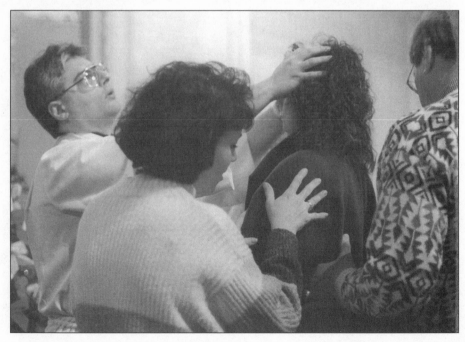

During Holy Week, parishioners join in song and prayer.

Easter sunrise mass at Nassau Beach.

*Chapter Twelve*

# "THE SIX"

The jumper cables began as Chuck Cutolo's little joke, a silly suggestion at a meeting where a bit of silliness often ushers in the desired creativity.

Cutolo was sitting in the religious education office of St. Brigid/Our Lady of Hope Regional School, a few feet from the large chapel where St. Brigid's offers its rock mass on Sunday evenings at six. The meeting included the director of youth ministry, Jennifer Gallagher; two key adult volunteers at the rock mass, Cutolo and his wife, Denise Pratesi; some of the young people who attend "The Six," and members of the band.

"I hate meetings," Gallagher said. "But I love those meetings, because we laugh like you can't believe. And part of it is the collective senses of humor involved between Chuck Cutolo and Denise and me and the kids."

Gallagher and Pratesi have a good reason for the adolescent turn of their humor: They work with students. In addition to her youth ministry job, Gallagher teaches music at the school. Pratesi teaches English and theater at Deer Park High School. But her husband has no excuse for his ability to think like a teenager.

Cutolo has an adult job: minority counsel to the Nassau County Legislature. Before that, he worked on public policy for Catholic Charities of the Diocese of Rockville Centre. Earlier, he was the top legislative aide to United States Senator Carl Levin, a Michigan Democrat. But one qualification that does not appear on his impressive resumé is the real secret of Cutolo's adolescent humor: his Muppet-mania.

The Cutolo–Pratesi home is a Muppets shrine, including a small, green army of Kermit the Frog dolls. And their cars both have Muppet-themed license plates—one focused on Kermit and the other on Kermit and Miss Piggy. On at least one level, this is a man who has refused to grow up.

"The formula that works for the Muppets works for St. Brigid's and works for the rock mass," Cutolo said. "The rock mass—the youth ministry—has to have a little bit of an edge of irreverence if it's going to be perceived as credible by the audience that you're directing it to."

That is the dominant spirit of The Six, a willingness to tiptoe on the edges of irreverence—by incorporating pop culture into the highly reverential setting of the mass, in order to help young people feel more at home with worship and Scripture. And that weekly liturgy, which draws from 500 to 600 people, is the center of the parish's extensive outreach to the young.

About every six weeks from September to June, the season when the parish offers the full band at The Six, Gallagher and the volunteer brain trust meet, examine the Scripture readings and themes for the coming weeks, and face the question, as described by Cutolo: "Is there any unusual, creative way to catch people's attention and still be consistent with the message of the readings?"

During Lent of 1996, for example, their overall theme was "The Heart of the Matter," focusing on "the many ways that we can prepare our hearts for Jesus, celebrate his great love for all of us and share that love with others." Throughout Lent, the band repeatedly used Don Henley's song, "The Heart of the Matter."

The subtheme for one week was getting people to stimulate their hearts to love more. Looking for physical objects to symbolize that jump-starting of the heart, they thought of coffee, vitamins, and breakfast cereal.

"The image in my mind at that point was a pacemaker," Cutolo said. "I put my head down and thought, 'We can't get a pacemaker. Why don't we get jumper cables?' The idea of the jumper cables was half mocking, if not two-thirds mocking, if not three-quarters mocking." To Cutolo's astonishment, his wife and Gallagher took him seriously. Before long, he found himself in an auto parts store, buying jumper cables.

At the mass, the guest celebrant, Father James Vlaun, preached about forces that make people more open-hearted and loving. Vlaun asked the congregation about everyday items that help jump-start the heart. He gave the people generous hints, prompting them to guess the items that he was carrying in a shopping bag, and then he gave the winners their prizes: the coffee, the vitamins, the cereal and, finally, the jumper cables. "That got a lot of laughter," Cutolo said.

In a similar spirit of innovation, the rock mass planners once decided that the band should repeatedly use "The Long and Winding Road," the Beatles song, as Christmas approached. "You know, the long and winding road that leads to the cradle," Gallagher said. She also expanded on that journey theme, using clown-foot-sized, fluorescent-colored paper cutouts of feet. Gallagher got some of the teenagers to take these feet out to their friends and ask them to write on the feet "what they were doing to prepare their lives for Christ," she recalled.

"So they'd write it on the feet, and each week, we would put more feet down in the chapel," Gallagher said. Imperfectly taped to the floor, they became foot-snaring obstacles. "Here I am taking up the collection, saying, 'Jennifer and her damn feet,'" Cutolo recalled.

People inevitably call this liturgy the rock mass, but the band likes to call it simply The Six. Rock is not the only contemporary music that it plays, and it doesn't want to scare anyone away with that word. But whatever it's called, it is central.

"The rock mass, I think, is the most important thing we do in the youth ministry," Gallagher said. "The rock mass reaches kids who are nameless faces, who come every week faithfully and would not come to mass otherwise."

St. Brigid's is not the only parish seeking ways to keep young people connected to the church and to pull them back once they have drifted off. Often, teenagers simply stop going to church after high school or even after confirmation, in eighth grade. That drift is widespread in the church.

Perhaps the simplest explanation is the disparity between the high-speed, flashing lights and booming sounds of the MTV culture that surrounds teenagers, and the slow, unexciting rhythms of the liturgy.

"Some people stop because they say it's boring, or they can't focus," said Kristen Gatto, a teenager who stopped going for a while herself, but who now attends the rock mass. "Not every church around here has rock mass."

Beyond boredom is the adolescent impulse to break free of confining institutions, often at the end of high school. "Part of it is a normal process," Gallagher said. "I think all of us go through it. You get to a point in your life where you're questioning the givens." One of the givens is the church.

"I think they don't see the church as relevant," said Sister Margaret O'Brien, who served until 1996 as director of young adult ministry for the Diocese of Rockville Centre. "I think they think the church doesn't have anything to say to them."

To many young adults, the church doesn't seem to have useful solutions to their problems with careers and relationships. "They go to other places for the answers: their friends, society, society's values, society's morals," O'Brien said. "We don't give an image like we can answer their questions."

The church recognizes this as a significant problem. So the National Conference of Catholic Bishops developed a plan for ministry to young people, a document called "Sons and Daughters of the Light: Ministry with Young Adults, a National Pastoral Plan."

The bishops themselves met with young people and talked about their needs, said Paul Henderson, associate director of the bishops' secretariat for family, laity, women, and youth. They said they wanted a sense of welcome, good liturgy, and good preaching. "We heard young people say, 'We want to make good decisions in our life, and we need some information to base our decisions on, and we really don't feel the church has given us that yet,'" Henderson said.

One problem that young people face is the church's emphasis on married life. Between the end of high school and marriage, they often feel they are all but invisible to the church. "They don't know where they fit in," Henderson said. "When they listen to the preaching, it's directed to families."

Confronting those realities, St. Brigid's has put together a comprehensive approach, from late elementary school through young adulthood. "There are a small number of centers in the diocese where young adult things happen," O'Brien said. "St. Brigid's is one of the ones that in my years of doing this has been able to build something and keep it ticking along nicely."

Like any parish, St. Brigid's reflects the interests and goals of its pastor. And Gaeta has been focused on youth since his earliest days as a priest. Beyond his natural affinity for the young, he has a deadly serious purpose for devoting so much parish energy to them.

"No youth ministry, no church tomorrow," Gaeta said. "Teenagers are really members of the church, and they deserve a fair shake. We have to be sensitive to their needs, and they have to be ministered to."

It was Gaeta who hired Gallagher in 1991. "Jennifer is beyond gold," he said. Her youth ministry runs from sixth to twelfth grade, starting with confirmation preparation. In eighth grade, the parish offers a "daybreak retreat" that runs from ten at night until ten in the morning.

If the retreat were ten in the morning until ten at night, Gallagher said, the students would reject it. But the all-night hours give it an air of cool. In addition to large-group activities, such as talks by retreat leaders, games in the school's gym, pizza, and the closing mass, the retreat offers students a chance to talk in small groups about their lives.

"I was surprised at how well these kids share," said one small-group leader, Nassau County Legislator Ed Ward, who became a volunteer at St. Brigid's through his friend John White, a leader in the establishment of the rock mass. "They shared relationship problems, not so much with the other sex, but with brother–sister," Ward said. "They're coming in with: 'My brother beats me up. How do I stop it?' 'My father drinks too much. What do I do?'"

After students receive confirmation in the eighth grade, formal religious education ends for most of them, but St. Brigid's keeps reaching out.

Every year, for example, the parish runs a retreat for high school students at St. Gabriel's Retreat House on Shelter Island. But perhaps the primary effort in high school is the RAP (Religion and People) program. It is totally voluntary, but the participation is high. "Last year, we had three-quarters of the confirmation class sign up for RAP," Gallagher said. It offers them a weekly opportunity to discuss issues in their lives with adults who aren't their parents.

"We get to talk about anything that's on our minds—school, family, friends," said Megan Perfetti, a student at Holy Trinity High School in Hicksville. "They, like, listen to us."

In RAP, religious issues don't often come up. "They're talking about their school life and boys and their classes," said Jack Cecere, one of the adult leaders of Perfetti's ten-teen RAP group. "Mostly, they talk among themselves, and we try to introduce things as we can."

The issues they do discuss can be very mundane. "One night, we sat there all night talking about school uniforms, because that's what was important to them," said the other adult leader, Katie Sheehan, who looks so young that officials sometimes mistakenly ask to see her student hall pass at Mineola High School, where she teaches.

The important thing is not the issue but the comfort that the teens feel in discussing it. "Whatever you say can't leave the RAP group, because it's confidential," Kristen Gatto said. "It's just kind of like a place where you can relax and have fun. It's kind of like a little family."

The "family" meets weekly in Sheehan's East Meadow home to share discussion and food. "The only two ingredients that we needed for the RAP group were: one, the kids, and two, junk food," said Sheehan, who learned early about the power of food over teenagers.

Growing up in St. Brigid's, Sheehan participated in a teen retreat program. Later, she joined in-home discussion groups that were like RAP. As a student at W. Tresper Clark High School in Westbury, she was part of a group who still wanted more from their experience of parish.

"This couple, Mary and Charlie Pinto, stepped forward and said they would do a three-week course on love and marriage," Sheehan said, recalling the abundant food that Mary Pinto cooked for them the first night. "We just kept coming back. Mary would always tell me, 'My mistake, Katie, was feeding you. . . .' If you feed them, they will come."

Food, of course, is not the only lure. "These kids are coming to this home where two adults are there for them every week," Cecere said. Even if religion doesn't come up formally in the discussion, the teens see a concrete reminder that the parish cares: the willing presence of two faith-filled adults. "If they have that awareness, it's already a positive thing," Cecere said.

It is also helpful to the teens to see Cecere and Sheehan regularly in leadership roles at the rock mass. Sheehan reads the Scriptures as a lector and distributes communion as a eucharistic minister; Cecere is a eucharistic minister. "Three of the kids in this particular group have asked, can they become lectors," Sheehan said, and Pratesi trained them.

Together, Sheehan and Cecere exemplify the interconnections among the rock mass, RAP, and other elements of the parish's work with the young.

As an adult, Sheehan found herself drawn into youth ministry by White, who exerted legendary powers of gentle, irresistible persuasion to attract "volunteers." She worked with him to set up the Shelter Island retreat, and she became involved in RAP—helping to coordinate an all-girl group. In September 1995, Sheehan joined Cecere in their current group.

Cecere's route into RAP was more convoluted. He grew up in Astoria, graduated from Fordham University, and went into computer retailing and servicing. But in the early 1990s, living in Rockville Centre, he was looking for something more.

"At the time, I was mostly focused on my working career," Cecere said. "There were things lacking in my life." As a Catholic, he had a sense that his answers were to be found within the church. But in the parish he was attending, he drew little spiritual nourishment from the liturgies. "I found them to be a little cold," he said.

Then, Cecere heard about Renew, a spiritual renewal program that St. Brigid's was running specifically for young adults, and he began going to the rock mass, which was anything but cold. "I got a whole different feeling," he recalled.

After the mass on Sunday evenings, Cecere took part in a Renew small group, discussing Scripture and life. "It was what I needed at the time," he said. "It helped to know that there were other people, my peers, who were also in the same situation." From there, he became a RAP leader.

The five-season Renew program, which ended at St. Brigid's in 1996, is not designed solely for young adults. But that is how the parish used it. Its reflection process is helpful for those who have run up against a wall. They are progressing in the career they sought, but it hasn't made them happy. And sometimes, they are also seeking to meet someone meaningful.

"They're looking in healthy places for healthy relationships," said Ward, who led a Renew group with Gallagher. "They're out of the bar scene. They're out of the kid scene. They're trying to find themselves."

What some of them found was the Renew program at St. Brigid's, even if they had to drive long distances to the weekly sessions. "If they see something good happening, they're going to travel to it," O'Brien said. "The word of mouth is what's drawing them there."

In the group that Eric and Palma Bauman ran in their home, for example, there were people from the Bronx in New York City, from Long Beach in Nassau County, and from Copiague in Suffolk County. "They were looking for something," she said. "They were in their early thirties, and they're tired of what's out there."

That is a fair description of what happened to Eric Bauman himself, in the late 1980s, when he was a decade into his career as a corrections officer at the Nassau County jail in East Meadow. "I went through a type of conversion; it was directly influenced by what was going on in the jail," he said. "I was taught to do things a certain way and treat inmates a certain way. Over the years, I got sick of that."

So he distanced himself from some of his co-workers and returned to the church, at about the time in 1989 when Gaeta arrived as pastor and White as his associate. "I took a big step, to walk into the new pastor in the parish," Bauman recalled. "I said, 'I want to work.'" Before long, Bauman became involved with White in the rock mass.

His conversion was so profound that he began thinking seriously about the priesthood. Then, as he stood in the rectory at St. Brigid's, helping Gaeta and White to decorate the Christmas tree, he met Palma, who showed up as part of a young-adult group, shepherded by her brother.

Palma's shyness put him off at first, but they soon became friends. Then he went on a seven-day retreat with his spiritual director, Fred Schaefer. He came home from the retreat with a decision to ask Palma to marry him.

His plan for the proposal revolved around the church. "We used to go to the tabernacle and pray before the Blessed Sacrament once or twice a week," he said. And that was where he would propose. "I had a dozen roses in the car and the ring in my pocket."

That scenario developed some flaws—first when Palma was delayed at the restaurant where she worked, then at the very moment when they knelt before the tabernacle. "Who comes walking around the corner but my mother, who's praying a rosary and who's always there," he recalled. Not knowing what they were up to, she started to interrupt, but Bauman's father sensibly steered her away. Bauman completed the proposal.

Later, when Bauman became a Renew leader, he persuaded his wife to help with the in-home meetings. During the five seasons, three members got married to people outside the group and two of them brought their new spouses into Renew. The group stayed virtually intact the whole time, sharing openly their concerns.

"People don't speak about things of this nature in the workplace, and if they do, it's a negative connotation," Bauman said. "It was safety that really drew them in. Confidentiality was a big part of the program."

This comfortable net of ministry to the young keeps spreading wider at St. Brigid's.

In the summer of 1996, Vinny Iannucci, a RAP leader, succeeded in reopening the teen center in the school basement, which had fallen into disuse. Iannucci studied youth ministry in the Pastoral Formation Institute run by the Diocese of Rockville Centre to train lay leaders. His final project was to pull together the teen center—complete with photo IDs for the teens and a full roster of adult volunteers.

"You need a lot of people to run this thing," Iannucci said. "We have about four to six adults there every time this place is open." In the summer, it opens once a month, and the rest of the year, about twice a month—with recreation, dancing, and guest speakers. "We tried to find a place for them to stay away from the street."

The parish has also kept up with the times by taking its youth ministry to the Internet. Costa and D'Souza worked to put together a listing of e-mail addresses for college students from St. Brigid's—an idea Costa got from Father Ralph Sommer at St. Thomas More in Hauppauge. Gaeta is famous for his computer ineptitude, but he knows a good idea.

"Father Frank wants to be very much able to reach out to the young adults in the parish who are away at school," Costa said. "As we get the list of people's e-mail addresses, then the parish will stay in touch with them."

St. Brigid's is not the only parish working on e-mail, not the only parish with RAP, not the only one with a paid youth minister. "Last count, I think we had about thirty-five employed youth ministry coordinators, some of them full time, some of them part time," said Michael

McCarthy, director of the diocesan office of youth ministries, which is separate from the young adult office and serves junior high and high school students.

And, like St. Brigid's, other parishes offer the Catholic Youth Organization. The St. Brigid's CYO provides team sports for 250 to 300 boys and girls, said its president, John Miller. In 1996, the sixth-grade and seventh-grade boys' basketball teams won a diocesan championship. "We've never had two," Miller said.

But what makes St. Brigid's stand out is the pivotal role of The Six on Sunday. "The rock mass is really the central focus of all of these ministries," Gallagher said. "It's not something that happens in a lot of places."

It happened at St. Brigid's because White and Vlaun had worked together on a rock mass at White's previous parish, St. Mary's in East Islip, and when White came to Westbury, he got Gaeta's enthusiastic approval and went ahead.

Even at St. Brigid's, with three high schools in the parish, there were few young people at mass. "The parents would come and say to us, 'Can't you do something?'" White said. "This idea of bringing good pop and rock music into the liturgy, careful evaluation of lyrics in the music itself, and involving the young people in planning the sermons and planning the special events at mass seemed to make so much sense."

Word about the new mass spread quickly. Rosanne Ausiello, who had been singing since Hicksville High School, heard about it from her cousin, Vinny Giovinco. Jamie Armanini, a self-taught musician who played guitar, keyboards, and drums, learned of it through mutual friends of his and Giovinco's. Though they became two of the earliest members of the band at St. Brigid's, they had not been regularly going to church.

"This was the mass that made me come to church," Armanini said. Ausiello said she had stopped going to mass regularly after hearing a series of sermons that she felt were not speaking God's word to her. When the rock mass started, they signed on and set to work.

"We practiced for about four months to get some songs together," Ausiello said. The first mass was in January 1990. Initially, Catholics United for the Faith, an ultra-conservative group, mentioned the new mass unfavorably in its newsletter. But the mass eventually drew primarily favorable notice. It started out in the church itself. That proved too difficult acoustically, and they moved it to the chapel at the school.

Like any band, the players at the rock mass were transient. But the new enterprise had a strong lure. "I've had to leave this a couple of times," Ausiello said. "I just can't seem to leave. Something pulls me back."

The pivotal event in its evolution was Gaeta's decision to hire a veteran pop singer, Tommy Ciotti Thorell, as the parish director of music—a few months after the rock mass began. In addition to the increased sophistication that he brought to the music, Thorell had a profound impact on the musicians themselves.

"The mass really took personal meaning for me with Tommy," said Armanini, who had left to work on a musical project of his own. "For some reason, I just came back. That was it. He just drew me in." Thorell, who had come through a long odyssey of his own to become a deeply spiritual person, kept reminding Armanini why he was there.

"It was not about music. It wasn't about ourselves. It was one reason: doing it for the church and for God," Armanini said. "Tommy always used to look at me and say that 'God wants you here.' He's right. I just keep coming back."

In addition to the secular popular music that they used, Thorell wrote memorable tunes for the mass, sometimes dazzling the young musicians with his on-the-spot inventiveness. Ausiello recalled particularly Thorell's "When He Returns," a song about forgiveness. "He wrote it while we were sitting there at rehearsal," she said.

At those rehearsals, they would do more than play music. Thorell also led them in prayer. "Tommy was a very good preacher to us also," Ausiello said. "He was very spiritual."

Then, in January 1996, Thorell died of a brain tumor, at age forty-eight. That was a crushing tragedy for the band, but Thorell continued to be a force even after his death, which Armanini said has motivated him to stay on and work harder. Similarly, Ausiello recalled: "He always said, 'If I leave this, don't let this fail.' It was very difficult for me, after he passed away, to actually go into that church. But I always hear him saying that to me in the background."

The mass still faces problems. To avoid copyright infringement, they have never been able to print out the words of the popular music, and that makes it difficult for the congregation to sing along. In 1996, they faced a new hurdle: adjusting to the transfer of Maffeo, who brought a youthful sense of humor to the rock mass, where he was a frequent celebrant, and to a variety of other youth ministries. But there were reasons for optimism.

"The mass has definitely evolved, it's grown up, it's matured," Armanini said. "It's still around, which is a good sign. . . . This is the mass of the future."

The mass continues to be inventive, in a tradition that has challenged the young people with speakers ranging from people with AIDS to Carolyn McCarthy, the anti-gun, anti-death penalty widow of an LIRR massacre victim, who spoke at the mass months before she decided to run for Congress. They continue to draw not only youth but mature adults as well. They still work hard to develop engaging themes, with a closer collaboration between the band members and the adult coordinators.

And The Six continues to serve as an anchor for the rest of the youth ministry, sending out a hopeful message. "There's really something powerful about a kid hearing a song that he heard on the radio in church," Jennifer Gallagher said. "What that says to that kid is, we're meeting you where you are."

*Chapter Thirteen*

# A NATION OF PARISHES

$\mathcal{S}$tanding tall and imposing in front of a large room filled with pastors, G. Richard Fowler was trying to make a simple point: that the Catholic Church has greater power to effect change than any other institution.

Fowler comes to that conclusion from an unusual outsider–insider perspective. He is a Methodist minister serving on extended temporary duty in the Department of Social Development and World Peace of the National Conference of Catholic Bishops. His job is to help dioceses and parishes to preach and practice social justice.

On this afternoon in late August 1996, he was carrying that message to a casually attired audience of more than forty, who had gathered for a Sunday-to-Friday conference on "Beginning a Pastorate" at the Malvern Retreat House in suburban Philadelphia. Some had just become pastors for the first time, some had been pastors before but had moved to a new parish, and some were expecting to be pastors soon. Most were priests, but the audience also included a nun, a laywoman, and two laymen. After spending a large part of almost two years with the people of St. Brigid's parish, I had come to Malvern to take a peek at what is happening at other parishes around the country.

The pastors listened as Fowler described the factors behind the church's ability to bring about change. He included such assets as its sheer size, its long experience in advocating for the poor, the strength of Catholic social teaching, and the willingness of the bishops to take difficult public stands. Then he mentioned a reality so obvious that people seldom think about it.

"The Catholic Church is the only institution on the face of the earth that's divided the globe up into little chunks of land that you call parishes,"

Fowler said. "You're everywhere. There's not a piece of dirt that's not in one of your parishes." The pastors laughed in appreciation.

All week, from one speaker after another, they heard not only a list of ways to lead more effectively those "little chunks of land," but also a litany of suggestions for helping their people to grasp the intersection between divine revelation and daily life.

"You are the ones who must help people make that connection," said Monsignor Philip J. Murnion, director of the New York–based National Pastoral Life Center, in his opening talk on Sunday evening. Among the many roles pastors fill, he said, they must act as an intermediary between the people and a phalanx of diocesan offices. "All of them want you to do something, and you're trying to relate to all these individual people," Murnion said. "It's the most complex position, I would suggest, within the life of the church, the most consequential position."

The position demands that pastors juggle the competing roles of administrator and spiritual leader. Every day is a tug-of-war between the call of the Gospel and the snares of what Murnion calls "The Killer B's" of buildings, budgets, boilers, and bingo, which trap pastors into constantly reacting to practical demands. "What everyone wants from you," Murnion said, "you do."

But Patricia Kelly, a psychologist who guided the pastors through a day of leadership training, challenged them to dig below the tyranny of detail to the core of what they are. "If you're only a manager, if you're only an accountant, if you're only a social director, what's the point?" Kelly asked. "You could be married. You could have a boat. The essence of the phenomenon is that you are calling others to know and love the Gospel."

Kelly, an outrageously energetic mother of twelve and a youthful-looking grandmother, excels at juggling multiple roles. While still raising her family, she completed her undergraduate education and acquired a doctorate in psychology. Now, she is a partner in a counseling firm in West Chester, Pennsylvania. In providing counseling to pastors and teaching them how to counsel others, she has gained a deep understanding of the difficulties they encounter. "I think a lot of them are very overwhelmed," she said after the conference. "That's why it's easier to talk to the plumber and to allow themselves to be immersed in the sort of details that you can feel useful. I think distraction is a tremendous temptation for all of them."

Her task in Malvern was to help the pastors analyze themselves and their leadership styles, to offer them ideas about managing collaboration and conflict, to nurture their ability to cope with a job that has not become any less complex since Vatican II.

Every pastor and every parish has to figure out its own approach to those complexities. In Westbury, for example, Gaeta uses a pastoring style that can't be confused with anyone else's, and St. Brigid's has crafted its idiosyncratic way of being a parish. But there are nearly twenty thousand other parishes in America, and the men and women at the Malvern conference represented a good cross-section of them, from the four corners of the country—joined by one person from Canada and five from Latin America, including an auxiliary bishop. Just as the conference itself was a microcosm of developments in parish life across the country, the stories of these pastors faithfully reflect many of the problems of pastoring in an era of fewer priests and more Catholics.

Bringing to the conference their individual problems, they examined together some knotty questions that, in one form or another, vex many pastors today: How do you survive the crushing disappointment when you invite lay people to a meeting to discuss the parish's social justice mission, and only seven show up? How do you exercise collegial leadership and encourage lay "ownership" of the parish, without surrendering the right to use a more top-down leadership style when the situation demands? How do you provide liturgy that allows the parish to celebrate as a community, when so many in the pews prefer a private, just-me-and-Jesus devotion? How do you comprehend the movement toward small church communities, and how do you connect those communities to the life of the entire parish? What do you do when a parish employee is using a relative's Social Security number for payroll records, because the employee herself is an undocumented alien? How do you make sure that a prospective youth minister has no history of sexually abusing children? How do you fire someone?

To address those issues and others, Murnion and Sister Donna Ciangio, project director at the National Pastoral Life Center, put together an impressively diverse group of speakers, on issues from liturgy to lawsuits. The gathering in Malvern was the sixth in a series of "Beginning a Pastorate" conferences offered by the center, whose own brief history sheds some light on the way the church in America handles parish life. Its story began almost two decades ago with a speech by Bishop Albert H. Ottenweller, the former auxiliary bishop of Toledo and later the bishop of Steubenville, Ohio, until his retirement in 1992.

"He got up at the bishops' meeting and lamented the fact that parishes were feeling, as he gave the image, at the bottom of a funnel, down which diocesan and national offices were pouring programs, pushing parishes into being more and more organizations responding to programs rather than communities building people," Murnion recalled. Ottenweller wanted to do something about it, and the bishops' conference referred his proposal to a committee. "I was one of the people asked to prepare a paper reflecting on various dimensions of parish life," said Murnion, who was then working in the Archdiocese of New York's Office of Pastoral Research.

The result was the appointment of a special committee in 1978, with Murnion as its staff. "Thinking that that wasn't a very exciting letterhead, I decided that the staff should be called the Parish Project," Murnion said. The project lasted four years, reconnoitering the country for good parishes and identifying what made them good. One of its fruits was a 1980 document that served as a vision statement for parish life, called "The Parish: A People, A Mission, A Structure."

The project later stimulated a variety of reflections on parish life, ending with a series of regional conferences that brought together bishops and the people of their dioceses. Then the project was supposed to end. "A number of people started to say, 'Gee, we really ought to keep something going at the national level for parish life,'" Murnion said.

At the time, the bishops' conference was trimming budgets. "They cut back on those offices that were service offices to dioceses and parishes," Murnion said. "What happened is that those entities became separate organizations." In that spirit, the leadership of the bishops' conference encouraged Murnion to start a center on parish life and urged the American Board of Catholic Missions to provide initial funding. With that money and some foundation support, the center opened on March 1, 1983.

So the bishops' conference itself does not have a separate office that focuses on parish life as a whole. There are independent national groups that represent constituencies within the parish, such as pastoral planners, pastoral councils, parish staff, priests, and others. But, aside from the Illinois–based Parish Evaluation Project, which has worked with more than 150 individual parishes, there is really no other national organization that serves parishes holistically. That mirrors the situation at the diocesan level.

"Some of the larger and more organized dioceses have somebody called vicar for parish life or secretary for parish life, or director of parish life and worship," Murnion said. "But that's the minority, by far." In some, the chancellor or vicar general assumes that generalist role. "But for the most part, parishes get dealt with by individual offices. That's part of their challenge: How do you take the multiplicity of offices that get funnelled into the one pastor and try to handle all these different specialties?"

Beyond the lack of structures that relate to them as a whole, parishes also face another hurdle. "It's very rare for there to be a prevailing set of standards in any diocese about what a good parish is," Murnion said. "The randomness of that is a real problem, because we don't know what the model is that we're working with, and therefore, changing pastors can change the parish radically."

For all those reasons, exercising parish leadership in the postconciliar era remains tricky. "Probably, for the most part, you won't feel too successful most of the time," Kelly told the pastors. "You have to accept the reality that leadership is a lonely job. One of the temptations is to withdraw into autocratic behavior. But I can guarantee you that the people of God are hungry and they need you. They're not very good at telling you that. It's kind of a crazy job. It's not empirically defined. It's a nutty job. You are wisdom figures, and people are hungry for wisdom."

―∞―

Sitting right in front of Pat Kelly was one wisdom figure, Father Bryan Brooks, who looked terribly young for the role, despite the slight maturing influence of his thick black beard. Just two months earlier, at the age of thirty-four and only three years ordained, Brooks had become the pastor of two Oklahoma parishes. Near the end of Kelly's morning session, speaking honestly about the pressures of being a newly minted pastor, Brooks told the group: "I feel a lot of expectations put on me that are scary."

After his ordination in 1993 for the Diocese of Tulsa, his first assignment was as associate pastor of St. John University Parish and Catholic Student Center in Stillwater, near his alma mater, Oklahoma State. Brooks expected a reassignment after three years, the normal term for associates in the diocese.

"My first request was to be an associate in another parish situation," Brooks said. "I had at first hoped to have a different kind of experience before becoming a pastor." Despite that hope, when his new assignment came in June 1996, it was a pastorate: at St. Anthony's and Uganda Martyrs, two parishes about a mile apart in Okmulgee, the county seat of Okmulgee County. The surprise was not entirely pleasant. "I kind of felt like maybe I'd been tossed into the deep end of the pool," Brooks said.

The first big difference for Brooks was the town itself, which is very different from Oklahoma City, where he grew up. Okmulgee was once a flourishing oil refinery town, but that industry is gone, leaving a technical school as the largest employer. The county unemployment rate is about nine percent, Brooks said, and the population has dwindled to 13,600. "It is a much smaller town than what I'm used to," he said.

The parishes are also small, with three hundred registered families between them. They are also are very different ethnically. St. Anthony's is mostly white and Uganda Martyrs heavily African-American. But that has not divided them. "The people get along here, in terms of going from one church to another," Brooks said. "We have one mass on Sunday at Uganda. They don't have a problem going over to St. Anthony's, and vice versa."

But they have had a problem of leadership continuity. "I'm the fifth pastor in twelve years," Brooks said. His predecessor was there two years and the priest before him three. Now, Brooks believes, the diocese should make a commitment to some stability. "I've spoken about that to the chancery and the bishop," he said. "Someone needs to be here for a while."

Even if Brooks stays a while, he'll still be younger than many of his parishioners. "I'm the youngest pastor in this parish since anybody can remember," Brooks said. "They're very excited about having a young priest. So they have lots of expectations of me."

And Brooks has expectations of himself, as he learns the ins and outs of leading two parishes, one combined pastoral council, and one school. "I've got a lot of work to do," he said. In addition, he faces a major adjustment in the way he lives. At Stillwater, there were three priests: the pastor and Brooks in the university parish and another priest in a nearby parish. Now, he is alone. "Before, the nearest priest was down the hall," he said. "Now the nearest priest is fifteen miles away." To cope with that, he meets once a month with a group of seven or eight younger priests from the Tulsa area for prayer and study, and he sees his friends in Tulsa and Stillwater.

With all that lies ahead of him, Brooks welcomed the chance to attend the Malvern conference. "It gave me a good sense of direction on what I should be doing and how I should be doing it," he said, a few weeks later. "I was really needing some kind of direction, rather than try to learn it on the job. I don't feel that fear now."

—⚏—

Among the pastors who attended the conference's workshops, walked meditatively through the leafy grounds of the retreat center, ate meals together, socialized in the evening, and sang heartily in unison at morning and evening prayer and at the daily Eucharist, Brooks was not the only young one. Though Father John Halloran had been ordained six years before Brooks, he is only a month older than Brooks. And, like Brooks, he was genuinely surprised by his appointment.

While Halloran was attending St. Charles Borromeo Seminary outside Philadelphia, his field assignment was at Incarnation of Our Lord parish in the city. It was an increasingly Hispanic parish, and Halloran knew little Spanish. But he worked there every Thursday for a year and began to pick it up.

Halloran was ordained in 1987 and assigned to St. Veronica's in North Philadelphia, another predominantly Hispanic parish. Five years later, he went to the cathedral parish, where he ministered to the Hispanic community. "It was all of the same responsibilities as a pastor, except for the ultimate one," he said. "If the roof caved in, I called the cathedral." There, he spoke Spanish constantly. He had also sharpened his Spanish skills by attending a linguistics program in the Diocese of Brooklyn and spending some time in Peru. That growing language competence turned out to be a major factor in the surprise that awaited him in 1996.

It began with a phone call from the office for clergy at the chancery, instructing him to come in and meet with Cardinal Anthony Bevilacqua. This could mean only one thing: Halloran was becoming a pastor. "I said, 'Are you sure?'" he recalled. He had been at the cathedral parish four years and expected to be there one more.

Arriving at the meeting, Halloran saw Bevilacqua with a group of priests, including Monsignor Richard Powers, who had earlier been his pastor at St. Veronica's and then pastor at Incarnation. Halloran still had no idea what pastorate he was about to get. But Powers, who was leaving Incarnation and speculating about his replacement, figured it out the moment Halloran walked in. "He said, 'Oh, my gosh, it's you!'" Halloran recalled. "'Who else could it be? Nobody else in the room speaks Spanish.'" Powers was right. Halloran, returning as pastor to the parish where he'd done his field work as a seminarian, was stunned to be leading such a complex, diverse parish, at such an early age.

"John would be probably one of the youngest ones we have," said Father Michael McCulken, of the archdiocesan office for clergy. The age for new pastors is declining in Philadelphia, as it is everywhere, with the decreasing numbers of priests. But most priests there still don't get to be a pastor until twenty years after ordination. So why pick Halloran, who is only nine years out of the seminary? "The facility with the language and understanding the culture of the Hispanic people was certainly a big factor," McCulken said.

The parish that Halloran now leads is incredibly diverse. It has mass in four languages: English, Spanish, Portuguese, and Malayalam, from the Indian state of Kerala. And it offers liturgies in three rites: the Latin rite, plus two from India: Syro-Malabar and Syro-Malankara. As a result, the pastor has a difficult time just coordinating the use of the buildings.

The Syro-Malankara community has a liturgy in the parish hall every Sunday of the month except for one, and they have specific physical requirements. "When their bishop comes, he really wants to say mass facing the altar," said Powers, who did all the juggling of needs before Halloran succeeded him. "He doesn't want to say mass facing the people."

In addition, a large number of Indian groups in the area want to use the church hall; the Hispanic and Portuguese communities—the two largest in the parish—also have significant needs for space; and a variety of groups constantly want to use the gym. On top of that, there's the school, with six hundred students from more than thirty nations.

"Guys would look at that and say, 'How do you do it? How do you survive?'" Powers said. But once the initial shock wore off, Halloran felt lucky to be the new pastor. "I said to the people, 'I feel like I've won the Olympic gold medal,'" he said. "To me, that is the most exciting thing anyone could have in a parish, to have all these cultures."

The ultimate goal is to get the language communities working together on liturgy and whatever else they can. "There should be a way for us to become one unified parish, at the same time celebrating our differences," Halloran said. "If I want to do anything, I think that's it."

That is not an easy task at Incarnation, or at St. Brigid's, or at any of the increasing number of multicultural parishes in America. But it is unavoidable. "Incarnation definitely looks like what the church in the United States will look like in the future," Halloran said. "Some people think that's a terrible prospect. I think it's wonderful. The universality of the church has been something I have always loved."

—⁂—

For all the pastors, young and old, much of the time at the Malvern conference became an earnest exploration of how to relate to their people. The most practical advice came from Monsignor Douglas Doussan, a New Orleans pastor with a Louisiana drawl, an endless repertoire of Cajun jokes, and a carefully crafted process for developing parish goals.

Doussan got some of his ideas from a three-day seminar based on Steve Covey's book, *Seven Habits of Highly Effective People*. Adapting those principles to the parish, he teaches pastors how to structure their own work more efficiently. On the broader question of developing the parish's goals, much of his training came from Management Design, Inc., an ecumenical group of organizational consultants established in Cincinnati in 1969.

In the post–Vatican II years, MDI helped religious congregations who were rethinking their structure in light of the council. Then it started working with diocesan assemblies of bishops and priests. "We direct and facilitate the processes whereby they learn to heal themselves and start talking honestly instead of bashing one another," said Father George Wilson, a Jesuit who has been with MDI since 1972.

From that background, Doussan has developed a goal-setting process that draws the entire parish into extended reflection on who they are and where they want to go. Early in his talk, he asked the pastors how many of them are the only priest in the parish. Then he discussed parish "personnel," making it clear that they should broaden their definition to include not just paid staff, but volunteers, the congregation itself, and even the unchurched. "We have to stop thinking in terms of, 'I'm alone in the parish,'" he said.

Those words came as powerful medicine for Father John Alvarado, who had recently become pastor of an urban parish in Perth Amboy, New Jersey, with no other priests and a minuscule staff. "Just as he started, it's given me a whole lift, because I've been in the dumps for eight weeks," Alvarado said quietly, as the the group broke for coffee. "It's just me and my secretary, Marie."

For Holy Trinity parish, getting by with one priest was a new experience. The previous pastor had left a few months before Alvarado arrived in the spring of 1996. And the other priests hadn't stayed much longer. "The day that I started, the two priests who were here left," Alvarado said. One of them had put in a bid to be pastor himself, and when he didn't get the assignment, he moved on. The other left for the missions in Ecuador. So Alvarado is the only ordained person on the staff. Holy Trinity doesn't even have a deacon.

Whatever their size, all the parishes in Perth Amboy face difficult times, as the town does. "People here really struggle," Alvarado said. "For many years, Perth Amboy could handle all the immigrants that came. There was work for them all. When industry left Perth Amboy, the immigrants didn't stop coming."

In 1900, when the founders laid the cornerstone for the original church, it was an overwhelmingly Slovak parish. Now, immigrants from the Dominican Republic are the majority. That requires some adjustment by both groups, but it is particularly difficult for those who have been dominant in the parish for so long. "The Slovaks are trying to be Christian," Alvarado said. "It's so hard for them to let somebody else in, because, 'This is mine. I built this.'"

In his first few months, Alvarado personally experienced that changing of the guard, presiding at the funerals of about a half-dozen elderly members of the early Slovak community. His secretary, Marie Sotak, who had been working full time in that job since 1949, gave him some historical perspective. "Marie said: 'Father, we've never had this many people die before,'" Alvarado recalled. "It's like I came and all the pillars fell down."

Sensing the strain that all this was placing on the new pastor, some parishioners told him, "Please come back," before he left for Malvern. "The people know that in the short time I've been here a lot has been thrown at me," Alvarado said, "and they just wanted to be sure that I didn't go away and never come back." He did come back, with a determination to put into practice what he'd learned at Malvern—if he could create the time for long-term planning in the press of daily business. "If you're just hanging by the skin of your teeth and running, running, running, how do you do that?"

Alvarado, who came to the priesthood from a career in the art and graphic design business, was ordained in 1988. Just before arriving in Perth Amboy, he had served four years at Immaculate Conception in Somerville, which had a thriving elementary and high school. In contrast, Holy Trinity had closed its school down before Alvarado arrived. That was part of a trend: To survive, the Perth Amboy parishes chose to "cluster" and do things together that they can no longer afford to do separately. "We're hanging on, and we're doing it together," Alvarado said. They closed their separate schools and launched one consolidated school, the Perth Amboy Catholic School. They also share one director of religious education.

That complex assignment, coordinating the religious education needs of nine parishes, belongs to Sister Elizabeth Crehan. She is originally from Ireland, but in her four decades in the Servants of the Mother of God, she has served all over the world, most recently in Venezuela.

When she got to Perth Amboy in 1992, she went to work for five parishes that had begun to consolidate their religious education leadership, including Holy Trinity. The idea later spread to all nine parishes.

"Once the decision was made that this was the best direction in which to move, we formed a committee of people involved in all of the existing programs and looked at what we were doing, in association with the diocesan syllabus, and agreed what we would do together," Crehan said. Step by step, they agreed on a range of issues. "That process took nearly two years," Crehan said. "We worked at it until we reached a consensus."

The process has worked, but not without bumps. The new system requires some parents to travel less than the old one, for example, but some have to travel further. "There are all the difficulties that go with change," Crehan said. "I would not say it was smooth, by any stretch of the imagination." But they put together a system that educated 1,500 students in 1995—in English, Polish, Spanish, and Portuguese.

"There is some diversity within the program, different emphases within the parish and different ethnic groups," Crehan said. Throughout the community, however, the basic requirements are uniform. "Mobility is the key word," Crehan said, because in an immigrant community, people move frequently within the town. "Wherever they go now," Crehan said, "people actually know now what's expected of them."

---

As it is in Perth Amboy, clustering is often a cold financial necessity. But beyond dollars and cents, cooperative arrangements among pastors can also provide psychological benefits, especially when priests end up living in isolated situations. It was that kind of friendly arrangement that awaited another Malvern participant, Father George Michell, the only priest at the conference from Long Island, when he began his first pastorate.

Michell was ordained in 1964, a year behind Gaeta. Since then, Michell had served six parishes from one end of the Diocese of Rockville Centre to the other: from Holy Spirit in New Hyde Park, at the western end, just east of New York City, to St. John the Evangelist in Center Moriches, just west of the fashionable Hamptons. For a decade, starting in the mid-1980s, he had been at Christ the King in Commack, in western Suffolk County.

Finally, in the spring of 1996, Michell ended up on the East End as pastor of St. Patrick's in Southold. Somehow, Southold and the rest of the North Fork have managed to remain more rural than the glitzier

Hamptons on the South Fork, where the pressure of second-home development has converted thousands of acres of farmland to expensive homes. The North Fork is filled with vegetable farms, vineyards, and horse farms. But priests for its Catholic parishes are in fairly scarce supply.

Though Michell had served primarily in busy, crowded parishes, he had also had some preparation for the sparsely populated East End. For about seven years before he became a pastor, he had studied the work of Father William Bausch, pastor of St. Mary's in suburban Colts Neck, New Jersey, a small, single-priest parish. After Bausch had become pastor, Michell said, the arrival of some large corporate headquarters in the area had brought an influx of highly educated Catholics. Bausch, a strong believer in Vatican II and the empowerment of the laity, had worked to draw the new residents into parish life. "I was very excited about the potential that a small parish could have," Michell said.

His other preparation had been three years of summer visits to Alaska, filling in for other priests. For two summers, he worked in Soldotna, on the Kenai Peninsula, southeast of Anchorage. "I was the only priest in an area the size of Long Island," Michell said. Another summer, he "did the circuit" of several parishes. So, when Michell arrived in Southold, he was prepared for a small, rural church. What he found was a cooperative arrangement with the pastors of three other North Fork parishes.

The other pastors were people Michell knew or knew about. Monsignor John Nosser, of Our Lady of Ostrabrama in Cutchogue, had been his seminary classmate. Father John Sullivan, of St. Agnes in Greenport, had been only a year behind them. Father Peter Allen, who leads Sacred Heart in Cutchogue and Our Lady of Good Counsel mission in Mattituck, had grown up in a parish where Michell's stepmother lived. So Michell knew the men. What he did not know was their working relationship. "It is probably the nicest unexpected thing that could have happened to me," he said. "I wasn't really aware of the level of cooperation or fraternity."

About once a month, the four pastors meet to talk parish affairs and share a meal. "We'll all have dinner at one another's rectories a lot," Sullivan said, on a cool, sunny, early fall afternoon, when they had finished the business meeting and were sitting in Allen's rectory, sipping drinks and munching on snacks before going out for supper. Earlier, they had set the budget for their outreach program. They also share a regional school and an adult education program. Two years before Michell arrived, the pastors had collaborated to hire the school's principal. "We interviewed five or six people at the time," Nosser said. They had no trouble reaching agreement. "Anything like that, we've always done together," Allen said.

In addition to the ministries that the four parishes operate together, there are others that two of them share, such as the Pre-Cana marriage preparation program that Nosser and Allen have in Cutchogue. They also cooperate, Sullivan said, on making sure that mass schedules don't conflict between Southold and Greenport or within Cutchogue. "If any of us needs help in any way, we can call," Allen said. "That can go for anything."

That close relationship suffered a setback in June 1997, when the diocese transferred Nosser to Montauk, on the South Fork. "We have to build a whole new relationship, because Jack was basically the leader," Michell said. "The unity had survived several changes already, me being one of them. There's a reason to feel that the cooperation will continue."

—◊◊◊—

On the next-to-last-day of the Malvern conference, one of the most affecting suggestions of the whole week came from Father William Griner, who directed the liturgy office in the Archdiocese of Louisville for eleven years and now leads liturgy as the pastor of St. Michael's parish in Jeffersontown, Kentucky. In a folksy, captivating style, Griner offered an array of practical advice for making liturgy work, including one step that he has regularly taken himself: telling the parishioners from the pulpit that he loves them. "I do it about every six months," Griner said. "They've got to know that we love them, and we've got to tell them that frequently."

But congregations don't always make the pastor feel loved, especially when the pastor represents change from settled routine, as Sister Mary Ellen Curl did for two rural Kentucky parishes. Curl, a Sister of Mercy, had run a retreat house in Crestwood, Kentucky, before starting to work in 1991 as a part-time minister to the sick and elderly at St. Francis parish in rural Marion County, south of Louisville. A year later, she also became director of religious education at the neighboring parish, Holy Cross.

Beginning in 1992, as a result of the region's priest shortage, the two parishes shared one pastor, Father Kevin Bryan. Confronting the diocesan shortage, the Archdiocese of Louisville began to plan. They wrote to community leaders, seeking the names of people who were ready to assume parish leadership. From the names submitted, they chose eight, to sit on a planning committee and to prepare for roles as parish leaders themselves.

Unfortunately for Curl, there was little time for preparation. Almost at the same time that she began sitting on the committee, she found herself the pastoral administrator of St. Francis and Holy Cross when Bryan left in June 1995. That made her the first woman in the archdiocese to become, in effect, the pastor of a priestless parish.

The announcement was sudden. "There was no preparation for the people, and there was only two weeks' notice for me," Curl said. The reactions in the two parishes were very different. "At St. Francis, there was a lot of anger, a lot of hostility," Curl said. At Holy Cross, people were receptive. "Their response was, 'We're just glad you're going to stay.'"

Some of the anger at St. Francis had to do with the past. Bryan had closed the school, and the parishioners didn't feel they'd had enough participation in the decision. "St. Francis was misdirecting their anger toward me," Curl said. "They were angry that they had no part in the process of my appointment. It was announced on a Sunday morning at mass. They had no arena to express anything."

It also did not help that she was a woman in a traditionally male role. "The biggest anger thing was that I moved into a rectory," she said. "It was just that, all of a sudden, here was somebody besides a priest living in the parish house." Early in her tenure as pastoral administrator, she preached, which caused a mini-scene. "This woman got up and walked out because I gave the homily," Curl said.

For the most part, Curl does not have to preach at mass, because after Bryan left, the archdiocese appointed an ordained "sacramental moderator," a priest who had once been a pastor, to live in the parish. He presides at mass and administers sacraments, but Curl is the pastoral administrator. Brian Reynolds, a layman who is the chief administrative officer of the archdiocese, said that there are advantages to the sacramental moderator's presence. "She's not there without someone who's been a pastor," Reynolds said. Still, it can be confusing for parishioners to have a priest living in the parish and a woman serving as pastoral administrator. Despite the occasional awkwardness, Curl said that the priest has been supportive. "He does not in any way undermine me," she said. "Whatever happened, he knows that I am the pastoral leader."

In the year between her appointment and the Malvern conference, a "real turnaround" took place, to the point that Curl feels a majority of the people at St. Francis support her. "My main goal has been to focus on the building of relationships," she said. "It's working. It's working."

Curl drove to and from the Malvern conference with a woman whose experience was less difficult. At St. Lawrence's, an urban-suburban parish in the south end of Louisville where Curl had grown up, Sharan Benton's designation as a pastoral administrator went smoothly. The pastor, Father Robert Stuempel, put out a letter to parishioners announcing that Benton would replace him temporarily during his four-month sabbatical in California. "The people don't seem to have a problem with it," Benton said.

Benton brought a long resumé to the role. She had spent eighteen years in the Sisters of Charity of Nazareth, teaching high school and working for a decade in an antipoverty program. She had also served as a director of religious education, participated in a family assistance program in Cincinnati, helped establish the House of Ruth for women and children touched by AIDS, and spent seven years as a teacher and facilitator of lay ministry in the archdiocese. At the time Stuempel designated her, she was in her seventh year on the staff at St. Lawrence's.

Her experience in the parish included presiding, unexpectedly, at an emergency communion service. "At 8:30 mass, we had a priest get sick on the altar," she recalled. "I had some medical people get up and take care of him." She decided to continue with a communion service and told the congregation that anyone who didn't feel comfortable with it could leave, if they chose. Only one person left, and the communion service went smoothly. "It was a turning point," Benton said.

Whatever the reasons, the announcement of Benton's role as pastoral administrator did not raise any hostility. "I haven't experienced that," she said. "I actually do believe in our archdiocese that, with some preparation, people will be accepted in this role."

Though the number of priestless parishes is growing, the number of female pastoral administrators is still small. In a study, the National Pastoral Life Center found that about ten percent of American parishes have no ordained priest. "Of that ten percent, though, which was about two thousand parishes, eighty-five percent of them were covered by a priest from another parish," Murnion said. "The remaining fifteen percent of them, two thirds of those were by women religious, and then a mix of lay people, deacons, and teams." So he estimated about two hundred parishes with women religious as pastoral administrators and ninety with deacons, lay people, or teams.

"The problem is it's not a clear role," Murnion said. "It's a role we're making up." It is such a recent phenomenon that scholars are just beginning to study it. Ruth Wallace, a sociologist at George Washington University in Washington, D.C., first became curious when she read that a bishop had appointed a woman pastor. "That made me ask around to see what was really going on," Wallace said. "Then I started to get systematic about it. It threw me for a loop." The result was a 1992 book, *They Call Her Pastor,* focusing on twenty parishes run by women. Later, she launched a second study, this time focusing on married men running parishes.

As dioceses appoint more and more lay administrators, they use widely varying approaches. "Some places, the lay administrator is forbidden to preach," said Sister Kathleen Hughes, a liturgist at the Catholic Theological Union in Chicago. "In some places, they're required. There are so many ways this is growing up, because this is not being discussed publicly at the bishops' conference, and it won't be until it hits the East Coast." For now, priestless parishes are not as numerous in the Northeast as elsewhere.

One diocese with a widely admired policy is the Diocese of Saginaw, Michigan. The shortage forced some priests to serve as pastor in two parishes, but Bishop Kenneth Untener didn't want to close parishes. "You know, they have a one hundred-fifty-year history, some of them," said Sister Janet Fulgenzi, the vicar for religious, who runs the pastoral administrator program. "So, the first four parishes where a pastoral administrator was assigned, she relieved the priest of two full parishes, and he remained the sacramental minister to that parish and was quite grateful not to be the pastor."

Before Saginaw adopted its policy in 1985, they checked extensively with other dioceses and experts. "We called everywhere," Fulgenzi said. "When we got all that, then we drew up our policy." One of the keys is the process for selecting the priests who will serve as sacramental ministers to the lay pastoral administrators. "Bishop Untener doesn't ask somebody to do this that isn't willing to do it," Fulgenzi said. "So that clears the way right away." And about three times a year, Fulgenzi calls together all of the sacramental ministers and pastoral administrators to iron out any problems.

"What we've experienced is those that are not doing it—the priests that are not assigned as sacramental ministers, or some who may come in for one liturgy while the sacramental minister is away—questions come from them," Fulgenzi said. "But the questions are not coming from those that are doing it week in and week out."

This relationship between non-ordained pastors and ordained sacramental ministers is essential, if the availability of the Eucharist is to be preserved. Without that arrangement, the phenomenon of communion services outside the mass will become more widespread, which many liturgists agree is not desirable. The bishops of Kansas wrote a pastoral letter in 1995 restricting such communion services to emergency situations only. They called regular reception of communion outside the mass "a short-term solution that has all the makings of becoming a long-term problem." Among the "disturbing" implications that they cited was a "blurring of the difference" between celebrating Eucharist and receiving communion.

"I would say that they are right on the money theologically, that this is not a good interim solution to the clergy shortage," Hughes said. Yet, she said, the Vatican quickly approved the ritual book for these communion services. "When a ritual book comes out that's hard cover with ribbons, it doesn't look very interim," she said. "The prayers sound as if we're doing Eucharist. The way the ritual book is set up is compounding the problem of people thinking this is mass."

But a communion service is not the Eucharist. "There's no preparation rite. So we're not bringing ourselves with the bread and wine," Hughes said. "For liturgists, for example, who think about more scientific things, we're not engaging in the death and rising of Jesus. We're not celebrating the core events that make us church." Murnion agreed that there are valid concerns. "If you resort to the communion service, you have a situation where people are consumers," he said. "The Eucharist is not just a reception. It's an action of identifying with the sacrifice of Christ."

Still, the communion services are happening, and they are forging odd alliances. "Interestingly, some of the more conservative bishops would side with the liturgists that the Eucharist and priesthood should be protected, and some of the more liberal bishops, who would normally be with the liturgists, might be open to the communion service," Murnion said. "I think what everyone would say is that, no matter how you feel about it, it's an anomaly that's just based on a situation that's undesirable."

—∽—

The appointment of pastoral administrators has not been the only method that bishops have used in coping with the priest shortage. Importing priests from countries that have a surplus has been another approach. At the Malvern conference, the embodiment of this trend was Father Mieczyslaw Bajek, a short, friendly man who announced puckishly during the opening introductions that, although he works in South Dakota, "I don't have any South Dakota accent." What he does have is a thick Polish accent that clings to him stubbornly.

Bajek grew up in Stalowa Wola, in a region of southeastern Poland. He entered the Oblates of Mary Immaculate in 1972, was ordained in 1981, and served as an associate in four parishes in Poland, eventually becoming a pastor in Koden, on the Russian border. Then the call came to America. "Our provincial superiors meet from time to time in Rome, and because the United States province has a personnel problem, the provincial asked the Polish provincial for personnel help," Bajek said. "My provincial in Poland spoke to me and another priest and we came here."

Since Bajek spoke no English at all when he arrived in the United States in 1991, he and another Oblate spent six months in Chicago, studying the language. "It was a small private school in a private house, and students from different countries," Bajek said. After that, his first assignment was a two-year stay as an associate at St. Mary's parish in St. Paul, Minnesota, where a tutor helped him with his English conversation. Then he went to Sisseton, in northeastern South Dakota.

When he arrived, there were three Oblate priests—Norman Volk, Gregory Gallagher and himself—to serve the three parishes, plus other ministries that the Oblates have in the area, a nursing home, and a treatment facility for teenage Native Americans with alcohol problems. A Sioux reservation is a dominant reality in the area, and one Sisseton parish, St. Catherine's, is predominantly Native American. The other, St. Peter's, is primarily European-American. So is St. John's, the mission in Veblen.

"Veblen is a very small town," said Volk, who is now assigned to the Newman Center at the University of Wisconsin at River Falls. "It's maybe three hundred people. The parish has about thirty families. For a while, it was a dying town. But in the last few years, with some things that have developed in Sisseton and a casino that the tribe built, it's turned up." Similarly, the economy has improved in Sisseton, raising housing prices.

What has not improved is the availability of Oblates. In the 1970s, Volk said, seven or eight were in Sisseton, with priests assigned to each of the parishes and each of the ministries. "That was in the days when they all lived separately," Volk said. Then, as the numbers of priests dwindled and they began to reaffirm the importance of community life in the order, they built a house in Sisseton where the Oblates could live together.

That was the situation that Bajek found when he arrived, still struggling with the language. "I thought he coped with it well," Volk said. "I don't have any doubt that it was hard, but at the same time he's a pretty balanced guy and pretty happy-go-lucky." Then Volk left for

Wisconsin and Gallagher became a vocation director for the order. Starting on July 1, 1996, a few weeks before the Malvern conference, Bajek became pastor of all three parishes.

"We had in our community three priests and one brother, all living together in our house," Bajek said. "Now there are two priests and one brother in Sisseton." He and the other priest celebrate mass and administer the sacraments. The brother runs religious education and the outreach program. With this group of three, they maintain their community life. "In the morning we pray and in the evening we pray," he said. "It is for us very important to have our community prayer."

Though the three Oblates are stretched thin to cover all the parishes and ministries, Bajek is optimistic that his order will not let their numbers shrink even further, leaving only one person for everything. The founder of the Oblates, St. Eugene, always emphasized work in community. "By a community, he understands at least three people," Bajek said. "The reason I became an Oblate was our community. We are never, so to speak, lonely."

But all around him in the Diocese of Sioux Falls, other priests are stretched even thinner. "So, very often, one priest must say mass in two or three parishes," Bajek said. It's not going to get any better for the diocese, and Bajek expects to remain pastor in Sisseton for six years or more. "We don't have too many people to rotate."

—⁂—

The pastoral team that Father James Shanley replaced was a difficult act to follow, an "experimental" collaborative ministry. At the invitation of their archbishop, a priest, a deacon, and a laywoman had formed themselves into a team, founded a new parish in suburban Hartford, Connecticut, and worked together with an unusual degree of collegiality.

The only question was whether it had worked. The team and the parishioners thought so, but the new archbishop, looking at the experimental teams launched by his predecessor, decided they had failed. That left Shanley in a potentially ticklish situation when he left his hospital ministry in New Haven for his first pastorate, at St. Elizabeth Seton Community.

It was a desire to plan ahead that had led Archbishop John F. Whealon to the idea for collaborative ministries. "The archbishop believed that there would be a serious clergy shortage overtaking the diocese in the near future," said Father Thomas Barry, former secretary to Whealon and now executive director of the Connecticut Catholic Conference. "In order to provide for the staffing of the parishes, he decided to experiment with the form of staffing parishes called a team ministry." If candidates for these teams passed a "period of evaluation," Barry said, the plan was "to hold them in readiness until a parish opened up where the people of the parish, through the parish council, would be willing to accept a team."

One of those who liked the idea was Father Robert Burbank, then co-pastor of St. Rita's in Hamden, which was Shanley's home parish. He approached the deacon in the parish, Dick Santello, and Gail Bellucci, a member of the choir who had just earned a master's degree in theology. "So the diocese put us through a whole testing thing, psychological testing for work compatibility," Burbank said. Once they were found compatible, all they needed was a parish. They gave Whealon a list of possibilities in the New Haven area.

A few months later, a parish became available, but the people told Whealon they didn't want a team ministry. Later, a second and a third parish rejected the idea. "The archbishop said to us, 'There is a leak in my office,'" Burbank recalled. Someone in Whealon's office was finding out which parishes were candidates for the team ministry, then lobbying parishioners against the idea, Burbank said, apparently "because there were lay folk, never mind women" on the proposed teams. Finally, about four years after the process had started, Whealon offered the team a chance to start their own parish in Rocky Hill, a suburb south of Hartford.

In 1984, they became the first of the collaborative teams, and set to work developing the parish, starting off with mass in a factory building, then putting up their own church. "Their big thing was first they built the community, then they built the building," Shanley said. Did it work? Burbank is positive it did. "I think the big thing—and the thing that I've said again and again and again—is that collaborative ministry set me free to be a priest," he said. Santello, with a background in finance, took care of those issues. Bellucci handled liturgical planning, music ministry, and eucharistic ministers. "We all did counseling and spiritual direction, all of those things," Burbank said. "We took our turns with prebaptism and all that kind of stuff. So that we were all doing various things."

The parishioners also felt it had succeeded. John (Jay) Montalbano, a Middletown attorney who is active in the parish, said that collaborative ministry worked because the team offered a variety of approaches and perspectives: a priest for the traditionalists, a married deacon for married people, a woman for women. "Everybody had something or someone that they could identify with," Montalbano said. "To ask a single celibate priest to fulfill all those roles, I feel, is asking too much of any person."

But when Whealon died in 1991 and Archbishop Daniel Cronin replaced him, Cronin made clear that he considered the experiment to have failed. "He is not appointing any new teams, and as their terms expired, he did not reappoint them," Barry said. "Others broke up totally on their own, without any intervention by the present archbishop."

The team at St. Elizabeth Seton broke up before their second term expired because Bellucci received an attractive, unsolicited job offer at a Catholic high school. She decided to take it. The team had agreed that they came together and they'd leave together. So they did. The archdiocese chose the single priest to succeed the team, but apparently after listening to the concerns of the parishioners. "I was on the committee that met with the priest who's in charge of appointing new priests to parishes," Montalbano said. "My impression of him was that he was a very good listener and he really seemed concerned about the needs and desires of the parish."

Shanley formally became pastor on November 3, 1995, but the team remained with him for liturgies that weekend, including a final prayer service and reception. During his first week, Shanley had a chance to see the parish in action, sense the "vibrancy and faith" of its collective personality, and hear its concerns. His antennae picked up their worries that he might reverse what the people and the team had chosen, by beginning to rearrange the building. "That was one of their big fears, that someone would come in and make them put kneelers in," Shanley recalled.

The following weekend, in his homily, Shanley reported on what he'd seen, what he was experiencing in his own transition, and what he hoped. "I come with no agenda except that of the Lord Jesus Christ, I have no sense of who we shall hire in the future until together we discern in what direction you want the parish to go, and I have no intention of putting in kneelers or additional stained glass, as some of you fear," he told them. "I intend to minister collaboratively."

In the months that followed, Shanley held thirty small-group meetings to get a sense of what the people liked and disliked about the parish, to ask them their hopes for the year 2000. "It was good, because they could talk about all the things they liked—the hospitality, the equality of women, good liturgy," he said.

As it turned out, despite the pain of the team's departure, the early months of Shanley's pastorate went well. The way the parish had grown up, the lay people had assumed their share of the responsibility for ministry, and they knew what they were doing. "They had good education, in terms of liturgy," Shanley said. And parishioners reacted well to him. "I can honestly say that the universal impression of Father Jim is that he is the perfect match for our parish," Montalbano said. "He comes with a very interesting blend of qualities. He's got a very good mind and he is a very good homilist. As a former chaplain, he comes with a very strong pastoral sense."

By the time he went to the Malvern conference, the parish had already begun planning for the next bold step: discontinuing collections during weekend masses in favor of leaving baskets at the doors, where people could drop their offerings at their discretion. The growth of the parishioners as a community, under the collaborative ministry, had laid a solid foundation for that initiative and whatever else the parish undertakes during Shanley's pastorate. "The transition was excellent," Shanley said, "because of the team."

In parishes all over America, there have been transitions that were less than excellent. There are troubled tales of pastors wreaking havoc on formerly functional parishes. With the numbers of priests declining, diocesan personnel boards and bishops have fewer and fewer options in choosing pastors, and they have been known to make mistakes. For that reason and others, there are reasons for pessimism.

"I think there's a rising awareness that maybe this parish thing isn't working, and that's because people are withdrawing," said Father Thomas Sweetser of the Parish Evaluation Project. Though there are some excellent models for success, parish life is turning people off in too many places. "I think the rising concern is, are we really touching people as we need to?" For Philip Murnion, the bottom line is still attendance at mass. "There are no more people going to mass today than there were ten years ago, fifteen years ago," Murnion said. "I mean, the decline has not been reversed."

Still, there are heartening stories of pastors who find ways to work with the people in building on what the pastor before them had done. That is what seems to be happening with Shanley and many of the other new pastors at the Malvern conference. And it is what happened at St. Brigid's.

*Chapter Fourteen*

# THE SEASONS OF
# ST. BRIGID'S

Flapping proudly on the flagpole at St. Brigid's rectory, the Star of David flag of the State of Israel was a sign that parish life was going on, with its inevitable ebb and flow, its rhythm of change, separation, loss, and renewal.

On this June day in 1996, the flag marked separation, the transfer of Michael Maffeo, who had arrived fresh and green from ordination and had been there for five years. It also signaled renewal, welcoming a new priest, Martin Klein, who had converted to Catholicism but remained proud of his Jewish heritage.

Maffeo's sense of humor had fit well into the Westbury parish's style, and he had developed an easy, wisecracking relationship with the pastor. But the Diocese of Rockville Centre requires new priests to transfer after their first five years. So, after several interviews with other pastors, Maffeo was on his way to Gaeta's former parish, St. Anthony of Padua in Rocky Point.

The new priest, one of Maffeo's seminary classmates, came to St. Brigid's with the story of an unusual odyssey. Klein was born on Manhattan's Lower East Side, to Jewish parents. When he was seven, they divorced, and he lived in a series of foster homes. Finally, he was placed with a Catholic widow in South Jamaica, Pearl Kirsch. "She introduced me to the church very lovingly, very beautifully, taught me the values that I needed," Klein said.

But it wasn't until he was thirty, in 1969, that Klein was baptized a Catholic, at St. Ignatius in Hicksville. "She introduced me to the church, but it was my journey," he said, "and it took me time to come to the realization that this is where I needed to be."

Klein spent twenty-five years in shopping-center management. But when his foster mother died in 1982, he took a year's sabbatical from his job at a mall in Valley Stream. "I volunteered to work at St. Ignatius, to help them raise funds," Klein said. "I was asked to become the full-time business manager."

While working in that position, he met Tom Costa, who arrived at St. Ignatius in 1984. They became such close friends that Costa's family unofficially adopted him. "His mother is my third mother," Klein said. So, when Klein sensed a religious vocation, Costa was a natural confidant. "I talked to him about becoming a deacon," Klein said. Costa asked whether Klein had considered the priesthood, and later Costa gave him an unexpected nudge.

The two friends went together to the Dominican sisters' mother-house in Amityville, where Costa offered mass and Klein proclaimed the Scripture readings as lector. There, Costa surprised his friend by telling the nuns that Klein was considering the priesthood and by asking them to pray for him. "Then he turned to me, and he said, 'When these sisters begin to pray for you, you'd better pack your bags,'" Klein recalled.

In September 1987, Klein entered the Seminary of the Immaculate Conception in Huntington. In 1991, at age fifty-one, he was ordained and assigned to St. Patrick's in Glen Cove. In the years that followed, he was a frequent visitor at St. Brigid's, where Maffeo had been assigned since 1991 and Costa since 1994. So in the spring of 1996, when the transfer rule forced him to seek a new parish, St. Brigid's was high on his list.

"I interviewed with seven pastors," Klein said. "I was comfortable with several of them, but I felt a draw to this parish. I wanted this experience of working with people of several different backgrounds."

In interviews with Gaeta, some priests had expressed doubts that they had the skills to minister in such a multicultural parish—but not Klein. "I think a big factor was his positiveness about coming to the parish and not in any way being intimidated by the complexity of the place and by the work level of the place," Gaeta said.

His dinner visits had already made Klein comfortable. "I really felt at home before I ever got here, but once I got here, it's like coming home to a family reunion," Klein said. On June 26, he drove up to the rectory and saw on the flagpole the American flag, the Vatican flag, and the Star of David—which Gaeta regularly uses to greet Jewish holidays, and in this case, to show hospitality to a Jewish priest.

"It brought tears to my eyes, because that's important to me," Klein said. "My Jewishness is very important to me."

As soon as he arrived at St. Brigid's, Klein preached at all the masses, introducing himself to the ethnic communities and telling the story of his own ethnicity and his faith journey. "I said, 'You know, this Jewish priest, I think, will fit in fine,'" he recalled. Quickly, he became simply Father Marty to the parishioners, who soon learned to enjoy his down-to-earth homilies, sprinkled with references to his favorite team, the New York Yankees. Klein is feeling comfortable in his new home. And his foster mother, who gave him the first nudge toward the Catholic faith, is close by, buried in Holy Rood Cemetery, adjoining the church grounds. "I can practically look out my window at her grave," Klein said.

—ππ—

The Maffeo-to-Klein succession was just one in a series of transitions for the parish in 1995 and 1996—some relatively smooth and some painfully abrupt. The life of every parish follows a cycle: Different ministries wax and wane, as people offer their services, give their energy for a time, then withdraw from a ministry for family or professional reasons. Others replace them, but not always in equal numbers or with equal fervor. As some ministries fade temporarily, others burst into renewed life.

On top of those normal changes, the people and the priests of St. Brigid's have had to cope with some especially painful losses—including the deaths of a uniquely charismatic music director, Tommy Ciotti Thorell; a pregnant young mother, Kerry Ann Wetter, who had played a key role in preparing parents for the baptism of their children; and a beloved former pastor, Monsignor Frederick Schaefer.

During the seventeen months when it was the focus of the Newsday series that is the basis of this book, the parish not only had to find a way to deal with these tragedies and subtle shifts in parish life, but it had to do that under the unaccustomed glare of public scrutiny, resulting from Newsday's series of occasional articles.

Before the series, the parishioners had already felt that St. Brigid's was livelier, warmer, more welcoming than the average parish. One indicator was that some people traveled considerable distances to worship there, rather than in their own neighborhood parishes. But the parishioners felt that, in the sudden spotlight that the stories provided, they had a chance to tell an even wider audience about St. Brigid's. After one piece described young mothers' prayer groups, one of the leaders, Catherine Cammarata, told Gaeta: "Think of all the people who are going to read that and say, 'We could start a prayer group.'"

During this period of increased attention, the three deaths hit the parish hard. The loss of Wetter was a shock because she was young and energetic and still involved with the life of St. Brigid's, even though she and her family had moved to Huntington. Schaefer's passing was a great sadness, but his year-long illness had given his former parish time to adjust and prepare. Perhaps the most difficult passage for the parish was the death of Thorell. Its impact was enormous, because he had profoundly shaped the parish's worship.

Toward the end of Thorell's illness, Gaeta felt that he had to do something to lighten the additional burden that it had placed on Stephanie Clagnaz, who already ran the children's choir, supervised the religious education program for the lower grades, and served as a cantor at many parish liturgies. In Thorell's absence, she also took on many of his duties as director of music. "It was just too much," Gaeta said. So he reached out for someone who had worked closely with Thorell and knew the parish's musical style: Mary Jane Witte.

For years, Witte had been singing in churches, including her own parish, Our Lady of Lourdes in Malverne. Then she heard about Father Robert McGuire's Spirit Life Center in Plainview, a ministry shaped by the charismatic renewal movement. She volunteered her voice at the center, and there she met Thorell and began singing his songs. Later, the center ran a retreat at St. Brigid's. That brought Thorell to the attention of Gaeta, who hired him as director of music.

Once Thorell was at St. Brigid's, Witte began singing at three weekend masses on her own and with Thorell at the monthly Jesus Evening, a charismatic healing mass. In that setting, she witnessed the spontaneous creativity that he had developed during his career as a pop music singer and composer. "You never knew what was going to come next," Witte said.

"Then I was offered a job at St. Vincent de Paul in Elmont as their lead cantor," Witte said. "I left here, which was very difficult." Even after leaving St. Brigid's, she still sang at the monthly Jesus Evening regularly. Then, after several months of Thorell's illness, Gaeta called to ask for her help. "She really was known to everybody before she came in," Gaeta said. "That was a big, big part of it. I knew that she was going to continue a philosophy—not totally the same, but at least there would be basic continuity." They agreed that she would come in and help as much as she could, and they'd continue to pray that Thorell would recover and return.

"The day I started, that's the day he passed away," Witte said. She began struggling with sleeplessness and worrying about the choir's reaction to her succeeding Thorell. "That had to be the hardest thing for me, because these people were so close to him and had been through so much," she said. "It was really, I would say, a nightmare for me, but they were wonderful. They opened their hearts to me."

For her part, Witte has simply taken things slowly. "I understood that they were hurting, and I understood that they wouldn't be so thrilled about having somebody come in," she said. "I would just go there and do my best quietly, and God would make it work."

The parish still uses Thorell's music often, and in a memorial liturgy in Queens for the victims of the TWA Flight 800 crash, Clagnaz sang two Thorell compositions: "Through It All" and "I Saw a World." Clearly, though Witte fit in smoothly, Thorell is still a powerful presence.

"Mary Jane is the most supportive and wonderful person. You could never have asked for Father Frank to bring in someone who is more supportive," Clagnaz said. "In terms of whether the choir could ever let go of Tommy, that's a different question."

—⟋ш⟍—

Losing someone of Thorell's charismatic abilities has been an extraordinarily difficult hurdle—one that does not often confront a parish. Now, over the next few years, a series of more ordinary but no less formidable challenges lies ahead of St. Brigid's and every other parish.

"One is that parishes are going to have to find ways to be much more effective in engaging people in personal commitment to their faith, and a faith that has consequences for their public life, besides their private life," said Monsignor Philip Murnion, director of the National Pastoral Life Center.

In that spirit, St. Brigid's has been seeking more effective ways to meet the needs of the poor. It already provides food, clothing, employment counseling, and other services from its outreach offices in the rectory basement and from the thrift shop below the church. But for months, the outreach director, Sister Judy Mannix, and the outreach advisory board had envisioned a presence in New Cassel, where many of the outreach program's clients live. Finally, they made it happen.

During a search of the neighborhood, Mannix and two lay volunteers, Anne Josey and Kay O'Brien, found a suitable space that was once a doctor's office. The advisory board and Gaeta approved. The office opened on a bright, sunny day in October 1996, with prayers and speeches. Al Peck, the chairman of the outreach advisory board, served as master of ceremonies, and Auxiliary Bishop John Dunne blessed the new office. Even on a weekday afternoon, the event drew more than fifty people, including parish staff, outreach volunteers, a group of nuns from Mannix's congregation, the Sisters of the Good Shepherd, and her mother Helen. "I think this is a blessed, blessed moment in the life of our parish," Gaeta told them.

At the time of the new office's opening, the plan was to keep the clothing and food operations on the parish grounds, where there is more room, but it was not clear how the parish would use the space. The key, Mannix said, was to listen to the people and use the new office to help them in ways that they specify. Whatever its uses, the mere presence of the office is important. "I think it's a statement to people that says, 'We want to be there,'" Mannix said. "I guess the question is, how is it going to change us? I think it will give us an opportunity to be able to get to know the families better."

One certainty about the new office is its name. Mannix suggested "St. Brigid's Well," after the widespread Irish custom of dedicating water wells to St. Brigid. Like those wells, this would be a place for people to gather. To that title, Gaeta added the name of his predecessor as pastor, who was known for his compassion to the poor. So the New Cassel office became St. Brigid's Well: The Father Fred Schaefer Memorial. "We thank you, Jesus, for his life, for his vision and for his example of love," Gaeta prayed at the opening. "Truly, Jesus, his fingerprints are here."

As for financing, the outreach program had enough money on hand to pay the rent for a while, with a large boost from the proceeds of Gaeta's book of Advent reflections and the prospect of further income from his new book about the parish, *From Holy Hour to Happy Hour*. Beyond that, Gaeta had announced, just before the opening of the New Cassel office, that the parish would give ten percent of its future collections to the poor. "Honestly, outreaches always do fine," Gaeta said. "I've never been in a situation where we don't have enough money. It always comes in."

But the good news for outreach is part of the story of ministries ebbing and flowing. When Mannix came to St. Brigid's in 1994, she served as a liaison to the Hispanic community and coordinated the parish's efforts in pursuit of peace and justice. Then outreach director Laura Rivera left, and Gaeta asked Mannix to take over outreach. The demands of outreach, including the additional effort in New Cassel, forced Mannix to tell Gaeta that she could no longer handle the peace and justice committee. "I think that you need somebody to be able to put a lot of time into that," Mannix said. "Nobody really had the time."

In most parishes, clergy and lay leaders have a hard time helping the people in the pews to see the connection between the Gospel and the hard work of peace and justice that it requires. That is the most difficult part of meeting Murnion's challenge to parishes: to connect faith and its public consequences.

"Peace and justice, in my experience in all my parishes, has always been underwhelming," Gaeta said. "But I do think it's something that we have to consistently be working on and hope that an awareness is going to grow." One of the peace and justice committee's efforts, to persuade children to turn in their violence-based toys, generated a disappointing response. "That doesn't mean we shouldn't do it this year and expand on it and explain more about it," Gaeta said.

In all parishes there is a strain of what Gaeta called "a hardness of heart to the pain and the needs of others." But at St. Brigid's, parishioners have been generous. "People will respond as they know how to respond, and I think it's part of the parish's responsibility to give people avenues and ways of responding," Gaeta said. "I would say you've got a tremendous part of the parish whose heart is absolutely in the right place, and truly want to do justice."

That nucleus of deeply committed parishioners includes such long-time activists as Isabel Lister, a feisty and energetic outreach volunteer who has also been involved with the peace and justice committee, and Ted Conlin, who is working on a long book that indicts war and writing a series of one hundred fifty reflections on spirituality, which he calls the key to peacemaking.

"We really have to rethink the work of peace and justice," Conlin said. "That is all self-defeating unless we are rooted in something deeper than ourselves. . . . The road to peace and justice and happiness must run through spirituality, and spirituality that is a consciousness of the sacred."

Beyond making practical connections between faith and life, Murnion said, parishes face another important task. "The challenge is going to be to make the parishioners much more responsible for the ministry of the parish," Murnion said. "It's going to have to be a community of disciples."

At St. Brigid's, lay people have taken important leadership positions since the time of Schaefer, who steadily nudged them toward taking ownership of the parish. Gaeta has continued that emphasis. Though the parish has a handful of lay people in leadership formation programs, he is concerned that it has not developed enough new lay leadership for the future. "I think that really is the thing that we have to be much more concerned about, given the fact that we have a shortage of clergy," Gaeta said.

The parish structure includes lay boards that provide Gaeta with advice in such areas as parish outreach, liturgy, finances, the regional school, and religious education. "He's sort of like the CEO," Lister said. "He not only is a good priest, with loving concern for people, but he is a damn good CEO. He always consults with people."

But for a time, the parish had not had a pastoral council to provide overall guidance. An earlier council had been large and unwieldy and eventually lapsed. After a pastoral visit to the parish in 1994, Bishop Dunne recommended that the pastor create a new one. "The importance of a pastoral council is to make sure you're really testing the waters and you're really trying to seek out the advice of a cross section of your people about what they see to be the needs," Dunne said. "A group of people, whether elected or selected, can keep your vision a little more sharpened."

Soon after the opening of the new outreach office, Gaeta called together the first meeting of a broad council that he hoped would help the parish focus its vision. "What I really want now is a coming together of the real leaders of all the ministries, and I want to use that as a consultation board," Gaeta said. "The parish has so much going on that people active in one area sometimes don't know what is happening in another. One of the things that we have to do is to come together to give people an experience of what exactly is going on in the whole body of the parish."

Another continuing challenge is to find ways of making St. Brigid's ethnic diversity work more broadly. The parish has mass every week in English, Spanish, Italian, and Creole. Several times a year, it has multicultural liturgies that involve all these groups, plus the smaller Filipino community. But parish leaders realize they still need to knit these communities together better in areas that go beyond liturgy.

"I think what they do well is provide welcome and opportunity for the different ethnic groups," Dunne said. "I think they also do well those moments when they pull them together. That's not the easiest thing to pull off, because people do enjoy their own identity."

Living with diversity is not easy, but the parish has overcome serious obstacles before. When Gaeta arrived in 1989, for example, the parish was $1,228,000 in debt to the Diocese of Rockville Centre. One large factor was the split of the parish to create the neighboring parish of Our Lady of Hope. That sharply cut revenue, without corresponding cost savings.

But in September 1991, the parish launched a fund-raising campaign with twenty receptions, hosted by parishioners, to encourage people to make pledges. The centerpiece was a Tree of Life in the back of the church, where parishioners could have leaves with their own name for an $1,800 pledge. "This was really all done in one month," Gaeta said. "It was a hell of a month." In 1996, five years later, the parish was debt-free.

"They have really rallied extraordinarily to take on the debt and to set goals for themselves at maybe a more rapid pace than most parishes would be able to do," Dunne said. "I dare say it is because people themselves have rallied."

Rapid debt reduction is not the only thing that has set this parish apart. Over the years, people in other parishes have somehow become aware of what goes on at St. Brigid's: its lively liturgies, its welcoming spirit, its ethnic diversity, and its profusion of ministries. But in seventeen months of 1995–96, the Newsday series resulted in an expanded public awareness, offering the parish both the pleasures and the pressures of the spotlight. That new awareness generated a large number of phone calls from areas outside the parish, often from people who had been away from the church and were seeking information on such parish strengths as confession or prayer groups.

"It gives them a forum to come back into the church," said Mary Grossi, the receptionist who answered many of those calls. This role as a possible re-entry point put added pressure on the staff to handle the calls kindly. "You're not even just answering for St. Brigid's," Grossi said. "You're almost responsible for the whole Catholic Church."

For Gaeta, the new notoriety served almost as a report card, helping him to reflect on what the parish could do better. It also triggered occasional criticism from outside. For the parish staff, the trick was to figure out how much of the criticism came from those who wondered why their own parish had not received similar attention and how much was genuine concern about the way St. Brigid's works.

But for Stephanie Clagnaz, those who are critical are missing the point about the warm, relational approach that St. Brigid's takes to parish life. "This is not like some theology that Gaeta dreamed up," said Clagnaz, who sees the roots of this approach in the Hebrew Scriptures. "This stuff dates back to ancient times," she said. "We're just bringing it to life."

Even in the religious education program, the approach is relational and experiential, rather than based solely on rote teaching of dogma. In the 1996–97 school year, for example, religious education classes planted, cultivated, and harvested a garden at school and gave the produce to Island Harvest and Long Island Cares, to feed the poor. "Our philosophy is providing the experience of church, so that later on they'll say, 'That was a loving place,'" Clagnaz said.

In the year between the end of the Newsday series and the publication of this book, the inevitable cycle of parish life has continued.

It has brought moments of sadness, such as the death of Agnes Kickham, one of the leaders of the small Christian communities, and the stroke that temporarily slowed down the irrepressible Deacon Phil Matheis.

It has also brought change, such as the retirement of the school's principal, Christine Lombardi.

And it has brought opportunity, such as the school's big leap foward: application for accreditation by the Middle States Association of Colleges and Schools. In that milestone process, Lombardi planned to serve as a consultant to the new principal, Paul Clagnaz.

Somehow, as it struggles with all the challenges that face modern parishes, wrestles with debt, celebrates diversity, and works out how best to serve the poor, St. Brigid's has managed to give out the message that it is a welcoming place.

Even young Michael Sparacino has picked that up, mostly by watching his aunt, Stephanie Clagnaz, rehearse with the children's choir. One day, at age two, he arose and expressed a strong wish to go to church. When his mother, a Methodist, asked him what church he meant, he clarified his destination: "The place where Aunt Stephanie is, where she sings and claps her hands and has fun."

For the people of St. Brigid's, working hard to keep the parish spirit alive as the millennium approaches, Michael's definition of church will suffice.

# PARISH!

## THE PULITZER PRIZE—WINNING
## STORY OF A VIBRANT
## CATHOLIC COMMUNITY

## ROBERT F. KEELER

*Photographs by Ken Spencer*

A CROSSROAD BOOK
THE CROSSROAD PUBLISHING COMPANY
NEW YORK

*For all the saints*
*of St. Brigid's*

1997
The Crossroad Publishing Company
370 Lexington Avenue, New York, NY 10017

Copyright © 1997 by Newsday, Inc.

Printed in the United States of America

**Library of Congress Cataloging-in-Publication Data**

Keeler, Robert F.
    Parish! : the Pulitzer prize-winning story of one vibrant
Catholic community / Robert F. Keeler
        p.    cm.
    ISBN 0-8245-1697-4 (hardcover)
    1. St. Brigid's (Church : Westbury, Nassau County, N.Y.)
2. Catholic Church—United States—Case studies.
3. Parishes—United States—Case studies.    I. Title.
BX4603.W517K44    1997
282′.747245—dc21                              97-14701
                                              CIP

# Contents

# Preface

# THE ORIGINS
# OF A PROJECT

*T*homas Merton led me to St. Brigid's.

In late 1993, I was working on a piece about the Trappist monk, for the twenty-fifth anniversary of his death. I'd read much of his powerful writing on subjects both inside and outside the monastic enclosure, such as contemplation, racism, and the evils of war. His books line my shelves, and a drawing of Merton by Newsday artist Bob Newman hangs over my desk at home.

So when I learned that Father Daniel Berrigan, the Jesuit peace activist and friend of Merton, would be speaking about him at St. Brigid's, I went. The warmth and energy of the people packed into that small church were overwhelming. Later, I had a similar experience when I went there to hear the Nobel Peace Prize laureate Rigoberta Menchu of Guatemala.

A few months after that, St. Brigid's was still on my mind. Phyllis Singer, the assistant managing editor of Newsday, had long wanted to launch a series on life in a Catholic parish, and I was doing research on Long Island parishes that we might consider as the focus of the series.

Finding the right parish was crucial. I'd had ample experience— raising funds, serving on a parish council, proclaiming Scripture readings at mass, and attending liturgies in many parishes. Over the years, I had developed a fanciful nickname for the kind of parish that provided the sacraments but very little in the way of liturgical warmth and emotional support, focusing more on the rules than on the Gospel. I called it St. Rigid's. And I knew that picking a lifeless parish like that would make for a painful year and a tedious series.

7

So I solicited recommendations, interviewed pastors, and gave my editors a memo listing seven parishes. In the end, the liveliness of the liturgy, the diversity of the people, and a strong recommendation from Father John White, who had served there, persuaded me St. Brigid's was the place. It was clear to me that St. Brigid's was nothing like St. Rigid's.

That decision was one key to the Newsday series that led to this book. The other was the attitude of parishioners and parish staff.

If the pastor, Monsignor Francis X. Gaeta, had declined to cooperate with the project, who could have blamed him? No parish really needs a newspaper reporter hanging around, like an annoying fly on the wall, at dozens of liturgies, meetings, and other events—especially a reporter for a paper sometimes viewed in the past as anti-Catholic. But he said yes, giving me complete access.

If the people had been hesitant to answer my questions, I'd have understood. To write about their spirituality, I had to ask questions that I'd never asked in covering politics: terribly personal questions about the deepest realities of their inner lives. Far from dodging the questions, people invited me into their homes, their prayer groups, and their hearts, answering knotty questions with thoughtful answers. In fact, one of my biggest challenges was retaining a journalistic detachment from people who had been so open and trusting.

During the long process of reporting and writing the series, I recalled some long-ago advice for reporters, written by the late, distinguished columnist Murray Kempton before he came to Newsday. Once I'd read it, I copied it down like a monastic scribe in my little ledger book of cogent quotes by clear thinkers. His point was this: A reporter never knows when someone might encounter a discarded newspaper in a subway, pick it up, and read the reporter's work. So every reporter had better be ready for inspection.

In that spirit, I imagined people that I'll never meet. I envisioned them reading one of my stories, learning how faith works at St. Brigid's, and finding a reason in that knowledge to make significant changes in their lives. After some stories appeared, the parish staff told me that people had called, asking about going to confession or starting a prayer group, as the people in the stories had. I know that being around the people of St. Brigid's has bolstered my own faith, and hearing about those calls made me think that perhaps the stories had done the same for someone else. For me, that made the whole enterprise worthwhile.

In the series, I was able to tell the stories of a few of the parishioners, but space constraints kept me from exploring many other stories and describing adequately the vital role of the parish staff. Among those who have made the parish work, but did not get sufficient acknowledgment in the series, are Adriana Miller, Marie Firenze, Lucy Rex, Ted Henderson, Bob Martella, Ita Levesque, and Tomás Evans.

Now, the series has become a book. In a few places, I've been able to add back some material that space considerations had kept out of the newspaper. I have also written two new chapters. Chapter two is a brief biographical look at the two pastors who had the most to do with making St. Brigid's what it is today: Gaeta and his predecessor, Monsignor Frederick Schaefer. Chapter thirteen, based on reporting that I did after the Newsday series had ended, tries to place St. Brigid's in a broader national context. There are nearly twenty thousand Catholic parishes in this country, and this chapter is designed to offer a sense of how some of them are coping with the complexity of parish life in the closing years of the millennium.

The publication of this book gives me an opportunity to offer some thanks. Let me start with the two people who had to live most closely with this project from the beginning. The first is my wife, Judy, who not only became a St. Brigid's widow for all the months that I spent evenings and weekends in Westbury, but also read my copy before publication and gave me excellent advice. The second is my good friend Ken Spencer, who contributed more to the series than his dozens of brilliant photographs, which somehow managed the incredibly difficult feat of capturing spirituality on film. He was also my wise advisor and good buddy, helping me through the difficult times with his understanding and common sense. And his wife, Kathy, offered valuable affirmation and support to both of us.

The idea for the series came from Phyllis Singer. But the Newsday editor who carried the greatest burden of editing the stories was Judy Cartwright. She treated them gently and sensitively from beginning to end. More than that, she and Phyllis together gave me one of the major ingredients of this series: time. While I worked on the series, I had little time for other stories, and they allowed me to focus heavily on St. Brigid's, with the full support of the editor, Anthony Marro, and the managing editor, Howard Schneider. My colleague Stuart Vincent helped immensely by covering many of the stories that I might otherwise have had to cover.

The other Newsday editors who deserve thanks include Rick Firstman, who helped edit the initial story before leaving Newsday for a book project; Deanna Hutchinson on the news desk, who shepherded the first huge package of stories into the news section; and Jack Millrod's Part 2 copy desk, especially Larry Striegel, Dick Wiltamuth, Sandy Miller, Annabelle Kerins, and Gus Dallas. In laying out the series, Miriam Smith did the bulk of the art direction, with help from Rita Hall and Joanne Utley. And, as always, Iris Quigley in the library offered help on too many occasions to count. In the process of nominating the series for a Pulitzer Prize, Joye Brown lobbied for the submission; Judy Cartwright wrote the nominating letter; Barbara Marlin put it together; Ken Spencer provided the official photograph; and Dan van Benthuysen, Gloria Sandler, Arlene Pallack, and Pat Byrne assembled the whole submission.

As for the book itself, I owe profound thanks to Lynn Schmitt Quinn, the managing editor of The Crossroad Publishing Company. Even before the first piece appeared, she offered me advice. Then, commuting to work from Long Island to Manhattan, Lynn began to read the series. A year before it ended, and well before it was even submitted for a Pulitzer, she proposed making it into a book. I can't thank her enough for her persistence and kindness. If this book turns out to be helpful to anyone, it will be because Lynn envisioned it and stuck to the idea until the end.

# THE MOTHER CHURCH

*B*eneath the drawing of St. Brigid's church in the weekly bulletin, a caption labels it "the Mother Church of all Nassau County." That little boast is typical of the parish's self-image, a gently brassy pride in both its antiquity and its style. Like all historical claims, though, it needs qualification.

To begin with, Nassau County did not come into existence as a separate county until 1898, when it split off from Queens, the easternmost county in the City of New York. The history of St. Brigid's easily precedes all that. But another Nassau County parish has antiquity claims of its own.

In Glen Cove, a small city in the middle of Nassau's wealthy North Shore, a few miles northwest of Westbury, loyalists of St. Patrick's parish have argued that it is really older than St. Brigid's. One priest assigned to Glen Cove, Father Martin Klein, took that position in friendly arguments with Father Michael Maffeo, who became the parish historian at St. Brigid's because he had a master's degree in history and worked as a substitute history teacher before his 1991 ordination and assignment to Westbury.

The development of the area itself is uncontroverted. It derives its name from Westbury, Wiltshire, England, the birthplace of Henry Willis, who first settled in 1670 in the flat expanse of land known as the Hempstead Plain. Willis was a Quaker, like many of the area's first families.

When the Roman Catholic Diocese of New York was created in 1808, it included Long Island. In 1850, in recognition of its growth and importance, it became an archdiocese. The same year, apparently convinced that the activity of Catholics in the area warranted an investment in the future, diocesan officials bought land in Westbury, south of the Long Island Rail Road tracks.

By then, people had already been attending mass at a farmhouse in the area for some time. In arguments with his Glen Cove friend, Maffeo liked to say: "Mass was said on the Hempstead Plain long before it was even thought of being said in Glen Cove."

A lay building committee converted a wooden farmhouse into the first church, in about 1850. The archdiocese kept growing, and in 1853, it was split, creating the Diocese of Brooklyn to cover all of Long Island. It wasn't until 1856 that Bishop John Loughlin, the first bishop of Brooklyn, formally dedicated the church in Westbury.

It started out as a mission, which meant that it did not have a full-time pastor. That circumstance created an interdependence between St. Brigid's and St. Patrick's, the other parish named for a patron saint of Ireland. The Glen Cove parish had not built its church until 1861, well after St. Brigid's, but St. Patrick's had its own priest, and St. Brigid's did not. So, for years, Westbury had to borrow a priest from Glen Cove. It was not until 1892, more than forty years after its church went up, that St. Brigid's got a pastor. "They put us rather late in terms of being a parish, because that was when the first resident pastor came here," Maffeo said.

The parish built a larger church in 1894, the current church in 1915, and the rectory in 1918. In the construction of the church and the rectory, builders used granite removed from the excavation sites for part of the New York City subway system. Soon after the completion of the church, the old church building was moved across Post Avenue and became the school.

As the population grew, the school became inadequate. Father James Sullivan, the pastor from 1944 to 1954, led two major construction projects: a new school building on Maple Avenue, about a mile from the church, and a chapel to serve the growing population of Carle Place, just west of Westbury.

In 1956—one year before the creation of the Diocese of Rockville Centre, to serve Nassau and Suffolk counties—the parish celebrated the centenary of the original church's dedication. At the time, the pastor was Monsignor Thomas Code, an Irishman with a strong singing voice and sharp sense of ecclesiastical politics. "Code was the epitome of the old-time Irish schmoozer," Deacon Jack Falls said. "He was a delicate, gentle, wonderful individual, with great compassion," said United States Circuit Court Judge Frank Altimari, who also appreciated Code's political skill. "He worked the room better than any person I ever saw."

But when the Second Vatican Council ended in 1965, with its call for renewal and greater lay involvement, Code was already elderly, and he was not speedy in adopting all the council's reforms. "I think some of the changes may have been a little difficult for him, but he did what he had to do," said Jack Graham, a key lay leader. Code moved the altar so that the priest could say mass facing the people, for example, but made few changes beyond that.

It was the arrival of Father Fred Schaefer in 1975 that began bringing the parish into the post–Vatican II era, followed by Monsignor Francis X. Gaeta in 1989. "Fred very much embraced Vatican II," Graham said. "He was really the one who brought to the attention of the laity that St. Brigid's was not his church; it was their church. Frank has done a magnificent job in following up on that."

The two pastors, strikingly different in personal style, somehow managed to shepherd one large community, made up of multiple ethnic groupings, into one decidedly post–Vatican II parish that somehow has continued to work cohesively and remain vibrant. That is no small accomplishment, and the purpose of this book is to examine how St. Brigid's does it.

## Chapter One

# LIVING IN
# ORDINARY TIME

*I*t is a nondescript winter Tuesday night in the third week of Ordinary Time, the gray expanse of not-Lent, not-Easter, not-Advent, not-Christmas that makes up most of the church calendar. No holy day of obligation, no palm, no ashes, no prospect of pageantry to draw the crowds.

Still, a respectably ample group of parishioners has slid into the wooden pews in the cozy, Norman-style confines of St. Brigid's church, to attend a "parish enrichment evening," early in 1995.

The pastor stands before his congregation in a plain black clerical suit. Officially, he has the honorary title of monsignor, but there are monsignors and there are monsignors. Some seem to enjoy sweeping grandly into a room, wearing the monsignor's red-fringed cassock and bright red sash. This monsignor doesn't even own one. In the bulletin, his name is at the bottom of the staff list, not as monsignor, but simply as "Rev. Francis X. Gaeta." Everyone calls him Father Frank.

"Parish is wonderful, because parish is people," Gaeta begins. Then he likens this parish in Westbury, in the center of suburban Nassau County, to the synagogue and the community in the Galilean hills that shaped Jesus. "This community transforms us and makes us into something we could never be by ourselves," he says. "Our spirituality is not just all by ourselves. Our spirituality is in community."

In that spirit, Gaeta asks people to think of moments when the parish has touched them. He begins by recalling an experience of his own in 1990, on his first Good Friday as pastor. The Italian community had staged its outdoor passion play, ending with the death of

Jesus, at St. Brigid's school, a few blocks from the church. Then the Hispanic community had carried a life-sized statue of the dead Jesus through the streets to the church, where others inside had been enacting a contemporary version of the Stations of the Cross. The Hispanic parishioners had carried the statue into the crowded, darkened church, lighting it up with their vibrant, emotional faith.

"It was one of the most extraordinary, liberating, life-giving moments of my whole life," Gaeta tells them. "Then I understood what it is to be in a multicultural parish."

To give others a chance to share their recollections, Deacon Phil Matheis—seventy-nine years old but still full of puckish humor and always ready to trade cracks with Gaeta—carries a wireless microphone around the church. Anne Josey takes the mike and tells of the day Matheis baptized her grandson, who was born weighing only a pound and a half. One woman tells of her granddaughter wanting to bring her puppy to a blessing of the animals at St. Brigid's: "She says, 'Maybe if God gets His hands on him, he'll last longer.'"

Gaeta introduces the guest speaker, a Jesuit priest named Thomas Sweetser, codirector of the Illinois-based Parish Evaluation Project. Sweetser has been in town only a few hours, but he has already gained a sense of the place, first from a bountiful, laughter-filled Italian meal at the rectory, and now from the enthusiastic, hands-raised worship style in the church.

"I have a feeling that you have a great spirit going here, right?" Sweetser says, stirring a ripple of applause. "I also have a feeling that your pastor has something to do with that. Am I right?" More applause. "What is it about you that you pray so well here? You pray a lot. You get a lot of practice."

In many parishes, people make little contact with those around them, except for a perfunctory handshake at the sign of peace. Here, the contact clearly is warmer. For example, the people tell Sweetser, everyone automatically joins hands to pray the Our Father. "Wow!" Sweetser says. "The word is 'Amen,'" says Josey, whose loud, distinctive "Amen" has become a signature of worship at St. Brigid's.

Toward the end of the evening, Lillian Morris asks for the microphone and offers a summation: "Personally, I think nothing is perfect, but this is almost a perfect parish."

St. Brigid's may not be quite a perfect parish, but in atmosphere and attitude it seems a fitting place to serve as the focus for an examination of parish life thirty years after the Second Vatican Council launched a major rethinking of what parishes should be.

There are 134 parishes in the Diocese of Rockville Centre, which covers Nassau and Suffolk, the two suburban counties lying just east of New York City. Some are lively and engaging, some staid and cool. And while any number of them could serve as a window into modern Catholic life, St. Brigid's, with its crackling energy level, its intriguing mix of ethnicities, its enthusiastic and emotional liturgies, seems particularly engaging. It is a parish that draws people from great distances, a parish whose reputation has somehow spread.

Despite national studies showing declining attendance at mass, parish is still a central focus of life for many Catholics. It is the place where they play out their distinctive "sacramental imagination, a tendency to see God as present in the world and to view the everyday realities of that world as revealing that presence," in the words of Father Andrew Greeley. So Catholics place great emphasis on community and ceremony, and parish is where they bring together the stuff of their lives with the ritual that brings meaning to it all.

"If there is any doubt about how important the parish is to those who live in it, one must merely consider the outrage that inevitably erupts whenever the chancery tries to close a parish or a school or tear down a church," wrote Greeley, a sociologist and novelist, in *The Catholic Myth*, a 1990 book that flowed from three decades of sociological inquiry into Catholic life. "The American neighborhood parish is one of the most ingenious communities that human skill has ever created."

But it is not a static community. Parishes are still working to figure out what they should be, thirty years after the Second Vatican Council initiated a movement toward more lay involvement. Ownership of the parish is shifting from pastor to people, and geographical parish boundaries are becoming less important, as Catholics display an increasing willingness to travel outside of their home parish to find one that meets their needs. The available number of priests is shrinking, which accelerates the shift of responsibility to lay people. And the number of parish schools is declining as dioceses economize by establishing regional schools to serve several parishes.

"The American Catholic parish is in the midst of a paradigm shift," Sweetser wrote with Carol Holden, codirector of the Parish Evaluation Project, in *Leadership in a Successful Parish*, a 1992 book. The project is an independent parish consulting group that helps parishes evaluate themselves and plan for the future. "The parish is at a most critical moment in its history."

At this pivotal moment, the parish is moving toward a firmer grasp of the concept that parish is people—not just a building or a hierarchy, but the place where the people gather together to *be church* for one another.

—⁂—

In the house on Lewis Avenue where they have lived for forty years, Bill and Mary Goode raised seven boys and five girls. Bill worked days at the Westbury post office and nights at Roosevelt Raceway's parimutuel windows. When he came home, Mary would head to her nursing job at Mercy Hospital in Rockville Centre. The demands of work and child-rearing didn't leave them time to be active in the parish. Once the children were grown, Mary became a eucharistic minister and, at Gaeta's request, started a hospital visitation ministry.

In late 1991, one of their children, Kitty Millan of Westbury, gave birth to a daughter, Megan, and the Goode children gathered for the baptism at St. Brigid's. Another daughter, Peggy Kilinski, came down from Schenectady with her husband, Paul, and their children, two-year-old Jay Paul and seven-year-old Lauren. On the eve of the baptism, Peggy put the children to sleep in the attic of her parents' home and returned downstairs to continue the reunion with her family.

Late that night, fire broke out in the attic, killing Jay Paul and leaving Lauren terribly injured. First Lauren and later her father were taken to the burn unit at Nassau County Medical Center, where Gaeta joined the family and kept vigil. "Peggy and Father Frank and I stayed until about five o'clock in the morning," Mary Goode said.

Over the next six weeks, as Lauren lay in the burn unit, the tragedy gripped the whole parish. Parishioners prayed for Lauren daily at mass and did what they could for the family. "I don't think we cooked one meal from October 26 to December 10," Mary said, her voice breaking. "Somebody sent a meal every night."

When this all began, the Goodes had not yet developed a close relationship with Gaeta. "Now he's like one of our family," Mary Goode said. "He came every single night to the hospital." When Lauren died, he sat with the family for hours, and later traveled to Schenectady to participate in her funeral mass.

In 1994, Gaeta baptized two new members of the family: James, the second child of Kitty and Chuck, and Francis, the third child of Paul and Peggy Kilinski, who named him for Gaeta. For the pastor, accustomed to dealing with death, this numbing level of tragedy was something he had never experienced, and he realized there were no adequate words he could say. But it drew him close to the family. "I just developed a bond with them," Gaeta said. "Honestly, their faith was just so incredible that I'd go there to be restored myself."

All this had a profound effect on Chuck Millan, who had grown up Lutheran but began thinking about conversion. "He saw our faith at work," Kitty Millan said. The Easter after the fire, he was received into the Catholic Church. Peggy's strength in coping with her grief and the parish's response helped all of them to grow in faith. "It changed all our lives so much," Kitty said. "We've all gotten so much closer to God."

—⁂—

The idea for a parish system arose in the fourth century, when the primary pastors, the bishops, could no longer adequately tend their growing flocks in outlying areas, away from the central worship center. The bishops divided the rural areas into parishes, each to be served by a resident priest. So the parish became the most local manifestation of Catholicism, where people gathered to celebrate the "dangerous memory" of Jesus, whose commands of selfless love and limitless forgiveness could be so costly to follow, and to participate in the mass, the central act of Catholic worship. In ways impossible to quantify, parishes have helped people to cope with life's unfathomable tragedies, to utter gratitude for its exquisite joys, to grapple with its most profound mysteries.

But there is no such thing as an average parish. Though they all offer the same sacraments and share the same mission, parishes can be very different—depending on the pastor, the people, and the synergy that they achieve together.

Vatican II and the 1983 Code of Canon Law moved the emphasis from pastor to people, making it clear that every member of the parish community, simply by virtue of baptism, has a share in responsibility for the life of the parish. But the pastor still sets the tone, for better or worse. The pastor is so crucial that some parishes have fallen into prolonged acrimony after a change at the top. For twenty years, however, St. Brigid's has not only survived but thrived under two pastors with sharply different styles.

Arriving in 1975, Father Frederick Schaefer was the educator who gave lay people a real role and nudged them into the training they needed. He was the community-builder, developing liturgies for the different language groups that had come to populate the Westbury area. He was the prophet who stood up and told the difficult truth: The Gospel of Jesus required the parish to reach out and help the refugees who flooded into Westbury from El Salvador in the 1980s. "He was a priest of the poor, and the poor knew it," said Joan Echausse, one of those who acquired a master's degree in theology with Schaefer's encouragement.

When Schaefer left in 1989 for St. Francis de Sales parish in Patchogue, feeling it was time for the people to hear the Gospel preached in another voice, Gaeta succeeded him. The primary lay leaders are still the people who received their theological training under Schaefer, and Gaeta acknowledges that reality gratefully. He also admires Schaefer's stand for the poor. "I think Fred was prophetic, and he just had a sense of the church and a beautiful compassion and love of the poor," Gaeta said. "I think he was right on the money." But stylistically, the two men could hardly be more different.

Gaeta has a far more emotional personality than Schaefer's, a more raucous sense of humor, a penchant for wide-open liturgies, a flair for the unusual. It was Gaeta who hired as music director a rock musician, Tommy Ciotti Thorell, with a life story full of twists and turns and stunning epiphanies that rescued him from the fast lane. Gaeta led the way to save the parish school and totally erased the parish debt. But his real genius lies in offering a wide variety of worship experiences, to attract different parts of the community. "Frank would say, 'If it leads you to God, let's do it,'" said Manuel Ramos, one of the leaders of the Hispanic community.

But ultimately, parish really is people. "Frank is a moving force behind it," said Father Michael Maffeo, one of the three priests assigned to work full time with Gaeta, "but if the people don't do it, it doesn't get done." With 23,000 Catholics, the parish is so huge the clergy can't handle it alone, even with four priests and five deacons—an unusually large collection of ordained staff in an era of dwindling clergy numbers. So lay people plan the liturgy, feed the poor, teach the faith to the children, comfort the elderly—in short, make the parish go.

The people are extraordinarily diverse. The parish got its name from a fifth-century abbess, one of three patron saints of Ireland, because when the parish started in the 1850s, the Irish were Westbury's predominant immigrant group. But its ethnic makeup now reflects later waves of immigration: Italians; Mexicans, Salvadorans, and other Spanish speakers; plus African-Americans from the South, Haitians, Filipinos, and others.

That diversity produces emotional events such as the epic Good Friday pageantry and multicultural liturgies several times a year, bringing all the language communities together. "We're working so hard to make our diversity not something that separates us, but something that unites us," Gaeta said at a Thanksgiving mass in 1994. "My dear sisters and brothers, what we are doing here in St. Brigid's parish is what the whole world is supposed to be about."

A few weeks after that mass, Gaeta gave a Sunday homily about a painting of the Last Supper. A young man just out of prison had come up to the pastor and presented him with the painting, which represented Jesus and his twelve apostles as black. Gaeta liked it and had it hung inside one of the entrances to the church.

During his homily, Gaeta told the congregation about the painting's origins and walked over to it. St. Brigid's, he said, is a black church. It is also an Italian church and an Irish church and a Haitian church and a Hispanic church and a Filipino church. As he spoke, the congregation started applauding—far from the usual etiquette for a homily.

"It was a Moment," said Joan Echausse, who as lector proclaimed the day's Scripture readings. "You knew you're part of something where time is standing still."

---

Who would be Jesus? That was the problem that kept vexing Vincenzo Iannucci, until one day when the door of his Post Avenue delicatessen opened, and Jerry DeLucia walked in.

DeLucia and Iannucci are both from Italian families that originated in Durazzano, a small valley town in the shadow of Monte Taburno, northeast of Naples. In fact, there are roughly as many people from Durazzano living in St. Brigid's parish as there are in Durazzano itself.

Most of them live just west of the church in a section called Breezy Hill, named for an area in Durazzano. Several have businesses along Post Avenue, including Giuseppe Telese, who runs Joe's European Haircutters and owns a home on the oldest street in Durazzano. "To me, over here is like living in Durazzano," Telese said, standing in his shop, beneath a photo of Durazzano.

People from Durazzano stick together. DeLucia's father, Vincenzo, for example, was a construction foreman and helped new arrivals from Durazzano to find construction jobs. They also work to preserve Durazzano culture. In their home, Vincenzo and Margherita DeLucia and their children spoke Italian. "When I started kindergarten, I didn't know a word of English," Jerry DeLucia said. Now he and his wife, Anna, are doing their part. Their children, Margherita and Vincenzo, students at St. Brigid's school, speak Italian at home.

With that devotion to the culture, DeLucia was more than willing when he walked into the deli more than a decade ago and Iannucci asked his help in staging an Italian-style Good Friday pageant. Iannucci had cast every role but Jesus. Everyone was reluctant. "I said, 'Yeah, I'll do it,'" DeLucia recalled. "He didn't believe me. I said, 'Vinny, I'll do it.' He said, 'But you have to carry the cross and you have to do this . . .' I said, 'Vinny, I'll do it.'"

Every Good Friday since, DeLucia, the owner of a plumbing business and the president of the Italian community at St. Brigid's, has carried the cross in the passion play—preserving a bit of Italian tradition that has become a keystone of the legendary St. Brigid's Holy Week liturgies.

—✠—

The question caught parishioners at parish enrichment night by surprise. "Are you any better than any other parish?" Sweetser asked. Some said no, apparently out of an egalitarian sense that it was the correct answer. But the negative sounded tentative. The people of St. Brigid's really do think other parishes could learn from them. And there's evidence that people elsewhere agree.

Traditionally, Catholics almost always went to church in the parish where they lived. But those who don't feel adequately fed emotionally and spiritually in their own parishes are more willing now to shop for a different parish. "I believe you have to do it, because in some places the church is dead, as far as I'm concerned," said Sister Joan Staudohar, who has often driven fifteen or twenty minutes from Hicksville to Westbury to attend mass. "I want to be in a place where there's worship going on."

That's why Chuck Cutolo and his wife, Denise Pratesi, decided to buy a house in Westbury: to live near St. Brigid's. Cutolo was once the legislative director for United States Senator Carl Levin, a Michigan Democrat, later worked as a public policy official for Catholic Charities, and is now the counsel to the Democratic minority on the Nassau County Legislature. Pratesi teaches English and theater at Deer Park High School. Their primary volunteer work for the parish involves the rock mass on Sunday evenings, which they say attracts young people who otherwise might not attend church.

"Many other parishes look to say no; this parish may not always say yes, but it looks for ways to say yes," Pratesi said. "There doesn't seem to be the fear of lay inclusion here that there is in so many other places. Here, they're asking you to be involved."

For all that, St. Brigid's has its share of financial and administrative struggles. It is also still learning how best to deal with its diversity, which is one of the parish's great strengths, but also a continuing challenge. Every weekend, in addition to nine masses in English, there are three in other languages: Creole, Italian, and Spanish. Several times a year, such as the feast of Our Lady of Guadalupe, the language groups get together for complex, uplifting multilingual liturgies, with sections in those four languages, plus some Tagalog, for the Filipinos. At the Guadalupe liturgy, for example, Father Thomas Costa, comparatively new to St. Brigid's, but not to foreign languages, preached in English, Spanish, Italian, and French.

Costa's language skill is a major asset to the parish, but even he agrees with others that the multicultural liturgies are an imperfect step toward unity. "Multicultural masses aren't really satisfying to anybody," Costa said. Because the liturgies reflect so many languages, they don't provide enough of any one language to satisfy. "Probably the English-speaking people of the parish are more positive about them than any of the language groups." At one meeting of the parish liturgy board, where the issue of multicultural liturgies arose, Estelle Peck, the director of liturgy and family life, acknowledged that although the parish is trying its best, "At times, people feel like they're being patronized and they're getting a bone."

Beyond the liturgies, Gaeta and lay leaders say, there is still work to be done to knit the different communities together in a continuing way. "Unity is the ultimate goal, certainly, but we have a ways to go," said Stephanie Clagnaz, leader of the children's choir and a composer of some of the parish's liturgical music.

Ethnicity is not the only form of diversity at St. Brigid's. The parish is also inclusive enough to address the concerns of many constituencies: such as carrying in the bulletin an affirmation of the dignity of gay people and offering a liturgy for their parents, arranging a Christmastime turn-in of violent toys, and providing statues and more traditional forms of devotion. Every parish has different constituencies to serve, but St. Brigid's seems to have a wider-than-usual spectrum and seems to invest more energy in addressing that diversity than do many parishes.

Its tent is big enough to include peace-and-justice liberals such as Cutolo and Pratesi, as well as conservatives such as Michael Posillico, a member of Catholics United for the Faith, a watchdog group that demands doctrinal and liturgical orthodoxy. Posillico, whose great-grandfather was one of the first Italians to migrate here from Durazzano, runs a disc jockey business with his twin brother, Marco.

Together with five or six members of his family, Michael attends mass daily at St. Brigid's, though he attends Sunday mass at a parish in Massapequa Park, to hear a more conservative preacher. He likes some of what Gaeta has done, but he thinks St. Brigid's, like other parishes, uses too many lay eucharistic ministers to distribute communion, which traditional Catholics feel detracts from the respect for the sacrament. He also thinks too many churches preach too little morality.

"Many parishes today, including St. Brigid's, talk about love, love, love," Posillico said, sitting in his basement, amid the huge speakers, vinyl records, and other paraphernalia of his disc jockey business. "My general complaint is priests in general should talk more about hell and about sinning." From the opposite end of the Catholic spectrum, Pratesi said: "That's precisely why we're here: a lot of eucharistic ministers and not a lot about sin and hell."

Tommy Thorell, St. Brigid's director of music, said the parish doesn't lock anyone out. And he should know. Thorell came to St. Brigid's after a career in rock, a dramatic conversion, a new life in Christian music, a falling out with the Catholic Church, and an experiment as pastor of a storefront church. Then Gaeta hired him, when a more mainstream music director left.

"I'm not liturgically correct or traditional at all," Thorell said. At first, not everyone liked his caress-every-syllable crooning. "They thought, 'Who's this guy? He's like this slick performer,'" Thorell recalled. But his singing is now a keynote of the parish's worship. "He's an entertainer, but he's also a man of prayer," Peck said. "It took a lot of guts for Frank to hire him."

This openness helps to draw people in and make the parish central to their lives. "St. Brigid's is a perfect example of a type of primal community," said Father Robert McGuire, a Jesuit who has given retreats at St. Brigid's and runs the Spirit Life Center in Plainview, which offers healing and prayer in a variety of settings. "The primary life of many people at St. Brigid's is the church."

The most visible dimension of that primacy is the public worship. But it also unfolds in quiet, less visible ways, away from the church building: in prayer groups, small church communities, in-home retreats, Pre-Cana marriage preparation, religious education, and in countless private acts of caring. For the people of St. Brigid's, parish is living out the command of Jesus to bind each other's wounds, to fill each other's needs.

"I feel that the church is the people and that we are here for one another," said Terry Patterson, who runs the parish's Ministry of Winter Grace, its outreach to the elderly, and also helps coordinate small church communities and the education of children for reception into the church.

Before she became so deeply involved in providing care, Patterson's family experienced receiving it, when her oldest son, Johnny, now an adult, developed a brain tumor at age ten. "It was a living nightmare," she said. "We had some insurance, but not enough to cover." So St. Brigid's had to help.

Every day, someone from the parish drove them to Nassau Hospital. And when they had to go into New York City for hospital visits, people at St. Brigid's School cared for her younger children. "We would drop them at the convent at six o'clock in the morning," she said. The school also waived the tuition and took up collections for the family. "I never had to ask," she said. "The parish was reaching out." It was the kind of experience that tests a family's faith. "Either you lose it or you just become stronger," she said. With help from St. Brigid's, their faith grew.

Once Patterson's children were older, she had to cope with some health crises of her own. In a six-month span, she had a hysterectomy and a gall bladder removal, on top of angina and hypertension. "I was flat on my face physically." Then she had a slight stroke, which left her with a leg brace. "I guess it was a turning point," she said. "I was always going, and it was very humbling being on the receiving end. I grew in my faith. I had more time to read the Bible. God said, 'Now, Terry, let's start over again.'"

At about that time, she saw in The Long Island Catholic, the diocesan newspaper, something about a new Pastoral Formation Institute, designed to give lay people further training for a variety of ministries. She checked with the pastor, Schaefer, who encouraged her to attend. It was in the institute that she put together a plan for a ministry to the homebound elderly. She presented her idea to Joan Echausse, who ran the outreach program, to Gaeta, who had succeeded Schaefer, and to the whole parish, at all the masses one weekend.

Her ministry reaches out regularly to people such as the two elderly sisters who had once made a comfortable living as executive secretaries, but now were old and infirm—one with Alzheimer's disease and one with heart problems—living in intolerable conditions of squalor that a neighbor discovered and reported to Patterson. She got one sister into a nursing home and the other into a hospital, followed by round-the-clock nursing care.

Now, Patterson sits in her home, with a portable phone by her side, and answers constant phone calls about elderly people trying to cope with the bureaucracy, the ravages of age, the bewildering complexities of small tasks that they once took for granted, such as shopping or going to a doctor. "The needs are so great," she said.

That cycle of need calling out to need is common. St. Brigid's has a way of pulling people in at a time of crisis in their own lives, then helping them to see ways of answering the needs of others. Ed Ward, a member of the Nassau County Legislature, is one of those drawn into the parish's gravitational pull. His father died at age forty, when Ward was eleven, and his mother's death in 1986 affected him deeply. He wasn't going to mass, and he wasn't coping well. It was a low point, emotionally as well as spiritually.

One day in 1989, near his mother's birthday, he was visiting her grave in Holy Rood Cemetery, adjoining St. Brigid's. "I heard the bells ringing; I went over to mass," Ward said. What he heard was not hell-fire, but love and forgiveness. "In terms of what I had been through, the loss of both parents, it was a punishing God I had grown up with," Ward said. "And here was this young, fresh, spiritually inspired guy, talking about the love of God."

The priest was Father John White. Over the next few weeks, Ward kept going to mass, and White always seemed to be the celebrant. Soon, Ward and White became friends. Though White has now been reassigned to diocesan Catholic Charities, Ward still drives from Seaford to attend St. Brigid's, where he helps run programs for young adults and is a regular at "The Six," the Sunday rock mass at 6 P.M.

That mass is one good place to see the parish's unusually high energy. In many Catholic churches, liturgies are staid, predictable, and proper, with hymns chosen from the same missalettes and song books that can be found anywhere. At St. Brigid's, for every Sunday and every special liturgy, Estelle Peck produces a pamphlet containing the songs and readings, and the worship itself bursts with spontaneity and high spirits.

Even the most solemn occasions turn out differently at St. Brigid's. In late 1994, Gaeta offered a funeral mass for Doris Matheis, the wife of Deacon Phil. She had been as active in the church as her husband. So, when Gaeta met her casket at the door and draped it in the cloth used at funeral masses, he said: "Doris, we clothe your body with this white

garment, which, by the way, you made, and did a very good job of it."
Later, he produced from the pulpit a bishop's mitre that she had made
for his St. Nicholas costume, put it on his head, then on the casket. Matheis, honoring his wife's request for a joke at her funeral, told one about
the length of the liturgies at St. Brigid's.

The church, patterned after Norman country churches in France,
holds fewer than five hundred people, making Sunday masses look full
and special liturgies look jammed. "What reinforces some of the theater of St. Brigid's is the structure of the church itself," Chuck Cutolo
said. "It has this Old World, Mediterranean atmosphere to it."

With its diverse constituencies and ethnic groups, its imaginative
clerical and lay leaders, St. Brigid's produces an astounding level of
activity—as reflected in a Sunday bulletin that often runs twenty-two
pages, compared with four to eight for the average parish. On one typical Monday evening, the peace and justice committee and the program
for bringing adults into the church met; the rock band and the children's choir practiced; boys played basketball; the church itself had an
Italian mass and a candlelight rosary; and the Haitian community offered
religious education.

The liturgies are also joyful, filled with small physical symbols. On
the feast of St. Patrick, Gaeta gives out shamrocks. On the feast of St.
Joseph, it's zeppoles. On one feast of St. Brigid, the parish distributed
small scrolls with a funny poem about the saint. At the end of that liturgy, as he often does, Gaeta reminded parishioners that there would be
food and drink in the parish hall across the street. Holding out his hand
to elicit a response, he offered the cue: "We of course go from holy hour
to . . ." The congregation, well trained, chimed in: "Happy hour."

And always there are jokes—often directed at Gaeta, on such subjects as the plastic Santa he displays over the rectory door. But for all
the laughter, it is a place of serious purpose.

"This parish absolutely is what the bishops had in mind when
they talked about what a Vatican II parish is all about: word, sacrament,
and action in behalf of justice," said White, who served in St. Brigid's
as a seminarian when Schaefer was pastor and later as a priest with
Gaeta, and now sees dozens of parishes in his diocesan job.

If St. Brigid's vibrancy is a hallmark, it is also ultimately a parish,
like others, where much of life revolves around the comfort of the routine. The central act of its worship, the mass, goes on day after day,
with the same essential words and actions. Three times a day on weekdays and a dozen times over the weekend, the people of St. Brigid's

celebrate the mass. You can set your clock by people like Jack Renison, now retired from the plumbing and heating business, who is a past grand knight of the Knights of Columbus and president of the Nocturnal Adoration Society, which several evenings a month keeps a prayerful vigil in front of the consecrated host, publicly displayed in the church. Most weekday mornings, Renison attends the seven o'clock mass, then says part of the rosary at church and part of it during his daily walk at Jones Beach. He is there because attending daily mass is a Catholic ideal, not because he expects anything out of the ordinary. But extraordinary things can happen.

---

In her hospital room after giving birth to a girl, Barbara Kellman was struggling to cope with the news that her daughter Carolyn had Down syndrome. A parade of professionals streamed through to offer advice.

"I said to my mother, 'Mom, I don't want to see another soul come into this room,'" she recalled. At the time, Kellman attended Our Lady of Hope in Carle Place. But her mother, Marie Verzi, went to St. Brigid's, and she persuaded her daughter to receive one more visitor, John White.

"That was the beginning of a whole new world for me, because Father John sat with me for maybe three hours or four hours," Kellman said. "I thought I'd never stop crying until Father John came and talked to me."

When she brought Carolyn home, Kellman started going to the nine o'clock mass on weekdays at St. Brigid's. "I listened to everything they had to say, because my heart was so broken, and I needed guidance," she said.

Before Carolyn was a year old, Gaeta told Kellman about the children's Christmas pageant and said: "We'd love your baby to be the baby Jesus." The day of the pageant, Kellman's mother sat in the front row and watched Carolyn as an ornate star of Bethlehem slid on ropes from the choir loft to the front of the church, where Carolyn lay. Verzi could see the child watching the star's progress—a promising sign of Carolyn's development.

Carolyn became a regular at the monthly healing mass, and in the summer, during Kellman's vacation from her teaching job in Carle Place, she took Carolyn to the nine o'clock weekday mass. There, in the summer of 1992, Carolyn's life intersected with the lives of Harry and Jane McLoughlin.

McLoughlin, a supervisor at a large mechanical construction company, had just been laid off after nineteen years, and his wife was losing her job, too. "I was in a very deep state of depression, and my wife said to me, 'Why don't we go to the nine o'clock mass,'" he said. "I thought God had forgotten about us." But he agreed to go.

A few days later, they noticed a young woman in the pew in front of them, trying to control her squirming daughter. "Suddenly, this kid just jumps over her mother's shoulder and into my arms," McLoughlin said.

Carolyn Kellman stopped screaming, put her arms around McLoughlin, and kissed him. "When I got a good look at her and saw she was Down syndrome, I just broke down," he said. "This poor kid has to carry all this weight on her shoulder, and I'm just out of a job. . . . Even though she had this affliction, God had given her the wisdom to know that what we needed at that moment was love. It was the most beautiful moment of our lives."

Kellman and her daughter are still regulars at the healing mass, and she also attends the charismatic prayer group. Carolyn is in the children's choir. In one Christmas pageant, Carolyn played an angel, her brother, Steven, played one of the three wise ones, and Barbara Kellman narrated. Even her husband, Howard, who is Jewish, often shows up at St. Brigid's. "He knows that the church means a lot to me," Barbara Kellman said.

McLoughlin later got his job back briefly, lost it again, got work repairing the World Trade Center after the bombing, and then was badly injured in an auto accident. But he and his wife, who later baby-sat for Carolyn for months, have only to look at her to put their problems in perspective. "Jesus was in Carolyn that day when she came across the pew into our arms and brightened our lives at a time when we needed brightening," he said. "I don't know anybody who doesn't love that child."

*Chapter Two*

# A TALE OF
# TWO PASTORS

$\mathcal{S}$omehow, even though Fred and Lizette Schaefer did not particularly push their children toward the religious life, three of the six felt the call and answered it.

Lizette was raised Lutheran, but when she married Fred, she converted to Catholicism. And, as the children grew up in Saints Joachim and Anne parish in Queens Village, in eastern Queens, Lizette took the convert's rigorous approach to her new religion. "She enforced us, confession every week, mass every Sunday," said Patricia Schaefer, one of their three daughters. The example of their parents, plus the positive influence they had in their parish school, with the Sisters of Notre Dame de Namur, was enough to plant the idea of a vocation, said another sister, Helen Schaefer.

The oldest of the six, Fred, was the first to detect a religious vocation— followed later by Helen, who joined the the Medical Mission Sisters, and Joseph, who became a Franciscan. After attending Andrew Jackson High School, Fred Schaefer enrolled at St. Mary's College in St. Mary, Kentucky, to prepare for the seminary. While he was there, he heard from a friend about a small missionary order of priests, the Fathers of Mercy. In addition to their missions, they also staffed four Brooklyn parishes.

After a year of novitiate in Washington, D.C., he went on to his seminary studies at the Catholic University of America and was ordained in 1953. His first assignment was to St. Frances de Chantal, then to Our Lady of Lourdes, both in Brooklyn. In 1957, he was assigned to start a new parish in the mountainous area of Utuado,

Puerto Rico. There he learned to speak Spanish and nurtured his life-long love of the Hispanic people and their culture.

During his eighteen months in Puerto Rico, he decided to leave the Fathers of Mercy and to become a diocesan priest. Late in 1957, he applied to the new Diocese of Rockville Centre, which had been established in April of that year. The diocese accepted his application in April 1958 and assigned him to St. Patrick's in Glen Cove. After five years there, he went to work at the chancery in Rockville Centre, running the diocesan religious education program from 1963 until 1975, when he became the pastor at St. Brigid's.

In the first years after Vatican II ended in 1965, Schaefer had been steeped in the postconciliar ferment. His job in the chancery had focused not only on elementary religious education for the young, but on the long-term educational development of the laity. When he came to St. Brigid's, he was excited by the spirit of the council, enthusiastic about the expanded role that conciliar documents had prescribed for the laity, and ready to put it all into practice.

But at St. Brigid's, the spirit of the council had not yet fully taken hold. The parish had not launched the process of education necessary to prepare people for the sweeping changes that the council had made possible. People were still kneeling down at the altar rail to receive communion, not yet receiving in their hands, and there were no lay eucharistic ministers. In general, the idea of the church as the people of God, with broad lay involvement in every aspect of parish life, had not yet come alive.

On top of that, Schaefer found people fearful about his intentions. "The rumor was—and the rumor was believed by a lot of people—that Fred had come to close the school," said Andy Simons, then the president of the parents' club at the parish school. The suspicion ran so deep that Simons recalled one meeting where parents asked the new priests pointed questions about exactly what they did and how they spent their time.

One way they spent their time, early in Schaefer's tenure, was to leave the parish for three days for a retreat at a house owned by a friend of Schaefer's on Shelter Island, between the North Fork and the South Fork of the island's East End. Of the five priests assigned to the parish, only Basil Ellard stayed behind to keep things together. Schaefer went on the retreat in May with the others: William Logan, John Malone, and Joseph Schlafer.

"We went out to Shelter Island and spent three days in prayer and reflection, in trying to put together some type of statement of where we thought we were at and where we thought we should be going," Schaefer recalled. "It was a simple statement about the building up of community." They decided to build community by focusing on liturgy, education, and social concerns.

One of the first things Schaefer did after his return from the retreat was to distribute a questionnaire to the parishioners about the schedule of masses. "There were twenty-two masses, and there were duplications," Schaefer said. "It was a crazy kind of schedule." The parish had masses in the main church, in the chapel at the school, and in the mission chapel in Carle Place. Schaefer considered that schedule unwieldy. "That had to be changed, but we didn't want to do it without consulting the people."

Eventually, after sorting through the responses to the questionnaire, they made changes, cutting the masses back to eighteen. "We decided that we would begin an Italian mass," Schaefer said. "We took the standard mass at nine o'clock and made that an Italian mass. Then we decided that we would also initiate a Hispanic mass."

As he got his feet on the ground, Schaefer began focusing on hiring paid professionals and on educating the laity. To start, the staff taught year-long courses in basic theology at the school. "Literally hundreds of people took this basic theology course for sixty hours—maybe more than hundreds, maybe a thousand or two," Schaefer said. "After the initial step, then we began to choose and select leadership types in the parish and suggest that they go for their master's in the seminary."

As many as twenty lay people completed a master's degree in theology and became the backbone of parish leadership. "It's such a blessing for the parish," said John White, who was still a seminarian when he spent his pastoral year working with Schaefer at St. Brigid's. "These are the people who stay. They live there. The priests are transient. We come and go."

One of those pulled in by the parish's new emphasis on education was Estelle Peck. One day in 1976, she went to mass at St. Brigid's and ran into one of the nuns Schaefer had hired, Sister Jane Halligan. The two women had met when Peck was briefly a postulant in the School Sisters of Notre Dame and Halligan was a novice. Soon after meeting Halligan at St. Brigid's, Peck began teaching as a volunteer in the parish's religious education program.

A few years later, after the birth of her youngest child, Timothy, Peck took the next step. "The church was becoming our social life as well as our spiritual life," she recalled. "I just felt the need to do something more with my life." It was then that Halligan encouraged her to get her master's degree in theology. She went to the seminary for three years, nights and summers, and finished her degree in 1985. Today, as director of liturgy, she is one of the key parish leaders.

In recruiting lay people for a greater role in the parish, Schaefer was relentless. Sandra Doscher, whose encounter with Schaefer launched her on years of work on in-home retreats and the Pre-Cana marriage preparation program, remembers receiving a blunt summons from him during confession. In that penitential setting, she recalled, he asked point blank: "'Why are you hiding yourself away? Why aren't you more involved?' I was a little taken aback. He was a very abrupt person."

His personality was an interesting blend of his Germanic upbringing and his acquired love for the warm, emotional Hispanic culture. On the surface, he could be Teutonically blunt, but below that surface was an Hispanically warm heart. "He could be as rough as a cop, if he wanted to be, and as gentle as a sheep," said Deacon Gordon Forester, who was ordained to the diaconate when Schaefer was pastor.

"He was gruff at times, but not with his family," said his youngest sister, Clare Watson. For his brothers and sisters and nieces and nephews, he was a constant, warm presence, including faithful daily phone calls to his sisters and his mother. But there was no question that he could be tough. "I don't know if that kind of developed over the years as a protection. In their lifestyle that they lead, you know, you have to put up a little bit of a barrier, or you're just consumed by everybody," Watson said. "I'm not sure if that wasn't it. But he truly was in his heart Hispanic."

Schaefer developed a reputation as a man's man and a priest's priest—someone more comfortable with men than with women. But he had insight into women and one skill that few men have. "At Christmas time, he did all the shopping for the women in his family and for the women on his staff in his parishes," his sister Patricia said. Somehow, he knew exactly what to buy for them, even in clothing. "He knew the size. He knew exactly what I liked."

Still, there is no question that he could be tough. Sister Mary Fritz, who worked with him in giving directed retreats to seminarians, recalled one of those moments. The retreat staff was discussing the progress of the seminarians in meditating on the passion, death, and resurrection of Jesus. Without giving the retreatant's identity, Schaefer reported that one seminarian had eagerly told him about imagining himself in the garden of Gethsemane and then suddenly at the resurrection. This, of course, let him skip the painful details between the garden and the resurrection, such as the crucifixion. So Schaefer commanded him bluntly: "Get your ass back in the garden."

Not everyone in the parish responded to him or to his style immediately. At first, the older parishioners found it difficult to adjust to their energetic new pastor. "They really didn't accept him; he was too different," Deacon Jack Falls said. "That old crowd, it took them a long time."

But Schaefer succeeded extravagantly at finding lay leaders and drawing out their talents. "He made sure the gifts of these people were used to build community," Manuel Ramos said. And he got people to respond in ways they might not have expected. "He was prophetic," Peck said. "He challenged you to think beyond yourself."

For Schaefer and for the people of St. Brigid's, perhaps the greatest challenge they faced together was a massive influx of Latin American refugees in the 1980s—many of them fleeing from the terror of war in El Salvador.

To this difficult struggle, Schaefer brought his natural affinity for Hispanic culture. "He really loved the Spanish people," said Adriana Miller, the parish executive secretary. One of the first things he had done in the mid-1970s was to launch a census of Spanish-speakers in the parish. That census turned up about 650 families. The influx in the 1980s would vastly increase those numbers, and Schaefer was convinced that St. Brigid's had a serious Gospel obligation of hospitality to the refugees. "There was no alternative," White said. "They were being hunted, they were being sent back to El Salvador, and they were being murdered."

For Schaefer, the dawning of awareness about the refugees took place in the early 1980s, at a time when the war in El Salvador was particularly ugly. Soon after Christmas, in the growing darkness of a bitterly cold afternoon, Schaefer was in the rectory kitchen, cooking. White, then nearing the end of his pastoral year in the parish before returning to the seminary, answered the front door and found three Salvadoran men standing there. Despite the cold, they were wearing warm-weather clothing: little more than tee-shirts on their backs. One of them carried a piece of loose-leaf paper, with "Westbury" written on it. "They'd been living in the train station in Westbury for three days prior to that," Schaefer said.

From the station, just a few hundred feet north of the church, they could see the cross on the steeple of St. Brigid's, and that's what finally led them to the rectory. They lived there for months. "There was one room in the basement that was furnished," Schaefer said. "We were using it as an office. So we moved the office out of there, and they used that."

In time, the men studied English, found jobs and a place to live, and moved out of the rectory. But they were not the last to need hospitality. "From then on in, we were inundated with Salvadorans— by word of mouth, I would presume," Schaefer said. "It was a tremendous influx, just a flood."

In the face of the flood, Schaefer essentially threw open the rectory doors, offering the refugees shelter and food. "For Fred, there always was room for everybody," Joseph Schlafer said. "Fred had an enormous heart." In the seminary, he had become an accomplished cook, who could throw together a gourmet-quality meal for a handful of people or for a crowd. "He would cook on Thanksgiving Day in those years for 200 refugees," White said.

Though the parish as a whole followed Schaefer's lead, not everyone in the parish or in the community saw the arrival of the refugees as an opportunity for Gospel service. "He used to bring people to the table, and many Americans were insulted by this," said Jennie Araujo, a Salvadoran who became a leader of the parish's growing Hispanic community.

In fact, the parish's openness to the refugees spawned a series of jokes: that there was a sign in El Salvador, pointing to Westbury, or that Schaefer had arranged buses to bring the refugees north. The jokes, of course, missed the point: Schaefer didn't bring the refugees to Westbury, but when they arrived, he had a clear idea of what to do for them.

Still, some people were seriously concerned that the refugees had placed too great a strain on the Westbury public schools and on the parish school, and they blamed the parish. "I only know that there were needs, and we were a parish who were able to answer their needs," said Joan Echausse, who ran the parish's outreach program. "Fred was a prophet. Prophets are never received well, unfortunately, in their own community."

That criticism over the refugees was not the only difficult time that Schaefer faced. One controversy arose from a proposal by Schaefer and the diocese to build about eighty units of senior citizen housing on parish-owned land near the school. Falls, who worked in the diocesan Office of Human Development, said that the idea arose in 1986. That year, they didn't get funding from the federal Department of Housing and Urban Development. The following year, they got a funding commitment, including about $300,000 to the parish for the land. They held a public meeting about the proposal in the local junior high school, and it wasn't pretty.

"The opposition was fierce," Falls said. "We were on the verge of calling the police that night." Monsignor Robert Emmet Fagan, who ran Catholic Charities in the diocese, was there that night to help explain the proposal, and he saw the effect that the angry opposition had on Schaefer.

"Fred was quiet that night," Fagan recalled. "He said to me, 'Emmet, I'm embarrassed. A lot of people sitting out there are my own people.'" Fagan was accustomed to angry meetings, and he tried to remind Schaefer that not all the opponents were parishioners. "I remember we took the break and he said, 'I feel like closing this thing down,'" Fagan said. "He really was hurt. I think he thought that he could carry it off because of all the positive feeling towards him."

Another source of pain for Schaefer was the way the diocese chose to deal with the parish's rapid growth. It had become clear that its Catholic population was just too big for a single parish to handle adequately. Already, the parish had something of a *de facto* split: Since 1938, St. Brigid's had served the people of Carle Place, just to the west, by scheduling Sunday masses for them in a mission chapel. In the mid-1980s, Schaefer did some thinking about how the church should provide leadership for parishes, and one idea that he advanced was to let deacons administer some. He asked Gordon Forester if he'd be interested in being the deacon administrator of a parish.

"As far as I know, there was no specific parish in mind," Forester said. He talked about it with his wife, Ann, and decided that he would be willing, in general terms—but not in whatever new parish the diocese carved out of St. Brigid's, where he would have been too familiar to the parishioners. "That would have been the worst possible parish for me to be an administrator."

The issue never really arose, because the diocese rejected the idea of using deacons as administrators. Schaefer himself had cooled toward the whole idea of a split. "There was a large contingent from the parish that was very opposed to the split," Schaefer said. "I initially was in favor of it, but then, after listening to these people and thinking it through a little bit more deeply, I also was opposed to it."

Finally, in 1988, the diocese decided to split the parish and create a new parish, Our Lady of Hope, based in the Carle Place chapel. In setting the border, the diocesan boundaries commission placed the line in a place that ended up hurting St. Brigid's. An area of relatively well-to-do homes wound up in the new parish, and revenue from collections at St. Brigid's dropped sharply, without a corresponding decrease in costs.

"Whatever line it had been, it would have taken a financial hit: When you create a new parish, you add expenditures," said Monsignor John Alesandro, then the chancellor of the diocese. "We kind of said, 'Shouldn't the small parish have a few more people, rather than the bigger parish?' We felt it was a reasonable line."

But the people who remained in St. Brigid's felt severely disadvantaged. "Financially, it was a disaster for us," Estelle Peck said. "It also cut off a tremendous amount of young blood we had in volunteerism. I remember myself feeling very angry about it all."

It is not clear how much the struggle over the senior citizen housing and the split of the parish affected Schaefer's thinking, but only a few months after the parish split took effect in September 1988, he made up his mind that it was time to move to another parish. That was not an easy decision. "It took me a year," Schaefer said. He believed that a pastor should always "be on the edge somewhat" and not get so comfortable in an assignment that he became a mere functionary. "Also, I think that the people deserve to hear the Gospel in another way, in a different way, other than my way."

Whatever had happened in St. Brigid's, there was something in Schaefer himself that made moving on seem like the right choice. "He was by nature restless, and he was ready for his next project," White said. "He wasn't sure what it would be, but he knew that he wanted to have another opportunity to do something with a low-income community and a community with new neighbors, with a sizable immigrant population."

The solution for Schaefer arose from his discussions with Father Thomas Haggerty, a young priest ordained in 1979, four years after Schaefer became pastor in Westbury. "He and I had been speaking for a number of years in terms of this whole concept of co-pastoring," Haggerty said. They wanted to "reimage the way parish could be done," with two priests serving as co-pastors and a clear role for the laity, so that everyone would know that "they were all pastors together."

Like Schaefer, Haggerty wanted to serve the Hispanic community. So, in 1989, they ended up as co-pastors of St. Francis de Sales, a parish considerably further east on Long Island from Westbury, with a large Hispanic community and a significant number of poor people. As Haggerty saw it, Schaefer had begun to feel a certain staleness in his ministry and was ready for the move. "He was hungry for a new time in his own life."

But for many of the people of St. Brigid's, it was a scary time. Schaefer had guided the parish solidly into the postconciliar era, but they had no guarantees about his successor. If the diocese sent the wrong pastor to replace him, they knew, it could cause chaos and unhappiness.

"It was a real fear of, 'Oh, my God, what are we going to get?'" Peck recalled. "What if we get one of these guys that all he thinks about is money, not people? I got a group of people together that I was very close to. We started meeting in the church to pray on a regular basis."

—⁂—

It took an Irish-Italian marriage, a rich and wonderful social phenomenon that became widespread in the great multicultural mosaic of urban America, to produce Francis Xavier Gaeta.

His great-grandfather, John McKenna, had come to this country from Ireland and fought in the Civil War, on the Union side. McKenna's granddaughter, Agnes Miller, married Pasquale Gaeta, born in this country of parents who immigrated from Bari, Italy. Agnes enjoyed joking about their Romeo-and-Juliet union of two cultures. "My mother just loved it, and she built it up," Gaeta recalled. His father worked hard at a variety of enterprises to support the family. "My father was in everything: garbageman, cesspools, cabs."

With his younger sisters, Rosemary and Agnes, Gaeta grew up in the Bedford-Stuyvesant section of Brooklyn. In later years, it became a blighted urban ghetto, the object of an ambitious redevelopment program championed by Senator Robert F. Kennedy. In Gaeta's youth, it was just another middle-class part of the city. "It was a mixed Italian-Irish neighborhood," Gaeta said. "For us, it was all we knew, and it was fine."

They lived at the corner of Kent and Willoughby avenues, just a short distance from the two Catholic institutions that helped shape Gaeta's early life: St. Patrick's parish, where he went to school, and the motherhouse of the Sisters of Mercy, a walled enclosure with a peaceful garden inside, in sharp contrast to the gray and gritty urban streets that surrounded it. "I used to serve mass in the motherhouse in the morning at 6:30," he recalled. "The best part of it was the sisters gave me breakfast afterwards."

In those years he drew inspiration from Monsignor Joseph Sweeney, chaplain at the motherhouse, and from Father Jeremiah Dineen at St. Patrick's. "I always remember wanting to be a priest," Gaeta said. "As a little kid and growing up, it was something that was always there."

With the support of his parents, he did what most young men did in those days if they were interested in the priesthood: He enrolled in Cathedral College of the Immaculate Conception in Brooklyn, a six-year prep seminary. Soon after that, when he was fifteen, his family moved out of Brooklyn to Long Island, settling in Ronkonkoma, in the woods of central Suffolk County. He continued to go to Cathedral, but now he had to commute every day, on the Long Island Rail Road—an hour and forty minutes each way. That long trip began to open him up to the world.

"It was really on the train that I began to read," Gaeta said. " I read The New York Times every day, from cover to cover. I read *Time* magazine." And he devoured the novels of Charles Dickens. All of that seemed like a more logical investment of time on a train than actual homework. "God forbid I study." Then, about halfway through the two-year college sequence at Cathedral, he wearied of the scholarly burden. "So I said to my father and mother, 'I want to get out of college awhile. I want to go to work.'"

His mother reacted strongly, calling him a bum and predicting that, if he didn't stay in school, he'd end up on the Bowery, a down-and-out Manhattan neighborhood frequented by out-of-work alcoholics. His father took the news more calmly. "My father at that time had a garbage route, his own private thing, and his own truck," Gaeta said. "So he said to my mother, 'He wants to see what he really wants to do, and he's tired of college. Let him come with me on the truck.'"

So, on a frigid Washington's Birthday, at about five o'clock in the morning, Gaeta and his father set forth in the sub-zero weather to sling garbage. "I went back to college the next day, and never doubted my calling to the academic life again," Gaeta said. "He was such a wise man."

Just before he completed his studies at the Seminary of the Immaculate Conception in Huntington, the first session of Vatican II opened, in 1962. "So, when I was ordained, the council was still on," Gaeta said. "It was business as usual, the whole Latin mass, the whole nine yards. But right after ordination, things began to just change and open up." As a young priest, he would have the chance to begin implementing the council's decrees. "It was very, very exciting."

After his ordination in 1963, his first assignment was to St. Joseph the Worker in East Patchogue, a few miles east of his family's home in Ronkonkoma. His pastor there was his mentor from the old neighborhood in Brooklyn, Jeremiah Dineen. In East Patchogue, Gaeta learned about "the terrible, terrible burden of poverty." In 1966, the diocese transferred him to St. Vincent de Paul, a middle-class parish in Elmont, in western Nassau County, where he began working with the youth ministry.

At his next parish, St. Margaret of Scotland in Selden, in central Suffolk, he worked with youth and with the religious education program, which was completely located in homes, because the parish had no school. Lay people ran the program and provided him with an enduring lesson: "If the lay people don't do it, it just cannot happen." In Selden, he was part of a three-parish consortium that pooled resources to hire the nuns who would direct the religious education programs in each parish. "It was a great sharing of personnel and real teamwork," Gaeta recalled.

From 1975 to 1977, he experienced a sharp change of pace, running the religion department at Holy Family, a diocesan high school in western Suffolk County. He also served as an assistant diocesan superintendent of schools, a bureaucratic job that he hated. "It was just a mistake," he said. "So I went to the bishop and I said, 'You know, I really don't think this is the right thing for me.'" After a brief tour at Our Lady of Lourdes in West Islip, he became pastor of St. Anthony of Padua in Rocky Point, on the North Shore of Suffolk County, in 1979.

His first task in Rocky Point was to resolve a conflict among parish groups over the dates of their summer feasts. Anger over conflicting dates was so high that people feared violence. "Of course, it's all centered around money, because they all had gambling at these feasts," Gaeta said. So he took simple, direct action, cancelling the feasts entirely. "That was all I had to do, and there was never another day's problem in the parish."

As pastor in Rocky Point, Gaeta showed his willingness to try anything to pull his parishioners more deeply into parish life. One technique he used, lifted from something that he had read in the Catholic press, was to mail out five dollars to everyone in the parish, challenging them to invest it and return the profits to the parish—an echo of the parable of the talents. "They just took it and went into all kinds of creative things," he said. "So many people came together. So many friendships were formed." Not incidentally, this little living parable brought in about $40,000 for the parish.

Gaeta grew intensely fond of his community, which he dubbed "Beautiful Rocky Point," with his characteristically emphatic pronunciation of beautiful. The name became tightly bonded to the community, and so did Gaeta. "I was very, very happy, very content, very fulfilled," he said.

The community responded well to his style, and together, they raised the money to build a new parish center. But soon after the center was finished, Bishop John R. McGann, the ordinary of the Diocese of Rockville Centre, asked him to consider leaving Rocky Point to accept a new assignment, as pastor of St. Joseph's in Ronkonkoma.

To begin with, Gaeta felt it would have been insensitive to the people of Rocky Point to leave them so soon after the completion of the parish center. On top of that, St. Joseph's was the parish where his family had settled after moving east from Brooklyn, and the Gaeta family had roots all over it. His mother had taught in the parish school for twenty years. His father ran a garbage-carting business in the area. And his sister Agnes and her family still lived in the parish. So he felt that it would be awkward for everyone if he returned as pastor. "I just didn't think it was healthy," he said. So he declined the honor and stayed in Beautiful Rocky Point.

About eighteen months later, in the spring of 1989, he was on sabbatical in Rome, studying theology and Scripture. While he was away, Gaeta received a series of phone calls from the diocese, both from McGann himself and from the personnel director, Monsignor James Kelly. In the diocesan personnel board's search for a replacement for Schaefer in Westbury, Gaeta's name had surfaced. Again, Gaeta was reluctant. "He was very much torn whether to leave Rocky Point," Kelly said. "He wanted to think about it."

For the diocese, Gaeta as the replacement for Schaefer made sense. "We wanted to have someone to go that was going to relate very well to the people," said Alesandro, then the chancellor. "We also knew that he had to have a quality of dealing with the finances. Frank had a very good history of doing that in Rocky Point." And the chancery had no desire to appoint a pastor who would destroy what Schaefer had created. "No one wanted to see a reversal," Alesandro said.

But for Gaeta, it was a painful change of plans. "I had no thoughts of leaving," Gaeta said. Besides, he knew almost nothing about St. Brigid's. Still, this was the second time in less than two years that his bishop had asked him to take an assignment. He had declined McGann's request that he become pastor at St. Joseph's, but this time, he felt he could not say no to the bishop again. "I really didn't have all that much of a choice," Gaeta said. So he agreed to leave Rocky Point. "I was devastated," he said. "It was the toughest thing I ever had to do in my life."

When Schaefer learned that Gaeta was to replace him, he reassured Estelle Peck, telling her: "He's a man of prayer, and he's not a cleric." And when Gaeta arrived in Westbury, he did some reassuring of his own. One of his first steps was to meet with the small group of people who had been praying for a new pastor compatible with the parish. Among other things, Peck recalled, they expressed a hope that Gaeta would continue the in-home retreats that had grown up under Schaefer and his staff. He told them he had been doing in-home retreats in Rocky Point. "Some of our fears were starting to be allayed," Peck said.

At the same time as Peck and others were trying to get used to the new pastor, he was also trying to adjust. One of the major differences that Gaeta experienced between Rocky Point and Westbury was the daunting size of St. Brigid's. At Rocky Point, almost every time he presided at a funeral, he had already known the person at least from a hospital visit, because the parish was small enough for the pastor to visit every hospitalized parishioner. "Here you can't," he said. "So you have to empower and create lay ministry in a whole different way."

Gaeta also felt that St. Brigid's did not emphasize families with young children as much as he was accustomed to doing in Rocky Point. "He has said that when he first came to the parish and went around to the masses, he was almost depressed because he didn't think there were any kids in the parish," said Paul Clagnaz, the assistant principal at St. Brigid/Our Lady of Hope Regional School. So Gaeta moved the Sunday family mass from the chapel in the school to the church itself and vigorously promoted the children's Christmas pageant and the children's passion play.

In another shift of emphasis, Gaeta moved to meet the needs of those in the parish who felt that Schaefer had gone too far in de-emphasizing the role of statues, during a 1984 renovation of the church. Gaeta sought a middle ground between what Schaefer had found when he arrived and what he had left behind when he departed.

That was in keeping with Gaeta's philosophy of providing a large variety of religious experiences. Many Catholics find statues distracting and unnecessary to their spirituality, but many others feel exactly the opposite. "As long as there's someone that does want it, he's for it," said Stephanie Clagnaz, the cantor and children's choir leader. "It's both/and, not either/or."

That philosophy emerges in his welcoming talks to candidates for admission to the church through the Rite of Christian Initiation of Adults (RCIA). "One of the things I say at the very beginning is that Catholicism is really a very simple religion," Gaeta said. "There's the Eucharist, the word of God, and the community." But beyond that, it also has a rich variety of traditions and worship styles. "You have the freedom to pick what's going to help you get closer to God."

In Gaeta's own spiritual development, two movements heavily affect-ed him: the charismatic renewal, with its emphasis on the presence of the Holy Spirit in daily life, and the Cursillo movement, the "little course" in Christianity. Among the first priests on Long Island to experience it, Gaeta made his Cursillo in 1966. "That absolutely blew my mind," he recalled. "I experienced for the first time in my life all the stuff that I had been learning about in Scripture, theology. It just absolutely came alive." In 1970, he went on a Marriage Encounter weekend, and he still feels its effects. "That's been a tremendously powerful part of my spirituality and theology and concept of family life and holiness and incarnational theol-ogy." Beyond the influence of those movements, Gaeta has continued his youthful habit of voracious reading, and he doesn't hesitate to borrow ideas that seem to have worked elsewhere. He will try just about anything.

So the parish's spirituality is an eclectic blend of traditional devo-tions, worship affected by the charismatic prayer style, and peace and justice—oriented activities, such as a turn-in of violent toys and a letter-writing campaign to toy companies to dissuade them from making still more violent toys. It's hard to categorize it neatly, because so many different people and different cultures worship there, and the parish reflects that.

"Frank's basic message to every single person in St. Brigid's is that, because you're human, you're holy," Stephanie Clagnaz said. Gaeta spelled that out one evening in a talk with couples preparing for the baptisms of their children. "Our holiness is in the ordinary," he told them. "Our holiness is in loving with everything we've got, and in loving the way Jesus loved. The church doesn't make me holy. The church doesn't make you holy. The church reminds us of what we already possess."

In setting the tone for the parish, Gaeta has in some ways shown a very different style from Schaefer, especially in the area of liturgy, where Schaefer was more restrained. "Fred liked everything in order. He didn't like any kind of gimmicks," Peck said. "He would take a fairly low pro-file. Frank doesn't take low profiles." Or, to put it another way, as Stephanie Clagnaz said: "You could put him on an elephant and send him down Post Avenue, and he'd be in his glory."

Gaeta also departed from Schaefer's way of using the rectory as almost a full-time open house. When Schaefer left, the parish offices were in the rectory basement, and there was a scarcity of space for priests to meet with parishioners, which forced them to use the recto-ry dining room and their own rooms for some of the meetings. So Gaeta and the other priests felt they were, in effect, living over the store. "It's very hard to live that way," Costa said. "Everybody needs their privacy. You need to have some separation." So they moved the parish offices across the street, to the former convent building, and Gaeta named the new parish center for Schaefer.

That public step mirrors Gaeta's private attitude toward Schaefer. "He's never, never, even in a personal discussion, ever taken Fred down," Peck said. "He's always supported everything he did." Despite the differences in their personal and liturgical styles, Gaeta makes clear that he sees his role as continuing and nurturing what Schaefer started. "I think he was right on the money," Gaeta said.

As in any change of pastors, this one brought difficult moments, such as Gaeta's decision, a little more than a year after his arrival, to replace the principal of the school and the two leaders of the religious education program. As Gaeta settled in, people noticed the differences between the two. Some saw Schaefer as more prophetic than Gaeta, for example, and looked back to that era, when a more prophetic stance was called for, as the best time in the parish's life. Some see Gaeta as warmer and more outgoing with his emotions than Schaefer, and more appealing to the Italian community.

But both men have a strong feeling for the Hispanic community. One of the leaders of the community, Manuel Ramos, remembered that Sister Carolann Masone, who ran the Spanish apostolate for the diocese at the time, had said that the best person the diocese could have chosen to follow Schaefer was Gaeta. "Fred had made them so welcomed and at home and had done so much there to initiate the ministry among Hispanics," Masone said. "I knew that Frank would just follow through on that."

For Gaeta, an assignment that started out in pain, because he had to leave another parish that he loved, has ended well. In 1995, he asked the diocese to give him a second six-year term, and he got it. "I really just know it's where I should be," Gaeta said. For Schaefer, the assignment to Patchogue also worked out well.

For the parish, the bottom line is this: Unlike some parishes that have dissolved in chaos after one pastor replaced another, the transition from Schaefer to Gaeta somehow worked. Despite their differences in emphasis, the two men share key commonalities. "They have the same ideas," Masone said, "the idea of hospitality in the name of Jesus, the idea of living the Gospel message, the idea of making all cultures feel at home."

*Chapter Three*

# THE LEAP OF
# FAITH: RCIA

*I*n the autumn twilight, Audrey Schencman steered her car into the parish parking lot, turned off the ignition and began to struggle with powerfully opposing impulses.

She got out of the car and started toward the Father Schaefer Parish Center. After a few steps, she succumbed to her fears, reversed direction, climbed back into the car, turned on the radio and sat there—undecided.

The journey to that indecision in 1993 had begun in another parking lot, nearly three years earlier. Driving home to Wantagh from her boyfriend's Westbury house, Schencman had fallen asleep at the wheel and awakened when the car slammed into a concrete divider in a shopping center parking lot. That accident, in December 1990, totaled her car and jolted her, forcing her to think about her attitude toward religion. Her father told her: "It's God's way of telling you to wake up."

Schencman's father is Jewish and her mother is Catholic, but they hadn't raised her in either religion. As an adult, she had tried various churches and a temple. "None of them touched me, including the Catholic Church," she said. But after the accident, she began attending mass, usually with her boyfriend, Nick Viscardi, who lived a short walk from St. Brigid's. Still, she couldn't fully participate. "I didn't know any of the prayers," she said. "I couldn't receive communion."

Then, in August 1993, Schencman received a letter from Gaeta, inviting her to an introductory meeting of a program for adults who want to become Catholics—the Rite of Christian Initiation of Adults (RCIA). "I couldn't figure out how he got my name," she said. At the time, she felt he must be "this spiritual, powerful being." (Only months later did her boyfriend admit he had submitted an application to the program for her.)

So she decided at least to try it. But as she began to leave her car that first night, second thoughts overwhelmed her. "I never had a really great comfort level with clergy," she said. "I was terrified." On the third try, she persuaded herself to cross the street and go to Gaeta's meeting, upstairs in the parish center.

When the pastor offered his bear-like handshake, she recoiled, fearful that the warm welcome implied a commitment that she wasn't ready to make. "I said, 'Look, I'm just here to check this out,'" she recalled. A few minutes later, it was her turn to introduce herself to the others. "I thought I was going to pass out," she said.

Another source of disorientation and mystery at the meeting was the presence of people who called themselves members of the RCIA team. "I couldn't figure out why the people who were already Catholic would want to just sit there and watch other people become Catholic," she said.

Impelled as much by curiosity as anything else, Schencman kept attending the meetings. "I thought, 'I'll just learn about the Catholic religion, and I can drop this at any time,'" she said. "In the very beginning, I had absolutely no intention of becoming Catholic." Months later, she heard a homily urging people to trust Jesus and let him act in their lives. Those words galvanized her. "At that point, everything changed."

On Holy Saturday evening in 1994, at the long Easter Vigil services, Gaeta anointed Schencman with oil, administering the sacrament of confirmation. "I felt like the happiest, cleanest, most wonderful person in the world," she recalled. "My life hasn't been the same since."

A few months later, she made a commitment that she could not have imagined. The lay leader of the 1994–95 RCIA program, Jack Graham, wrote to ask if she would be one of the sponsors for a new group. "I jumped all over it," she said. "This is my chance to give back to someone what the team gave to me."

At the start of her own conversion, she had not understood what RCIA team members were about. But then she began to develop strong ties to the other candidates and catechumens, as well as to the team. Her initial desire to make her confirmation and then melt into the background had turned into a need to remain part of the process and the community.

In fact, community is a key element in RCIA. Only twenty-five years ago, a person who wanted to become a Catholic would usually go through weeks or months of instruction by a parish priest, in private.

That provided information, but not a sense of community. But after Vatican II, the church adopted a new rite for receiving adults, emphasizing community. "It's not just Father and me," said Sister Sheila Browne, who coordinates the RCIA program for the Diocese of Rockville Centre. "It's Father and me and all of us."

The year-long RCIA process is designed to prepare people to receive at Easter the sacraments that they need to enter into full communion with the church. Those who need to receive baptism and confirmation are called catechumens. Those who have already been baptized and need only confirmation are called candidates. They meet weekly throughout the year, to study Scripture and life, to learn about spreading the Gospel and building Christian community, rather than focusing primarily on dogma, as in the past. Often, a priest supervises the process, but they receive significant support from the lay members of the team, who are already Catholics—either from birth or from going through the RCIA process themselves.

The small RCIA community connects with the larger community of the parish by attending parish events and being visible at liturgies. "It's in the community where they come to see and know and understand a living faith," Graham said.

During Lent, as they near their reception into the church, they are the center of attention at a series of liturgies. That begins with the rite of election, the first Sunday in Lent, when they declare formally to a bishop their intention to acknowledge God's call and join the church. In 1995, in the Diocese of Rockville Centre, 681 people declared that intention.

The 1994–95 class donned their white robes at an exuberant, richly textured, four-hour Easter Vigil liturgy. By then, they had developed a real unity with each other and with their mentors on the RCIA team, but they had all come to the process with their own stories and sharply contrasting personalities. The parish had sown the seeds of that unity in the summer of 1994, with the annual bulletin item about the start of a new RCIA group.

In past summers, Michael Lynch had regularly shown that item to his wife. Lily had grown up in Taiwan, with a Buddhist father and a Christian mother, but she was not actively religious. In 1980, she and her family immigrated to America and soon moved to Westbury. There, a neighbor introduced her to Michael, then an import–export clerk, later a postal worker. He was Catholic from infancy, but at the time they were married in 1981, he was not a frequent churchgoer.

Their lives had begun to change when their daughter, Christina, entered St. Brigid's school in the second grade, asked to be baptized a Catholic, and joined the children's choir, where she later became a regular soloist. Over those years, her singing drew her parents more and more often to St. Brigid's. Lily didn't feel quite right going to mass, but a Catholic friend of hers told her: "Don't feel awkward going to church. Maybe some day, when the time is right, Jesus will call you and you'll become Catholic."

Something about St. Brigid's and its pastor appealed to Lily. "A couple of times, Father Frank's sermon really touched me," she said. Still, when Michael annually raised the subject of her studying to become a Catholic, she hesitated. She was attending mass often and becoming more interested, but even in the summer of 1994, she didn't jump at the idea. "I filled out the application anyway," Michael said. "She went along with it. I think, deep down in her heart, she felt that she was ready."

The parish had also worked its charm on Jennifer Dowden Stokes, a banking consultant originally from Tennessee. She had come to Long Island more than two years earlier on a contract, and the assignment has just kept on going. During the week, she lived in a hotel. Most weekends, she left the island—first to travel to her home in Phoenix and later, after selling the home, to Syracuse, where her boyfriend lived. Some weekends, she stayed on Long Island to entertain out-of-town friends, many of them Catholic, and occasionally she took them to mass at St. Brigid's.

"The first time I went there, I said, 'This place is great,'" Stokes recalled. But she was a Methodist, not eligible to receive communion. "The last couple of years, I've been thinking about converting." So she joined the RCIA at St. Brigid's, despite the uncertainties of her nomadic career. "I just thought I'd take a chance that I would be here long enough to complete it."

For them and the others, the primary guide for the journey was Jack Graham, a lay leader with master's degrees in both business administration and theology, whose personality blends the silver-haired self-assurance of a Central Casting corporate executive and the uninhibited, speaking-in-tongues spirituality of the charismatic renewal movement.

Unlike the candidates and catechumens, Graham is a cradle Catholic. In high school, he attended a preparatory seminary briefly, but decided against the priesthood. After earning his master's degree in business at Hofstra, he launched a business career, specializing in marketing. He and his wife, Marilyn, moved to the parish in 1958, becoming heavily involved in its life.

Marilyn was among the founders of the charismatic prayer group in 1974, and she continued going even after Graham decided that its worship style was too demonstrative for him. But he soon saw how the group's spirituality seemed to make her even more warm and caring. "I said, 'I don't know, I've got to get some of what she's got.'" From that time on, he rarely missed a Tuesday night prayer meeting.

When Schaefer was pastor, he nudged Graham to get a theology degree. In 1987, he persuaded the Grahams to run the RCIA. For years, they led the weekly sessions together in their Westbury Gardens home—a non-threatening environment for catechumens who might still be uncomfortable meeting in a church setting. Some of them would come early to ask questions and some would stay past midnight. With his training, Graham handled the theological questions. "Marilyn focused on welcoming them into the church community," Graham said. "It was a good mix."

Even when Marilyn was diagnosed with cancer, she continued with the RCIA. But by her fifty-ninth birthday, in September 1992, it was clear that she was dying. For her birthday, Gaeta showed up at their home with his brother priests—Malcolm Burns, Michael Maffeo, and John White—carrying a dozen roses and a pan of baked ziti. "She just cried tears of joy," Graham said. That December, she died. Gaeta promptly proclaimed her an uncanonized saint, installed her photo and a plaque in the chapel at St. Brigid's school, and declared: "She did ordinary things with extraordinary love, and that's what we're called to."

Graham took a leave of absence from RCIA during the 1992–93 class—a time when he suffered not only the death of his wife but the loss of his position as a corporate president, after a member of the firm's controlling family took the job. In 1993–94, Gaeta asked him to fill in occasionally. Then, in the summer of 1994, Gaeta asked him to lead RCIA again.

One of his tasks, even as he continued his search for employment, was to assemble a team of sponsors. "Each candidate has a spiritual friend," he said. "It's easier for a catechumen or a candidate to relate to someone who made the journey a year or two ago." Some had just received the Easter sacraments, such as Schencman, Tracey Tiberia, and Floyd Rosenberg, an intense bundle of energy who had come to the church from Judaism and told his life story in a powerful, moving testimony at Pentecost.

Rosenberg grew up in the East Bronx, taught English in the city, and later became an accountant. Though he had grown up in a non-religious family, when he moved to Long Island in 1969, he eventually became active at Suburban Temple in Wantagh.

His journey toward the joy of the Easter Vigil began in years of misery, brokenness, and what he described as a comprehensive disregard of the Ten Commandments. After a particularly difficult divorce, he dated a woman who had problems with drugs and alcohol. He put her through a rehab program, but when it was over, she left him for a twenty-year-old man she met in the program.

Stunned, Rosenberg went into a deep slide. "I would go to a bar and pick the three biggest guys in the bar and pick a fight with them," he said. One of his accounting clients bought him a boat, and Rosenberg dropped out of society, living on the boat for almost two years, reading the Bible and the Qur'an. "I was searching for why I had been deserted by the Lord."

Then, at the end of 1992, Rosenberg's fortunes suddenly reversed. Invited to a wedding, he found himself sitting with a divorced woman who was very active at St. Brigid's. For him, she was the incarnation of stability and steady virtue. "All I saw was a glow around her," he said. "We spoke for hours that day."

They began dating, Rosenberg attended mass with her regularly at St. Brigid's, and he thought more and more about conversion. The humanity of Jesus, portrayed in the film *The Last Temptation of Christ*, had attracted him, and the goodness of his girlfriend, plus the spirit of St. Brigid's, drew him in. He joined the RCIA, formed close bonds with the others, became calmer, more in control of his temper, and channeled immense energy into parish activities such as the parish newspaper, RCIA, a men's prayer group, and the family mass.

After his time of alienation, he had found a home. That became especially clear after he suffered a heart attack in early 1995. While he was in the hospital, a stream of parishioners visited him. On his first day back in church, when Rosenberg went up to receive communion, Maffeo offered him the host and didn't simply say "Body of Christ," as he would for anyone. "He smiled and said, 'Floyd, it's great having you back.' I never felt as at home as I did then."

Along with the newly accepted Catholics, Rosenberg, Schencman, and Tiberia, the team had a mix of others. The recent converts included Linda Schoenberg and Liz Hegarty. Schoenberg had come from the same temple as Rosenberg and was entering her third year on the team. The cradle Catholics were Maria Sarra, a friend of Schoenberg; Arthur Solar, whose wife had been through RCIA, and Mary Teddy-Freedman, who had joined the team in 1993, after her husband Eliot's baptism.

Eliot Freedman grew up in Lakeview and went to high school in Malverne, in an observant Jewish family. He didn't contemplate conversion, but he liked what he saw of Jesus in popular films. "There was something positive about it that stayed with me," he said. In 1984, when he was working in the pathology lab at Winthrop-University Hospital, he met Mary Teddy, a social worker at Creedmoor Psychiatric Center. She had grown up in a Catholic home in Westbury, but was not then a practicing Catholic. At their wedding in 1985, a rabbi and a Presbyterian minister presided, in a Unitarian church, with a Unitarian minister present. "Neither of us had any strong faith," Mary said.

Just before that wedding, Eliot's father and Mary's father died within six weeks of one another, and the young couple began going to church occasionally. But it wasn't until the arrival of their son, Andrew, in 1990 that they became more serious.

"I remember being pulled back in during Lent and being in awe of the [post–Vatican II] changes," Mary said. Then Eliot expressed an interest in attending Good Friday services, even though that has always been an uncomfortable time for Jews. He even went up to the altar with the others who were kneeling to kiss the crucifix. "It was a new experience," he said. "I didn't have any conflict."

In 1990, they also took a suggestion from Gaeta and were married in the church. But perhaps the most dramatic event for Eliot was Andrew's baptism at the weekly family mass, when Gaeta took the boy from their arms and paraded up and down the aisle holding him, inviting the applause and welcome of the community. The family mass was getting to Eliot—the sharing of love and the sounds of children's voices in the choir. "I remember one day saying, 'This feels like it could be heaven. If there was a heaven on earth, this could be it,'" he said. "That kind of feeling just tipped the scale."

So he joined the 1992–93 RCIA group. Mary decided to attend the weekly sessions with him, which turned out to be almost a conversion process for her. "It was also a good bond for us," Eliot said. His baptism in 1993 was a moment of high exhilaration. "He had such an incredible look on his face as he was being baptized," Mary said. "It was just the most beautiful moment that I can remember."

At Pentecost, the end of the RCIA process, Eliot offered a public testimony about his conversion. "I can see Jesus was always there, creating a path before me," he said then. When it was all over, they were both reluctant to let go of RCIA. So they became part of the team that guided Schencman and Rosenberg's class. Mary stayed on the team for the 1994–95 class, but Eliot's work prevented him from continuing.

At first, Graham worried that the new group wasn't bonding or responding to the Scripture sharing. For some, such as the slight, soft-spoken Lily Lynch, the prospect of opening up before other people was intimidating. "Father Frank said, 'Don't worry. Just come to the class and relax and see how you feel,'" she said. But at first, when Graham would ask the catechumens to share their views on the Scripture, Lynch would routinely say: "I have nothing to add."

Normally not inclined to cry, Lynch found herself growing increasingly sentimental. One night, she tearily expressed a sense of unworthiness, of inability to live up to Catholicism and the example of Jesus. But after the session, a group of the others soothed her and told her that Catholics make plenty of mistakes. "Everybody tried to calm me down, saying, 'Don't worry. Relax. Just do whatever you can.'"

For the chatty, self-confident Jennifer Stokes, speaking out in a group comes naturally, but she surprised herself at the first meeting she attended, by tearfully recounting her pain over the suicide of a close friend. "I cried in front of them the first time out," she said. "I bared my soul to people I don't even know."

That sharing caught Stokes by surprise. "I thought I was going in for instruction, that they were going to sit down and say, 'Now these are da-da-da-da-da and this is what you're supposed to do,'" she said. "All the things that are kind of easy to be seen about Catholics, I thought those would be the things that I would learn. And it turned out to be completely the opposite."

They did get factual information, but mostly in readings assigned outside of the sessions. "The key thing is not going to be how much Catholicism any of us knows, but how much of Jesus we know," Gaeta told them one night. "Ultimately, if you don't personally know and love Jesus, there's no sense in going through this." At another meeting, Mary Teddy-Freedman told of her own growth. "I never could have imagined ten years ago that I could say I have a personal relationship with Jesus," she said. "This is like the best relationship I've ever had."

By the end of Lent, they had detected genuine growth. "I feel myself changing," Lynch said. Once, she could not express herself. "But right now, I cannot hold back the feeling I have." The process also affected her husband and daughter. "I've been getting closer to God," said Christina, glowingly happy that her mother was joining the church. Michael said: "It's made me more open to Jesus. That's for sure."

Throughout Holy Week, the catechumens and team members were heavily involved in the liturgies. On Palm Sunday evening, for example, at the first of three nights of candlelight services called Tenebrae, Tracey Tiberia was the prayer leader and Linda Schoenberg the preacher. "Conversion is not only about changing our religion," Schoenberg said in her homily. "It is about being touched by the Holy Spirit and becoming something more and better."

On Monday evening, after Tenebrae, their last meeting before the Easter Vigil, Gaeta tried to calm them down about the prospect of making their first confession on Wednesday evening. And the team members reassured them. "That sweating and that nauseous feeling will pass," Schencman said, recalling her own nervousness. "It's not scary," Mary Teddy-Freedman said. "It's a very comforting sacrament."

Somehow, they got through that first confession and arrived, renewed and relieved, at the Mass of the Lord's Supper on Holy Thursday evening, the start of the stunning swirl of liturgies that would culminate Holy Week.

At St. Brigid's, Holy Week had become almost an Olympic event—a liturgical endurance test that offered a bracing reinforcement of faith to those who stuck with it, and a time of fatigue for the parish staff—especially for director of liturgy Estelle Peck, director of music Tommy Ciotti Thorell, organist Susan Porteus, and children's choir director Stephanie Clagnaz. Still, in the middle of it all, Peck smiled and admitted: "I can't get enough of it."

All parishes have Holy Week, but few pack as much into it. Not every parish has three nights of candlelight services called Tenebrae. "Lay people are your leaders in prayer, Sunday, Monday, and tonight," said Manuel Ramos in his Tuesday homily. "A woman—a black woman at that, with a French accent—is the celebrant. What this reflects is a profound sense of what church is all about."

Not every parish has a priest translating the readings at the Mass of the Lord's Supper from English, Spanish, and Creole into sign language, as Costa did, or a candlelight procession through the streets afterward.

Not every parish has children's versions of both the Palm Sunday procession into Jerusalem and the Good Friday passion service—with a girl, Caitlin Cassidy, playing Jesus in both.

Not every parish has Good Friday services from 9 A.M. to almost 10 P.M. The evening requires precise timing, as the Italian community's passion play winds from the church through the streets of the Breezy Hill section to the school, and the Spanish community goes from there back to the church, carrying a life-sized statue of the dead Jesus, arriving just at the end of the young adult community's Stations of the Cross inside the church.

And not every parish has an Easter Vigil so long that it almost runs into the Sunday sunrise mass. One year, it lasted five hours, with a break in the middle.

As the vigil approached, the RCIA group had shared jokes about its traditional length. But in the actual event, they found that the hours slid by lightly, in the uniquely Catholic kaleidoscope of sounds and sights: the lighting of the paschal candle from a fire on the lawn outside, the procession of the candle into the darkened church, with Deacon Phil Matheis chanting in a gravelly voice, "Lumen Christi, Christ Our Light," and the series of seven scriptural readings. Through much of the evening, Costa translated the proceedings into sign language for Bruce Geffen, who has a hearing impairment and received his instruction from Costa.

At the end of the readings, all the lights in the church came on. Just before 10:30, two hours into the vigil, Gaeta began his homily. "The church is not asking you to reject who you are and what your traditions have been," he told the catechumens. "God has led you tonight to take another step. We hope and pray that you will always be Jewish and Protestant, that you will always keep these holy traditions living in your hearts." Then he invited the catechumens to gather around the altar for the blessing of the water to be used in the baptisms.

The catechumens knelt in a circle around the altar: ten adults, joined by three school children who had received their instruction through the Rite of Christian Initiation of Children, led by Terry Patterson. Members of the RCIA team went to each of the catechumens and placed hands on their heads in blessing. Then the catechumens returned to their pews and began coming forward, one at a time, with their sponsors and families, to receive the sacraments—starting with those who needed both baptism and confirmation, then those who needed only confirmation.

Costa baptized and confirmed Geffen, simultaneously saying aloud the sacramental words and signing for Geffen. Then Gaeta took over. Those to be baptized knelt at a miniature waterfall installed near the altar for Easter, and Gaeta poured the baptismal waters with a silver dish. Then, using spiced oil blessed for the occasion, he liberally anointed their heads, administering the sacrament of confirmation.

"He was holding onto our hands very tight," Jennifer Stokes said. "He's a very strong person, and you get a lot of feeling coming through his hands. . . . It was just me and Father Frank and the Lord. I didn't even think about people watching or people being there."

Following the confirmation, Gaeta helped each to don a white robe, handed each a lit candle and said, "Receive the light of Christ." Accompanied by loud applause, they took their places behind the altar, holding the candles.

"When I went back to standing behind the altar and the oil was dripping on my face and everything, I was just very happy," Lily Lynch recalled. "I don't know how to describe it. I felt so happy to become Catholic, like a part of the family."

After they had all received the sacraments, they took candles and spread the light among the congregation. Then, Gaeta invited people to come forward and sprinkle their own faces with baptismal water. After this watery ritual, the brand-new Catholics stood there in their white robes, offering towels to members of the congregation. Only then did Jennifer Stokes realize she had already begun to spread the faith. For weeks, she had been telling her manicurist about St. Brigid's. So the young woman had showed up for the young adult community's Stations of the Cross on Good Friday and now for the Easter Vigil.

The vigil finally ended past 12:30. At 1 A.M., Gaeta was preparing to go to another event, but Maffeo was ready to go to sleep, knowing that they'd be up again at 4 A.M. for the sunrise mass. So Maffeo, poking fun at Gaeta's inexhaustible energy, did his Gaeta impression, crowing: "I'm so excited, I could never sleep."

Gaeta stopped in briefly at a coffee-and-cake reception, where many of the catechumens and sponsors stayed awake all night. From there, they went directly to the 5:30 sunrise service at Nassau Beach. But Stokes went back to the hotel with her out-of-town guests and got to sleep at about 2 A.M. She didn't set the alarm. "I said, 'God, if you wake me up at four o'clock, I'll go,'" she recalled. She woke at exactly four o'clock. Her mother declined to stand in the cold, but her boyfriend, Jim Gavin, joined her for the two-hour liturgy.

After his painfully brief sleep, Maffeo was at the beach parking lot by 5:30, greeted by a chorus of "We came to see Mikey," and "For he's a jolly good Father." Minutes later, standing beside Gaeta at an outdoor fire, Maffeo started the chilly liturgy with a comment on Easter that could well be the motto of St. Brigid's: "Celebration seems to be the only thing that makes sense at this moment."

Later, at the end his homily, Maffeo took off his shoes, walked briskly into the cold surf, and filled an urn with water to be blessed.

As Jennifer Stokes watched, her hair was still wet with the sacramental oil. "I didn't want to wash it, because it smelled so good, and it just reminded me of what had just happened to me," she said. Her boyfriend, the son of a devout Catholic family, stood there, with his arms around her, taking in the sunrise and the joy. And at the beginning of the week, he called her from Syracuse to say how much the weekend had meant to him.

"He was very happy for me," Stokes said. "The other thing is he was really envious, too. When he was young and confirmed, you're a child. It's so different when you're an adult and you see adults making a choice to live their lives a certain way and to join something that you've always been a part of. It kind of makes you proud that you're part of it and kind of renews your faith."

After Easter Sunday, the new Catholics still had a few weeks of study left before the year ended at the Pentecost Vigil on June 3. But on the Monday following their reception of the sacraments, they celebrated mass together, spending nearly two hours sharing their reactions to RCIA. Even the quietest had a lot to say, such as Barbara Garaguso, who had been reticent in the weekly sessions, but spoke up to thank Audrey Schencman for getting her through the process. Then they adjourned to the rectory for supper, ending with a cake made by enthusiastic new Catholic Heide Cherubini. The message on the cake put a period to their year: "Catlics R Us."

*Chapter Four*

# A SCHOOL OF MANY COLORS

$\mathcal{A}$s she struggled toward a pivotal decision about sending her daughter to a parochial school, memories of her own Catholic school childhood lurked in Lynn Kennedy's mind.

At the time, 1989, Lynn and her husband, Michael, were not very active Catholics. But Michael felt it was time for a change for their oldest daughter, Morgan. She was in pre-kindergarten at a Quaker school, and he wanted to enroll her in St. Brigid's in Westbury. But Lynn had formed some negative images about Catholic school as a child in Peekskill.

"I definitely felt that I did not get the math and science background that I needed, but at the same time, I had such a wonderful time then, in some ways," Lynn said. "I learned to love literature, and I learned to love writing in Catholic school." Her love of literature led to a career as a high school English teacher, but her schooling had another side. "There were a few teachers—very few, when I think of the whole spectrum of teachers I had—who loomed in my memory as being cruel, uneducated, and very frightening."

This was on her mind as she checked out the building. "I looked at the school, and it looked fifties," she said. "So what I did was I walked into the school and didn't announce myself and started sort of snooping around. I wanted to see whether there were cheerful pictures on the wall that reflected a happy population. I wanted to see whether the rows were neat, and therefore the teachers would be too rigid. I wanted a mingling of chaos and order."

Later, Lynn asked some probing questions of the principal, Sister Carlann Buscemi. "She looked at me very deeply and she said, 'You're

57

looking for something for yourself, aren't you?'" Lynn recalled. "She was right, and as I grew to know her, she encouraged me very much on my own personal journey, and I'll always love her for that."

That journey was shaped by the decision to enroll first Morgan and then her younger sister, Sarah, in St. Brigid's. The school converted both parents from skeptics about Catholic education to high-profile players in the struggle to save the school's life—Michael as a former president of the school board and later leader of the bingo operation that raised $20,000 to $30,000 a year for the school, and Lynn as the vice-president of the Parents Association. It also enlivened their faith. "Our children really brought us back to the church," Michael said.

Andrew and Eileen Simons also wrestled with the decision to send a child to St. Brigid's, even though their two older children had already gone there and thrived. Michael had graduated from the eighth grade at St. Brigid's in 1978, went on to Chaminade High School in Mineola, the College of the Holy Cross in Worcester, Massachusetts, and Harvard Law School. Katie had graduated from St. Brigid's in 1983, went on to Sacred Heart Academy in Hempstead, and was a Phi Beta Kappa graduate of Holy Cross. While they were at St. Brigid's, their parents were very involved. Andrew, an attorney, served as president of the Parents Association and, at another time, as president of the school board. So did Eileen, who teaches math education at Hofstra.

But from Katie's graduation in 1983 until young Andrew was ready to start in 1986, the Simonses had not been as active in the school, and they were hearing rumors it had declined. "I asked around to a lot of people: 'What do you think?' There was not a great deal of enthusiasm," Eileen said. But her own observations convinced her that it was sound educationally. It also had something they couldn't find in their public school district—diversity.

"The atmosphere in the school is what we wanted," Eileen said. Though the East Meadow public school district had become more diverse in recent years, she said, at the time of their decision on Andrew, it was virtually all white. "That's not the reality of the world." In Andrew's reading group at St. Brigid's, however, there were children of several ethnic groups, all doing very well. His parents liked the lesson: Ethnicity has nothing to do with talent.

But in an era already marked by increasing tuition, that atmosphere wasn't attractive to enough other parents. "The enrollment went down every year from 1977 until 1993," Eileen said. The question for her was: "Is the school going to be there long enough for him to graduate? I had to answer: I don't know. I'm not sure."

So they threw themselves into the survival struggle. When parents had to raise large amounts to plug the budget hole, Eileen led the fund-raising. When the school became a regional school with Our Lady of Hope parish in September 1994—a key step in the fiscal salvation of the school—Andrew agreed to be on the regional school board. The past few years had been a turbulent time. "We almost went out of business," he said.

For now, with the funding situation improved as a result of the regionalization, times are calmer. St. Brigid's has the qualities that attract parents to Catholic schools: educational excellence in a caring, value-laden environment. But it faces the same problems that have troubled Catholic schools for thirty years: rising tuitions that depress enrollments, plus inability to pay teachers salaries competitive with public schools. On top of that, it has the challenge of being a proudly multicultural school that finds it hard to attract students from mostly white areas nearby. In early 1995, there were new signs of hope: more financial stability and increased enrollment in the two most recent school years, to a total of 435, at the same time as Catholic school enrollment was increasing nationally as a result of a new push by Catholic leaders and an aggressive marketing campaign.

Over its first half century, the school grew steadily. It opened in 1918, with 150 children and five nuns from the School Sisters of Notre Dame. To accommodate increasing enrollment, the parish opened a new building on Maple Avenue in 1955, with 934 children. Within a decade, enrollments soared to 1,600, and in 1965 the parish opened a fourteen-classroom addition and a new convent. That was the zenith for St. Brigid's, right after national Catholic elementary and secondary enrollment peaked at 5.5 million in 1964.

Soon after, new religious vocations dwindled and thousands left the convents, cutting the number of nuns by 74,000 in three decades. Many nuns left teaching for other ministries. Catholic schools had to hire more lay teachers, at salaries well above the stipends of the nuns they replaced (though below public school wages). With the increased costs, schools could no longer rely solely on the traditional source of revenue, Sunday church collections. Tuitions rose, and enrollments fell almost constantly, until they began to increase consistently early in the 1990s. Elementary and secondary enrollment stood at 2.6 million in the spring of 1995.

On top of these national factors, St. Brigid's faced another overwhelming reality in the 1980s: the wave of Central American refugees. Many could not afford the tuition. Schaefer had put together a scholarship fund—starting with $10,000 left in a will by one of his priests, Basil Ellard—and used it to help refugee families. "So they weren't being carried by the other children," Schaefer said.

Despite that, some parents saw the refugees as a financial drain, and some worried that their language problems would take teaching time away from other children, even though the school had a staffer to teach English as a second language. But the parish did not flinch. "We felt we were carrying out the Gospel message in doing this," said Sister Marie Patrick McDermott, who came to St. Brigid's in 1980. "I think it caused some of the people to take their children out of school and, I think, to get very upset with Fred."

It is not clear how much of the enrollment loss was attributable to this Gospel commitment to the poor, and how much to tuition increases. But tuition did increase. It was $500 when Sister Carlann became principal in 1984. In the fall of 1995, it was $1,500 for each in-parish child, kindergarten through eighth grade, and $2,195 for each out-of-parish child. There were reduced rates for families that send more than one child and slightly different rates in nursery and pre-kindergarten. And enrollment did go down during Sister Carlann's seven years as principal. "It continuously declined, roughly by about forty each year," she said.

In the eighties, the school hired a full-time computer teacher, started a nursery school and pre-kindergarten program, and expanded its kindergarten to a full day—making it a nursery-through-eighth-grade school. But enrollment losses spawned annual rumors of closing. "I've heard it since I started here," said Kathleen Battistini, a teacher recruited by Sister Carlann to start the pre-kindergarten.

In addition to the school's problems, the division of the parish in 1988, creating the new parish of Our Lady of Hope and sharply cutting revenues at St. Brigid's, hit the parish hard. "Worse than the finances, in my estimation, it drew the color line," Schaefer said, "and it affirmed Carle Place as being lily-white forever and a day."

In 1989, Schaefer left and Gaeta became pastor, and he had to make debt reduction a priority. One step was to lease the mostly empty convent to the Nassau County Police Department for office space. Four nuns moved to a house owned by the parish, and two retired to the motherhouse. The lease was painful, but it brought in revenue. "It was a logical move," Sister Carlann said.

The next decision meant more pain. The school board members liked Sister Carlann, but they felt they needed a new principal to turn around enrollment losses. "It was a consensus," said Michael Kennedy, then board president. But in his own home it was a controversial decision. His wife Lynn had grown very close to Sister Carlann. "The only way we ever survived at that time is we agreed not to talk about it," Lynn said, "because I disagreed very strongly."

On the first school day of 1991, Gaeta showed up at the school, looking uneasy and asking to speak with Sister Carlann. "He called me a holy person, a wonderful person, a prayerful person. I kept waiting for the punch line," she recalled. "He was wonderful about the whole thing—very gentlemanly, very nervous." The message still hurt: At the end of the school year, the parish would have a new principal.

Gaeta called it one of the most difficult things he has ever done. "She really was just a beautiful, beautiful lady, a very compassionate heart," he said. "But I just felt that she didn't have what was needed for basically a crisis kind of a time." He also replaced the leaders of the religious education program, Patricia McDonough and Sister Barbara Schwarz.

McDonough, a psychologist who now serves as the coordinator of marriage programs for the diocesan Office of Family Ministry, still looks back at Gaeta's painful decision with an uncompromising toughness. "Now it so happens, the three pastoral leaders were all women, all strong, intelligent, and talented women," she said. "Without any consideration for their rights, for the years that they had faithfully served the people of God in Westbury, Monsignor Gaeta dismissed them and replaced them with women more to his liking. . . . Perhaps some pastors try to meet their emotional needs through a staff that will provide them with childlike affirmation rather than mature challenge."

To succeed Sister Carlann, Gaeta and the school board chose Christine Lombardi, who had been an assistant superintendent in Port Jefferson for twenty-five years and retired when the district began to downsize. They liked her educational knowledge. "She already knew what the cutting edge of research was," said Eileen Simons, a teacher of teachers. Though Lombardi is Catholic, she did not attend or work in Catholic schools, but she had a spirituality of her own.

"Having been in the public system, you realize how much of Gospel values and values in general are missing," she said. "I really feel that this is ministry here, and that I've been called by God to do this, because there were circumstances in my life that led to a deepening of my faith."

She believes in the injunction in the teacher's handbook to "teach as Jesus taught," but she has also focused on updating the curriculum and keeping teaching standards high. She asked some teachers to leave, and some left on their own. "Three-quarters of the staff is basically new."

The other reality the school had to face was tight finances. It couldn't raise tuition too high without further eroding enrollment, and the new pastor couldn't increase the parish's subsidy to the school without shortchanging other parish needs. So Gaeta set an annual ceiling of $215,000 on the subsidy. To fill the gap, the parents would have to raise $90,000 a year.

"What Father Frank did was he threw down the challenge: 'How much do you want the school?'" Eileen Simons said. Parents wanted it enough to do almost constant fund-raising in 1992–93 and 1993–94. "Eileen was our commander-in-chief at the time," said Nancy Silvestro, whose twin sons Bryan and Scott sold their share of chocolate and wrapping paper to fill the gap. "There was just one event right after another."

Not all parents were happy. Some grumbled about the fund drives, because they already pay tuition. "It's just part of the Catholic school experience," said Paul Clagnaz, who sees the issue from both sides, as a parent and as a teacher and assistant principal at the school. With improving finances, the 1994–95 goal was only $50,000. "The resentment has diminished, because the number of fund-raising activities has diminished," said Luis Navia, the former president of the Parents Association.

—ɷ—

The reason for the financial improvement was regionalization. "We had to regionalize," Lombardi said. "Otherwise, we were going to close." Knowing that many parishes could no longer afford their own schools, the Diocese of Rockville Centre in 1990 set up twenty-seven regions, in which several parishes could combine resources to run a regional school.

St. Brigid's was in a region with Our Lady of Hope, St. Aidan's in Williston Park, and Corpus Christi in Mineola. Since Our Lady of Hope had no school of its own, it had to give a share of its collections—eventually fifteen percent—to the three parishes with schools. Then the diocese agreed to a plan that would create a new St. Brigid/Our Lady of Hope Regional School in the Westbury building, allow St. Aidan's and Corpus Christi to keep running their parish schools, and permit Our Lady of Hope to give its entire subsidy, nearly $65,000 a year, to St.

Brigid's. That helped St. Brigid's financially and didn't cause real pain, as plans in some regions had. "There was no closing of any school," Clagnaz said. "There was no loss of staff."

The regionalization also helped win a three-year, $100,000-a-year diocesan grant for St. Brigid's. (Despite the school's jaw-breaking new official name, most people still use the simpler old one.) To get the grant, schools must have a legitimate deficit, must be regionalized, and must have a minority population of more than forty percent. In effect, the school's diversity has saved it and become its guiding spirit. Teachers, parents and students see that spirit in the way the children get along, without racial or ethnic division.

"To me, this school represents the world, the United Nations," said Idali Arnes, the mother of four St. Brigid's students. The children notice diversity, she said, but positively. "They're aware of it in its beauty," she said. "I think it excites them and intrigues them and makes them more tolerant."

The students agree. "They try to bring everybody together—not just teaching math, one plus one," Morgan Kennedy said. One 1995 graduate, Andrew Simons, said: "It really depends what kind of tastes you have, who you hang out with. It's mixed that way, not by race." Two of his classmates were Scott and Bryan Silvestro. "When I see my friends, I don't really see their race; I just see my friends," Scott said. "It makes you color-blind," Bryan added. "You just see what's inside a person."

But Navia and others believe the diversity also causes some parents to choose other schools. "There are sometimes white parents who come, take a look at the school and say, 'Thank you, no,'" Navia said.

Even though it is a two-parish school, for example, it has had few students from Our Lady of Hope. Parents there send children to St. Brigid's for pre-kindergarten and nursery, which the Carle Place public schools don't have, but they don't keep them in the school later. "Carle Place is lily-white," said Sister Carlann, who now teaches at Our Lady of Victory in Floral Park. "They don't want to send their kids to this multicultural school. I openly spoke at school board meetings of racism." Gaeta agreed. "That is definitely a big part of it," he said. "But there's also another big factor, that the Carle Place schools are excellent."

The quality of the Carle Place schools, plus finances, were the key factors for JoAnn Moreno, one of two lay representatives from Our Lady of Hope on the regional board. She sent three children to the public schools and not St. Brigid's. "I would not have been able to afford the tuition," she said.

When Donna Fitzgerald came to St. Brigid's as a teacher in 1990, she was hesitant about teaching in Catholic school. But the diversity helped bond her to St. Brigid's. "To me, this is what school desegregation was supposed to lead to," she said. "It's very hard to explain to people who are not here how important it is." As assistant principal, Clagnaz often speaks with parents who have opted against St. Brigid's. "I think that if people would just come in and take a look, it would serve them so well, because the kids get along beautifully," he said.

In fact, Jennifer Gallagher, a music teacher, said that teaching children to love one another is the whole point: "I think that's the mission of Catholic education. It isn't better discipline anymore. It isn't better education."

Though the school does have a code of conduct, the ruler-swinging nun image does not fit. "I tell parents very clearly, if they're coming to this school because in their minds is the old, traditional Catholic school discipline, they're not going to find that," Lombardi said.

She also has to face stereotyping of teachers. "People are under the impression that we have uncertified people, just warm bodies in the classroom," Lombardi said. That isn't true, but even Donna Fitzgerald remembers having that impression before she arrived. "I expected to walk into a school with people who couldn't find jobs anyplace else," she said. "That's not what I walked into."

In fact, parents who are professional educators applaud the educational quality. "My children have had teachers whom I consider to be master teachers," Lynn Kennedy said. "I would want to student-teach under Sister Marie Patrick," the last remaining nun teaching in the school. Consistently, Lombardi said, 100 percent of the students score above the state reference point on program evaluation tests of reading, math, writing, and social studies.

Navia, dean of the School of Liberal Arts and Sciences at New York Institute of Technology, is also an evaluator for the Middle States Association of Colleges and Schools, an accrediting agency. His goal was to see St. Brigid's apply for and win accreditation, which not even all public schools have achieved. "If Middle States were to come to St. Brigid's, they would be very impressed," he said. They might want better computer education, but he said that is solvable. "The most critical thing is the spirit, the commitment, the enthusiasm. It is here."

Nationally, a federal study showed that Catholic school students spent more time on computers than those in public schools, said Robert Kealey, executive director of the Department of Elementary Schools at the National Catholic Educational Association. In the federally sponsored National Assessment of Educational Progress, Kealey added, Catholic school students scored higher than public school students in the fourth and eighth grades.

"The Catholic schools in the past didn't have to be competitive educationally; today they do," said Eileen Finn, a former St. Brigid's teacher. Her parents never had any doubt that they'd send her to Catholic school, but these are different times. "I don't think anyone today, at the prices the Catholic schools charge, could say that."

Finn is an example of one area in which Catholic schools cannot compete: salary. The starting pay in the diocese for 1995–96 was $14,558, and the top pay after twenty-eight years of experience was $38,625. As a single parent with four children after her separation from her husband, Finn decided to go into teaching. But when she finished her master's degree at Queens College in 1991, she could not find work in public schools. So she accepted a job at St. Brigid's. "I wouldn't have thought of working for that kind of money unless I had to," Finn said.

Like other good teachers who can't find work in public schools and decide to take jobs for less pay in Catholic schools, Finn ended up loving it. But then, out of the blue, she was offered a New York City public-school job. Her salary at St. Brigid's was just under $19,000, and she would start in the city at about $32,000, with a chance for considerable overtime. Still, it was tough for her to leave St. Brigid's. She had an emotional discussion with Lombardi, an advocate of better teacher pay, who understood why Finn had decided to leave. "We both cried," Finn said.

Finn's son, Jimmy, was accepted at a Catholic high school, Chaminade, and they could finally afford to think about it. "If I was still teaching in Catholic school," she said, "my son couldn't [afford to] go to one." But she missed St. Brigid's, where she had state-of-the-art books and the freedom to spend her time and energy on teaching, rather than on enforcing discipline. In public school in Far Rockaway, she has neither.

It is difficult for single people to live on Catholic-school pay. Donna Fitzgerald, who lives with her parents, manages. Her friend, Donna Krauss, lives alone. She lost her job at St. Anne's in Brentwood when the school closed in a regionalization in 1993, then found work at St. Brigid's. But she had to supplement her $15,000 teaching salary by waitressing. "I make sure I work at a restaurant that's not anywhere near here," she said.

"The teachers who are involved in Catholic education see it as ministry, because they cannot survive on this pay," Lombardi said. That ministry teaches values, starting early. "We don't have any religion textbooks, but we live our religion every day," said Kathy Battistini, one of two pre-kindergarten teachers. The children pray before snack, they learn not to fight, and at Christmas they get to put hay in the manger if they've done a good deed. "We talk about Jesus and the love of Jesus."

The lessons take hold early. Lynn Kennedy remembers Morgan's insisting in first grade that she wanted to give her piggy bank to the poor. Morgan made Lynn take her to the rectory, where Morgan presented it directly to Gaeta. Nor have the school's values been lost on Sarah, a charming, friendly child who often tells Lynn: "Sister Marie Patrick is close to Jesus."

About twenty-five percent of the students were non-Catholic in the 1994–95 school year. Lombardi explains to the parents that the school imparts Catholic values, and that non-Catholic children learn religion with the others. It has not been a problem. "To teach them to be good Christians is to teach them to be good people," Fitzgerald said.

For all that, the school is still not out of the woods. In the spring of 1995, projected enrollment for the fall dropped below expectations, and Lombardi had to delay for weeks giving letters of intent—promises of employment—to some teachers. The school's diocesan grant expires after the 1996–97 school year, and there was no guarantee that they could get it extended indefinitely. There was also the uncertain impact on enrollment of two changes in the fall of 1995: a five percent tuition increase and a $200 participation fee. Parents pay at the start of the year and get back all or part of the fee, based on how much they volunteer.

But the parents and teachers remain optimistic that the worst of the school's travails are behind it. Sister Joanne Callahan, the diocesan schools superintendent, is also hopeful. "I do think they're going to make it," she said. "St. Brigid's is a wonderful school and should be saved."

At the Lessons and Carols service, Cynthia Stein leads the Italian children's choir.

At a family mass in June 1996, Msgr. Francis X. Gaeta baptizes Grayce Marie Nix.

Makenzie McIntosh, left, and Mary Vargus, during a field day at the school.

Eugenia Bradshaw of Port Washington with Msgr. Francis X. Gaeta in the reconciliation room, where some parishioners receive the sacrament face to face, while others prefer to kneel behind the traditional screen.

On Holy Thursday, Deacon Jim Morris washes the feet of children.

During a parish staff meeting at a diner, Father Tom Costa, Father Michael Maffeo and Msgr. Francis X. Gaeta enjoy a laugh together.

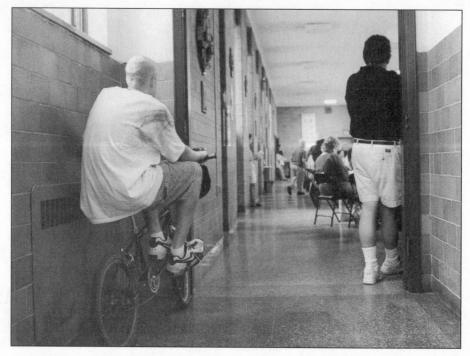

A teenager sits on his bike outside Our Lady's Chapel during the rock mass, The Six, on Sunday evening.

Anne Josey distributes communion. Her fervent, high-volume "Amen" at liturgies has become a parish trademark.

Some of the parish's Filipino community at the multicultural Lessons and Carols service during Christmas time. From left, Cely Varias, Lulu Biazon and Leonora Rances.

At a men's prayer group gathering, from left: Lou Marchesi, Eliot Freedman, John Castellano, Peter Haarmann and Jose Renter.

Msgr. Francis X. Gaeta prays with a family at a mass for expectant parents.

## Chapter Five

# HELLO, YOUNG LOVERS

The question for the small group of engaged couples seemed simple enough: In their marriages, what would they do about credit cards?

It was one of several questions posed by two married couples who were leading a Pre-Cana group for Catholic couples preparing to be married at St. Brigid's. The object was to get the couples talking about their relationship. But Ron and Mary Grossi, who were hosting this session in their basement, didn't expect the answer they got.

One man spoke up and said that they wouldn't be using credit cards. His fiancée disagreed. "She said, 'Of course we're going to have charge cards. In fact, I have two now, and I have $20,000 on them,'" Mary recalled. "I think he was in shock. The only thing I remember him saying was: 'And you *will* pay that off before we get married.'"

The questions don't usually evoke such pyrotechnics. But that answer, early in the Grossis' sixteen years of Pre-Cana work, shows how the process can help. "We felt if that question hadn't been there," Mary said, "they might have gone all the way to the altar and gotten married without him finding out."

Sometimes, after the self-examination that Pre-Cana fosters, couples decide not to marry. "Now is the time to break it off, if it is not meant to be, rather than wait," said Herb Doscher, who has been a Pre-Cana volunteer since about 1980, with his wife, Sandy.

In the Doschers' first group, one young woman decided that the marriage was a bad idea. The groom-to-be telephoned the Doschers, frantic. "He wanted us to call her and convince her to go back to him," Herb recalled. "We said, 'We can't do that. That's what the whole purpose of this is. We are here to make sure that you're not doing something that's wrong.' It was hard. It really was."

Virtually every diocese requires engaged couples to undergo some form of marriage preparation program before they can be married in the Catholic church. Pre-Cana, named after the site of the first recorded miracle of Jesus, the changing of water into wine at the wedding at Cana, is perhaps the most familiar term for marriage preparation. A more recent development is Engaged Encounter, an intensive weekend experience for engaged couples. In either case, the goal is to prepare the couples, not to break them up. But honest discussion can produce that result.

At St. Brigid's, the program begins with an opening liturgy and general meeting. It also closes with two general events: a night of prayer one week and a concluding mass the following week. In between, in a series of four small-group sessions, four to six engaged couples in each group meet in the homes of two married couples to discuss communication, conscience formation, sexuality, and spirituality.

Young couples don't initially find it easy to discuss these issues with married couples they've just met. But this approach, with engaged couples in dialogue with married couples, offers a better chance of improving the relationship than the old system did.

Before their marriage in 1969, the Grossis attended a Pre-Cana conference in Queens that lasted three or four hours. "It seemed like a very long time—I mean, to be talked at," Mary Grossi said. The engaged couples sat passively in a large group, without married couples. "A young priest spoke for most of the afternoon, and then a doctor came in with some charts and talked about sexuality," Ron Grossi said. "No dialogue at all."

The experience of the Doschers, who teamed with the Grossis in the Pre-Cana cycle for the spring of 1995, was even more cursory: an hour with a priest in an upstate rectory in 1968. He asked them if they'd raise their children Catholic, even though Herb was Protestant. They said yes. "Then he told my husband that it really wasn't important that he convert, as long as he's the best Methodist he can be and I'm the best Catholic I can be," Sandy said. "That was the extent."

Sometimes the program entailed a session with a married couple, but in a large room, with no real opportunity for intimate dialogue. "It was totally impersonal, it was totally boring, and it was totally dictatorial," said Schaefer, who ran the religious education program and the family life bureau for the Diocese of Rockville Centre in the 1960s and early 1970s. "It was felt that there had to be a better way of communication."

The key move was taking Pre-Cana out of large halls and putting it into the homes of married couples. The germ of this idea came from the way St. Thomas More parish in Hauppauge had reshaped its high school religious education program.

Meeting in the parish's large public room, in a former factory, the St. Thomas More program had dropped from 150 students to thirty-five. In 1970, Father John Cervini asked some married couples to "open their homes to the kids one night a week and just love them to death," discussing values, Scripture, and anything else the teenagers felt important. The RAP (Religion and People) program drew thirty-five students the first night and four hundred in the second year. "The word started to spread," said Cervini, who tried it again when he was transferred to St. Martin of Tours in Amityville. He is now pastor of Our Lady of the Miraculous Medal in Wyandanch.

Schaefer liked Cervini's in-home approach and began applying it to Pre-Cana. Then, in 1975, Schaefer left the diocesan staff and became pastor of St. Brigid's. There he started recruiting couples for an in-home Pre-Cana ministry. The Doschers and the Grossis were among the volunteers.

For the Doschers, the impetus to join was a request from Schaefer, who also played a pivotal role in Herb's conversion to Catholicism. For the Grossis, the path to Pre-Cana ran through Marriage Encounter, a program designed to help couples communicate better and strengthen good marriages. After an encounter weekend, they were anxious to become more involved in the parish. They chose to work in Schaefer's Pre-Cana program.

"His program became the model for the diocese and beyond the diocese," said John White, who worked in the parish as a seminarian in 1980–82 and again later, as a priest.

But over the years, the number of married couples has dropped off. All parish ministries wax and wane, as volunteers grow tired or move on to other ministries. "So many leaders who began in Pre-Cana are now doing other things," said White, who was the moderator of the program under Gaeta. And recruiting new couples isn't easy, because in so many marriages both husband and wife work. In 1995, the program was down to between twenty and twenty-six married couples, from a high of about fifty-five, Ron Grossi said. The Grossis coordinated Pre-Cana with another couple, Dick and Diane McIver.

With White in a new assignment at Catholic Charities, Gaeta and Maffeo moderated Pre-Cana together in 1995, hoping for a new burst of energy. Gaeta cares about Pre-Cana because young families are one of his top priorities, and the program is about giving new marriages the strongest possible start.

"The plan of God is that in each of your relationships the church is born again," Gaeta said at the first general meeting for the spring cycle, after mass on a Sunday late in April 1995. "The building block of the church is the Christian family."

For the engaged couples in that room, the program could be "four of the most important weeks of your life," Gaeta told them. Pre-Cana is mandatory, and some couples grumble about it, taking an attitude that Gaeta described as: "What have they got to tell me? We're in love. Nobody has ever been as in love as we are." Gaeta conceded the uniqueness of each relationship, but argued that they can profit by exposure to the "wisdom of the community," found in its married couples.

In the group of five young couples who went through Pre-Cana with the Doschers and Grossis in the spring of 1995, some were more talkative than others, but none of them displayed hostility to the process. One couple, Michael Rafanelli and Stephanie Ann Vivona, were positively eager. "We were looking forward to having Pre-Cana that was structured and not one afternoon, as some churches do," Michael said.

In recent years, most engaged couples in Pre-Cana have seemed mature. "They're so much more sophisticated now," Sandy Doscher said. "They have their careers on course, they have their houses bought. They're set." In fact, Michael and Stephanie Ann not only had firm ideas about where they're going, but an engaging sense of mission. "I believe God put us together," she said.

Stephanie Ann had grown up in Bayville and moved to Westbury at fifteen with her father, when her parents separated. Michael grew up in Holliswood. They were both Catholic, but she had attended public schools and he had been in Catholic schools through college.

They first met on February 9, 1991, while visiting a mutual friend, Michael Terranova, in his hospital room. "I knew when I met him there was something special," Stephanie Ann said. Michael was intrigued, but Terranova thought their age difference might be a problem. She was nearly twenty-one, and he was nineteen. Eventually, Stephanie Ann told Terranova he could give her phone number to Michael. He called her immediately, and they talked for forty-five minutes. That was June 7, 1991. "I know all the dates," she said. On their first date, they saw the film *City Slickers*, then sat in the car for three hours, talking.

Three years later, on the day that Stephanie Ann graduated from Queens College, Michael asked her to marry him. The engagement was not a surprise. "I knew on our first date that we were going to get married," Stephanie Ann said. The timing, however, caught her off guard. So did his method of making the proposal: He bought her a VCR for her graduation, played a romantic videotape about their relationship, then knelt before her with an engagement ring.

They started planning immediately. "That's all we do, is plan," Michael said. They settled on the wedding date: February 9, 1996, five years from the day they met. And they decided to see Maffeo to make the arrangements.

"I really had only started going back to church the year before we got engaged," Stephanie Ann said. In that time, she had been drawn to Maffeo's down-to-earth style. "I just always love what he has to say," she said. "St. Brigid's makes religion, God, spirituality human. When we met him, he was in a shirt and a pair of jeans. . . . He told us he could sense that there was God in our life and that there was something really special about us."

A week after the opening Pre-Cana liturgy, the Grossis opened their home on a Sunday afternoon to Michael and Stephanie Ann and four other couples: Robert Siri and Irasema Amaya, David Vargas and Adriana Mejia, Ronald Winicki and Kerry Upton, and David Schrage and Donna Verderber. This was the first of four sessions: two at the Grossi home and two at the Doschers'.

Though the married couples in Pre-Cana receive diocesan training for the program, to put the engaged couples at ease the married couples try to make clear that their role is simply to talk about their own marriages and elicit discussion. "The whole premise of this is the honesty and the fact that we don't have a special marriage," Herb Doscher said. "We're not here to pass judgment or teach or lecture. We're just here to tell them, 'This is what it's going to be like.'"

Sometimes that preview sticks with a young couple. One couple who went through Pre-Cana with the Doschers in 1991, John and Lois McCourt, still remember those talks, now that they have an active young son, Tyler. "I remember Herb and Sandy said when they had children they set aside Thursday night every week," said John McCourt, a vice-president in regional administration at Chemical Bank. "That was their date night. We just started doing that. That's something that really stuck out."

The first session at the Grossi home began with the couples describing how they met. Then they completed an ice-breaker questionnaire, to help them figure out how much they know about each other and where they may disagree. Finally, the Grossis asked for someone to read some questions on communication issues, and Winicki volunteered. The questions, each written on a separate piece of paper, formed the core of the four sessions.

Another key to making the discussion fruitful is the honesty of the married couples about their own ups and downs.

"I told them I can be impatient, I can be bitchy, I can be not a morning person; I tell them I'm not easy to live with," Sandy Doscher said. "There are couples who go into marriage thinking that it's going to be just as wonderful for the rest of their life as it is right now. . . . That's why we tell them, this is what we've been through. This is what twenty-seven years can bring. . . . We're not divorced. We do fight, but we're still together."

For the Grossis, one of the most difficult hurdles was Mary's diabetes. The initial diagnosis came during her first pregnancy, but it wasn't until fifteen years into the marriage that she began to realize that Ron didn't comprehend what the disease was doing to her emotionally.

"I wanted Ron to understand that so desperately," Mary said. "He listened and he heard it, but he just couldn't grasp it." If her blood sugar numbers were on target, he felt things were fine. "That's what I wanted him to understand, that even if everything looked okay on the outside, it didn't always feel okay on the inside. We were just starting another Pre-Cana group, and I just felt very distant from him."

Then, at the opening talk for Pre-Cana, something that Schaefer told the engaged couples struck Mary. "He said, 'The married couples will teach you how to pray,'" she recalled. But she didn't feel equipped to teach prayer. "Even though we went to mass together and we had been on retreats together, we never actually formally prayed together."

So they began a habit that they still follow: Every night, before going to sleep, they hold hands and say the Lord's Prayer together. Mary no longer has the sense that Ron doesn't understand her diabetes. "And it's gotten us through even more difficult things than that," she said.

Even though the Grossis and Doschers were sharing honestly, there were times when the engaged couples seemed not to feel as comfortable sharing, such as the second session, on conscience formation, dealing with the couples' views on difficult issues such as euthanasia. "I think they sometimes feel that we're asking them what their morality is," Herb Doscher said. "They're a little bit more on guard about that."

The sexuality session can be tricky. "We were scared of it," Michael said. But it turned out fine. "It touched on topics that people don't think of when they think of sexuality," Stephanie Ann said. "It was more about being a human being. It was very spiritual also."

In the sexuality session, the conversation does not focus as much on the physical aspects of sex as on developing emotional intimacy. And it is not a forum for the married couples to beat the drum for the church's opposition to artificial contraception and abortion. The engaged couples receive written material on that teaching, but it is not a major topic of the sessions.

"We did not put our personal feelings or stands on abortion or birth control in front of them," Sandy Doscher said. "Unless we are asked directly about these matters, we don't really discuss them. I am, of course, anti-abortion, and so is my husband, but you can waste a lot of time and get into heated discussions about right to life."

The priority, in other words, is not studying doctrine but helping the engaged couples to examine their relationships intelligently and to realize the centrality of those relationships for the church and the world.

The in-home session that Michael and Stephanie Ann seemed to find the most rewarding was the final one, about spirituality. In their relationship, Michael is more knowledgeable about the facts of the faith, due to his Catholic education, but Stephanie Ann is more spiritual. "She's been like that since I met her," he said. It was just before he met her that her life turned. "God came into my life," she said, "and then He brought him into my life."

From their first date, they talked seriously about issues, and they began developing a plan for life. As they prepared for marriage, she studied for a master's degree in social work at Adelphi University and worked with mentally ill adults at Hillside Hospital in Queens. He taught pre-kindergarten children in special education at a private school in Brooklyn and worked on his master's in education at Queens College. But as focused as they are, they still felt Pre-Cana had something to offer. "I feel it deepened our communication to another level and made the love and the commitment even deeper," Stephanie Ann said.

In the church's view, the program wasn't just for them, or just for the other couples. "Your marriage is a sacrament that Christ is going to use to touch the whole world," Gaeta told them on the evening of prayer after the in-home sessions were over. "There are so many people that you haven't even met yet that are going to know that there's a God of love because you're in their life. This sacrament isn't just for the both of you."

The following week, at the closing mass, Maffeo and Gaeta gave crosses to the engaged couples. Michael and Stephanie Ann planned to use theirs in the wedding ceremony. They also planned to attend the weddings of the other four couples in the group, as the married couples usually do.

Sitting in the back of the church at these weddings, the married couples get to see the first step on the journey. They get to hear young couples exchange words of commitment—words that Gaeta used in crafting a good summary of what Pre-Cana really means, in his homily at an end-of-cycle liturgy just for the married couples. "When they say those words," he told the married couples who make Pre-Cana happen, "they mean more than they would have meant without you."

# Chapter Six

# THE SPIRIT OF RECONCILIATION

Stepping nervously into St. Brigid's Church for the seven o'clock weekday mass, Perri Caldera decided that the only suitable place to sit was the last pew. "I didn't feel like I belonged any closer," she recalled.

Her Catholic upbringing had provided the positive example of nuns, which had launched her on a long teaching career. But it had also contributed to her image of God as judge—all-knowing, ever-lurking, recording every sin—and of herself as unworthy. "I was very hard on myself," she said. She had reinforced her feelings of unworthiness by marrying a divorced man and divorcing him eleven years later. Religion had been absent from her marriage.

For years, she was what she calls an absentee Catholic. But then she worked as a campaign volunteer for Nassau District Attorney Denis Dillon, a committed Catholic who became her friend and began a gentle campaign to nudge her back into the life of the church.

One day, as she wrestled with some difficulty in her life, someone suggested that she go to a church and just sit there for a while in silence. She dropped in briefly at Sacred Heart Church in North Merrick and later started going to mass there.

At about that time, Caldera drove her sister, Josephine Beaudoin, to the Westbury railroad station, passing St. Brigid's. She was already familiar with the church, and on this morning she happened to notice people entering for the seven o'clock mass. "I said to myself, maybe I should come to St. Brigid's."

75

Later that week, she walked in and sat in the last pew, feeling like an outsider, as White celebrated mass. "John was talking about God's love and God's forgiveness, and lift up your heart to God," she recalled. "I said, 'This is a man I have to talk to.'" Her schedule and his didn't mesh right away. But she kept going to daily mass and finally decided that she should go to confession, even if it weren't with White. After her years away, she approached it with dread.

Even though she made her confession face-to-face in a reconciliation room, a far friendlier environment than the old dark confessional box, she was still nervous. "I looked like death," she recalled. "I think I cried through the whole confession." She hadn't yet finished her long, tearful self-accusation when the priest, Father Robert Fulton, held up his hand and said gently: "That's enough." She had expected him to assign her some heavy penance to perform. But he didn't. "He said to me, 'I want you to go home, and I want you to stop beating up on yourself.' I remember coming out of there and feeling this tremendous relief."

She wrote to White, thanked him for the impact that his words at mass that day had made on her life, and volunteered to work in the church's youth ministry. Later, she gave her time for three years to develop a garden behind the rectory, dedicated to Mary. Now, long after that confession, she still travels often from her East Meadow home to take part in the parish's life—as a lector, a eucharistic minister, and a member of the liturgy board and the outreach advisory board.

During Holy Week in 1995, Caldera was asked to preach at one of three evening services called Tenebrae. Her homily, an emotional account of the events leading up to that confession, set off sustained applause and, at the end of the liturgy, an outbreak of hugs. "I was amazed at the reaction of people," she recalled. "They were so supportive, just accepting everything that I said."

For her audience that night, confession is still a vivid reality. In fact, confession flourishes at St. Brigid's—despite a national decline in reception of the sacrament of penance and reconciliation. Beyond the normal Saturday evening setting, St. Brigid's priests hear confessions every day after the 12:10 P.M. mass. At the Jesus Evening, a healing mass held on the first Friday of every month, long lines of penitents often occupy priests until midnight. And during Holy Week and just before Christmas, there is a day of morning-to-night confessions.

"I think we probably have far more opportunities to celebrate the sacrament than most parishes," said Costa, who has heard many of those confessions since he was assigned to St. Brigid's in 1994. "I don't know any place that has the all-day marathons that we have."

That abundant availability is a key reason why confession still thrives at St. Brigid's. "People really do come if they see that you believe in it," Gaeta said. "It sets a precedent that every single day anybody can just walk in and say something to a priest."

Another crucial element is the palpable sense of welcome and forgiveness that the parish radiates. "The whole theological atmosphere in this parish is one of: 'God loves you. There's nothing you can do that will ever change that love,'" said Jack Graham, who sees that theology in practice in his work as a leader of the RCIA program and the Jesus Evening.

In many American parishes, however, the practice has declined. Only four decades ago, weekly or monthly confession was the norm. But in a 1990 report by a committee of the National Conference of Catholic Bishops, only four percent of the lay people surveyed said they go weekly, five percent monthly, seventeen percent every two or three months, fifty-five percent once or twice a year. Almost one Catholic in five surveyed, nineteen percent, said that they never go to confession.

What makes that survey more striking is that the respondents seem not to be alienated from the Catholic Church itself—just from confession. Of those surveyed, eighty-six percent reported going to mass weekly, and eighty-two percent said they receive communion weekly.

The roots of the sacrament lie in the preaching of Jesus. He scandalized religious leaders by offering forgiveness of sins, a prerogative that they held to be reserved for God. Nonetheless, Jesus forgave bounteously and gently: the frequently married woman at the well, the woman caught in adultery, the men who nailed him to a cross. And he told his apostles: "Receive the Holy Spirit. Whose sins you shall forgive, they are forgiven; whose sins you shall retain, they are retained."

The Catholic Church teaches that the sacrament reconciles penitents with God and with the church itself. Even if a penitent has only minor sins to confess, the *Catechism of the Catholic Church* says regular confession "helps us form our conscience, fight against evil tendencies, let ourselves be healed by Christ, and progress in the life of the Spirit."

In the first five or six centuries of the church, when people received baptism late in life, if a person committed a serious sin after baptism, penance was available, but usually only once in a lifetime. It was a public event, reserved for serious sins such as murder, adultery, and heresy. Those who committed lesser sins sought forgiveness through such practices as almsgiving or fasting.

The practice of private confession grew up in Irish monasteries by the seventh century, and it later became the norm for laity. At the Council of Trent in 1551, the church's leaders adopted a theology of the sacrament that has lasted four centuries. It required the penitent to be sorry and determined not to sin again, to present all serious sins to a priest, and to perform some kind of penance to make up for the sins.

The sacrament is based on a mystery truly to be celebrated: the endless mercy and compassion of God, made visible in Jesus. But many Catholics approach it not as mercy to be celebrated, but judgment to be feared. To many, it has been the scariest sacrament: a sweat-inducing ordeal in a dark, closetlike box, where the sinner kneels and waits for the sound of a small panel to be slid back, revealing behind a screen the fuzzy outline of a priest who may or may not act with compassion.

This accretion of dread around a sacrament of mercy has created a whole narrative genre for Catholics of a certain age: Confession Stories.

Take Maggie McCartin, a theologically sophisticated woman who serves on a committee that plans the weekly family liturgy at St. Brigid's. She can still recall a confession that she made three decades ago, in fourth grade. For the first time, she and her younger sister, Eileen, had made chocolate chip cookies. They'd eaten a lot of the batch as cookie dough, and when the cookies had come out of the oven, they'd set upon them voraciously. That night, their mother, Agnes, asked them to produce the dessert, but they had nothing to show for their labor.

"My mother sat us both down and explained to us that this was a sin of gluttony," McCartin said. It was already too late that Saturday night to go to confession, but the following Saturday, Agnes drove them to Notre Dame Church in New Hyde Park and sat there, to make sure they went into the box. "My knees were shaking when I was standing on line," McCartin recalled. "This was the worst sin I ever had to confess in my life." When they reached the confessional, Eileen went in on one side of the priest and Maggie on the other.

"I went first," McCartin recalled. She recited a thin litany of pallid childhood sins, then mentioned the gluttony. "He said, 'Wait a minute, wait a minute. What was that?' He said, 'How exactly did you do that?'" And when she explained, his reaction was swift. "He burst out laughing." At that moment, she might have been a bit humiliated, but he had helped her to put it into perspective. "It didn't harm me. I wasn't scarred by that. That's the way the church was."

But some people do carry away scars. "I can remember having a very bad experience as a child going to confession," said Mary Kennedy, a co-coordinator of the parish's small Christian communities, who still goes to confession three or four times a year. "It upset me terribly, and it was a long time before I could really go to confession. The priest was extremely nasty, and he screamed at me and yelled at me. He complained I was not speaking loud enough, and he couldn't hear me, and didn't I realize he had a war disability."

Priests themselves condemn that kind of behavior. When Costa was in the seminary, one of his teachers offered this advice to any penitent who encounters an angry, abusive priest in the confessional box: "If a priest yells at you in confession, get up and walk out. And if he asks you where you're going, tell him, 'I'm going to find a priest.'"

So, for Costa and many others, there is no excuse for harshness in the sacrament of God's gentle mercy. "If I'm a priest and I'm supposed to be there continuing the mission of Jesus and receiving sinners the way Jesus would receive them, how could I possibly yell at someone?" Costa said. "I also think it's a tragedy that people would deprive themselves of the benefit of the sacrament because one priest had a bad day and yelled at them."

The seriousness of the offense itself is no excuse for yelling. It would be a rare sinner who could present a priest with a sin so heinous that it hasn't come up before. "Within the first year I heard everything," Costa said. "Within the first year, I heard things I never thought I'd hear."

Father Claude D'Souza, who came to St. Brigid's in 1994 after serving in three other parishes since his arrival from India in 1983, approaches the sacrament as a healer—appropriate for the author of a book on Indian country medicine. He likes to tell penitents: "God is our father, not a tyrant." And when people come in after being away from the church, he reminds them about a Francis Thompson poem, "The Hound of Heaven," which depicts God as a relentless, loving pursuer. D'Souza tells them: "'God has caught up with you today. He is the one who has brought you to confess.' And they begin to weep."

In the past, whether a priest was gentle or sharp, the penitent still faced another stumbling block: the notion that people had to go to confession every week in order to receive communion on Sunday.

That was the attitude of Graham's late father-in-law, Andy Eschmann. One Saturday, Eschmann had not made it to his own church, St. Joseph's in Garden City. His daughter, Graham's late wife Marilyn, told him that he still had time to get to confession at St. Brigid's chapel in Carle Place. So he went. The priest, Basil Ellard, greeted him by asking how old he was, and Eschmann said he was nearing 80. Ellard asked him why he was there and what an 80-year-old could do that would separate him from God's love. Eschmann insisted on confessing. Ellard heard his confession, told him that he really hadn't done anything to lose God's friendship and assigned him an unusual penance: Go out and walk the dog and think of God's love.

Weekly confession could be especially excessive for small children, who had few real sins of any importance to confess. "I always found out that I told the same sins over and over again, like stealing out of the refrigerator and taking the black-eyed peas out of my grandfather's bin," said Anne Josey, who grew up Catholic in heavily Baptist Georgia.

Between the old approach to confession and the current practice, the great divide was Vatican II. Its Constitution on the Sacred Liturgy, promulgated at the end of 1963, contained a sentence that led to major change: "The rite and formulas for the sacrament of penance are to be revised so that they give more luminous expression to both the nature and effect of the sacrament."

In 1974, the church published a new document outlining the rites of the sacrament. Among other things, it provided a setting for face-to-face confession, leading to the development of reconciliation rooms, where penitents can either kneel and confess through a screen or sit in a chair facing the priest.

That change offered relief from the atmosphere of the confessional box itself, which had been a central element in the scariness of the sacrament. In fact, even for the priest, the box wasn't always a comfortable setting. For a rookie priest, the box could be as nervous-making as it was for the penitent, as Costa demonstrated in a Confession Story of his own.

Soon after his ordination in 1978, he offered a weekday mass at St. Patrick's in Glen Cove, and when mass was over, a parishioner wanted him to hear her confession. This caught him by surprise. He had never heard a confession before, hadn't had much training for it, and hadn't memorized the prescribed words of absolution. "I was, like, panicking," Costa said.

Rummaging around in the sacristy, he managed to find the requisite purple stole and a printed card that contained the words of absolution. Then he walked nervously out into the church to take his place in the confessional box. Not only had he never been in one of the boxes as a priest, but he hadn't even entered one in years as a penitent. In college and in the seminary, he had made his confessions face-to-face, while seeing a priest for spiritual direction. Now, he was expected to hear his first confession in an unfamiliar space.

When he stepped into the priest's compartment in the confessional, it was pitch-dark. He could find neither the light switch nor the handle to the sliding panel between himself and the penitent, but he was too embarrassed to open the door again to let light into his compartment. Finally, he was able to slide open the panel to begin the confession, but it was still too dark to read the words of absolution from the card. As she told him her sins, he struggled to position the card at the bottom of the compartment, where it could catch a few rays of light coming in through a louver at the base of the door. That kept him so busy that he didn't really hear her sins.

"I realized I didn't have a clue as to what she confessed," Costa said. "I was too embarrassed to say, 'Could you run that by me one more time?'" He gave her absolution anyway. When she left, he was so humiliated by his performance that he didn't want anyone to see him leave the box. "I hid in the confessional until I didn't hear another sound in the church," he said. "I was too embarrassed." He could only hope it was a good experience for the penitent. "God knows, it wasn't a good experience for me."

For those who felt uncomfortable with the confessional box, the new availability of face-to-face confession was very welcome. "I think some of those changes were made for people like me," McCartin said. "I always had difficulty going into the little black box and not being able to look at somebody. I'm more relational than that. I see confession and the sacrament of reconciliation as part of my whole relationship with God and my brothers and sisters in Christ. I need to be able to look at another person in the eye."

Once, after going face-to-face with a confessor in another parish regularly, she went at Easter to her own parish at the time, Our Lady of Loretto in Hempstead. Expecting to find the confessional altered to allow face-to-face confession, she was shocked to find the traditional dark box. She knew the priest, Father Thomas Coby, but she couldn't see him through the screen. She said: "Tom, it's me. It's Maggie. I can't do this in here." So they both stepped outside, and he heard her confession face-to-face, as they sat in the pews.

The face-to-face approach does not appeal to everyone. At first, it seemed like a good idea to Linda McGowan, but now she's not so sure. "When you talked to that screen, you were focusing in on a relationship between you and God," she said. But for her, face-to-face confession changes that emphasis. "It's so much more a person-to-person situation now, rather than a person-to-God situation."

Nationally, about half of the penitents choose face-to-face, and half prefer anonymity, the report to the bishops said. Whatever setting penitents choose, and whether they go to priests in their own parish or are so active in the parish that they prefer to go elsewhere, they now find priests handling the sacrament differently.

"The old approach was very juridical; the new approach is much more relational," Gaeta said. Formerly, the priest's role was primarily to determine whether the penitent had made a good confession and whether to grant absolution. "No longer is the clergyman a judge and jury dispensing sentences," Graham said. "Today they seem to focus on bringing the person closer to God through the actions of their lives."

In that spirit, when priests decide what penance they want penitents to perform to demonstrate sorrow for their sins, they don't always simply assign a few Our Fathers or Hail Marys as penance. "I have told people to tell each person in your family that you love them," Costa said. "I have told people to do something nice for yourself."

Josey recalled a similar penance from another priest. "Once, one told me to go out and the first stranger that I saw, to walk up and introduce myself to them and just say something about God to them." Never hesitant to proclaim her faith, she found a suitable stranger. "I said, 'Hello, my name is Josey. I just want to say to you, God bless you, and I hope you have blessings all the time.'"

In the face of changes that make the sacrament seem less fearsome than before, the level of participation has still been declining. In 1983, the world's bishops held a synod on the sacrament, and the following year Pope John Paul II issued an apostolic exhortation based on their work. In that document, he acknowledged a statement frequently made during the synod's work: "The Sacrament of Penance is in crisis." Among other things, he cited a "lessening of a sense of sin."

It isn't that people don't like talking about themselves—with talk-show hosts or bartenders. "There is a phenomenon in our society of people wanting to 'confess' to lots of other people," said Monsignor Philip Murnion, director of the National Pastoral Life Center in Manhattan. "There seems to be no diminishment of the need to have a forum for being able to voice one's weaknesses and failings."

So why do so many people go to psychotherapists, at the same time fewer people are going to confession? "Psychotherapy explains why you're not responsible for the way you're behaving," Murnion said. One expert, Father Peter Fink, who teaches sacramental theology at Weston Jesuit School of Theology in Massachusetts, said: "There's a growing cultural dispersion of responsibility. It's 'The devil made me do it.'" He also pointed to the spread of the victim mentality, which allows people to feel they are not individually responsible.

It is one thing to hear a paid professional or a friend affirm your worth. But Catholics believe that a priest, for all his faults, is acting as God's representative. "It's the priest as another Christ, *alter Christus,* standing in for Jesus, saying you are valuable, you are worth something in God's sight, you are precious," Costa said. "We have the opportunity as priests to say that in a way nobody else can say it."

For priests, even though it can be tedious to listen to the same grubby sins over and over, and to sit alone for long stretches between penitents, confession can be a powerful experience, especially when they witness the relief of someone returning to the church. D'Souza recalled hearing a little girl's confession in preparation for her first communion. Her father, waiting outside, saw the smile on her face as she emerged from confession and was stricken by it, because he'd been away from the church. Minutes later, he came to D'Souza and told him: "I don't have that joy in my heart." Then he made his confession.

Though the quantity of confessions has declined, there are some good side effects. "What we call the quality of the confession is vastly improved," Gaeta said. Instead of simply listing a "scorecard" of sins, he said, people are taking a more relational approach, examining more deeply how they have fallen short in their relationships with God, with the people in their lives, and with themselves.

With shorter lines and more use of face-to-face, priests can give more spiritual direction and guidance. "What's happening, I think, is that the rote confession for many people is a thing of the past," Fink said. "With the numbers diminishing, the context is becoming more and more conversational. I, as priest, can react to you according to your needs, not according to the line that's waiting outside."

Even for those who still find it difficult, it has real benefits. "You say 'confession' and I squirm," McGowan said. "On the other hand, confession itself, intellectually I think it's a very good thing. It makes you stop and seriously think about what you're doing."

It could be better, of course, and in a 1987 volume of the *Alternative Futures for Worship* series, Fink and others tried to imagine new ways of celebrating the sacrament.

The church already has a public penitential rite at which people also confess individually. But with a shortage of priests, that is difficult. So Fink's book imagined a public penance service that would let people confess individually to specially trained lay people, who would then present the penitents to the few priests present for absolution. He also imagined a ritual based on the Jewish feast of Yom Kippur. Catholics could atone for the social sins that don't come up in individual confessions—including the sins of the church. "If the model only allows you to pin down personal responsibility, all of those larger things remain untouched," Fink said.

Whatever it looks like in the future, Fink imagined confession as playing a significant role in a world where forgiveness is in short supply. "The real challenge and the real need of the sacrament is only secondarily that we be forgiven but primarily that it become a school of forgiveness, that we be formed into reconcilers," he said. "The only way I can forgive you is if I'm humble enough in my own life to feel as if I have been forgiven."

## Chapter Seven

# DEACON,
# AS IN SERVANT

The Gospel of the day was about Zacchaeus, a rich tax collector who was short of stature but long on curiosity about Jesus of Nazareth. Knowing that Jesus was passing by, Zacchaeus climbed a sycamore tree for a good view. Jesus saw him, called him by name and invited himself to the tax collector's home.

For weeks before Deacon Bob Broyles was to preach on this reading, he kept turning it over in his head. As he thought about it, he recalled a story about his grandson, Michael DeSantis, who had heard this Gospel in nursery school and told his teacher: "I know someone like Zacchaeus: my grandfather. He's short, he's always running around doing things, and he climbs trees with us."

Whatever else Broyles decided to say in his homily, he was certain that he wanted to include the story of his grandson. And why not? One of the strengths of deacons is precisely that they are married men, who can enliven their homilies with parenting stories or tales from the world of work.

"I like to preach, because I think I have something to say," said Jim Morris, another of the five deacons at St. Brigid's, who taught in New York City schools for thirty-five years and now works three days a week for the United Federation of Teachers. "I have a perspective from my life's experience."

The deacon lives in two worlds. Like laymen, he has a job, a mortgage, children, and often grandchildren. But he is not a layman. His ordination makes him a cleric. He has powers to baptize, to preside at

85

weddings, to preach the homily at mass. When he vests for liturgies in a long white alb and drapes over it a stole, the symbol of clerical office, he looks like a priest and is often mistaken for one. "The minute you put your 'pajamas' on, you're 'Father,'" said Deacon Jack Falls.

But the deacon cannot offer mass, hear confessions, or administer the sacrament of the anointing of the sick. Some of that may change, though. In November 1995, the Vatican's Congregation for the Clergy met to discuss questions about the future of the diaconate, such as: Should the church allow deacons to anoint the sick? Should it ordain women as deaconesses? That meeting could turn out to have been an early step toward broadening the deacon's role.

Up to now, the restored diaconate has been totally male. But the Canon Law Society of America, a group of lay people and clerics that studies church law, accepted a report in October 1995 saying that canon law could easily be amended to make possible the ordination of deaconesses. One reason offered by those who oppose ordination of women as priests is that there is no evidence of female priests in Christian Scripture or tradition. But there is clear scriptural and historical evidence of women serving as deaconesses.

Ordination of deaconesses is not the only question. As the number of deacons increases and the number of priests declines, the hierarchy is looking anew at the roles of clergy. "I think the diaconate is really in a serious transition situation, because the church itself is going through a significant redefining of ministries," said Deacon John Pistone, executive director of the National Association of Diaconate Directors.

The origins of the diaconate lie in the Christian Scriptures, which refer to the office of deacon—from the Greek *diakonos,* meaning servant or helper. For centuries, the diaconate had ceased to exist in the Western church as a separate, permanent office, though seminarians were ordained deacons as a temporary step on the way to priesthood. Vatican II set in motion a restoration of the permanent diaconate. In 1967 Pope Paul VI issued guidelines for this ministry, and in 1968 the American bishops received permission to establish the permanent diaconate.

Since then, it has expanded rapidly. In late 1995, the Diocese of Rockville Centre had 199 deacons and 359 active diocesan priests, and the Diocese of Brooklyn had 141 deacons and 492 active diocesan priests, and there were 11,452 deacons in the United States, with 1,938 in training. "They've grown about five percent a year," Pistone said. That growth is in sharp contrast to the declining numbers of priests, a decline that is partly related to mandatory priestly celibacy. If both trends continue, early in the next century deacons will outnumber priests. It seems clear the role of deacons will keep growing.

"I see them as a tremendous possibility for the church," Gaeta said. Falls added: "I think now is the time to say, 'Here is this body of men. How can we better employ them?'"

The deacons at St. Brigid's were all very active in parish work before they applied for the diaconate, which fits the national pattern. "Most men who are called to the diaconate are already serving the church through ministries of service," Pistone said. Usually the men have stable families and stable jobs, which means they are mature—at least in their late thirties and early forties—when they decide to apply.

Falls, Morris, and two other St. Brigid's deacons, Bill Byrne and Phil Matheis, were in the first class to study for the diaconate at the Seminary of the Immaculate Conception in Huntington, starting in early 1977. Broyles was in a later class. Other dioceses had established the diaconate several years earlier.

"We watched while some other dioceses got started first, and we saw the need and saw the value of having it in our own diocese," said Auxiliary Bishop Emil Wcela, who served on a diocesan committee on the diaconate, in his role at that time as rector of the seminary.

For St. Brigid's, the first formal step toward the diaconate took place when Schaefer was still pastor, a few months before the training began. Schaefer arranged a meeting at the School of the Holy Child in Old Westbury, which included Byrne, Falls, Matheis, Morris, and two others who were later ordained deacons but have since moved out of the parish. Each of the men had a firm grounding in parish life, and each felt a call to the diaconate.

"There are two people responsible for the call, as far as I'm concerned: my wife Eileen and Fred Schaefer," said Byrne, who had worked his way up from office boy to executive vice-president in a Manhattan advertising firm by the time he felt the call.

For years, Byrne had been going to daily mass at St. Brigid's, but he still sensed a lack in his spirituality. One morning after mass, Schaefer invited him to the rectory for coffee, and they talked about prayer. Later, Byrne's wife became involved in the charismatic prayer group, but its emotional worship style was not to his taste. Then Eileen was diagnosed with cancer. The evening before her surgery, she went to the prayer group, but he stayed home.

"I'm sitting here saying to myself, 'You bastard, you know that she wants you to be with her,'" Byrne said. So he went to the meeting.

"It was all the weird stuff that I imagined it was, and yet, in the midst of that weirdness, there was obviously a love and a warmth in that room." He kept going. Not long after, Schaefer called and asked if he'd thought about the diaconate. Since his family had already put up with his ten years as a Village of Westbury trustee, Eileen and the kids were amenable to this new demand on his time. "She said, 'If that's what you want to do, by all means,'" he recalled. "The kids said to me, 'You ought to do that, Daddy.'"

The charismatic prayer group was also an element in Jim Morris' growth toward the diaconate. He and his wife Dorothy had long been active in the parish, launching a high school religion program and working in Pre-Cana instruction for engaged couples. But Morris also felt an incompleteness. "There was a point in my life when I said, 'My spiritual life is not as good as it used to be when I was in high school or college,'" he recalled. So he started going to mass daily at Elmhurst Hospital, where he worked with emotionally disturbed children. Together, he and Dorothy went on a number of couples' retreats. "We were looking for more," he said. "There was a yearning that we had."

At a training day at the seminary, Morris met a nun who taught at Holy Trinity Diocesan High School in Hicksville. She invited him to a charismatic prayer group at the school. "It was just such a beautiful experience," he said. But Dorothy, coping with five kids, was reluctant at first. "This one night, I had everybody ready for bed," she recalled. "I just said, 'I'll be going with you tonight.'" Then they began having charismatic meetings in their own home, which evolved into the parish charismatic prayer group.

His attraction to the diaconate grew from that quest for a deeper spirituality, combined with a sense that it would be an opportunity for service to others, as teaching had been. In the years after he was ordained, doctors, nurses, therapists, beauticians, and others at Elmhurst Hospital began to seek him out for spiritual counseling. For Morris and his wife, who has always worked closely with him in his ministry, the diaconate is not an isolated reality, in some separate box. "My work life and my spiritual and diaconal life are one," he said.

The oldest of the St. Brigid's deacons-to-be was Phil Matheis, who turned eighty in 1995. His long career included a Silver Star in World War II, high visibility in the Long Island building industry as a vice-president of Title Guarantee Company, and an array of volunteer projects, such as work at the A. Holly Patterson Geriatric Center in Uniondale. He had also volunteered for Catholic Charities, winning its

Caritas Award, and served as the diocesan chairman of the Nocturnal Adoration Society. But he had never felt any attraction to ordination.

One weekend, he and his wife Doris were having lunch at the Shelter Island parish of Monsignor James Griffin, the director of the Nocturnal Adoration Society. Some visiting nuns said that they had just attended the first ordination of deacons in another diocese. "Jim Griffin says to me, 'Did you ever think of becoming a deacon?'" Matheis recalled. "I said, 'I don't even know what the heck they are.'"

But once he learned that the diocese was accepting applications, he signed up—even though he was nearing retirement age. It seemed a natural progression. "I've been a very fortunate person that's never been separated from his church," he said. "I never had a period of being angry with the church or being out of step with the church."

Like Matheis, Falls came to the diaconate with experience in the military, business, and volunteer work. After World War II, his Marine Corps battalion was on a Mediterranean cruise when a small launch sank and he saved the lives of eight men, winning the Navy and Marine Corps Medal. Back home, influenced by Thomas Merton's autobiography, *The Seven Storey Mountain*, Falls thought about becoming a Trappist monk. He hitchhiked to Merton's monastery in Kentucky and spoke with him. "He told me go out and get some life experience, fall in love," Falls said.

Falling in love was easy. In 1951, after a second tour in the Marines, he married someone he had known since elementary school in Ozone Park. As he began his business career, as a buyer at American Can Co., he and Ginny started what became a family of seven girls. Then, through a Trappist friend, they became involved in a lay apostolate among the poor of Chile. In 1962, they sold their twenty-two shares of American Can, their house in Seaford, and their car and moved with their first five daughters to work in the slums of Chile for three years. "It solidified our willingness to give of ourselves," Falls said.

That commitment to service made a decision for the diaconate easy, and it led Falls to leave the private sector to work for ten years at the diocesan level as associate director of human development. Only one element seemed jarring: the requirement that, if a deacon's wife should die, he must not marry again. "It sounded very adolescent," Ginny said. To at least one of their children, the concept was confusing. When Jack started his training, Rosemary, then eight, expressed reservations to Ginny. "She put her arms around me and said: 'In two years, when Daddy becomes a deacon, do you have to die?'"

The classes at the seminary, open to both the deacons-to-be and their wives, began in January 1977—every other Saturday from nine in the morning until nine at night. In June 1979, Bishop John R. McGann ordained the first class of deacons for the Diocese of Rockville Centre: twenty-four for Nassau and twenty-five for Suffolk. At the start, there was some uncertainty about what their roles should be.

"Pastors asked me, 'What am I supposed to do with this guy?'" said Byrne, who began working in the diocesan office of the diaconate right after his own ordination, then became the first deacon to serve as its director, from 1980 to 1988.

The most visible role was to assist the priest at mass, by proclaiming the Gospel and reciting some parts of the liturgy. They also began presiding at baptisms, weddings, and at wakes. But in the early years, some parishioners complained about having a deacon officiate instead of a priest.

During one baptism, a man raised his hand with a question. "He said, 'Where are the priests today?'" Matheis recalled. "So I said, 'I've been assigned to do the baptisms.'" The man persisted. "'What authority do you have to do baptisms?' I said, 'By the faculties granted to me by Bishop John McGann after my ordination.'" They went on with the baptism, and later the man's wife apologized to Matheis. "I'm sure he said, 'My kid's getting second-class treatment,'" Matheis said.

Similarly, Morris recalled the wake of a local public official, whose relatives made their feelings clear to the pastor. "They called down and told Fred, 'We don't want a deacon. We want a priest,'" Morris said. Schaefer, supportive of the deacons' role, responded: "The deacon is going to do the wake, or else you're not going to have anybody."

In the years since, that has changed. "There's less and less of that kind of story," said Deacon Gerard Wilson, the director of the diaconate for the Diocese of Rockville Centre. "I think the support is getting much, much better."

When the first class of deacons was ordained after two and a half years of study, they were permitted to preach at weddings, wakes, and baptisms, but not to preach at Sunday mass, for which they had to take additional training. But in 1995, Wilson asked McGann to change that, so the diocese wouldn't ordain deacons not fully prepared to give homilies.

"We asked that it become a three-year program where all the training would take place before ordination," Wilson said. McGann agreed. Before entering the program, deacon candidates must first complete two years in the diocesan Pastoral Formation Institute, which trains lay people for a variety of roles. Once they have completed that, they go through the three years of the diaconate program, receiving training for preaching throughout those three years.

In effect, it now takes five years to become a deacon. Then he becomes available as he is needed: during the work week at his secular job, for counseling people who ask for help; in the evenings, for wakes, meetings with engaged couples and parents preparing for baptisms; on the weekends, for marriages, baptisms, proclaiming the Gospel at mass, and preaching.

For deacons, as for priests, preaching well is not easy. "I agonize. I'm up all hours of the night," Falls said. "I drive Ginny crazy." The priests preach weekly, but the deacons only once a month. That gives them more time to prepare, but it has drawbacks. "We don't preach enough," Broyles said. "To me, it's like bowling. You've got to play enough to get a decent score."

Another difficult role of the deacons is comforting mourners at wakes. "I accomplished it by saying, 'Here's a chance to be with people who are really hurting,'" said Matheis, who lost his wife in 1994 and feels that the loss made him more compassionate. His wit, down-to-earth style, and wide circle of friends make him a comforting figure. "Phil is like family to us," said Anne Josey, after Matheis had led the prayers at her daughter's wake in October 1995. Such relationships often help. Broyles recalled one wake for a young woman. "My daughter played ball with this girl," he said. "I knew the family, and I could relate to it."

At baptisms and weddings, the deacons also frequently have connections with families. One of Matheis' employees had a baby and waited until after Matheis' ordination to have the baby baptized, "the first sacrament I ever celebrated," he said. Matheis officiated at the wedding of his own son, Felix, Jr., and at the weddings of five children of his niece, Anne Marie Nataro. He often reminds John, her only remaining unmarried child: "I'm getting closer to the Lord every day. Get going. Get somebody."

When couples come in seeking a wedding, the parish's executive secretary, Adriana Miller, assigns them to either a priest or a deacon, on a rotating basis. Whoever interviews the couple later performs the wedding. If the couple ends up with Broyles, they sometimes have a surprise when the wedding date approaches and they show up for a license at Hempstead Town Hall: Broyles works there, and he issues licenses. He also serves as an advocate for couples seeking annulments.

Broyles spent most of his business life working in the office end of the construction industry, until downsizing struck. He went to work in the Nassau County senior citizen department, then took the Hempstead job. Broyles grew up in a large family, the youngest of eight children—including one who became a Christian Brother, the principal of Bishop Loughlin High School in Brooklyn, and one who became a Dominican nun. His wife Millie is the oldest of eight. They have eight children.

For years, Broyles had been active in the parish, serving as president of the Holy Name Society, working in the Catholic Youth Organization, and running a variety of fund-raisers. "I was not too aware of the diaconate," he said. Then he heard that Matheis was becoming a deacon. "I said, 'What is that old renegade doing?'" Broyles recalled. "I got very interested in it. I applied for it." He was ordained in 1985.

Millie Broyles is shy, but her support has been pivotal to her husband's ministry. "She's the rock in back of me," he said. The same is true of the other deacons' wives. Doris Matheis, for example, made her husband's albs and stoles, but she made no fuss about the time he had to spend on his ministry. "She made it possible, by making it comfortable," Matheis said.

Now that he is a widower, Matheis must stay unmarried if he is to remain a deacon. "I didn't know that Doris was going to predecease me, but I knew if it happened, this was the way it was going to be," he said. "I was willing to take that chance, even if Doris died two days after I was ordained."

The death of Byrne's wife, Eileen, put him in the same position. "The church does not understand the void that is created by the loss of a partner of over fifty years. Particularly when you're married to a babbling brook, as she was, the silence is sometimes deafening," he said. "I really have no interest in getting married. I have a real need for companionship, for somebody to hug and be hugged by."

Whatever their marital situation, the deacons have also assumed the role of sympathetic listeners—both in the parish and at work. Byrne remembered a colleague who approached him on the fairway. "He said to me, 'How'd you get mixed up in this church stuff?'" Byrne told him it was through prayer. The man said he never remembered to pray. "I reached down and picked up a pebble," Byrne recalled. "I said, 'Put this in your pocket. Every time you touch it, just say, 'Jesus, help me.' I said, 'That's prayer.' For five years, the guy walked by me in the locker room and said, 'I still have it.'"

One of the most moving moments of Matheis' diaconate was in one of those quiet interactions. It was during a hospital visit in Glen Cove, with Maffeo. The priest is young enough to be his son, but they have similar senses of humor and enjoy each other's company. While the two men were visiting a terminally ill woman, she and her husband celebrated their fiftieth anniversary, with the whole family present, and renewed their marriage vows. Then Maffeo went to his car, got the anointing oils, and administered the sacrament of the sick. "It certainly was a very touching moment," Maffeo said.

Administering the sacrament of the sick is one role that many deacons would like to perform themselves. In addition, Broyles said people seeing him in church before daily mass have sometimes assumed he is a priest and asked him to hear their confessions. "Why shouldn't I be able to help somebody like this?" he said. "I absolutely wish I could do it for them."

Whether or not deacons acquire a larger role, the key to the diaconate will not be its liturgical functions, but the spirit of service to others that is the root of the word *deacon* and the core of the Christian Gospel.

"The most important thing I am is a sign of what the whole church is called to be," Morris said. "When you think about that, it's an awesome responsibility. This is what I want people to understand, that what I am, what I'm called to do, is what the whole church is supposed to be."

*Chapter Eight*

# MAKING A
# JOYFUL NOISE

*M*oments after the last notes of the multilingual recessional hymn had closed the Thanksgiving liturgy at St. Brigid's, Eileen Ruesterholz turned to someone in her pew and asked: "Where would you see something like this?"

The unique "this" was a resounding liturgy that filled the small church to overflowing with parishioners from different cultures, praising God in English, Italian, Spanish, Creole, and Tagalog. The offertory procession, usually a staid affair in which a family brings to the altar the bread and wine to be consecrated, was a rhythmic dance: Three Haitian girls carried baskets of fruit and two carried bread and wine, swaying toward the altar to the beat of a drum and a Creole hymn.

These multicultural celebrations are among the many crescendos of the year-long symphony of liturgy at St. Brigid's, where public worship is the pastor's top priority, where a larger-than-usual liturgy staff spends an immense amount of time planning and executing liturgies that have set a standard for innovation, spirit, participation, and length.

That length is both a fond parish joke and a sure sign that people care enough about their public worship to stay as long as it takes to say the words and offer the gestures that express the parish's exuberant prayerfulness. Even when the liturgies end, parishioners seem reluctant to let them go, moving smoothly from the "holy hour" to the "happy hour" of refreshments, such as coffee and cookies, that follow many liturgies.

The symphony of liturgy at St. Brigid's is a richly varied work, rising and falling with the changing seasons of the church year and always filled with color: a Holy Week schedule that tests endurance but provides a powerful, palpable experience of the sacrifice–death–resurrection cycle that lies at the heart of the Christian mystery; shamrocks on the feast of St. Patrick; zeppole on the feast of St. Joseph; special services thrown together hastily, but with equal care, for the illness of a parishioner or the sudden martyrdom of Jesuits in El Salvador; rock music that packs the school auditorium with young people every Sunday at a mass called simply "The Six."

This is not the place for Catholics who want an easy-in, easy-out liturgy, quiet and sterile, devoid of interaction with the others in the pews. St. Brigid's embodies the Vatican II vision of the church as the people of God and its worship as an act of people in community, not a collection of individuals who happen to be in the same space but focus on their private prayer, isolated from others. This parish is about being together in prayer, and the multicultural liturgies are a particularly effective example.

"It's holy ground; it's spirit-filled," said Ruesterholz, who worships at St. Brigid's, although she lives in North Massapequa. "The liturgy and the congregation are so blended. You don't feel that you're separated racially."

But creating meaningful liturgies for a parish with so much diversity is not easy. Liturgy, the public worship of the church, comes from a Greek word meaning "work of the people." And multilingual liturgies, like all good liturgy, really do require work.

Only two and a half weeks before Thanksgiving, the parish's newly created multicultural planning team had met in a small upstairs room at the parish center, to figure out ways to involve the language communities more in liturgical planning, to give them each a larger role.

"How do we do that in a predominantly English-speaking world?" asked Estelle Peck, the liturgy director, who chaired the meeting. "Do we make sure that it's equally distributed? It's really, really hard. I don't want to just throw bones. I'm trying to get everybody together, so that everybody can own it."

One evidence that not everybody "owns" the multicultural liturgies yet is attendance. Every Sunday, the parish offers mass in four languages: English, Spanish, Italian, and Creole. Those masses are well attended— especially the Spanish liturgy, which draws about seven hundred people to the chapel in the school. But when the language communities all come together on such occasions as Holy Thursday, Thanksgiving, and others, it becomes obvious who is still in the majority.

"It's predominantly the English-speaking community that comes to the multicultural celebrations," Peck told the planning group. "How do we celebrate a liturgy that's really going to get to the hearts of all our people?"

In the past, the parish staff had done the planning, but Peck made it clear that in the future, the communities should take the lead. "This is going to be a working committee," she said. "I expect us to laugh and to struggle and to fight. If you think you're getting deprived of something, let's get that out in the open."

The first step was a suggestion from Sheila Dunphy, a representative of the English-speaking community. She proposed that one language community should take responsibility for planning a whole multicultural event, with another community planning the next event, throughout the year. The others quickly agreed, and the Haitians volunteered to plan for New Year's Day.

With the liturgy for Thanksgiving of 1995 fast approaching, however, they had no time for long-term planning. They had to do it right then, sticking close to the format of the 1994 liturgy and dividing up the parts among the communities. The result was like a friendly horse-trading session.

Peck started with the basic question: Do all the communities actually celebrate Thanksgiving? The Haitians acknowledged that they don't have a November feast, but that they have adapted to America. "We eat a lot of turkey," said Yvenet Decessa, one of the Haitian representatives. The other, Darly Allonce, said the Haitian community would like to do the offertory procession. The previous year, it had been in English and Italian.

"Domenic, you've just given up a song," Peck told Domenic Abbatiello of the Italian community, who answered: "We're going to get something in return, right?" And Jose Castillo of the Spanish community, apparently tongue in cheek, added: "We'll give you the Amen." Not much of a prize, since it is essentially the same in all the languages.

In the end, each of the communities seemed satisfied with the distribution of readings and hymns for the liturgy. At a final rehearsal the Sunday before Thanksgiving, they all worked at blending their voices, so that when one of the communities sang in their own language, the others tried to join.

"For the Anglos to have to struggle to learn to pronounce Tagalog is the experience of the other communities, who struggle to learn English," said Stephanie Clagnaz, who leads the children's choir, acts as a cantor at many liturgies, and directed the Thanksgiving rehearsal because the music director, Tommy Thorell, was ill.

Trying to blend the different languages into one choir, as they did on Thanksgiving, is less disruptive to a liturgy than trying to move around 100 to 150 singers from different choirs. "It's just unbelievable, just the logistics of getting the people where they're supposed to be," Clagnaz said.

The homily also is a knotty problem. If the priest preaches only in English, many non-English speakers won't understand much of it. But preaching in four languages also poses problems. At an ordinary mass, the homily would usually run ten minutes, but at the multicultural liturgies, if the celebrant preached ten minutes in each language, the homily would run forty minutes. So the only realistic alternative is to preach a briefer homily in each of the languages. On Holy Thursday of 1995, for example, Gaeta did exactly that. He wrote his homily in English, got help translating it into the other languages, worked on the pronunciation, and spoke it all himself.

"I think you should try to do as much as you can to give people a sense of being included, but they have to be charitable towards your limitations," Gaeta said. That is what happened. "What I've heard from the other communities is that they're just so touched that he would give that much time," Peck said.

The apportioning of parts, movement of choirs, blending of voices, and preaching of homilies are some of the liturgical complexities that accompany the parish's ethnic diversity. Beyond that, in creating its liturgies, it also must cope with the same challenges that face all parishes after Vatican II, which considered liturgy so important that the first document it completed was the Constitution on the Sacred Liturgy.

One of the pivotal insights of the council was its teaching that Jesus is present at the mass not only in the consecrated bread and wine, but also in the assembly itself. This places stronger emphasis on the worshiping community than on individual piety. For many Catholics who grew up before the council, this emphasis on community, including such rituals as an exchange of a hug or handshake of peace, has been such a jarring distraction that some have even stopped going to church. Not all who have stayed are happy.

"I do think that there are people who are in our pews on Sunday that are longing for a contemplative experience that sets them apart from other people," said Sister Mary Alice Piil, who teaches liturgy at the Seminary of the Immaculate Conception in Huntington. The challenge is to remind people that they find God in each other, not alone. "Liturgy is about the corporate body at prayer," she said. "It's not just that we're together praying personally. We are together praying as one body."

Explaining the essence of liturgy to her students, Piil gave them an article by Father Robert Taft, a Jesuit liturgist. His opening metaphor is Michelangelo's fresco in the Sistine Chapel, showing God, the creator, reaching out but not quite touching Adam, the created.

"That space is what liturgy needs to fill," said Clagnaz, who was studying with Piil, working toward a master's degree in theology. "That analogy of bringing the believer closer to God is sort of how I walk into every liturgy. . . . Our focus is to teach people week after week what the face of God looks like."

At St. Brigid's, no other activity has a higher priority. "To me, liturgy is number one," Gaeta said. "You've got people for an hour a week. You've got to give them the best you can give them." That involves engaging the emotions as well as the intellect. "Liturgies that really mean anything are the ones in which people leave the church and they've touched the sacred, they've experienced forgiveness, they've experienced healing," Gaeta said. "There has to be a personal engagement where you feel you have entered into something and you're part of it, and you've been touched by God."

Toward that end, whatever it takes, no matter how unorthodox it may seem, St. Brigid's does it—even hiring a rock singer to lead the people in song.

—꿰—

The defining prophecy in Tommy Ciotti Thorell's life came from his grandmother, Theresa DeFilippo, who taught him about Jesus, exerted a profound spiritual influence, and often told him: "Tommy, one day you're going to sing for God."

As a boy, he was so serious about being a Catholic that he even got into fights with people who violated church law by eating meat on Friday. For a time, he thought of becoming a priest, but other influences prevailed. "The world drew me in," he said, "and my dad."

Peter Ciotti, a singer, began early to nudge his son toward the music business. Thorell studied tenor saxophone at the High School of Performing Arts in Manhattan, but grew tired of commuting from Queens. So he graduated from Francis Lewis High School in 1965. He started Queens College, but soon left to travel with a rock band as a lead singer.

Then, when he was eighteen, his grandmother died. Among her final words was a reminder of her prophecy: "Never forget what I told you." But in his bitter grief, he had no desire to sing for God. His attitude toward God was: "If you're that kind of guy, I don't need you."

In the years that followed, his life was a blur of travel and relationships, of starts and stops. The further he got into his career, the
more he had to mold his image to what his managers wanted, like wearing his hair a certain way and adding a less ethnic name than Ciotti. He
took the name Thorell from a business associate of his brother, Peter.

By the early 1980s, his career was going well. Doing benefit work
for St. Francis Hospital, he wrote a song called "One Heart." In 1984, he
was booked to sing it before an audience of three thousand, including
Nancy Reagan, at the Waldorf–Astoria Hotel. Before the concert, Thorell
stood in his suite, wearing a white tuxedo and looking down at Manhattan's dazzling lights. At this moment of apparent professional triumph,
he felt empty. "I said, 'There's got to be something more,'" he recalled.

Almost two decades after his grandmother's dying reminder, Thorell
felt a summons from God. "There was no way, as far as I could see, to walk
away from His calling," he said. "I couldn't get away from Him. I tried."

Faced with a sudden health problem that required serious surgery,
Thorell became intensely focused on his effort to straighten out his life.
Awaiting the surgery, he bargained with God. "I said, 'Lord, you got me
one hundred percent. If I get out of this hospital alive, I give you every
song I ever write and give you my entire life. You got my attention.'"
Soon after that, he told his manager: "I'm leaving to sing for God."

In his new life, he began to sing in the ministry of Father Robert
McGuire at the Spirit Life Center in Plainview, an outgrowth of the
Catholic charismatic renewal; started a traveling music ministry, Just
for Jesus Ministries; dropped out of the Catholic Church and became a
music leader at St. Thomas Episcopal Church in Malverne; married Clau-
dia Grappone, whom he had known since childhood; took a job at North
Shore Assembly of God in Oyster Bay; studied at an Assembly of God
institution; got ordained, and started his own church in North Hempstead. In a few months, he realized he wasn't meant to be a pastor. So
he returned to working with McGuire.

Thorell joined McGuire in giving retreats, or missions, in Catholic
parishes. One of them was St. Brigid's, where Gaeta saw what Thorell
could do. Soon after, when Gaeta was seeking a new music director,
Thorell was on his short list. Estelle Peck wrote Gaeta a long letter from
her vacation in Maine, urging that he hire Thorell.

There were good reasons for Gaeta to resist. Thorell wasn't a traditional
organist, for one thing, and he had once left the Catholic Church. "That
didn't bother me at all," Gaeta said. "I was very, very taken with Tommy
from the beginning, simply because he really brought people into prayer."

Still, Thorell didn't fit right in. "The first six months was a little rough," Thorell said. "I wanted to make St. Brigid's into a charismatic church. They weren't ready for that music."

Some parishioners also disliked his emotional, crooning style of singing. "People will still comment on that, but from what I've seen working with him, it comes from his desire to minister to people," said the parish organist, Susan Porteus, who met him through the Spirit Life Center and came to St. Brigid's with him. "He sings it with feeling. He doesn't just sing and count measures and notes. That's not ministering to people."

Thorell had to learn some of the daily duties of a music director almost from scratch, such as singing for funerals. "It took a good six months, and Susan was a very big part of it," Gaeta said. "They worked very hard together on that. She's been playing in churches for years. So she has that whole sense. But Tommy didn't have that sense at all."

Gaeta, who didn't want Thorell to be a traditional music director, has been open to the rock singer's creativity. Once, Clagnaz recalled, Thorell asked Gaeta if he could put secular songs in the Christmas song book. Gaeta answered: "Tom, you're the doctor. I'm the patient." Thorell also offered to play soft piano during the eucharistic prayer at the mass, which is usually silent. Gaeta gave it a try. "When I go someplace else now and I don't have it, I feel like I'm flat," Gaeta said. "There's something missing."

The bottom line is prayer. "He has called us into another way of praying—the expression, the feeling, the humanity," Gaeta said. "I ultimately feel that that is what people are looking for, when people come here, when they come from other places. They want to experience something. They want to be communicated to, in the whole package: the preaching, the liturgy, the singing. Tommy's a very, very big part of that."

—⁓—

For the average parish, the liturgy staff consists of a volunteer choir and one paid music director, who usually doubles as organist. At St. Brigid's, the lineup includes a children's choir; an adult choir; Italian, Spanish, Haitian, and Filipino choirs; a director of liturgy; a director of music; an organist; and a children's choir director, Clagnaz, whose duties also include religious education.

That means there are four paid, professional parish staff members focusing on the public worship of its people. Despite the sparks that sometimes fly, they mesh well. "Although we don't have things written out that we're each individually responsible for, I think each of us recognizes each other's gifts," Clagnaz said. "It's not like we're four people who are all strong in the same thing."

At the center is Peck, who has been running the liturgy since 1986, now in close coordination with Gaeta. "He gives me tremendous freedom and leeway to be able to be creative," she said. Peck brings to it a master's degree in theology, a profound love of liturgy, a cherubic smile, an artistic touch with a computer, and a flair for organizing. She pulls together the planning meetings and coordinates everything. In church, she hovers gently around the periphery, making sure it all works.

Clagnaz, who studied voice at Juilliard, has a master's degree in education and a gift for teaching. That uniquely suits her to run the children's choir and the sacramental liturgies, such as first communion and confirmation. She has a powerful voice and a strong personality. Sometimes, she and Thorell differ on musical issues—quick flashes of harmless, short-lived lightning between two highly charged people.

Thorell is a multi-talented musician who composed much of the parish's trademark music—from the traditional "Agnus Dei" and "Kyrie Eleison" to the catchy, triumphant "He's Alive"—and also has a genius for improvisation. Influenced by the charismatic renewal movement, which emphasizes the everyday presence of the Holy Spirit, he flourishes in situations such as the monthly Jesus Evening, a free-form healing mass that allows him to take the music where he feels the Spirit is leading.

Porteus, the only one on the team proficient on the organ, provides a steady, disciplined musical anchor and a counterpoint to Thorell's piano. "Musically, we blend, because of my training in reading and organ and his ability to just play off the top of his head," she said.

With so many players and so much going on liturgically, St. Brigid's does a prodigious amount of planning. The average parish gets by with one liturgical committee. St. Brigid's has a liturgy board that sets policy, a committee that meets monthly to plan the weekly family mass in minute detail to make it meaningful and engaging for the children as well as the parents, a group that plans the rock mass, and the multicultural committee. "I just think it's important that everybody has a say in it," Peck said.

The parish provides more printed liturgical material than most, which Peck produces on computer. One unusual touch has been Gaeta's daily reflections during the Advent season. In 1994, they appeared weekly in the bulletin. In 1995, Peck compiled them into a booklet,

"What Shall I Give Him, Poor as I Am?" She creates song sheets for the masses every week. She finds them a good planning tool, but they also convey a subliminal message to parishioners.

"It's wonderful, because it really personalizes it for that community," Piil said. "People take it much more seriously, I think, when they see that people have put that much into it."

Thorell chooses the music for the adult masses. The overall tone of that music reflects his background in the charismatic renewal—uplifting, emotional, spirit-filled. That music is one of the parish's widely loved hallmarks.

But one worshiper, who drives to St. Brigid's from another parish specifically for the liturgy, said that her only complaint is that the lyrics of the music sometimes focus too much on individual relationships with God, not enough on the community. "It's too privatized for me," she said. "It's community worship and it's supposed to lead us outward."

As crucial as the music is, however, it is only one element in the liturgy. "You need good prayers, you need good leaders of prayer, you need good ministers," Peck said. The parish has been lucky in having pastors—Gaeta and Schaefer—who place a strong emphasis on good liturgy, and priests who are open to the liturgy's spirit and capable of powerful preaching. But good liturgy needs more than priests. Those who distribute communion must look people in the eye as they say "the Body of Christ." The ushers must smile, offer a palpable sense of welcome, and pray with the assembly before taking up the collection, to help sanctify the moment.

In addition, Peck said, liturgical leaders need to focus on events that are preoccupying the people, such as Mother's Day or Father's Day, and issues that have engaged their attention. When Israeli Prime Minister Yitzhak Rabin was assassinated on a Saturday afternoon, for example, she rushed to the church to include prayers for Israel in the prayer of the faithful. "To me, those little things speak very clearly to people that we are concerned about the whole world," she said.

Another hallmark of the liturgy is willingness to try something different. In Advent of 1995, for example, the leaders of the Sunday evening rock mass distributed "Give Peace a Chance" slips, inviting people to write their own name and the initials of someone with whom they are trying to make peace. The idea is to get people to make a commitment to peacemaking, and the identity of those represented by the initials remained confidential. The slips were used as chances in a drawing for an appropriate rock mass Christmas prize, a Tower Records gift certificate.

Above all, though, the liturgy touches people on an emotional level. Frank Pesce, an attorney and a former editor of the parish newspaper, *The Spirit of St. Brigid's*, recalled how closely Peck, Thorell, and Father John White worked with him in planning and personalizing his mother's funeral in 1993, and how comfortable the parish made his family feel. His daughter, Jeannine, read one reading, and his son, Danny, read the prayer of the faithful.

"After the funeral, it was amazing how many people were coming up to us and saying how beautiful it was," Pesce said. One of them was his uncle from the Bronx, Ted Tobia, whose reaction was the kind of review any liturgist would want. "His statement was: 'Love was bouncing off the walls in there.'"

## Chapter Nine

# BEHIND THE
# RECTORY WALLS

Serious and proper in a clerical black shirt and crisp white Roman collar, Michael Maffeo stood nervously outside the door of the rectory at St. Brigid's, where he would soon begin his career as a priest.

This was to be his first real meeting with his first pastor, Frank Gaeta. As long as there have been veteran pastors and newly ordained priests, this initial meeting has been a nervous-making moment—and for good reasons: Even in an era of greater lay involvement in the work of the church, the pastor still sets the tone for the whole parish, including the happiness and productivity of the priests in the rectory.

Before ordination, Maffeo had happily spent his pastoral year, a kind of internship, at Our Lady of the Snow, a small parish in Blue Point. But now he was walking into a different rectory, in a huge parish, to live with priests he hadn't chosen. Ordination doesn't guarantee congeniality, and priests can get on each other's nerves as much as relatives do. So the rectory atmosphere can make a parish assignment joyful or painful, sanctifying or stultifying. And the quality of that private life can be crucial to the public role in the pulpit.

Maffeo had no reason to suppose Gaeta would be difficult, but he knew little about him. A week earlier, minutes before Maffeo's ordination, they had gotten a glimpse of each other as they waited for the entrance procession, outside the rectory at St. Agnes Cathedral in Rockville Centre. The new priests would not formally learn about their first assignments until Bishop John R. McGann met with them after the ceremony, but Maffeo had a strong idea that he would be going to Gaeta's

104

parish. So he asked someone to point out Gaeta, who turned out to be easy to find: All the other priests were wearing white stoles on their shoulders, but Gaeta had somehow shown up wearing the prescribed color from years gone by, red.

That brief look, plus a bear hug from Gaeta after the ceremony, had been Maffeo's only exposure to his first pastor until he stepped into the rectory a week later. "He looked scared to death," said Mary Underwood, then the rectory receptionist. She said to Maffeo: "Oh, you're our new priest," and then he heard a loud, exuberant greeting from a nearby room: "Mi-i-i-i-ke-e-e-y, come i-i-i-i-i-n."

The voice was Gaeta's, and he soon appeared at the door, wearing an unmonsignorlike outfit: casual white pants and a T-shirt. The buoyant greeting and informal style were Maffeo's introduction to life in the St. Brigid's rectory. In the years that followed, he grew comfortable in that rectory, even in the midst of significant change.

The most lasting change was the decision to move the parish offices out of the rectory and into a former convent building across the street, to give the priests some privacy and provide office and meeting space for the growing lay ministries.

The most jolting was the 1994 transfer of two well-liked and charismatic priests, John White, who had come to the parish at the same time as Gaeta, in 1989, and Malcolm Burns, who arrived along with Maffeo. Both moved on to other assignments. "If you lose one guy, it's tough, but to lose two guys, it is a very, very difficult thing," Gaeta said. "When the parish is too priest-dependent, a turnover can be just devastating. The more people are involved in the parish, the less traumatic it's going to be for the whole body of the parish."

Burns and White had helped keep the parish from becoming too priest-dependent, by continuing to nourish a tradition of lay activism that began under Fred Schaefer. "They were building the Kingdom," Gaeta said, "not their own kingdom."

The priests who replaced them in 1994, Tom Costa and Claude D'Souza, bring impressive intellectual and pastoral strengths of their own to the rectory. Though it has a new mix of personalities, the rectory remains what priests call a "good house," where they can practice their ministry without the burden of excessive tension.

In some rectories, the emotional tone is cooler, more hotel-like. "This is exactly what Frank does not allow to happen at St. Brigid's; he creates a home," said Monsignor Joseph Nagle, who served until late 1996 as director of the Immaculate Conception Pastoral Center in Douglaston and regularly offered mass at St. Brigid's. "We genuinely enjoy being with one another," Costa said. "There's a lot of good-natured kidding and fooling around."

In that atmosphere, the dry wit that lurks below Maffeo's serious surface has shown itself. Almost constantly, in the house and even on the altar, Maffeo and Gaeta trade gentle digs. Maffeo is more liturgically traditional and less emotionally expansive than Gaeta—differences that provide ample ammunition for good-natured shots across the bow.

As they left a diner after one staff breakfast, for example, Gaeta and Maffeo exchanged wisecracks about their different theological approaches, a frequent subject of their jibes. Gaeta said something about the younger priest's lack of theology, and Maffeo told Gaeta that the pastor's theology, like a display of cakes near the door, was "sweet and syrupy, with no substance."

In some rectories, a priest wouldn't even dream of making a crack like that about his pastor, but Gaeta has created an atmosphere that encourages his associates to rib him. He is very serious about the Gospel message, but in proclaiming it, he is not above using funny hats, broad humor, and practical jokes.

One favorite tale from the rectory relates a prank that Gaeta once played on White. In addition to playing sacred music over the church's outside loudspeaker system to edify passersby on Post Avenue, Gaeta had been playing more secular selections, including a collection of nautical tunes. White had repeatedly urged him to stop. One day, as White was hearing confessions after the 12:10 P.M. mass, Gaeta struck again.

"I said, 'I'm going to get John,'" Gaeta recalled. "I put the nautical one in, and it starts playing 'Harbor Lights' and 'I Left My Heart in San Francisco.' And he's hearing confessions. So he's ready to come out and kill me." In the confessional, White heard the music clearly and said to himself: "He's still at it."

Moments later, a woman came into the confessional and told White she hadn't confessed her sins in a long time, but when she passed by and heard "I Left My Heart in San Francisco," she decided this was a church where she could comfortably make her peace with God. "So she goes to confession," Gaeta said, recalling his triumph over White. "He comes out later, and he says, 'I give up. I give up.'"

Somehow, the laughing works for St. Brigid's. It fits Gaeta's philosophy about rectory life. "The most important thing is it has to be everybody's home," Gaeta said. "It is not *my* home, where the associates happen to live. There's no special status for anybody. It's *our* home."

But rectories aren't always comfortable. The wrong chemistry among priests, like lingering squabbles in a family, can be draining. In feuding families, however, the workplace can be a refuge from trouble at home. In parishes, priests not only live together but work together. "So it's always a little strange," Costa said. "You're not always going to get along. You're not always going to like everybody's personality."

The relationships in the rectory, which most parishioners don't see, can affect the priests' more public life. "I think guys who are happy priests do good ministry, and I think guys that are unhappy in the rectory, their work suffers," said Monsignor James Kelly, chairman of a diocesan committee on priestly life and ministry. Bishop McGann appointed him to the post in 1994, acting at the request of the priest personnel policy board and the priests' senate.

In McGann's initial letter to priests explaining the committee, one area of inquiry he proposed was "living arrangements for clergy." The committee sought the views of priests in the diocese, and about 350 responded. Some expressed interest in alternate living arrangements, such as living in one parish and working in another— or living alone. The committee is looking at that and other issues, but setting up alternatives won't be easy.

Kelly wondered, for example, what if all the priests in his parish, St. Aidan's in Williston Park, moved out of the rectory? "What happens to this house?" he asked. "If you live someplace else, are you under that pastor, or are you a free agent?"

For priests who have lived in painful rectory situations, living alone can look attractive. But it would also have drawbacks, such as the loss of room and board in the rectory, which supplements their modest salaries. (All priests in the diocese get a transportation allowance of $290 a month, plus a base salary that ranges from $405 a month for priests ordained up to nine years, to $608 for pastors and administrators, and sacramental stipends for such events as weddings and funerals.)

"I think a lot of guys are totally unaware of the many benefits they get from living in a rectory," Kelly said. Most rectories, for example, have cooks. In the few that don't, the priests often cook and shop for themselves, which takes time away from their ministry. "The bishop doesn't like that," said Monsignor Frank Caldwell, diocesan director of priest personnel.

The cooks also provide some continuity to a situation that is by nature transient, because priests come and go as their fixed terms of five or six years expire. The cook at St. Brigid's is a good example of this dual role. Michelina (Mickey) Gambale offers more than just steaming bowls of meatball soup and brimming plates of pasta. She gives the house an element of stability.

"Mickey is the head of that rectory, and Frank [Gaeta] sees the absolute need of that," Nagle said. "Most rectories in our diocese might have a cook for dinner five nights a week. Breakfast and lunch, you're on your own. Mickey cooks lunch and dinner. The food is plentiful, and to her, it's an act of love."

Only the housekeeper, Sophie Sawczyn, with more than four decades of service, has been there longer. Gambale came to St. Brigid's to work for Schaefer, at a time when she was working part-time as a hairdresser, had two teenage daughters, and had recently been divorced. She got the job through Sister Helen Rooney, who worked in the parish outreach program. "I used to do her hair, and she happened to say to me that they were looking for a cook," Gambale recalled. "I fell into the best job that I could have imagined."

Though she came with her own cooking skills, she also picked up culinary training from Schaefer and one of his priests, Robert Fulton, both known as excellent cooks. Sticking with what she knows best, Gambale cooks primarily Italian food. "It seems we always go back to a pasta dish," she said. "If I made six different pastas at a meal, they would love it." She also makes a lot of soup in winter, and all year she uses the barbecue on the patio.

Gambale works five days a week, arriving before lunch, shopping in the afternoons and leaving after supper. She buys breakfast food, which the priests prepare for themselves, and cooks food for the weekends, leaving it for them to heat up. When they need haircuts, she provides those, too. "The period in the rectory that Frank hates the most is when Mickey has to go on vacation," Nagle said.

From her vantage point in the kitchen and dining room, she observes closely the interaction among the priests. They're all different personalities, she said, "but they tend to give each other their space, to give each other the air they need."

—◆—

The mix of personalities in the house is indeed diverse—from Gaeta's ebullient, outgoing, bear-hugging nature to D'Souza's quieter, more scholarly temperament.

Like Gaeta, who could not remember a time when he didn't want to be a priest, D'Souza seemed destined for the priesthood. He was born into a large Catholic family in southern India. "I am the last, number eleven," D'Souza said. Of the five brothers, four became priests, and of the six sisters, five became nuns.

The family received an award from Pope Pius XII for producing more priests and nuns than any other family in the world. D'Souza's father had hoped that his youngest child, the last one living at home, would stay there to help run the family's coconut plantation. But he decided to follow his brothers into the priesthood. "When I said I'm going, my father couldn't speak for three days," D'Souza recalled.

After his ordination in 1964, D'Souza served as principal of St. Aloysius College in Bangalore and as a pastor of a Bangalore parish. In addition to his theological training, he has master's degrees in educational psychology, sociology, political science–public administration, and a doctorate in education. He has written a book about herbal remedies and a geography text series for elementary grades.

D'Souza came to America in 1983, for treatment of a head and neck injury that he had sustained years earlier. A doctor told him treatment might take several years. So, with permission from his bishop in India, he stayed. His first parish was St. John the Evangelist in Center Moriches, followed by assignments to Our Lady of Loretto in Hempstead and St. Louis de Montfort in Sound Beach before coming to Westbury in 1994.

Though he doesn't have Gaeta's broad sense of humor and is more of a theological traditionalist, D'Souza fit in well, in his own low-key way. "I am quite at home here," he said. It is a busy parish, and he likes staying busy.

—〰—

In contrast to Gaeta and D'Souza, both Maffeo and Costa have maneuvered through detours on their way to the priesthood.

Maffeo grew up in Lindenhurst and graduated from Adelphi University in 1978 with a history degree and a secondary education certificate. Later, he got a master's degree in history from Adelphi. But he couldn't find a full-time teaching job. So he taught as a substitute and kept working part-time in the deli department at King Kullen in Lindenhurst, where he had first worked when he was in high school. "You do get to see the good and the worst of people—people yelling at me because the price was too high," Maffeo said.

Eventually, he was substitute-teaching almost daily, but he still could find no full-time job. So, in 1982, he and a friend went to Virginia, his friend seeking work in horticulture and Maffeo in teaching. In his year there, Maffeo worked in a real estate office, helped a builder put up a house, and subbed. But he couldn't land a full-time teaching job.

Still, the journey had value. It began to focus his mind on another career plan: His older brother, Joe, had been in the Montfort order, had left the order, and was later ordained a permanent deacon. "I had heard a lot about what the priesthood was all about," Maffeo said. "When I was in high school, I had seriously thought about being a priest." The time in Virginia helped him mature and make up his mind about the priesthood.

"I did not want to go into the seminary *because* I couldn't find a teaching job," Maffeo said. "That's one of the reasons I delayed even longer than I should have." But he entered the seminary in 1986 and was ordained in June 1991.

Costa decided on the priesthood earlier in his life, attending Pius X Prep Seminary in Uniondale and Cathedral College in Douglaston before entering the Seminary of the Immaculate Conception in Huntington. But he left, angry with the seminary but not with the church. "I never really thought I would go back," Costa said. He got a job working in Wallach's, a clothing store in the Roosevelt Field shopping mall. In the evenings, he attended Hofstra University, working on a master's in secondary education, focusing on teaching English as a second language.

Teaching made sense, because his father, James, had taught for thirty-eight years in the Levittown schools, retiring as an assistant principal. Teaching language also made sense. Costa had already studied Latin, Greek, Spanish, French, and Italian in high school and college, and later would go on to more language study.

But his plans changed when the Newman Club, a Catholic student organization at Hofstra, held a retreat and Costa signed up. When the club had to change its plans and hold the retreat at the seminary, he wanted to back out. "It was the last place in the world I wanted to go on retreat," he said. He went anyway, and the nun who led the retreat said some insightful things to the group about making life decisions— things that seemed to apply directly to him. "It was so powerful," he said.

The experience jolted him. "Maybe I decided too quickly never to return to the seminary," he thought. "I started to rethink the whole thing. Then I was in a great deal of turmoil about it." Finally, he re-entered the seminary. "By the end of that first year, I decided that this is where God wanted me." He was ordained in 1978.

After assignments at St. Boniface in Elmont, St. Rose of Lima in Massapequa, and St. Ignatius in Hicksville, he became a co-pastor at St. John of God in Central Islip in 1988. But in 1993, his paternal grandparents were admitted to a nursing home in Glen Cove, and the long trip on the Long Island Expressway to visit them became too much. "I said, 'I can't do this. I can't live like this.'"

So when his first term in Central Islip expired and there was an opening at St. Brigid's, much closer to the nursing home, he decided that visiting his grandparents was more important than remaining a pastor. In religious orders, people regularly serve as superiors, then return to the ranks. But among diocesan priests, stepping down as a pastor to become an associate again is still rare.

"To me, being a pastor is a very beautiful ministry, but it's one of many ministries that are available to us," Costa said. During an interview, Gaeta asked him whether no longer being a pastor would be difficult for him, and Costa said no. Costa's gift with languages, Gaeta knew, would help him minister to the Spanish and Italian communities in Westbury. Costa had first worked at St. Brigid's as a seminarian, and after his ordination had often presided at the Italian mass as a visitor. "I was just so delighted to get someone like Tom, with those blessings," Gaeta said.

So Costa moved to St. Brigid's, looking forward to being closer to his grandparents. But on the day he reported for duty in June 1994, his grandfather died. "Shortly after his burial, my mother went into the hospital with chest pains," Costa said. She had a heart attack and a triple bypass and later learned that she had lung cancer. In this series of health emergencies, from which his mother ultimately recovered, his brother priests gave him the time he needed to be with his family.

"I could not ask for more wonderful people than the guys I live with," Costa said. "They've taken all the anxiety. Everybody just said, 'Go. You belong there.' Nobody's guarding their turf."

Costa's experience is a reminder of what parishioners sometimes forget: Though priests are not married, they do have family obligations.

"It's not a vacuum that we live in," Maffeo said. Duty and family sometimes conflict. He will often, for example, agree to preside at a funeral mass on his day off. But if he has made promises to his own family for that day, he also owes something to them. "If I'm taking my mother to the doctor or my father to the hospital, I can't tell them no either," he said.

At St. Brigid's, each priest gets a day off. Gaeta usually visits his sister's home in Ronkonkoma. D'Souza sits at his computer in the parish center, working to update the books he has written, or cares for his canaries, or creates stained glass. Maffeo visits with his family or arranges an event with one of his classmates. Costa visits family or spends time at a house in Smithtown that he owns with another priest.

On one of his days off in early 1996, Costa spent most of his time at the pastoral center in Douglaston, at a retreat for deaf people who may have religious vocations. While he was still in the seminary, Costa had added to his language skills by learning to sign. Since then, he has worked regularly with the deaf, and he sits on the board of the DePaul Deaf Vocations Project.

Whatever they do on their days off, it is important for priests to have some privacy. That is why Gaeta decided to move the parish offices out of the rectory basement and across the street. Older rectories were built before the growth of lay activism, and they just don't have room for all the offices that a parish now needs. So much was going on that Gaeta ended up doing marriage interviews in his private room. The move has changed that, leaving only the outreach offices downstairs.

"It helped a lot, because then you got the feeling the rectory was your house," Maffeo said. "This has enabled us to better serve the people of the parish. No one's going to go through the dining room while I'm interviewing a couple. This improves our productivity in many ways."

---

In late 1995 and early 1996, the rectory at St. Brigid's faced another stressful time. A brain tumor had struck Tommy Ciotti Thorell, making him desperately ill, stunning everyone into a deep sadness and leaving the parish without a full-time director of music. "So many people have shared with you, as they have with me, how devastated they all are, and hurt," Gaeta told the choir, during a mass to pray for Thorell's recovery.

The other issue was not nearly as tragic, but it was a source of concern: Maffeo's impending transfer in June 1996, mandated by diocesan assignment policy. Reassignments are like that. "We grow into a genuine love of one another," Gaeta said, "and when the transfer comes, it's a real family pain."

The diocese wants to give its priests two or three different assignments before they become pastors. So all new priests must move to a different assignment five years after ordination. "There is almost never an exception," said Caldwell, the priest personnel director. For second and subsequent assignments, the term is now six years, with the possibility of extension for an additional year or two. Pastors, who used to serve for life, now get two six-year terms.

The first transfer is often the most difficult. "Usually, your first assignment is a very happy assignment," said Costa, who was trying to help Maffeo cope by sharing some ideas about what to expect. "Your first parish is special. It's like your first girlfriend or your first car. It's where you learned how to be a priest."

In the old system, priests had no control over transfers. Now, the diocese puts out a list of parishes that will have vacancies and associates who are being transferred, and asks associates to call pastors and set up interviews. Then the priests list their top three choices of parishes, and pastors list their top three choices of priests. That process usually starts in March and culminates in transfers in late June.

"I'm not looking forward to a whole series of interviews," Maffeo said. "I'm not a good interview. I tend to be more serious and more quiet when I go for an interview." In that setting, his dry wit doesn't show up. He recalled one interview, before his ordination, when he was looking for a teaching job. Afterward, the interviewer told him: "You don't seem like the kind of guy who likes to have fun."

Gaeta was not looking forward to it either. In replacing Burns and White, he spent about twenty hours interviewing. "I have to honestly say that I don't like it," Gaeta said. "I don't like to say to six people that I'm not interested. That's not an easy thing to say."

The other problem is that every time a parish loses a priest these days, with priests in declining supply, the pastor has to worry whether the diocese will replace him. In this case, there was another complication: Father Augustine Savarimuthu, a Jesuit whose permanent assignment is teaching at a seminary in India.

Savarimuthu lived in Costa's rectory in Central Islip from 1990 to 1992, while studying for his master's in communications at New York Institute of Technology and working as a hospital chaplain. Then he returned to India. In the summer of 1995, he came back to this country to enroll in a doctoral program at Rutgers. He needed a place for the summer, and Costa needed someone to replace him while he took a one-semester study sabbatical in Chicago. Savarimuthu moved into St. Brigid's.

"As if I had been here for a century, people accepted me just like that," he said. "It is my experience in life when you totally place yourself in the hands of God, things do happen. The best people I could meet in America I met." Gaeta felt the same. "He's a wonderful guy," Gaeta said. "I love having him, and he's a great, great blessing for the parish."

But when Costa returned, Savarimuthu had difficulty arranging another place to live while waiting for admission to Rutgers. Gaeta feared that the diocese would consider Savarimuthu as Maffeo's replacement, and Savarimithu would soon leave for New Jersey. So Gaeta called Caldwell, who promised that the diocese would permanently replace Maffeo.

"I can honestly say now I wish it were one more year," Maffeo said. "Now I practically know everybody." Looking out in the pews, he knows the specific problems that people are enduring and makes those problems part of his prayer. In a new parish, he would have to look out in the pews and see strangers for a while. "That's really the sad part of going."

As it has in the past, the rectory at St. Brigid's would find a way to adjust to the changing faces and continue as before. But the parish would miss Maffeo's wit, his down-to-earth personality and his kindness. Maffeo knew he would miss the parish, and, for all their wisecracks, he would miss Gaeta.

"The old saying, 'You become like your first pastor,' I think is true," Maffeo said. "When I'm no longer here, he's going to be one of my lifelong friends."

*Chapter Ten*

# THE PARISH
# REACHES OUT

The steady flow of human need begins when the door opens in the rectory basement at ten o'clock each weekday morning, and the earnest parish outreach volunteers start sorting gently through the clients' lives and figuring out how to help.

On a sub-freezing Tuesday, the volunteers sat in the outreach office's small interview rooms and listened to the wide variety of ways in which life's nasty surprises have produced need where once there was none.

One client, a tall, elderly man who made his living driving a truck, now has cancer and can no longer work. After he takes out the cost of rent and medicine from his income, which comes entirely from Social Security and food stamps, he has about $60 for the whole month, to cover food, transportation, and miscellaneous expenses.

In addition to his cancer, this client has a more bureaucratic malady: Born in the rural South, he lacks a birth certificate. "This man is an honest man in hard luck," said Isabel Lister, a regular Tuesday volunteer. Since the client has no birth certificate, social services workers in Manhattan turned him away. Lister feared that local social services officials would do the same. She gave the man food and then sat down to try to figure out a way around the birth certificate impasse.

One diminutive woman struggled to lead three children and carry three bags of St. Brigid's food to her well-worn Volvo station wagon, parked behind the rectory. Hers is clearly a middle-class life that only recently descended into need. "As soon as her husband has a good-paying job, she won't come here anymore," said Lillian Morris, another volunteer.

Later in the day, Morris met with another client, a woman who would be homeless except for the hospitality of friends, but who looked nothing like the stereotypical image of the homeless. "She looks so good to be so homeless," Morris said. The woman left with a supply of St. Brigid's food.

That is about as close as Morris can get to skepticism. She knows that some clients may not be totally truthful, but she is a trusting person. So she finds it hard to detect deceit in those who come looking for help.

"I can't tell if they're telling the truth or not," Morris said. "So I think they're all telling the truth." When she is in doubt, Morris resolves it by applying a principle starkly simpler than the complex regulations of the secular bureaucracy: "For the few that take advantage, what would Jesus do?"

The same attitude pervades the whole program, from the volunteers to Al Peck, who in early 1996 became chairman of the outreach advisory board.

"We're not using taxpayers' money," Peck said. "So I don't think we have to say with any assurance that anybody who walks through our door has met some admissions criteria. If they say they're in need, they're in need."

In the initial interview with new clients, the volunteers do not even ask about the person's religion. The program provides help to people of all religions and no religion, the churched and the unchurched. The volunteers do seek proof that a new client lives in the Westbury area and refer those who live outside the area to an outreach program closer to home. But wherever the client lives, St. Brigid's also provides immediate help: food and, if it is needed, the right to purchase used clothing in the parish's Nearly New Shop.

"Nobody walks out of that door with empty hands," said Katie Rodriguez, the program's secretary. Rodriguez retired in 1992, after working for twenty years for the Department of Social Services in Manhattan and Queens. She moved to Westbury in 1993 and heard that St. Brigid's needed bilingual help in the outreach program. She began as a volunteer and now is a paid employee, second-in-command to Sister Judy Mannix, the director of parish outreach.

Wise in the ways of social work, Rodriguez sees a strong contrast between St. Brigid's and the tough, often harsh bureaucracy of the government. "We don't treat people like that here," she said. "We act like Christian people. This is a church. So we have to reflect what we are."

What they are is reflected by what they do. In a parish that stretch-es from the wealthy enclaves of Old Westbury to the poor neighbor-hoods of New Cassel, the outreach program collects food, clothing, and cash from those who have and distributes them to those who don't have enough. "We're in the Jesus business, and we take care of people," Lister said. "We feed them."

They have no trouble collecting food. To begin with, the people of St. Brigid's have demonstrated a reliable generosity. And, in recent times, a member of the outreach advisory board, Dan Fisher, who developed a crisp and efficient style in his career as Hempstead town clerk, has turned that efficiency to the creation of a highly organized food collection system.

Outreach does not lack willing hands, with more than sixty vol-unteers. Most of them are women, and some have felt tragedies of their own. "In this life, to understand other people in need, you've got to suffer yourself," said Rose Cangialosi, who grew up in the inflation and hunger of wartime Italy, lost her husband to a cerebral hemor-rhage when he was forty-six, and raised two sons, with help from her mother. At the start of the busy Tuesday, she was packing donated rolls into small bags, working with Florence Parisi, who lost her hus-band twenty years ago. Lister, Morris, and Rodriguez also have endured the pain of losing a husband.

Nor does the program have trouble finding money. On top of the weekly proceeds from the poor boxes in the church, outreach can rely on periodic cash infusions from the fund-raising ventures of the pastor. The sale of St. Brigid's coffee cups raised about $10,000, for example, and Gaeta's booklet of Advent reflections drew another $20,000. In 1996, the parish also offered his booklet of daily Lenten reflections.

What St. Brigid's does need is to grow beyond meeting direct needs and evolve into a more effective advocate for the poor.

"I think that we are where most good Catholic parishes are," Gaeta said. "I think that we're doing a really wonderful job in the Mother Teresa model of direct aid to people who are in need." But Gaeta and Mannix would like the parish to move toward a model of advocacy patterned after such courageous champions of the poor as the late Archbishop Oscar Romero of El Salvador and Dom Helder Camara, a Brazilian bishop. In a statement often quoted by peace and justice workers, Camara said: "When I give food to the poor, they call me a saint. When I ask why the poor have no food, they call me a communist."

Sister Judy Mannix has had significant experience with both models of serving the poor. As a laywoman, she taught math with the Peace Corps in Malaysia. Then, in 1982, she joined the Sisters of the Good Shepherd, an order that specializes in social work with women and children. She worked in the order's residences for teenagers in Manhattan, did legal assistance for Central Americans in Brooklyn, and later set up a literacy program in El Salvador. So she has seen both direct service and advocacy.

"I don't think you can separate one from the other," Mannix said. "If somebody needs food, you need to provide food. Then you can address the reasons why they're hungry."

The food and clothing are the most visible and quantifiable services that outreach provides. It does help people deal with bureaucracies, with such services as translating government documents into Spanish, setting up appointments with immigration counselors, and making mental-health referrals. But outreach leaders want to expand that advocacy work.

St. Brigid's is not the only parish in the Diocese of Rockville Centre that has not yet advanced to a higher plane of advocacy. Outreach is just one way that parishes can respond to the sweeping commands of Catholic social teaching, but it is the most widespread.

"That is the clearest and most easily understood part of the work," said Tom Ulrich, who served as director of parish social ministry for Catholic Charities until early 1997. "It tends to generate the quickest response among parishioners."

Of 134 parishes in the diocese, all but fourteen had outreach programs in early 1996. Fewer parishes are using other social justice tools, such as the Campaign for Human Development, a national agency that helps low-income communities help themselves (sixty-seven parishes), and peace and justice committees, which promote nonviolence and concern for the poor (thirty-five parishes, including St. Brigid's). "The social action end of parish social ministry is still in the developmental stages," Ulrich said.

At St. Brigid's, the parish leadership has an urgent sense that outreach could be doing so much more. But expanding into new roles is difficult in the face of what Gaeta called "the day-to-day tremendous demands." Those demands are not likely to get any less, as governments continue to shed the burden of caring for the poor, leaving more and more responsibility to voluntary agencies.

"I've seen government use charities, use churches, in a most inappropriate way," said John Castellano, who preceded Peck as chairman of the outreach advisory board. "Folks who are eligible are illegally or wrongfully denied benefits, cut off [from] benefits, or just made to wait." So they have to rely on places like St. Brigid's. "To be asked to supplant the responsibility of government is a misuse of our church resources," Castellano said. "And that's happening."

The outreach program does give emergency cash, but usually only after government sources have failed the client. "We always use public money before we do private money," Lister said. That runs counter to the efforts of government to rely more on private charity. "This is what Mr. Newt Gingrich would like us to do: Pick up the bill for everything. No way."

Over the years, increasing demands have forced the parish to expand its response. One pivotal event was Schaefer's arrival as pastor in early 1975. "We didn't have any food pantry," Schaefer said. "There was a group called St. Brigid's Human Services, which did a wonderful job, and they worked very, very hard." But the group was small and had no paid staff. Almost immediately, Schaefer began expanding parish staff in several areas, including outreach.

In June 1976, Schaefer hired Sister Dorothy Lynch, who had just received a master's degree in social work from Adelphi. In three years at St. Brigid's, she focused heavily on advocacy. "We try to make a difference in the lives of people and not just pass them through, giving them food, because the food is just for today, and they live longer than today," said Lynch, who now runs outreach at Our Holy Redeemer parish in Freeport.

By 1983, when Lister sold the business that she had run with her husband and started volunteering in the outreach program, its office was still in one small part of the rectory basement. At that time, she said, one volunteer "core worker" was enough to handle the flow of clients each day. Now, three or four are necessary. And other parish offices have moved to the parish center across the street, leaving outreach in sole possession of the rectory basement.

In the late 1980s, two women who had met on a parish retreat, Rosemary Mucci and Anne Josey, added a new dimension. Mucci saw disorganized piles of donated clothing in the church basement and decided to hang them up, to make it easier for people to go through them. Her father, Anthony, suggested that they call the place the Nearly New Shop, and then he constructed its sign.

At first, the parish gave away the clothing. Then, to defray some of the costs and to give clients a sense of dignity, they began to sell it at nominal prices. "When they come in for the first time of the month, they can buy a $1 bag or a $2 bag, and then they can take anything they want that's on the racks," said Mary Woods, who took over the shop from Mucci and Josey. For second and subsequent visits during a month, clients have to pay for each item.

In the past few years, Woods and the three women who work with her on Tuesdays—Helen Gathmann, Norma Henderson, and Jane Hulle—have clothed thousands of recipients. Until recently, the shop was open only on Tuesdays. That helped make Tuesday the busiest day for the outreach offices in the rectory basement, where clients must go to get a letter of authorization to buy clothes. Though the shop is now open four days, Tuesday is still the busiest day for outreach volunteers. On one Tuesday early in 1996, outreach served 48 clients in the tiny office.

As the outreach effort grew, Gaeta saw a need for a group that could envision its future. In 1994, he created the outreach advisory board and offered the chairmanship to Castellano, who lives in Garden City and practices public-service law in Manhattan, serving the mentally ill.

"My main reason for the advisory board was to get a group together who really had a sense of the community and a sense of the parish," Gaeta said. "We really could make a tremendous gift and be a tremendous help to the community."

It was into this expanding ministry that Mannix stepped in 1995. Gaeta had hired her to work with the Hispanic community, and she also had been working with the peace and justice committee. Then the outreach coordinator, Laura Rivera, left to take another job, and Gaeta asked Mannix to take over. She had never before run an outreach program.

"I don't even know what I don't know," Mannix told the advisory board in March 1995, a week after she had taken over from Rivera. In the year that followed, she worked hard to learn what resources are available to the clients and how to help them navigate through labyrinthine bureaucracies. She also had to find a replacement for Castellano, who asked to be relieved of his chairmanship because of other demands on his time. So she asked Peck, a board member, to succeed him.

Since the volunteers usually work only one day a week and the clients' needs are constant, Mannix has to provide the continuity. She spends a lot of time out of the office, helping clients cope with government agencies and acting as a translator for the Hispanic clients. One cold day, she showed up at the home of a Spanish-speaking client to help her deal with a county investigator who wanted to check her case. The investigator wasn't there. Using the client's phone to call the government agency, Mannix had to make another appointment for a few days later. They resolved the questions then.

"No place should be dependent on the director," Mannix said. "I should be able to leave at any moment and outreach continue to move along quite smoothly." So she has asked volunteers to make themselves experts on different services available to clients.

Since Mannix took the job, the ambitions of outreach have continued to expand. One key change has been in the food collection system. The parishioners have always been generous in bringing food to the church, for distribution to outreach clients, but that alone is no longer enough—not even supplemented by government-supplied food.

Then, in 1995, the parish found a series of better solutions. The architect was Dan Fisher, the Hempstead town clerk. He had grown up Catholic, attended St. Brigid's school, and watched as his father and mother, Daniel and Lorraine, volunteered in the parish for years. But as an adult, he had drifted away from the church.

"About four years ago, I really felt strongly that I wanted to get back involved in my religion," Fisher said. His nature is to jump in and do something, but he feared that volunteer work for the parish might raise suspicions that he was doing it for political reasons.

"I had to be very careful," Fisher said. He spoke with Deacon Bob Broyles, who works in his office. Broyles spoke with Gaeta, who asked Fisher to serve on the new outreach advisory board. "I see my role predominantly as the supplier of food," Fisher said.

His first effort was a food drive in April 1995, patterned after Boy Scout drives. It involved about a hundred volunteers. One Saturday, they went to homes in the parish to deliver five thousand plastic bags with information about the drive printed on them. (Fisher persuaded American Ref-Fuel Company, which runs an incinerator in Westbury, to donate the bags and the printing.) The following Saturday, using twenty-six vans and drivers on loan from the Central Nassau Athletic Association, they picked up one thousand bags filled with food.

The parish ran a similar drive in November 1995. In rainy weather, they picked up fewer bags of food, but the bags actually had more food in them. In addition, Fisher and other volunteers have stood outside a Foodtown supermarket in East Meadow, handed out leaflets about the needs of outreach, and reaped 100 to 120 bags of food each time. "People are very good," Fisher said.

If he needed any proof of the program's value, Fisher got it one day when he dropped by the rectory to see how the food was holding up. Outside, in the grassy area between the rectory and the church, he saw a woman and several children who had just received food from outreach. "Anything that the kids could eat right away, they were just [eating] hand over fist," Fisher recalled. "There is some real need here."

Despite his efforts, that persistent need at one point diminished the food on the shelves in the rectory basement faster than expected. "All of a sudden, the food disappears; the shelves are empty," Rose Cangialosi said. "It's scary."

Eventually, Fisher's goal is to put in place a system that supplies a steady flow of food all year. "Then, when the demand goes up, we have the ability of simply turning the dial, so to speak," he said.

In early 1996, outreach expanded into a new area: employment counseling. It covers everything from finding job openings to preparing resumés. The volunteers attended seminars by Catholic Charities and by other parishes that provide the service. "We basically got a lot of ideas from different places," said Esther Weintraub of Woodbury, an employment volunteer. "We're just a brand-new baby, and we're playing it by ear."

For the future, outreach has no shortage of visions. Mannix would like to develop a women's sewing cooperative that would produce high quality crafts and give women a dependable source of income close to home. And, as they looked forward in 1996, Gaeta, Mannix, and Peck were unanimous in wanting to find the right office space to establish a presence in New Cassel, where many of the outreach clients live. Peck wants to generate revenue for that initiative by setting up a thrift shop on a shopping street in Westbury.

"We need a whole marketing scheme," Peck said at an outreach board meeting, holding up as an example a marketing plan used for Salvation Army thrift shops. "We can change it to meet our needs, but it's a start."

That is typical of Peck's crisp, no-nonsense, let's-just-do-it approach, which serves him well in his role as director of homeless services for the Salvation Army in the fourteen lower counties of New York State. In his first meeting as chairman of the advisory board, he characteristically urged action.

"I think the whole theory of this board will be summed up in one word, and that's momentum," Peck said, pointing to Fisher's food drive as a prime example. "You take an idea, and you actualize it, and you make it work." Then he outlined a series of working committees to push for action. "The outreach program right now does an enormous amount and is complex," he said. "What we're looking at is to make it even more complex."

One major test of that would be finding the right place to set up an office of outreach in New Cassel, where the need is great. Often, clients walk from New Cassel to the outreach office in Westbury because they lack transportation. A New Cassel location would help, but at the start of 1996, it was not clear yet how it would work.

"I don't know what we would do there, other than initially just be there," Mannix said. "We need to be shaped by what people tell us they need, not by what we think they need."

One of the issues for the parish was finding extra volunteers to work in a New Cassel office, despite the fears that some have expressed about the drug problems in the area. "What's so horrible about New Cassel?" Isabel Lister asked. "Some of the present workers would be uncomfortable. They would lose their uncomfortableness after a little while." Anne Josey, an advisory board member who volunteered to serve on a committee examining potential sites there, said: "I've been here thirty-three years. I've never had anybody mug me."

Beyond the question of the site and the volunteers is the issue of finding revenue to pay the rent in New Cassel. There was no question that the leaders of outreach wanted it to happen, just as they wanted to move further toward advocacy, in addition to direct service. They also trusted that, if they worked to meet the needs, the means would be provided.

"If this is where God wants us to be, then the money comes," Mannix said. "That's not my job. It'll come. I don't presume to know how. If there's a need, it gets addressed somehow, and usually in ways that I could not have imagined."

# Chapter Eleven

# TOGETHER IN PRAYER

*I*n the living room of Maura Goodwin's home, a television issued the muted but steady rhythm of cartoon noise, a mostly ignored pacifier for a few of the eight children who played while their mothers prayed.

A few feet away, six young women sat at the crowded dining room table, holding some of the children, and began to recite the rosary. Catherine Cammarata uttered their common prayer: "Help us to understand our vocation of motherhood."

The rosary did not impress Matthew Cammarata, who sat in his mother's lap, pressed a spoon against her mouth, and massaged her face with a toy, bending her head backward at a sharp angle not normally associated with prayer. A few moments later, Mary Kahl, holding red-headed Scott, prayed: "Lord, give us the strength to get through our everyday dealings. Give our husbands also the strength, as they make sacrifices each day for us."

The women's fingers glided over the beads as Kahl led them through the ten Hail Marys of the rosary's second decade. While they prayed, Chris Wetzel had to get up from the table to retrieve her son, Matthew, from the living room. And Vickie Russini's son, Richie, seized his mother's hand and dragged her away from the table, toward the living room.

The eight children, ranging in age from eight months to five years, created only a moderate level of chaos on this warm, sunny morning at the Goodwin home in Westbury. But they didn't hesitate to speak up. As Jean Ottoson led the women into the fourth decade of the rosary, Sean Goodwin sounded off loudly in his high chair, and the hasty hands of the mothers hurried a bowl of Cheerios down the table in his direction.

"Some days are better than others," Russini said later. "Some days, we get a rosary in, and that's about it." On this comparatively calm occasion, they followed the rosary with a time for reading Scripture and sharing reflections about its meaning in their lives.

"Many times, we find something very relevant that Jesus and Mary would like us to talk about that day," Maura Goodwin said. Unlike many groups, they do not focus on the readings for the coming Sunday, but on whatever passage they feel led to read. "It's more like instruction from the Holy Spirit," Goodwin said.

These young women are stay-at-home moms, like most members of young mothers' prayer groups at St. Brigid's, where small prayer communities of all kinds flourish, reflecting the growth of small faith communities throughout the church. In a parish that heavily emphasizes the sanctity of family life, these women embrace full-time mothering. But that vocation has its challenges.

"Mothers tend to feel so isolated," Cammarata said. So the weekly meetings of the mothers' groups provide a connection with others experiencing that isolation, a chance to share Scripture and daily struggles. "This gives a whole new dimension to your life," she said. "These friendships just last, because you not only talk about yourself, you talk about God."

The difficulty of their vocation as mothers makes the sharing in the prayer groups essential to them. "It strengthens my faith to hear God's strength in your life," Russini said seriously, sitting near a toy horse perched playfully on the table. "By sharing these stories, my faith deepens."

As they talked, Chris Wetzel told of a time when she lost patience with her family. "I was a crank," she said. "I had no patience with the kids. No matter what my husband did, it was not the right thing." Soon after that, at Sunday mass, she had received communion and prayed: "Lord, you've got to fix me." Then she experienced a sense of peace and a clear insight that her impatience had been a glimpse of what she would be like without God's help. "That's how I am without God in my life, a raving lunatic."

The family stories they told were gentle, without an edge of complaint about their husbands. "We don't put down the men," Cammarata said. In fact, Lynn Kennedy's husband, Michael, tells her that her evening mothers' prayer group is one gathering of women he knows won't gossip about men. "He's very affected by them and he knows that his own spirituality has been prayed for and has grown as a result of that," Kennedy said.

Cammarata's husband, Rob, experienced the value of the group intensely when a miscarriage left her bedridden for weeks. Members of her own prayer group and other groups did all the cooking that her family needed, and he didn't have to do any. "It really blew my husband away," she said.

The idea for the young mothers' prayer groups came from Gaeta, who had started them in his previous parish, St. Anthony of Padua in Rocky Point, and had seen their value. With Cammarata and Russini as the coordinators, the idea grew from one group in 1991 to five morning groups and one evening group in 1996.

Every six to eight weeks, the leaders of the groups meet. The full membership gathers for a summer picnic and also for a liturgy. "Usually, once a year, Father Frank has a mass and all the mothers' prayer groups come together," Russini said.

The mothers' groups are just one manifestation of a pervasive St. Brigid's phenomenon: prayer breaking out in small gatherings. Though the weekly liturgies are unusually warm and lively, they are big. So the people of St. Brigid's feel a need to gather in smaller groups, where they can look together at life, through the lens of Scripture, and build their own smaller communities within the larger parish.

"As central as the Sunday assembly for Eucharist is, it is very difficult for that to carry the full weight of generating community, because of the size of it," said Brother Robert Moriarty, of the Archdiocese of Hartford, the chairman of the National Forum for Small Christian Communities.

Just as the answer at St. Brigid's has been small groups, similar communities are developing nationwide, under any of several names: small Christian communities, small church communities, base communities, house churches, and others. "It's like little green shoots emerging all over the country," Moriarty said.

One catalyst is society itself. "The culture has destroyed the nature of community," said a strong advocate of small communities, Monsignor John Cervini, pastor of Our Lady of the Miraculous Medal parish in Wyandanch. "It is so individualistic and self-centered that people's lives are so isolated from one another. In the isolation is a yearning for recapturing a sense of community."

The state of the church has also spurred the growth of the groups. "I would say it's primarily related to the church not working the way it is," said Father Arthur Baranowski, president of the National Alliance for Parishes Restructuring into Communities. "Our whole goal is to create a structure in the parish where the ordinary people of the church help each other connect everyday life with faith regularly."

No one can say how many communities have sprung up. But the Lilly Endowment is funding a study led by Father Bernard Lee, a theologian at the Institute for Ministry of Loyola University in New Orleans, and William D'Antonio, a sociologist at The Catholic University of America.

"We've completed the first stage of a national census," D'Antonio said. "We've found some evidence of them in all but two states."

In the Diocese of Rockville Centre, D'Antonio sees strong representation. "They're one of the hot spots on the East Coast," he said. "We have evidence of every possible type of small faith community existing in Rockville Centre."

To Cervini, that is no mystery. "Over the years, the diocese has been very open to bringing in people from throughout the United States who are experts in assisting the development of it," he said. In addition, small Christian communities are one "track" of the diocesan Pastoral Formation Institute, which trains lay people for a variety of ministries.

The national study has identified ten to twelve types of groups, but the national organizations agree broadly on what a true small Christian community should look like.

"There are four commonalities," said Rosemary Bleuher, a past chairman of the National Forum for Small Christian Communities, who supervises small communities for the Diocese of Joliet, Illinois. "The people come together and they pray and reflect on Scripture. The second is they support and care for one another. The third is that they continue their learning. The learning comes from one another, as much as it does from materials. What they're learning principally is how to live out their role as disciples, how to connect faith to life. The last is that they have a mission or outreach."

Baranowski would add a fifth. "That would be having a person or a couple who would serve as pastoral links," he said. These "pastoral facilitators" provide liaison between the groups and the parish staff.

Some local parishes have focused more intensely than St. Brigid's on the formal structure of small communities. Miraculous Medal, for example, has divided into regions and is developing small communities in each of its regions. Good Shepherd in Holbrook has nineteen small communities, with pastoral facilitators for each, and it has included in its parish vision statement Baranowski's goal of helping people to connect faith with everyday life. "Our approach is to try to color the whole way of being church with that principle," said Good Shepherd's pastor, Monsignor Thomas Spadaro, who sits on the board of Baranowski's organization.

Though St. Brigid's does not say it in so many words in a formal document, the parish works hard at connecting faith with life, and the parishioners exhibit a bountiful prayerfulness that seems naturally to result in the growth of small groups. Gaeta encourages that, with a minimum of formality.

"As guidelines, I always tell the groups to be centered on the Scriptures of the Sunday," Gaeta said. "I'll always suggest that they have a review of the week, kind of a sharing of their experiences, a time of intercession, a time of sharing the word as they've read. . . . I don't particularly feel that any of these groups should be doing the same thing, or that they should have the same format. I think the best way for them to form is when people have a common need or a common interest and want to come together. . . . I think the structure has evolved from the need of the group, rather than the other way around."

Only five of the groups at St. Brigid's would probably call themselves small Christian communities, in the strict sense that movement leaders use. But whatever they are called, small groups are thriving in the parish.

"I really feel if people are coming together in a group to pray, to reflect where Jesus is in their life, I don't care what you call it," said Terry Patterson, who is co-coordinator, with Mary Kennedy, of basic Christian communities for the parish. The huge size of the parish— about 23,000 Catholics—is an inducement for the growth of small communities. "I think that, by breaking it down, sharing becomes more personal," Patterson said, "and God speaks to people in different ways."

The groups also came to life in different ways. Among the earliest were those that flowed from in-home retreats, a spiritual program that lasts for several weeks but leads to permanent groups. "Probably every single in-home retreat has in one way or another continued," Gaeta said.

One of those who built up the in-home retreats in the mid-1970s, Sister Christine Mulready, now lives in Brooklyn and works at a parish in Queens, but she is still part of a group at St. Brigid's that is more than twenty years old. "This particular group is an offshoot of maybe three or four different home retreat experiences," she said.

The group's members have shared Scripture and life, worked in service to others, and seen each other through widowhood and other hard times. "Every one of us went through a major tragedy," Bea Patti said. "It was like the Lord was getting us ready through this group for what we had to face."

One example occurred fourteen years ago, when Julia Waszkiewicz' husband, Edward, was dying of cancer. During those seven months, members of the group did not let them suffer alone. She particularly remembered Helen Sheehan, who recently had been widowed and still had six of her ten children at home. "She would put them to bed and then come over at ten o'clock at night and sit with me," Waszkiewicz said. "She doesn't talk very much, but she's got a kind heart and a loving heart."

That spirit of service actually cost one member of the group her life. Rita Posillico joined after she had made an in-home retreat and her daughter, Margo Messina, steered her toward the women. "As a result of being in the group, she blossomed," Messina said. "She came into her own and got very involved." Among other things, she brought communion to the homebound and worked in the parish outreach program. Then, on a February morning in 1995, she was driving through Westbury to help another member of the group when she was killed in an auto accident. "It was a real story of laying down one's life for a friend," Waszkiewicz said.

All of that sounds like the definition of a small Christian community. But the members don't seem to worry about fitting anyone's labels. "We're not a small church community," Isabel Lister said. "We're just a small group that prays."

At one meeting during Lent of 1996, in a sun-flooded interior porch at the rear of Lister's home, the group began with a prayer for Mulready, who had fallen ill the night before and was not present. Then the seven women took turns describing how their prayer life had been going.

Dolores Dominioni talked about using a daily book of Lenten meditations by Gaeta. Sheehan reported that her prayer life was sometimes as simple as reminding herself once or twice daily of God's existence. "It's no great shakes, but it's me," she said. And Edna Clavin said she had felt very low a week earlier and prayed simply: "Lord, just help me to get out of this." Then a friend had invited her to a movie and dinner, and she was out of it.

Clavin belongs not just to this group but to three others. One is a larger Tuesday evening charismatic prayer group, which has produced many of the parish's leaders. She also belongs to a Saturday evening group, the Sacred Heart Community—most of whose members are Filipino—and a weekly Wednesday group of women that has been going for more than two decades. "It just seems like you see Jesus more in people after you have spent time in prayer," she said.

Lister, who joined the group in 1983 after her husband's death and the sale of their family business, offered the group a litany of her prayer life. "I love Frank's book," she said. "Monday, of course, is Bible study, and my life is enriched through that. Very often, God talks to me through study. Tuesday is parish outreach."

One of the earmarks of true small Christian community is a sense of mission, of obligation to serve the community. Lister and another member, Jeannine Henderson, have both worked in the parish outreach program, for example, and other members of the group serve in other ways.

From discussing prayer life, the group moved on to talk about films, books, and articles with moral content. They ranged over the films *Il Postino* and *Dead Man Walking* and articles on such subjects as corporate downsizing. "I think that it's immoral what some of the companies are doing to people," Henderson said.

Then they went to the petitions. As each woman named people who needed prayers, the others wrote them down in a list to be kept as a reminder. Waszkiewicz keeps her list in a prayer jar. "Every morning when I get up, I go over to it and I just pray for all the people who are in that jar," she said. Dominioni keeps the names in mind during her rosary. "There are so many people to pray for," she said. "Each bead, I pray for a different person."

After the petitions, the women closed the day with a simple lunch and a time for further bonding of a group that has already shared so much. "We ourselves refer to one another as our sisters," Sheehan said.

—⚏—

A few years after this group had started, at a time when the small Christian community movement was building steam nationwide, Gaeta's predecessor, Fred Schaefer, took an interest. He sent Sister Jane Halligan for training in small Christian communities by Bernard Lee, who is now running the national study of small communities. Halligan and a small core group of parishioners created several communities at St. Brigid's.

That was about a decade ago, Mary Kennedy recalled—not long after her daughter Peggy, who earlier had beaten cancer, died in an automobile accident at twenty-two. At the time, Kennedy was already active in the parish, working with a committee that provided food and hospitality for parish events. One night, she was in the church, and Halligan summoned her. "Jane said, 'Mary, why don't you come with us? We're having a meeting.'"

So Kennedy soon found herself heavily involved in the development of small Christian communities. When Halligan left the parish for another assignment, Kennedy became one of the coordinators. Over the years, the groups have dwindled from eight or nine to five, but they have remained faithful to the founding ideas.

# LORI
# FOSTER

## Sisters of
## Summer's End

HQN™

**HQN**™

ISBN-13: 978-1-335-00768-1

Sisters of Summer's End

Recycling programs
for this product may
not exist in your area.

This edition published by arrangement with Harlequin Books S.A.

For questions and comments about the quality of this book, please contact us
at CustomerService@Harlequin.com.

® and TM are trademarks of Harlequin Enterprises Limited or its corporate affiliates.
Trademarks indicated with ® are registered in the United States Patent and Trademark
Office, the Canadian Intellectual Property Office and in other countries.

www.HQNBooks.com

**Printed in U.S.A.**

To all my readers,

Thank you for *everything*—for the positive reviews you've posted, for visiting my Facebook page with comments and most especially for purchasing my books.

I'm convinced I have the nicest, smartest and most considerate readers in the world. :-)

I hope my stories never disappoint you!

*Lori Foster*

Dear Reader,

I hope you enjoy the vacation setting, first with *Cooper's Charm* and now in *Sisters of Summer's End*. I certainly enjoyed writing the stories of friendship, family and romance with the ambience of nature in the unique setting of an RV resort.

Many of you have asked me about the basis for the resort. Because I needed certain things for my characters and the plot, the setting is largely fictional, but it is influenced by an RV resort I visited for many years. In fact, I wrote a few books in my own RV, parked near a beautiful creek with mature trees making it feel like I was all alone in the woods, even though an entire campground surrounded me.

It's a lovely, quaint, welcoming place…and if you want to know more, look up naturalspringsresorts.com.

Just like in my books, they have scuba diving, a lake formed from an old stone quarry, an amazing camp store and grill, and so much more.

My characters are 100 percent made-up, not even remotely drawn from any living person at the resort, but there are strong similarities to the layout. Have fun finding them.

My "happy place" is anywhere in nature, most especially near water. I haven't been back to the resort since we bought our lake property. Now when I want my fix of sunshine and fresh air, I head to our lake house and take a boat ride, swim or occasionally water-ski.

My husband and I also love Hocking Hills, Cumberland Falls and the Great Smoky Mountains. Of course, anywhere we go, I take a book!

Here's wishing you lots of happy reading—in your own happy place.

*Lori Foster*

www.LoriFoster.com

# CHAPTER ONE

After dropping her son off at school, Joy Lee returned to Cooper's Charm, the RV resort where she worked and lived. It was backtracking since she had an appointment near the school later this morning, but it wouldn't do to show up a half hour early.

Actually, nothing in the small town of Woodbine, Ohio, was too far away. In fifteen minutes she could drive to the school, the park, the grocery...or visit the new owner of the drive-in, who she'd be meeting today.

Hopefully Mr. Nakirk would continue to work with her. As the recreation director of the park, she and the past owner had put together various events with a lot of success. Halloween was coming up and she didn't want to have to completely restructure a tried-and-true camper favorite.

Coming through the grand entry of the resort, Joy couldn't help but admire the beauty of it. She'd been seeing the same gorgeous scenery for six years now, yet it never failed to soothe her.

She'd found peace here, a kind of peace she hadn't known existed. Now she couldn't imagine living anywhere else.

Large trees, currently wearing their fall colors, lined the property and served to add privacy to the costlier campsites.

A wooden walk bridge divided a pond from the large lake. Wooden cabins were scattered about, with plenty of lots for RVs and level, grassy areas for campers who preferred a tent. Even the playgrounds were well maintained, colorful and attractive.

Deciding a cup of coffee wouldn't hurt, Joy headed for Summer's End, the camp store. Maris Kennedy, a woman close to her own age, always had coffee ready. She also worked nonstop and treated everyone like a friend.

When Joy came into the camp store, Maris was busy wiping down the tops of the dining booths. She glanced up and said, "Hey."

In so many ways, Joy admired Maris. For one thing, the woman never seemed to tire. She opened early, kept it open late and rarely slowed down throughout the day. During the busiest season, Maris employed part-time help, but she handled the bulk of the responsibility herself.

Maris apparently preferred it that way.

Another admirable thing? Maris *always* managed to look fantastic with her dark blond hair in a high ponytail and a shirt at least a size too large over her jeans.

Unfair, but Maris was so incredibly nice, and she took such great care of all the employees, Joy forgave her the perfection. "Good morning."

"Is it?" Maris turned her gaze to the window. "Ah, sunshine. Better than rain and clouds, right? Coffee?"

Joy hated to pull her away from her task. "Yes, but I could—"

"I'll get it." Toting her little carrier of cleaning supplies, Maris headed to the kitchen. Joy heard her wash her hands, and then a moment later she reappeared with two cups. "I just made a fresh pot."

Of course she had. Smiling, Joy shook her head.

The café in Summer's End offered a menu of sandwiches, soups and daily specials. Positioned on the walls behind the seating area, packed shelves held basic grocery necessities and emergency items, as well as things like pool floats, sunscreen and fishing tackle. Campers didn't have to leave the park once they arrived, and if they didn't want to make use of the grills, Maris always had something to eat.

Joy took a sip of the coffee, fixed just the way she liked it, and sighed.

Instead of moving on to another chore, Maris stood there with her own coffee. "I'm wondering something."

"Oh?" She and Maris were friendly; Maris was too nice for anyone *not* to be friendly with her. But Joy wouldn't say they were close.

Sadly, it had become Joy's habit to keep some measure of distance from everyone.

"How the hell do you always look so put together?"

Surprised by the question, Joy looked down at her cotton skirt and button-up sweater. "It's a casual skirt." At least five years old, like the majority of her wardrobe. She'd updated only a few pieces since moving to the park.

"Yeah, but everything you wear looks like it came from a fashion magazine. Always, no matter what, you're styled head to toe. There are days I can barely get my hair into a ponytail, and yet you never have a wrinkle."

Feeling suddenly self-conscious, as well as amused by the irony, Joy laughed.

"Why's that funny?" Maris asked, looking genuinely curious.

It wasn't like Maris to linger, so Joy hastily explained, "I was literally just thinking how great you always look. Especially your ponytail! No matter what's going on, you...glow."

"Me?" Maris snorted. *"Glow?"*

Even more embarrassed and feeling completely out of her el-

ement, Joy continued. "You don't need makeup or anything. You always look fresh, even when you've been working all day. There's an energy about you." A wholesomeness that few other women could pull off. It was probably attitude as much as appearance that was responsible for that vibe. Maris personified friendliness, but she owned the space around her in a way Joy could never manage. "Believe me, the natural look works for you."

When Maris laughed, it made her even prettier, but before Joy could say so, she asked, "So what are you up to today?"

Hmm. Had Maris just deflected? Maybe she was as uncomfortable with compliments as Joy. "Meeting the new owner of the drive-in."

"That's right. I heard it changed hands."

"Very recently," Joy confirmed.

"Heard the new guy was a gorgeous hunk, too."

"You...what?" Joy sputtered. *A gorgeous hunk?* Definitely not what she'd hoped for, although it absolutely wouldn't matter. A man's appeal meant nothing to her—and good thing, since the guys at the park were all very handsome in varying ways. "Who told you that?"

"I'm like a bartender, you know?" Maris bobbed her eyebrows. "Everyone talks to me. You should try it sometime."

Generally the small town shared everything about everything. If a squirrel dropped a nut, someone announced it and the gossip spread like wildfire—though Joy was usually the last to hear it since she didn't cultivate those close relationships. Maybe she *should* chat with Maris more, if for no other reason than to keep up on current affairs in Woodbine. "I don't know about the hunk part since I haven't met him yet, but it's not an issue. My only interest is—"

"In recreation for the park, I know." Maris rolled her eyes

in a playful way. "But there are all kinds of recreation, and I'm thinking you should try the kind that involves a man."

A nervous laugh trickled out. Since when was Maris Kennedy interested in her lack of a love life? Joy's next thought was whether or not the lack was that obvious.

Did she seem...lonely? Or, oh God, *needy*?

No, Maris more than anyone else at the park understood that a woman didn't need a man to complete her. Joy's life was already full, thank you very much.

To keep things friendly, Joy said with a smile, "Jack gets all my free time. I don't even know when I'd fit in a date." Just to clarify, she added, "Not that anyone is asking."

"Hello," Maris said. "You realize you have a big old blinking *not available* sign on you, right? Guys would—" she pinched the air "—if you'd give them just a teeny tiny bit of encouragement."

"But I don't want to encourage anyone. I mean, not for that reason."

"Why not? Jack's in school now, so don't tell me you can't eke out an hour or two."

"Hmm. Well, I guess technically I could..." Joy sat at the counter and finished with, "But I won't."

"Spoilsport." Maris joined her, taking the stool to her left.

Well, that was new. Sure, Maris conversed with Joy, but usually while she worked. She didn't sit down and join her.

She didn't focus on her.

Unsure what was going on, Joy said, "I don't mean to hold you up..."

"Already got through my routine, so I was ready for a break."

Curious, she asked, "What type of routine?"

"Coffee first—that's as much for me as it is for anyone who might drop in. Then I turn on the oven so I can make cookies from the dough I prepared the night before."

"Wow."

"I dust again, make sure all the chrome shines. Face up the shelves so they look orderly." Maris looked around her store with obvious pride. "There's always food stuff to prep, too. Soup to get in the pot, tea to make. Oh, and I have to put money back in the cash register. I like to take inventory each evening before I head home, so I know what I need to replace the next day. That means sometimes I have to restock the hot dogs or condiments."

Joy shook her head. "I have no idea how you do it all."

"Listen to who's talking, Super Mom."

"I'm not—"

"Yup, you are. I see plenty of moms here at the park, but you make it look effortless."

"Oh. Well, thank you." What else did someone say in this situation? Joy had no idea. Before moving to Woodbine, she hadn't had any friends like Maris. Her social group had been superficial, not down-to-earth. They talked about the latest high-end fashions and the next important social function. None of her so-called friends would have ever owned a wonderful little camp store like Summer's End—and none of them would have ever ended up as a single mom. Losing them hadn't been a hardship.

Other things had been hard. So very, very hard.

Like finding herself alone.

Over the years she'd adjusted, but now she shied away from getting too personal with anyone. Life felt safer that way.

"So." As if she'd been privy to her innermost thoughts, Maris gave her a direct smile—one filled with warmth and sincerity. "I'm just saying if you ever want to go out, or even if you just want some time to yourself, let me know. I'd be happy to help."

Touched by the offer, Joy laid a hand to her heart. After all her effort to keep real friendship at bay, Maris still reached out to her. It meant a lot and made Joy rethink some of her choices.

Honestly, since turning thirty, it had played on her mind, anyway. Perhaps she should begin to open up a little.

Jack certainly had. Then again, her son was one of the most personable, engaging, adorable people…and maybe she was just a tiny bit influenced by the incredible love she had for him.

Jack liked Maris a lot, and vice versa.

That didn't explain why Maris was suddenly so keen on Joy dating. "So…what's going on?"

Maris lifted her brows. "What do you mean?"

Ha! That innocent look didn't cut it. "You're up to something. We've known each other five years now and you've never asked me about dating."

"Sure I did. You just didn't answer much, so I let it go."

Ouch. That could be true.

"Gawd, don't look guilty," Maris said. "Here's the thing. You were quiet, I was swamped, so we let it go, right? But know what? I'm thirty-one now. Freaking *thirty-one*."

"Oh my God," Joy said, amazed that their thoughts seemed to be on the same track. "I'm thirty now, so I know exactly what you mean."

"Yesterday," Maris said, "this lady came in with three kids, one of them a newborn. She and her husband were frazzled and happy, and they said it was their first vacation after buying their house. Guess how old that woman was."

Joy said, "Um…thirty-ish?"

"Twenty-nine. Two years *younger* than me."

"Younger than us," Joy corrected.

"Right, but you have a kid. A *great* kid." Maris propped her head on her hand. "My point is, I can't do the whole family and home thing—but you can. Heck, you're already halfway there."

*Family?* Joy almost choked, since her family didn't want anything to do with her. She knew that wasn't what Maris meant, though. "You can't do it…why?"

"It's not my thing." Maris shrugged that off with haste. "You're great at being a mom. Heck, you're great at everything

you do. So the least *I* can do is lend a hand, and maybe give you a push."

After all that, Maris smiled, as if she'd explained everything to her satisfaction and Joy should be jumping on board.

When Joy just blinked at her, Maris said, "Consider this your push."

It was almost laughable, but also very sweet. Joy said with feeling, "Thank you so much. Even though I don't have any hot prospects, I appreciate the offer."

"That's what friends are for, right?"

Joy had no real idea, but she nodded, anyway. "The same from me. If I can do anything for you, please just let me know."

"Great. Know what you can do? After you meet with the new owner, let me know if he's as gorgeous as everyone says he is. I'm dying of curiosity."

"Right, okay. Sure." Wondering if she'd misread this entire conversation, Joy offered, "If you want, I could mention you to him…?"

Maris blinked at her, then laughed. "We're talking about *you*, not me, but thanks." She nodded at the coffee. "Good?"

After another, more cautious sip, Joy sighed. "Mmm. Of course. You make the best coffee."

"True story." Maris suddenly sniffed the air. "Be right back."

*So much for Maris's break.* "Whatever that is smells delicious." Through the last five years, Joy had taught herself to cook by trial and error, but she didn't come close to Maris's skill in the kitchen. From full-blown formal dinners to the soup of the day, Maris worked magic.

Less than a minute later, Maris returned with a plateful of warm chocolate chip cookies. "Fresh from the oven. Want one?"

"I wish I could, but if I don't get going, I'll be late." Joy prided herself on her professionalism. Showing up tardy for an appointment was unthinkable.

"We stay too damn busy, don't we? We should carve out more time to visit." Maris wrapped two in a napkin. "For the road, then."

Joy's mouth already watered. "They won't last five minutes. Thank you." Smiling, she stood and slipped her purse strap over her shoulder. Hesitating, she said, "This was nice. Us talking more, I mean."

"Right?" Moving the cookies under a covered dome, Maris remarked, "We need to do it more often."

Surprised by the idea, Joy nodded. "That would be terrific."

She loved her role of recreation director at the park, and she appreciated all the wonderful people. She thought she did a good job—and yet, she'd never truly fit in. This morning, for a few minutes, Maris had been much more like a friend than an acquaintance. She didn't know if it was seeing the other couple with the three kids, or because Maris was suddenly more aware of her age.

Whatever the reason, Joy liked it. She liked it a lot.

Twenty minutes later, cold and miserable, Joy peeked in the small door window of the concession stand at the drive-in.

How had things changed so quickly?

The meager overhang barely shielded her from the pounding rain of the pop-up storm. Not that it mattered since she was already soaked to the skin.

*If you could see me now, Maris...*

There wasn't anything fashionable about her drowned-rat appearance. Joy couldn't remember a time when she'd been more of a wreck.

Freak rainstorms could do that to people.

Instead of knocking, she peeked inside again. People didn't usually catch her off guard like this, but for once, she felt totally flummoxed.

Royce Nakirk was everything Maris said he'd be—and more.

He stood over six feet tall, his body very...*fit*, and his dark hair reflected the blue of the concession lights.

Didn't matter. Men, attractive men in their prime, held no significance to her.

She was a mother.

A dedicated employee.

A once-burned, never-again divorcée.

My, oh my, the gossips hadn't exaggerated.

Joy wanted elderly Mr. Ostenbery back. She could deal with him. She could charm and bargain and coerce him without noticing his thighs. Or his shoulders.

Or his...butt.

All she'd ever noticed on Ostenbery was the impressive size of his nose and his genuine smile and kindness.

But this new owner was a different animal. Denim companies should pay him to wear their jeans. The way his T-shirt fit his body—snug in the shoulders, loose over a flat midsection—caused her ovaries to twitch. Until this moment, she'd forgotten she had ovaries.

*Mother.*

*Employee.*

*Divorcée.*

The mantra marched through her brain without much effect. She wondered what Maris would say when she told her about this.

*Would* she tell her?

Yes. It might be fun to share her shock. No doubt Maris would have some witty comment to contribute.

With his back to her, the owner squatted to rinse a cloth in a bucket of soapy water.

Biting her lip, Joy let her gaze track over him.

*Stop it*, she silently demanded, and she wasn't sure if she spoke to herself or the new, much too young and attractive owner.

When he turned, she saw his intent concentration as he scrubbed at a corner of the counter.

Joy almost envied the counter. How long had it been since she'd garnered that much concentration from anyone? Five years? Closer to six?

Scowling, he glanced at the clock, a jolting reminder that she was already fifteen minutes late.

Joy shoved wet hair away from her face and straightened her sodden clothes. No chance now for a good first impression. If the day hadn't dawned with sunshine and clear skies, she wouldn't have left her umbrella behind. The weather had held long enough for her to almost arrive at the drive-in—and *then* the black clouds had rolled in, tumbling one over the other as if racing for a finish line. A deluge split the skies, flooding a crossroad so she'd had to drive around, making her late.

The irony, of course, was that she could have walked through the woods and arrived at the drive-in within five minutes. Driving meant going around the long way, but she'd considered walking too informal. Her skirt and cute flats, which Maris had admired earlier, wouldn't have survived the woods.

Now it didn't matter, since the look was ruined, anyway.

Before she made things worse, Joy stepped to the side of the little window and gave a brisk knock.

It opened exactly two heartbeats later, making her think Mr. Nakirk must have reached it in one long stride.

Dark eyes went over her in a nanosecond and his frown deepened. He rubbed his mouth—then his gaze pinned her. "Joy Lee?"

Rain blew against her back but she barely felt it as she tried to summon professional confidence. If looking at him through

a window had been disturbing, it was nothing compared to seeing him face-to-face.

He waited.

"Yes." Fashioning her frozen lips into a smile, she lifted her chin. "I'm sorry I'm late." Good. That sounded formal and sincere. She cleared her throat. "A road was closed and I had to take a detour." Pretty sure her lips were still smiling, but she turned it up a bit, anyway.

He looked at her mouth and nodded. "Come in." Belatedly, he stepped back, making room for her. "Wait on the mat. The floor can be slippery when wet. I'll get you a towel."

"Thank you." So he wouldn't belabor her tardiness? She appreciated his restraint.

After watching him disappear into a room behind the concession stand, Joy glanced around the interior. She couldn't help noticing that the counter was spotless. The glass fronts of the candy cases sparkled, and even the black-and-white tiled floor shone. Admiring the fresh new appearance, she looked up...and found the same old stained ceiling tiles there.

"Next on the list," he said as he walked back in, startling her. He had an orange striped beach towel in one hand, a utility towel in the other. He stepped into her spreading puddle.

This close, he was taller than she'd realized. At five-nine, few men made her feel small but she had to tip her head back to meet Royce's inscrutable gaze. *And...*her thoughts fled once again. "Pardon?"

His mouth twitched. "I haven't heard that expression since my grandmother passed a decade ago."

*Ohhh, he mentioned his grandmother.* How sweet was that?

No, wait. Joy prided herself on her professionalism, on making a good appearance.

She did not lose her poise over a man's butt or his mention of a grandmother.

But his eyes…they were incredibly dark, framed by short, dense, ebony lashes. In a less welcoming face, she'd have labeled his eyes sinister, but the only thing deadly about this man was his bold appeal.

"Pardon," he said, as if explaining. "It's something Nana used to say. Most people aren't that polite anymore."

He called his grandmother Nana—and why would that make him more appealing?

Joy cleared her throat. "I see." Ah, yes, way to bowl him over with scintillating conversation.

He pointed up. "I meant the ceiling. I'll be replacing the tiles when I can, probably sometime over the winter so it's done before the next season." He held the beach towel out to her.

Making sure not to touch him, she accepted it, and noticed that his hands were large, his wrists thick, his forearms sprinkled with dark hair.

*What is* wrong *with you? So the man has hands. Most men do.* It was no reason for her temperature to spike.

She could probably blame her new distraction on Maris. If she hadn't steered the conversation toward hooking up, maybe Joy wouldn't be thinking about it now.

While she patted at her face, trying to look delicate instead of desperate, he dropped the utility towel into the puddle and moved it around with his foot.

Rain continued to drip from her hair, her clothes, even the tip of her nose. Her brain scrambled for conversation, a way to ease the awkward moment.

His nearness made that impossible.

"Well." Joy plucked at her clinging sweater. Maybe if she didn't look at him, it'd be easier for her brain to function. "I hope you've been properly welcomed to Woodbine."

"I've only met a few people."

*Enough to make an impact,* she thought.

"Mostly I've been stuck in here all week, trying to get it spick-and-span before movie night on Friday."

"Mr. Ostenbery was a wonderful person, but not a stickler for organization."

"Or cleanliness," he said with a smile.

For a second, Joy stared, caught in that smile, before regaining her wits. "You've done a great job. Everything shines."

The drive-in ran on Friday and Saturday nights, from March until the end of October, but Mr. Ostenbery had often hosted other events during off-hours. Joy hoped to continue that practice, and maybe even add to it.

Suddenly Royce flagged a hand toward her face. "You're washing away. Did you want to use the restroom? I can put on coffee while you do that."

She looked at the towel where she'd patted her face and saw it smudged with makeup. Oh good Lord. Cold and embarrassment nearly took out her knees. "Yes, if you don't mind."

"In fact—" He ducked back behind the counter, snagged a folded T-shirt from a stack, and offered it to her. "You look... chilled."

Apparently being faced with a sodden woman in ruined makeup didn't faze him. She accepted the navy blue shirt with the drive-in's logo on the front. "You want me to change?"

"I want you to be comfortable. Doesn't seem possible while you're shivering." He pushed aside the half door that allowed her behind the concession stand. "This way."

As they walked, Joy gave herself a pep talk. Never mind that she hadn't had sex for nearly six years. Forget that he was a specimen with a capital S, for *Sexy*. Disregard that she was sometimes lonely.

She would cease daydreaming about his jeans, and that fine backside in his jeans, and she wouldn't notice anything else about his body. Or his face. Or even that deep voice.

She would concentrate only on the purpose of this meeting.

"Right here," he said, pushing open yet another door to show her the most sanitary business restroom she had ever seen. The white porcelain toilet and sink shone, as did the floor and wall tiles. "There's a dryer around the corner if you need it. For your skirt, I mean."

That surprised her enough that she almost slipped on her own trail of water. "You have a dryer here?"

"I brought in a small stack unit for convenience. The mop head and cleaning towels get laundered regularly."

The positives were adding up. Joy mentally tallied them: butt. Nana. Neat freak.

Oh, and those sinfully dark eyes.

*Poise*, she reminded herself. *Professionalism*. "I'll only be a minute."

Accepting that, he turned away. "I'll go get the coffee started."

*And...* She watched him walk away, already forgetting her lecture.

When he glanced back to say, "Take your time," she knew that he knew she'd been staring.

Mortified, Joy quickly closed the door, muttering to herself about decorum. One glance in the mirror and her heart almost gave out.

Her pathetic attempts at smiling couldn't have had any impact at all, not when mascara created comical black stripes down her cheeks. Add her long, light brown hair plastered to her skull, throat and chest, and she was hideous.

The worst, though, was her sweater.

Opaque, yes, but through the soft material her chilled nipples seemed to beg for attention. *Look at me, look at me.*

She couldn't really blame them, not with a man like that standing around as if such a thing happened every day. She'd

certainly never seen anyone like him before. Even in a Photoshopped magazine ad, the men weren't so...perfectly *manly*.

It was indecent.

Her nipples were indecent.

Her standing in front of a mirror carrying on a private, one-sided discussion about her nipples was indecent.

In an attempt to recover, her lungs grabbed a deep breath. *Being a good mother is your number one focus. Period. You don't care about attracting men.*

No, she didn't. So what did it matter if she looked like a murdered body washed up on the shore? It didn't.

As of right now, her hormones were going back in hibernation.

And yet, she frantically scrubbed her face and fretted over her hair.

Royce poured himself a cup of coffee and tried to quit glancing at the clock. *What was she doing in there?*

Changing her shirt and removing the tracks from her face shouldn't have taken twenty minutes. He rubbed the back of his neck and tried not to think about her tall, trim body in wet clothes, but yeah, he may as well tell himself to stop breathing. Pretty sure that image would stick with him for a while.

Funny thing, how a woman nearly drowned in rain and ruined makeup could still look so classy. She had a calm deportment that defied circumstances.

Gifting her with the shirt had been an act of self-preservation, to make it easier for him to refocus on the important stuff.

Not that breasts weren't important. They just weren't important right now.

For several reasons, this meeting had to be his priority. One, he'd just taken over the run-down drive-in and, for some ridiculous reason, he wanted to hear her opinion on his improve-

ments. Two, he needed to first be accepted to the small, intimate town. Working with her would be a start. Three...damn, he'd forgotten three the second he'd opened that door.

He couldn't tell the true color of her hair, not with the wet hanks clinging to her face, but there was no mistaking the green of her eyes. Not just green, but a light green with shades of amber, all ringed in blue.

Pretty eyes. Startled eyes. Joy Lee had stared at him as if he'd somehow surprised her.

She'd sure as hell surprised him.

From everything Ostenbery had told him, he'd expected a polite but formal businesswoman. Maybe she was...usually.

But not today.

Not with the way she'd looked at him.

Damned if he hadn't looked back.

A foolish move since he had zip for free time. Only a month remained of the season for the drive-in, but he planned to make the most of it, to send it off with a bang so that when he re-opened in the spring, the locals would remember. Plus he had some ideas for off-season activities, if he could get Joy Lee on board.

First, she'd have to emerge from the bathroom.

He drank more coffee, stewing over the impressions Osten-bery had given. Though the retiree hadn't mentioned Joy's age, his descriptions of her had led Royce to expect someone older. Someone not so attractive.

Someone austere and aloof.

Instead, Joy Lee had openly gazed at him while her face and throat flushed pink.

*Focus*, he told himself. After far too long taking care of oth-ers, this was his turn and he wouldn't get derailed by wet clothes clinging to a sweet body, or bold, mesmerizing eyes.

With that in mind, Royce strode to the door and called back, "You okay in there?"

Her head poked out, not from the bathroom but from his utility room. "Yes, sorry. You said I could use the dryer, so…" She smoothed back a long hank of still-damp hair.

Royce realized he was doing it again, allowing his brain to go down paths it shouldn't. At least this time he had good reason for staring.

She stood there in the logo T-shirt, knotted at the side so it'd fit her waist, with the beach towel tied like a toga skirt around her. The colors clashed, but that was the least of the fashion disasters.

Yet somehow, on her, the hodgepodge outfit looked like a trendy statement.

When she laced her fingers together and smiled, he felt it like a kick. Luckily, a kick was just what he needed to get back on track.

Royce cleared his throat. "I pulled some chairs up to the counter for us." The building had a small break room, but it felt too isolated for this meeting.

He gestured for her to precede him, then wished he hadn't as she moved past, slim legs parting the overlap of the towel, giving him a glimpse of calf and thigh.

*Calf and thigh?* he repeated to his libido. This wasn't the 1700s. A man could see legs—gorgeous legs, not-so-gorgeous legs, young legs and old legs, plus a whole lot more—any damn time he wanted. Just because they were *her* legs didn't make them special.

Sure, the past year had been…rough. No sex, no dating. Nothing but all-consuming responsibility, focused around sickness, culminating in the inevitable end of life.

But legs?

Royce followed her, doing his utmost to keep his gaze on the back of her head and not anywhere else.

Being here in Woodbine, rebuilding the drive-in to what it could be, was *his* turn and he wouldn't let pretty green eyes and shapely legs muddle his plans.

Keeping that in mind, Royce got down to the task of building a business relationship, and absolutely, one hundred percent, nothing else.

As Royce parked at the entrance to the RV park three days later, he paused just to enjoy the view. Fall painted the landscape a breathtaking pallet of hues, from bright orange honey locusts, red maples and the purple sweetgum trees, to the softer yellow of aspen trees. The pale blue skies, interrupted by only a few fluffy clouds, met the darker surface of the rippling lake.

As a kid, every tree was a challenge to climb. Now, as an adult, he took in the colors and understood how others would see them—and why his mother had been so single-minded in her pursuit to catch the image.

Dispelling the pang of that memory, he inhaled the crisp scent in the air and glanced around at the plentiful fall flowers.

Without meaning to, he searched the various people moseying around the grounds. Most of them were likely campers, but the second he saw the slender woman, a long, patterned skirt drifting around her legs as she walked, he knew it was Joy.

He'd done his utmost not to dwell on her, but still a tension fell over him that had nothing to do with stress and everything to do with awareness. A gentle breeze teased her long, fawn-colored hair and she looked like a woman with a purpose, striding toward the back of the grounds where she disappeared into a building.

Would he run into her? Would he get close enough to see those remarkable eyes again? It seemed likely, and damned if he didn't hope he would.

*Goals,* Royce reminded himself, starting down the slanted drive from the extra parking area to the park itself. He was here for an appointment with Cooper Cochran, the park owner, not to indulge a juvenile infatuation.

A few campfires burned outside RVs and tents, the wood smoke scenting the air. People waved to him as he passed, friendly in the extreme. The play areas were still and empty, but Cooper had explained that with school back in session, weekdays were naturally quieter now. Weekends, though, the park would fill, especially toward the end of the month when Joy helped facilitate a site-by-site Halloween event. Guests decorated their campers, kids wore costumes, people handed out candy and the lodge hosted a "friendly" haunted house, appropriate for kids of all ages.

The evening would end at the drive-in with campers getting discounted tickets and a free bag of popcorn. According to Joy, that got the kids settled before dark, when mishaps could happen if they were still out going door-to-door for candy.

His visit to the park today was just to get to know another businessman, since he and Cooper were neighbors of sorts, with the drive-in just through the woods that bordered the property. If it weren't for the tall trees, campers would be able to catch a free movie every weekend, minus sound.

Suddenly Joy came around the corner only a few yards away from him. She had her arms loaded down with more boxes, a large scarecrow under one arm and her sunglasses were slipping.

Royce stepped into her path. "Joy."

She stopped so abruptly the uppermost box toppled, spilling fall decorations around her feet. Glasses askew, she blinked at him. "Royce."

"Here." He reached for the remaining load she still held, setting everything aside while squatting down to collect the things she'd dropped. "Sorry if I startled you."

"You didn't," she said a little breathlessly. Pushing her glasses atop her head, she looked him over in that same intent way she had at their first meeting.

"Just throwing things at me, huh?" Trying to ignore the charge of her nearness, Royce replaced everything as neatly as he could, although he had no idea how she'd gotten it all in the boxes in the first place.

Her lips parted. Soft lips. Naked lips.

He was thinking things he shouldn't when she suddenly rushed into explanations.

"I'm running late and I'm afraid my mind was elsewhere..." She trailed off and then knelt, too, quickly rearranging things. "What are you doing here?"

She smelled nice, Royce thought, her scent subtle but sexy. Stirring. Maybe it was the October sunshine on her skin, or the warmth of her hair. He breathed her in before explaining, "I'm meeting Coop in the camp store. I'm a little early yet. Let me help you carry this stuff."

As they both reached for the same box, their hands bumped.

She jerked back to her feet. "Oh no." A nervous laugh. "That's okay. Really."

*Why* she was nervous Royce couldn't guess. He watched her, trying to figure her out—trying to figure himself out, too. He had no business lingering here, deliberately running into her and then prolonging his time with her.

Yet there was a pull, opposite of what he told himself he should be doing. Business, that was number one. Building a relationship in the community. Establishing himself and, therefore, the drive-in needed to be his goal.

So why was it so hard to look away from her? Seeing the flush on her face, he had to assume she felt it, too.

Like him, did she find it equally alarming and exhilarating?

Without taking his gaze off her, he slowly stood with two

boxes in his hands as a natural barrier so he didn't do something really dumb. Like step up against her.

Breaking the spell, Royce asked, "Where to?"

After a deep inhalation, she forced a bright smile and snagged up the scarecrow. "This way."

Following her through the grounds, Royce continued to admire...well, the area, sure. It really was a well-laid-out, nicely tended park. But he also admired Joy. The sway of her hips. The flow of her hair. How everyone greeted her with smiles.

That is, everyone except the guy who pulled up on a golf cart, a toolbox beside him on the seat. Shoving sunglasses to the top of head, he frowned at Joy. "Hon, I told you I'd get this stuff for you. Don't you need to go?"

Royce remembered her saying she was running late. He waited, unsure who the young man might be, but assumed he worked for the park.

"I'm leaving as soon as I drop this stuff off at the lodge." She gestured back to him. "Royce is helping."

The man eyed him. "Royce, as in the new owner of the drive-in?"

"One and the same." Juggling the boxes in one arm, Royce reached out a hand. "Royce Nakirk. Nice to meet you."

"Daron Hardy, handyman extraordinaire, or so I'm told." He accepted the handshake. "You going to do a horror night for Halloween? Something really scary that'd make a sexy lady friend want to cuddle?"

Royce glanced at Joy.

She gasped, then quickly denied, "Not me!" as if that idea were the most absurd thing she'd ever heard.

Daron grinned. "Could be you, hon. You fit the bill." To Royce, he said, "Sadly, Joy gives me the cold shoulder. To hear her tell it, there's only one guy in her life."

Well, shit. Royce automatically looked at her hands, though

he already knew she didn't wear a ring. Not married...but that didn't guarantee she wasn't involved in some other way.

Not liking that idea at all, he gave his attention to Daron. "We'll have a double dose of kid-friendly flicks that night, but leading up to it we're playing movies that'd probably work for you." He mentioned the latest blood-and-gore movie that'd hit the big screen.

"I'll take what I can get." Back to Joy, Daron asked, "So you'll be there Halloween weekend for the kids' flick, right? If Jack can stay awake long enough?"

Jack? Royce watched her get more flustered. "Yes, we're planning to attend that weekend, along with many of the families from the park." She adjusted her purse strap. "Speaking of Jack, maybe I'll need your help, after all, or I really might be late." She strode around to the back of the golf cart. "Drop this stuff off for me, okay?"

"Sure thing."

Royce watched the younger man, and realized he had no real interest in Joy. He was friendly in a flirting way, but he wasn't at all serious about it.

Already walking away, Joy said over her shoulder, "Royce, thank you for your help. Just give the boxes to Daron. He'll take care of it." She practically jogged away, her skirt dancing around her calves as she headed toward a parking area.

Daron cleared his throat in an exaggerated way, drawing Royce's attention. "Seriously, dude, you're wasting your time."

"How's that?" Pretending he hadn't just been watching her, Royce unloaded the boxes onto the rear-facing seat, then secured the scarecrow there.

"Joy doesn't date. Her whole focus is on Jack."

"And Jack is...?" he asked, trying to sound casual.

Judging by Daron's wide grin, he wasn't fooled. "Her five-year-old son. Cute kid. A little shy."

Royce forgot that he wasn't interested in a relationship. He wasn't even interested in dating. He felt like he'd just taken one in the gut. "She's a mother?"

"Head to toe."

"But...single?" His brain stuck on that fact, regardless of how Royce tried to block it.

"Always has been, far as I know."

Royce looked back and saw her driving out of the park in a small yellow Ford hatchback. It took a strong woman to raise a kid alone. He knew that firsthand.

"Again, fair warning," Daron said. "Joy assigns all men to the 'casual friendship' zone. In all the time she's been here, plenty have tried to get past it with no luck."

Royce shot him a look. "You?"

Laughing, Daron tugged off his hat to run a hand through messy brown hair, then jammed it back on his head. "Not me, no. I could say I don't play where I work, but truth is, she's a mom through and through. She's also a really nice person, a hell of a hard worker and she's never given me a single hint of interest. Fact, most times she treats me like a bigger version of Jack."

Huh. From what Royce could tell, Daron was a midtwenties, fit, decent-looking *man*—but Joy saw him as a kid? Fascinating.

She sure as hell hadn't looked at *him* that way. Royce was rusty, no doubt about it, but he figured he could still pick up on sexual tension. "So she's going somewhere to get her son?"

"Kindergarten. If you're into lost causes, she'll be back in half an hour."

He wouldn't mind seeing her again, but it wasn't the reason for his visit. "Actually, I'm meeting with Coop, and now *I'm* late." But only by two minutes. "Hope I'll see you Halloween night, if not before."

# CHAPTER TWO

It was cowardly, Joy knew, but she didn't trust this new version of herself. So instead of heading directly back to the park, she took Jack to a restaurant for fried chicken and biscuits.

Even though he was thin, Jack was a bottomless pit and he finished off two legs and a biscuit while Joy nibbled on a wing.

Her thoughts refused to veer long from Royce.

Now that he knew she was a mother, what would he think? It didn't matter, but still...

"What's wrong, Mom?"

Joy gazed at her son's big brown eyes and smiled. "Nothing. I just have a busy day yet ahead."

Warily, he eyed her around a third piece of chicken. "Will I get to play?"

Unable to resist, Joy stroked his fair hair. "We play every night, don't we?"

"Could I play longer?"

Oh, that wheedling tone. Jack was at the age where he negotiated everything. She loved each new facet of his growth,

watching him expand his horizons. He was still shy, but kindergarten had helped him to make friends. And thank God for that because while the summer had provided constant entertainment, the park would now be incredibly quiet until spring. If it weren't for school, he'd spend all his days without peers.

For the thousandth time, Joy questioned her decision in moving to the Cooper's Charm resort. At the time, she'd been desperate for work that would accommodate a baby and allow her to be both caregiver and breadwinner.

Because there was no one else.

Cooper Cochran hadn't owned the park long when she'd shown up largely pregnant with a nonexistent résumé and promises that she'd be perfect for the job, vowing that she'd work harder than anyone else possibly could. At that time, promises and determination were all she had to offer. She'd felt so fragile, so utterly alone, that when he hired her, she'd broken down into tears.

Badly needing a positive focus, and grateful for his confidence, she'd thrown herself into the job, going above and beyond the requirements, and in that process, she'd found a new love: organizing recreational activities for kids and adults alike. Jack had grown up with the other employees as family—more so than her real family would ever be. She, however, still kept others at a distance.

Trust, once broken, instilled a very real fear.

"Tell you what," Joy said, leaning an elbow on the table and smiling at him. "We'll grab an ice cream at the camp store first, then play for an hour if you promise to help me with some of my work afterward." On her strict budget, ice creams were a treat, but she needed to see Maris, anyway. Jack didn't know that, and she'd found he was really great at sorting craft items, as long as she gave very clear instructions. He liked helping out, plus it kept him busy—and close.

"Deal!"

The way Jack's face lit up had Joy grinning, too. With their frugal lifestyle, it wasn't often he got to eat out and have ice cream. She'd grown up the opposite, indulged to a ridiculous degree. Rarely were there meals at home, and if she'd chosen a diet of jelly beans and milk shakes, no one would have denied her.

Only in hindsight had Joy realized it was lack of interest, not an excess of love, that had motivated her parents. The hard truth was forced on her at twenty-four, and in some ways, it felt like her life truly began after that moment.

Now, without her family's influence, she lived on a shoestring budget—and it didn't matter. Her life couldn't be happier. She had Jack, so she had everything she really needed. She'd give her son the more important things in life, like her attention, guidance, protection and supervision. And yes, unconditional love.

And if occasionally, when in her bed alone, she felt an undefined yearning...well, that didn't matter, either. She wouldn't let it.

Cupping her son's face, Joy put a smooch on his forehead. "You are the most perfect little boy I could ever imagine."

*"Mom,"* he complained, wiggling away as his dark eyes quickly scanned the room, ensuring no one had witnessed her affection. He didn't mind hugs, cuddles and kisses, but only when they were alone.

Hiding her smile, Joy cleared away their mess, and within minutes they were headed back to the park. Of course, with Jack buckled up in the back seat with a picture book, her thoughts returned to Royce.

The morning after their first meeting, she'd given her report to Maris, who'd been suitably interested and impressed. But as far as Joy knew, Maris hadn't met him in person yet—unless the introductions had happened earlier today, after Joy left for the school.

Would Maris be as impressed with his looks as Joy had been?

Somehow Joy doubted Maris would lie awake at night thinking about him. And for sure, Maris wouldn't have let his presence at the park chase her away.

Or more accurately, Joy had let her attraction for him get in the way of her responsibilities.

Since she'd be seeing him more all through October, she had to figure out how to keep her physical reactions to him in check.

*Or you could just grab one more indulgence?*

*Oh no.* Definitely *no.* Royce hadn't shown any particular interest, and when would it be possible, anyway? Ruthlessly, Joy snuffed that idea.

But after she parked and she and Jack headed for Summer's End, she spotted Cooper Cochran standing near the scuba shack, at the edge of the boat ramp. Two others stood to his left on the shore, their wet suits rolled down to their waists.

One of them was Baxter, the scuba instructor. Joy had seen him and his very fine physique a great many times. She took in the sight of him the same way she admired art—with an eye of appreciation, but nothing more. *He* didn't keep her awake at night.

However, the other man was… Royce.

Seeing him like that, chest bare, dark hair slicked back, sun glinting off his wide shoulders, caused a very different sort of appreciation. Her heart raced, her stomach seemed to take flight and she couldn't breathe.

She forgot her resolve. She forgot everything.

Good God, she felt…*alive.*

"Well?" Coop asked him.

Now that they'd peeled down the wet suits, Royce felt goose bumps assault his torso. "Other than freezing my balls off, it was awesome. I haven't done this since college. I'd love to visit

again, longer next time." He'd forgotten how good it felt to just relax. After the endless obligation, he'd been elbow-deep in the effort to restart his life. Fun and recreation hadn't factored in.

It still couldn't, not in any significant way. But the occasional swim? Losing his worries while exploring the bottom of the lake—a lake that had once been a quarry so it still offered a unique underwater landscape? That he could manage.

"You're a natural." Baxter set his gear aside, tossed Royce a towel and used one himself. "The water is colder now than in the summer, but clearer, too, since we don't have any swimmers churning it up."

It wasn't the water that bothered Royce. The wet suit had insulated him from that. But the chilly October air? An altogether different matter. The fins made it tough to walk, so going into the shack to change wouldn't have made sense. If he did this again—and he hoped to—he'd be better prepared for exiting the lake.

Coop took Royce's mask and tank. "The season ends for guests after Halloween, but Baxter still dives as long as there isn't ice."

While briskly drying, Baxter shrugged. "Some men jog. I dive."

Royce looked out over the rippling surface of the lake. A bird skimmed low, squawking, and in the distance a large, silver fish jumped. Something about the combo of sun and water and sand filled him with peace. "If you don't mind, I'll join you a few more times before winter lands."

"I'd be glad for the company," Baxter said.

"Thanks." As Royce turned, he roughly ran the towel over his head. The sun warmed his shoulders, but the sharp breeze cut over him.

The park was a thing of beauty this time of year. He gazed around the empty beach and foamy shoreline—then paused

when he noticed Joy some distance to his left, standing by the entrance to the camp store, a small boy holding her hand.

She seemed surprised to see him, almost frozen...and then he remembered he was shirtless. Joy wasn't staring at his face.

Her gaze was on his body.

The sight of her chased away much of his chill. In fact, as he watched her, he forgot about everything, including the two men standing with him.

"You've met Joy, right?"

Drawing his gaze from her, Royce glanced at Coop. It wouldn't do to give the wrong impression. "Yeah, she came by the drive-in the other day." He snagged his T-shirt from the picnic table and pulled it on. The wet suit, rolled down to his hips, would have to stay in place for now. All he wore under it was his boxers, but he sat to remove the fins.

When he glanced up again, he saw Joy and the boy darting into the store.

It had been a hell of a long time since he enjoyed a woman's attention. Too damn long. Yet he couldn't deny what he felt: pleasure that she looked at him, pride that she appeared to like what she saw and, worse, an almost instinctive urge to reciprocate her interest.

"That's Jack."

Hearing the fondness in those two words, Royce turned to Coop. "Her son?"

"Good kid," Baxter said as he stripped off his suit without a care. Of course he'd thought ahead and worn compression shorts underneath. "Friendly but shy with strangers."

"Joy's protective of him." Coop moved around to the other side of the table. "We all are."

A warning? Royce wasn't sure how to take that.

While he was trying to decide on a reply, Coop said, "No one's around. You're good to go."

Royce realized that Coop had his back to him while he kept watch for anyone who might come along. Joy and her son were nowhere to be seen.

"Might take me a minute. I'm not as practiced as Baxter." He struggled out of the wet suit and quickly drew on his jeans. As he zipped up, he said, "Thanks." The T-shirt stuck to damp places on his body, so he shoved his arms into his flannel shirt before sitting down to pull on his socks and shoes.

Was it his imagination or had the temp dropped ten degrees?

Baxter clapped him on the shoulder. "Have Maris pour you a cup of coffee and I'll store the gear."

Not wanting to start off on the wrong foot, Royce shook his head. "I'll help."

Baxter offered a friendly smile. "Not this time."

"For today only," Coop explained, "you're a guest." He indicated the open door of the camp store that Joy and Jack had entered. "Next time you can learn the ropes."

"Ask Maris to pour me one, too," Baxter said, already striding off with the tanks and fins. "I'll join you in a few."

Royce looked at Summer's End. Sunshine bathed the entry, shielding the doorway like a yellow curtain so that he couldn't see anyone inside. The faint strains of country music drifted out, along with the low drone of conversation. And, damn it, he couldn't deny the jolt of...excitement? Anticipation?

He wanted to see Joy again.

With another absent, "Thanks," for the men, he started forward.

The unwelcome, heated interest intensified as he neared. Everything else faded away; he no longer heard the squawking of gulls, the constant washing on the shoreline or the rustling of drying leaves in the trees. The closer he got, the deeper he breathed and the warmer he felt.

And then he heard her voice.

"What do you mean?" A nervous denial. "I wasn't staring."

"Give it up," another woman said. "You were eyeballing the new guy big-time. Your face is still hot, too." He heard a laugh that was both soft and husky. "It's not a crime to admire a nice bod, you know."

Flattered, Royce looked down at himself and gave a mental shrug. Yes, he'd stayed fit, mostly through strenuous physical labor. As a mobile sawmiller, he'd been able to tailor his hours to make a living wage while also meeting his other obligations.

Joy's pause sounded loud in Royce's ears.

Yes, he'd picked up on her scrutiny, but it had been so long since he'd done the whole man/woman thing, he liked having her awareness verified by someone else.

Suddenly Joy groaned. "All right, so I stared." In a lower voice, she added, "I thought he'd be gone by now, so I hadn't expected to see him, and then he came out of the lake half-naked..."

"And lookin' fine," the other woman said with humorous admiration. "I'm glad to know you still have a pulse. And before you get offended—"

"I wouldn't," Joy said, her tone tinged with self-directed disgust. "I know I come off as cold."

"Not cold at all. You're one of the nicest, most considerate people I know. But around men, you're always disinterested. Maybe even oblivious. God knows plenty of campers have tried to get your attention."

Joy dismissed that. "Not seriously."

"Come on." The other woman guffawed. "I get that your big focus is on Jack, and he's a sweetheart because of it. But every single guy—and some of the not-so-single guys—do their best to get your attention, and they all fail." Her voice went lower, soft with understanding. "I've been trying to tell you, Joy. You're allowed to have some fun, too."

Stopped just outside the doorway, Royce paused. So he was expected to be fun? Hell, fun had been absent for so long he wasn't sure he'd recognize it anymore. But now, finally, he was close to having a new life.

This was no time to lose sight of his end game.

"I know what you've been telling me," Joy said. "And I've explained that I can't get involved. Between my job and being a single mom, I have zilch for free time."

"I'm not saying you have to get involved. Offer him a night. An afternoon. Hell, I'll watch Jack for you right now and you could—"

Joy laughed while shushing the other woman at the same time. "You don't even know if he'd be willing."

The woman gave a soft snort. "Oh, he'd be willing. Men are *always* willing."

Not necessarily true, Royce knew. He had a stretch of celibacy to prove it. But was he ready now? He couldn't deny the way his cock jumped at the idea, though as a grown man, he made decisions with his brain. Still, other parts of his body rallied persuasions, ganging up against better sense and—

"Who are you?"

He'd been so enthralled by the women's conversation Royce hadn't noticed the little fair-haired boy approaching until he spoke.

Silence swelled around him until it picked up a pulse beat. Or maybe that was his own guilty conscience now drumming in his head. Listening in equaled eavesdropping...and he only just realized he was doing it.

In his defense, he'd been so surprised that he hadn't even thought about it. Instinct alone had kept him standing there, taking it all in.

Avoiding looking toward Joy, Royce turned his attention down to the kid. Chocolate ice cream dripped over the small

pale hand gripping a cone. It also smudged the boy's mouth, and even the tip of his button nose.

Grinning, he held out his hand. "I'm Royce Nakirk, a neighbor of sorts since I own the drive-in."

Big brown eyes rounded comically wide as they stared at Royce's hand. Though he felt the women watching, no one said a word. Finally Jack shoved the cone into his left hand and held out his very sticky right hand. "I'm Jack Lee."

Royce took one step in the door, snagged a few napkins from the first booth and then knelt down. "Nice to meet you, Jack." He took the boy's hand—melted ice cream and all—and gave it two careful pumps. That done, he asked, "Mind if I mop up a bit?"

Narrow shoulders rolled in a shrug…and Jack thrust his face up for Royce to clean.

Nonplussed, Royce's grin widened more. He'd meant to tend his own hand, but he wasn't a novice at this sort of thing—although his experience wasn't with kids.

He carefully wiped the boy's mouth and chin.

Suddenly Joy was there, protectively close to her son as she took over, efficiently swabbing his face and hands.

Jack was quick to say, "I'm not done yet." Then to Royce, "She usually cleans me up when I'm done." And back to his mother, with firm insistence, "I'm *not* done, Mom, okay?"

Fighting a laugh, Royce said, "I'm sure your mother will understand that I interrupted things." He looked up at Joy, saw something like panic in her eyes and smiled. *Yes*, he wanted to say. *I heard every word.*

But that would only get him in deeper, and he figured he was already mired ass-deep in feelings he didn't recognize.

"See, Mom," Jack said. "I saw him standin' there and that's why I'm not done." Again to Royce, "Ain't that right?"

The kid was a charmer with his blatant honesty. Royce gave a solemn nod. "Exactly right."

"*Isn't*, not *ain't*." Joy's face softened. "And I'm not rushing you, but if you want time to swing we need to get going soon."

Royce, *still* on one knee, watched Jack jam as much of the cone in his mouth as he could, determined to get every bite.

Instead of getting annoyed as ice cream dripped down his shirt, Joy stroked the boy's hair. "Jack," she said softly. "You'll have Mr. Nakirk thinking you're without any manners at all."

That tone reeked of affection, as did the gentle touch, and it took Royce a moment to refocus.

Coming back to his feet, he looked past Joy—a necessary break from her impact—and asked the woman behind the counter, "Do you have coffee?"

"Do I have coffee," she scoffed. "Only the best coffee in town. Grab a seat and I'll bring you a cup."

"Thank you. One for Baxter, as well, please. He'll be joining me shortly." This woman he could deal with. She was pretty in a more practical way, with dark blond hair held back in a bouncy ponytail, and brown eyes that weren't at all as innocent as Jack's, yet held an all-business mien when she met his gaze.

As Royce moved around Joy, Jack fell into step behind him. Mouth full, he asked, "Do you get to watch movies every night? Do you pick the movies? Do you have a favorite?"

Because her son followed him, Joy did, as well…though she held back a few steps.

"At the drive-in, you mean?" Royce chose a booth in the middle of the store. "Since I run it, I'm usually working when they play. And we only have movies on the weekend, though I wouldn't mind changing that a little, maybe in the future. I pick them, but I base it on what's popular because it's not about what I want to see, right? It's what will bring in an audience."

Jack took all that in, chewed it over in his head and nodded.

"I'd like to own a drive-in." Taking the position across from Royce, he balanced his knees on the seat and his elbows on the tabletop. "When my windows are open, I can hear the movies. Sometimes moaning, sometimes screaming."

Lifting his brows, Royce wondered exactly which movies the boy had heard. A horror flick...or something else? "Is that right?"

He nodded and grinned. "Since I can't see it, I make up my own movies to go with the moans."

Royce choked. "Fascinating."

"Jack." Joy tried to interject while still not getting too close. "Mr. Nakirk is expecting a guest. Let's move to another booth."

"Not a guest," the kid argued. "Just Baxter, and he likes me, too."

Too? The boy didn't lack for self-confidence, something Royce considered a good thing. "I'm pretty sure everyone around here likes you," Royce said.

"Of course we do." The other woman reappeared with two cups of coffee, a coffeepot, creamer and sugar on a tray. "What's not to like, right?"

"Agreed." Royce waited until she'd set everything down, making sure it was all out of Jack's way. "I'm Royce—"

"Nakirk, new owner of the drive-in." She winked. "Listening in goes both ways." After drying her hands on an apron skirt, she held one out. "Maris Kennedy. I run Summer's End."

Her hand was warm, small but strong. "It's nice to meet you." As they each pulled away, he looked around. "Seems you have quite the business going here."

Maris took it upon herself to nudge Jack over so she could sit beside him. "I have all the staples campers might need, basic food stuff, camping items and even a few things for the lake. Plus I run the café. With the end of the season, I won't pre-pare daily specials anymore, but if you're ever in a pinch, let

me know. I often throw together lunch or dinner for everyone who works here."

That didn't include Royce, since he wasn't a camp worker. "I wouldn't want to impose."

"No imposition. Coop supplies me with what I need to keep the coffee going for employees—or friends." Maris smiled at him, putting emphasis on how she said *friends*...as if she expected him to be more?

When her gaze slanted to Joy, he caught her meaning. The lady was a matchmaker, and oddly enough, Royce didn't mind.

Now that Maris sat, only Joy remained standing—and it felt awkward. "Thank you," Royce said. "I appreciate the warm welcome." So far, everyone at Cooper's Charm had proven to be friendly and easy to like.

Standing, Royce turned to Joy. "Why don't you sit with us?" *Next to me.* He gestured at the booth seat.

Their gazes held a moment before she forced a smile.

Royce knew she would refuse. Maybe, like him, she was wary of the attraction. He couldn't blame her. At least on his end, it felt out of place and somewhat disconcerting.

"Jack and I should get going."

Accepting that, Royce retreated back to his seat.

"But I'd rather talk to Mr. Nakirk," Jack announced.

The way both Maris and Joy stared at the boy, this must be an unusual request.

"We're going to the playground to swing," Joy reminded him.

Jack grabbed more napkins now that he'd finished his ice cream. They quickly shredded against his sticky little hands. "We can swing anytime."

Without planning it, Royce heard himself say, "You can visit with me anytime, too. I'll be back to the park off and on, and I don't live that far away."

"I can?" Jack bounced. "Can I see how the popcorn machine works?"

"Jack," Joy said firmly, her tone a mix of reprimand and exasperation. "It's definitely rude to invite yourself over."

Maris chuckled.

Royce wondered what Joy objected to most, her impetuous son or the idea of visiting him without the excuse of business.

Or maybe she didn't like for her son to get too close to men. He gave that brief thought, but given how Coop and Baxter reacted, Jack didn't lack for male figures in his life.

It would be different, though, for a man who wasn't a coworker. The other men in the park would be a constant in Jack's life.

But a man interested in *her*? That would be a risk for a dedicated mom.

Hoping he didn't overstep, Royce offered, "I'd be happy to show him around. Maybe that'd be a good field trip for his class?"

Jack cheered, almost toppling the pot of coffee. Royce caught it. "Careful."

Abashed, Jack bit his lip. "Sorry."

"I like your enthusiasm, but we don't want anyone to get burned, right?" He glanced up at Joy—and caught her staring, her expression almost dazed.

Had she expected him to snap at Jack? Hell, he liked kids being kids. That's how it should be.

Whatever Joy had been thinking, she shook it off. "Jack, we really do need to go."

"You're the only one who doesn't have brown eyes, Mom. Did you know that? But Mr. Nakirk's eyes are really dark." He leaned over the tabletop, this time with more caution, to closely study Royce. "They're maybe even black."

Grinning at the near nose-to-nose scrutiny, Maris patted Jack's

back and left the booth. "I have to get back to work." With a touch to Joy's shoulder, she whispered, "Sit, drink the coffee. I'll bring Baxter another," before she walked away.

It occurred to Royce that he was enjoying himself. *Again.* Joy's son was pure entertainment with his frank, inquisitive manner. He was so close now Royce felt his breath.

"Jack," she said again, sliding into the booth. "That's enough."

To let Joy know she shouldn't fret so much, Royce flashed her a smile, then took Jack by the chin and did his own scrutiny.

"Your eyes are pretty dark, too. But you're right. They're not as dark as mine." He turned Jack's face this way and that to study him. "I got my grandmother's eyes. Looks like you got your mother's…ears."

Mouth dropping open, Jack clapped both hands on his ears to feel them, then scrambled over to examine his mother's. Despite his sticky fingers being in her hair, Joy laughed, and that made Jack suspicious.

He shot Royce a look. "You serious?" Again, he felt his ears.

"Cross my heart."

Baxter stepped through the open front door, spotted Royce with Joy and hesitated. Instead of joining them, he went to the counter to speak with Maris.

Damn. Was everyone at the park trying to push them together?

Joy turned to follow his gaze, spotted Baxter and apologized. "I'm sorry. We've interrupted your—"

"My what?" Royce sat back, wanting her to stay a little longer. "My visit was to get to know everyone, and I did." He smiled at Jack. "Including this character."

Frowning slightly, Jack still felt his ears.

Joy let out a slow breath. "I saw you in the water with Baxter."

Hoping she wouldn't be embarrassed, he nodded. "I know."

"Were you cold?" Jack asked. "Mom said I can't swim because it's too cold."

"Your mom is right. Even I won't go in too many more times."

Jack fidgeted. "If you can't swim, do you think you'd want to swing?"

Immediately, Joy was on her feet again. "He has a meeting with Baxter, sweetie. Come on. Time for us to go."

Well, damn. Now that Jack had mentioned it, Royce kind of wanted to swing. He definitely wanted to visit more with Joy. And he hated seeing the disappointment in Jack's eyes.

He got to his feet, saying, "Next time, okay?"

"You mean it?" Jack scrambled out. "You might be too big for the slide. Mom says she is."

Joy rolled her eyes and laughed.

Leaning in, Jack said, sotto voce, "I think she'd fit, but she's chicken."

"Challenged by my own son?" She tickled his ribs. "I'll show you who's chicken!"

Jack squealed with laughter, and that brought Baxter from the counter. "I hope I didn't break up your visit?"

"Jack and I are off for the swings." She clasped her son's hand, silencing his arguments with a firm, "We've lingered too long already, especially since I still have a lot to get done."

"Anything I can help with?" Royce offered, before he could think it over.

Taken by surprise, she shook her head. "Camp stuff. But thank you."

Inspiration struck, and Royce again knelt down. "Jack, it was nice meeting you."

"I don't want to go yet."

His mouth twitched. It was nice to be liked. "Your mom is the boss, though."

"I guess."

"But I was wondering, since you seem like an expert on swings, maybe you could give me some pointers on the old playground equipment at the drive-in. What do you think?"

"Pointers?"

"On what needs to be replaced, what I should add, what rambunctious little boys like most. That sort of thing."

His whole face lit up and he turned to Joy in a rush. "Can I, Mom? Can I?"

Flushed—likely because she saw through his ploy—Joy waffled. "Um..."

"I'd enjoy seeing you both." Royce felt it necessary to offer that dose of honesty. Yes, he wanted to see her. Against all logic and in direct opposition to his plans, he wanted that a lot. But he'd also like to visit more with Jack.

For whatever reason, the boy had taken to him.

To let her off the hook for now, Royce said, "Not tonight. Seems we're all busy. But maybe over the weekend? That is, if your mom has the time?"

Baxter contributed to the cause, saying, "Good idea. Jack is the foremost swing set expert in town."

"I... Okay." Taking two steps back, Joy nodded. "I don't have my calendar with me, so I can't check my schedule—"

"No problem." From behind the counter, Maris said, "I can give him your number. And, Royce, you could leave yours. That way one of you—" she lifted her brows at Royce "—can check in with the other to see what works."

"Fine by me." Royce saw Joy's expression and knew she wasn't quite as eager as Maris. It didn't insult him. Given what he'd heard, this was a big step for her.

And he respected that Jack was her number one priority.

"Well, then." With that vague response and a harried expres-

sion directed at Maris, Joy turned to go, prodding a reluctant Jack to follow.

The boy waved and said, "I'll see ya, Mr. Nakirk."

Once they were gone, Maris shook her head. "He never got past Mr."

"I noticed." Baxter sipped his coffee. "Took Joy a month to let Jack call me by name, and only after she knew for sure I had nothing but friendship in mind for her."

"You," Maris said to Royce, striding toward the booth with a plate of cookies, "are different."

"Am I?" Just that morning, Royce would have said he wasn't. The idea of inserting himself into a woman's life, into her son's life, would have been roundly rejected.

But now... Well, now he felt an invisible pull, a need to know her better, to befriend Jack. The things he'd heard, the way he felt when she was near, how much he enjoyed talking with her, even just watching her...it wouldn't go away.

Royce wasn't one to fight a losing battle, and that's what it would be if he tried to resist her. Add in Jack, and he knew he had to pursue things, at least to see where it took him.

He had a better understanding than some exactly how it would be for a single mother, and for a lone boy. Maybe Jack reminded him of himself—though Royce was pretty sure he hadn't been as cute and precocious at that age. Whatever the reasons, he already looked forward to seeing Joy again.

When Maris offered a cookie, he gladly took one. "Will you tell me more about Joy? Jack, too?"

"I'll tell you anything she wouldn't mind you knowing."

Royce laughed at that diplomatic reply. "Spoken like a true friend."

"I'm working on it." Propping a hip against a booth top, Maris shrugged. "Given how I pushed her today..." She grinned, clearly unconcerned. "I might be back at square one, but Joy

is the forgiving sort, and she deserves a night off, so here's her number." She took a slip of paper from her apron pocket, then held it out of reach. "Just be sure you don't abuse it."

"I get it." Royce gave her a level look. "I wouldn't pressure her if she's not interested." Besides, he wasn't sure he wanted to move too fast, anyway. He wasn't one hundred percent sure of anything—except that he did want to see her.

"She's interested," Maris assured him. "I could tell. She's just out of practice."

That made two of them, then...yet some things a man never forgot. "Thanks." Royce tucked the paper into his back pocket.

Satisfied, Maris asked, "You guys need anything else?"

Baxter shook his head. "Ridley and I are heading out for dinner tonight."

"And I need to get going soon."

"Then I better get to my chores. Put the plate and cups on the counter when you finish, and give a yell if you need me."

Once Maris disappeared into the back room, Baxter shook his head. "If you think Joy works hard, she's got nothing on Maris."

Royce knew Coop and Baxter were both married, but he wasn't sure about Maris. "Don't misunderstand—I'm not personally interested—but she's single? Maris, I mean?" He looked around the store again. "She runs this alone?"

"Sunup to sundown, yeah." Baxter finished off his coffee. "Now that we're heading into the off-season, she'll do any repairs and upkeep that's needed."

"I thought that was Daron's job."

"Ha! Yeah, it is, but those two butt heads a lot. It's pretty damned amusing actually. He'll do what he can to help, but he flirts with her the whole time so Maris will do what she can to keep him away. If you're around enough, you'll see what I mean."

That gave Royce another idea. He was good with his hands,

and he wouldn't mind pitching in around the park. For one thing, it'd give him an excuse to be around more, which meant he'd have opportunities to see Joy. Plus it'd help shore up his standing in the community, since the entire town seemed curtained around the resort. But mostly, he'd enjoy repaying Maris's kindness.

Things were coming together nicely. Not quite as he'd expected, but each day his optimism grew.

Smiling, Maris locked up behind everyone and began her evening routine that included starting the dishwasher, a thorough cleaning of the seating area and switching out the entry rug, which had collected dirt from shoes during the day.

She lived for her routines, morning and night. They reminded her that she alone guided her future, and because of that, she'd never again have reason for shame.

Growing up, there'd been no order to anything, no planning, no...pride.

Maris had plans. As soon as she'd gained her independence, she'd set up goals and never, not once, had she veered from them.

Tonight, though, she smiled because of Joy.

How had she known Joy so long and yet never known certain things about her—like her sense of humor, her modesty over her appearance...and her willingness to expand their friendship?

Maybe, like Maris, age had inspired that last part.

Damn it, her routines were starting to feel tired, but today, chatting with Joy had renewed her.

No, she couldn't get involved with anyone—that'd definitely put a kink in her goals. But Joy? There was absolutely no reason for Joy to avoid dating, and every reason for her to finally have some fun.

Maris planned to encourage her in every way she could, and she'd start with Royce.

# CHAPTER THREE

Hours later, Joy peeked in on Jack and saw he was finally asleep. Meeting Royce had gotten him so hyped that she'd had a difficult time getting him to wind down.

It wasn't like her son to get so familiar so quickly. He was generally a shy boy, at least until he knew someone well. Before kindergarten, he'd often hidden behind her when they met new people. Yes, he'd come out of his shell some since the interactions at school, but not like he had today.

She thought of how Royce had knelt down to talk to him, how earnest Jack had been in meeting him almost eye to eye. And *how* Royce had spoken, not like he humored a little kid, but in a more respectful way.

He'd won her son over with very little effort.

Resting a hand over her heart, Joy stood in the doorway, looking at Jack's small body curled under his favorite Ninja Turtle blanket. The few toys he owned were scattered about. Luckily, Jack didn't ask for a lot, because she didn't have much to spend on indulgences.

However, she'd given him everything she knew he needed, including love, security, affection, guidance and boundaries.

But had she cheated him out of a father figure? Had she let her own insecurity about involvement negatively affect her son?

Jack had always chased after Coop, Baxter and Daron, but she'd been careful not to let him get too close. She'd feared for his disappointment.

And her own.

The ringing of her cell phone in the other room startled her. No one called her after nine p.m.

Leaving the door open a tiny bit, as was her habit, she hurried down the hall and to the small living room. There on the desk, her phone buzzed.

For only a heartbeat, she warred with herself before snatching it up and saying a soft, "Hello?"

"Joy? It's Royce. Am I calling too late?"

She eased out the desk chair and sank into it. "No." Dumb. *Say something else.* "I was just about to shower." *No. Not that.* Catching her breath, she rushed on, explaining, "I mean, Jack is asleep now, so—"

"I understand."

He'd sounded amused...and now he was silent.

She briefly closed her eyes. Damn it, she was an intelligent adult, a divorced woman, a single mother. She could carry on a coherent conversation. "How was your day?" *Gawd, so bland and clichéd.*

"Good. Yours?"

"Jack was excited. He enjoyed meeting you." That, at least, was sincere.

"I enjoyed meeting him, too. He's a smart kid. Cute."

Smiling, Joy said, "Once we got home, he stayed in front of the mirror for ten minutes studying his ears. Then he tried

drawing them a dozen times. He's not yet satisfied that he's got it right."

Royce laughed. "Does he have any features that resemble family members?" He paused, then asked lightly, "His dad, maybe?"

Shadows filled their apartment over the rec center. Only the glow from her laptop screen and a small light over the stove lit the interior. Floodlights from outside, stationed around the park, filtered in through the windows.

Joy always made their home dim and quiet in the evening when it was time for Jack to sleep. Her chair squeaked as she sat back and curled her feet beneath her. "Actually, he does look a little like his father, at least from what I can remember. I haven't seen Vaughn since...well, six months before Jack was born actually."

Silence stretched out. "He knew you were pregnant?"

"He'd already talked of divorce. Finding out I was pregnant only shored up his arguments to leave."

Royce gave a low curse. "I didn't realize. I'm sorry if I overstepped."

"You didn't. It's fine." What wasn't fine was her talking about her ex to a...what? Prospective date? Joy shook her head, hating how pathetic that seemed. "I should apologize for saying so much. It's just that Jack rarely asks about his father. I'd prefer that you not mention it when he's around."

"No problem." After a second or two, Royce asked, "You're divorced now?"

"Yes. We were already having issues—" what an understatement "—when I found out I was pregnant. Vaughn walked out the day I told him, and I haven't seen him since the divorce became final shortly after that."

"How old were you?"

If Royce had sounded too sympathetic, it would have bothered her, but he seemed only politely curious. "I was a very im-

mature, very dependent twenty-four." That made her laugh a little. She knew a lot of people, Daron among them, who'd been far more mature at a much younger age. "Nothing makes you grow up like becoming responsible for someone else."

"A hard truth."

He sounded like he understood something about that. "Have you ever been married?"

"No." Then he asked, "How long were you with him?"

Had he just changed the subject to get it off him? Joy considered pressing him—did he disapprove of marriage, or had some woman broken his heart? There were so many things she wanted to know about Royce, but this was nice, just talking to him, and she didn't want to chase him off. Chatting on the phone instead of looking at him made it easier for her.

Oh, she had a vivid image of him in her head, but her imagination didn't quite replicate his potent impact on her senses.

"Vaughn and I were together for a year. My parents detested him. Actually, *detest* might not be a strong enough word."

"I suppose that made you want him more?"

Why was she telling him all this? She never discussed Vaughn with anyone. Not since the last big blowup with her parents.

Not since they'd disowned her.

She put her head back and closed her eyes. "Like I said, I was immature."

"It's human nature. Don't beat yourself up over it."

Too late for that. Following his lead on topic changes, she prompted, "Did you want to get together this weekend? Jack's talked about it a lot."

"That's part of why I called."

Did she hear a hesitation? Would he back out now? Jack would be crushed. She never should have—

"I was thinking maybe I could take you both to lunch Saturday. Afterward we could stop at the drive-in so I could show

Jack around. That'd still give me time to get you both home and get back before sunset when I need to prep for the showing."

Like a teenager being asked out on her first date, Joy felt exhilarated, excited—and so disappointed that she had to refuse. "That sounds wonderful, Royce, but until the season officially ends, I do activities from afternoon to evening here with the campers. This Saturday we have fall crafts."

Without missing a beat, he asked, "Sunday works better for me, anyway, since the drive-in is closed that day. What do you think?"

She bit her lip to suppress the smile, then cleared her throat. "Sunday we're free." Perfect. She sounded calm and mature and not like a woman whose toes had just curled in anticipation. "It's a school night so I'd have to be back early."

"Done." She heard his smile, too, when he asked, "Any chance I can get in on that afternoon craft action?"

Laughing, Joy hugged herself and savored the new freedom of flirting. "Oh, I think that can be arranged."

"Perfect." His voice went a little deeper. "Fair warning, though. If at all possible, and with due respect to your son, I plan to steal a kiss before I go."

More than her toes curled over that statement. "Oh, um…"

"Good night, Joy."

"Looking for someone?"

Startled, Joy ducked her head to hide her guilty face. "Hmm?" She *had* been watching the door, wondering if Royce would really show, and when. She hadn't even heard Maris come in from the back entrance.

Maris openly laughed at her in that easy, friendly way she had. "I'm on to you now. That particular expression has something to do with Royce, doesn't it? Is he coming by today?"

Straightening, Joy stared at her in wonder. How could Maris

read the situation so easily? Joy had known her for a while now, and never before had she read her mind.

Of course, never before had Joy been infatuated with a man. Plus Maris was usually too busy working to waste time wondering about anyone else.

In the past week, something had shifted in their friendship. Whatever it was, Joy enjoyed it.

"I was only putting out craft supplies." She gestured at the bins on the round table filled with glue and markers and yarn. "Just that. Nothing telling or obvious. So how did you know?"

Setting aside a tray filled with cookies, Maris crossed her arms and leaned on the wall. "I'm a woman. You're a woman. That gives us some common ground." She shrugged. "Call it female intuition."

"But we're nothing alike."

At that, Maris's brows rose up. "You don't think so?"

Hoping Maris didn't take that as an insult, Joy glanced around to ensure they weren't overheard. Luckily none of the kids had shown up yet. Jack sat alone coloring at a smaller table toward the back, and everything was ready for afternoon crafts.

Drawing a breath, Joy stepped closer to Maris. "I didn't mean that how it sounded."

"It's all right. I get it. You're always polished, while I'm something of a mess and it doesn't bother me."

"We already discussed this. You're beautiful."

"And you're generous with compliments, but come on." Maris nodded at Joy's long skirt and ballet flats. "I can't even remember the last time I dressed up."

Joy stared at her, surprised yet again. "That's not at all what I meant. My wardrobe is just what I have left from… Never mind." Once, long ago, she'd thought clothes mattered. Now, she wore what she had because investing in the newest fashions

wasn't feasible. Was it the same for Maris? Somehow she didn't think so. "It's just... I admire you, you know."

Maris snorted. "I can't imagine why."

"Are you serious? I have a hundred reasons!" And Joy didn't mind listing them for her. "You're so confident and self-assured. You always know what you're doing and why. You accomplish more in a day than most people do in a week. You're completely self-reliant. Plus my compliments were honest, not generous. You look *amazing* in jeans—and no makeup. That's just unfair, because you're right, makeup is a pain. If I had your flawless skin or dark eyelashes, I wouldn't wear it, either."

Maris blinked at that outpouring of compliments. "Thank you. I admire you, too." With a laugh, she wrinkled her nose. "Though I have to say, this conversation is a little embarrassing."

Right. People didn't walk around detailing attributes. They met, became friends, and it was all more natural.

Twisting her mouth, Joy pointed out, "That's another way we're different, I guess. I'm...awkward." That wasn't precisely the right word, so she shook her head and tried again. "Awkward on the inside, I mean. I tell myself to be confident, but you just *are*. You always seem to know the right thing to say or do to put other people at ease. You're so together and take-charge, but also comfortable and friendly."

Maris took her hands. Joy realized that Maris's were work-worn, her fingers a little roughened from all the dishwashing and cooking she did.

"I think we're both misunderstanding. I've never seen you look or act awkward. What I meant is that the flattery embarrasses me because I'm not used to getting compliments like that. Compliments that matter."

Joy searched her face and saw the truth. "You mean, compliments for something other than looks?"

Maris nodded. "It shows what a nice person you are that you

see beyond the surface. Especially since my look is usually some shade of permanent determination and stubborn will."

"It's a good look," Joy promised her with a laugh. *Much better than deep-rooted insecurity.* Honestly, Maris looked like the woman Joy wanted to be.

Maris grinned. "You're those things, too."

"I want that to be true, for myself and Jack." It was important for Jack to know she'd always take care of him. Her confidence was as much for him as for herself. She did what she could to ensure he'd never have the same worries she'd had. "I work at it, but it seems so effortless for you."

Laughing, Maris reached for a cookie. "I've been working for as long as I can remember. The day I turned eighteen, finding a job was my top priority. By now it's second nature for me— still difficult, but part of my life."

Shame hit Joy, thick enough to make her throat tight. She didn't know what type of childhood Maris had, but it was surely different from her own. Joy knew she'd been given far more advantages than most, so what right did she have to complain? "I'm sorry."

A smile teased over Maris's mouth. "Don't be. I've enjoyed talking to you. We need to do this more often."

When? They both stayed busy, but Joy vowed she'd make time—if Maris could. "I'd like that."

"Maybe we should start our own little club where we drink coffee, eat cookies and praise each other."

Oddly enough, that sounded like a very good time. "Count me in."

"But someone also has to share fun stories that involve a hunk. Since I'm out—" she tapped Joy's shoulder "—you're it."

It? Wondering what that meant, Joy asked, "Why are you out?"

"I don't date," Maris stated. "Never have."

"You say that like it's part of your religion or something." Joy crossed her arms. "Why can't you date?"

Maris choked on a laugh, quickly covered her mouth and shook her head. "It's not that I can't, it's that I don't."

True. Joy couldn't recall a time where Maris did anything other than...work. "Okay, but *why*?"

"Let's just say I have other priorities. Financial security tops the list. Independence is right behind it."

Joy couldn't help but wonder about Maris's background—and why those two things were so important. "Doesn't everyone want to be secure?"

"Sure, I guess. But since I've personally felt the bite of dependence, I'll do what I can to never end up there again." She pointed her half-eaten cookie at Joy. "And no, I'm not talking about any of that right now, so stop deferring. You're it and that's that."

Giving up, Joy said, "Fine," and then she felt a small thrill when she thought of Royce. "What do I have to do?"

"Something..." Maris gave it thought, then grinned. "Something *scintillating*."

"Um...okay. Define that."

Maris rolled a shoulder. "If Royce shows up, steal a kiss." She quickly clarified, "Not a peck. Those don't count. Make it something substantial, something with *tongues*."

At that, Joy outright laughed. Royce had said he wouldn't leave without kissing, so... "I might be able to make that happen."

"Perfect." Maris nodded toward the door and whispered, "Make it hot and wild, and then you can tell me all about it. I'll get some vicarious thrills, since I'm not getting anything else." As she backed up, she thrust a fist in the air and said, "To the Summer's End club!" then turned and ducked through the back door again, no doubt returning to the camp store.

Everyone working at the park would be happy to lend her a hand now and then, but Maris delegated only the most insubstantial tasks to others. Anything of importance she handled herself.

When it came to her livelihood, Maris considered nearly everything important.

Laughing, Joy glanced to the entrance and found Royce walking in with Daron. Jack spotted him right off and with a happy cheer he raced over. Daron said something, ruffled Jack's hair and left again.

Probably chasing Maris, if Joy had to guess. Why Maris didn't orchestrate her own wild night, she didn't know. It seemed obvious to her that Daron was anxious, willing and able.

With a hand to her son's back, Royce crossed the room. His dark gaze moved over her, lingering a heartbeat on her fitted sweater before meeting her eyes. "Hey."

She'd taken extra care today with her appearance, wearing a little more mascara, choosing clothes that flattered her figure. She'd wanted him to notice—and he did. "You made it."

Those dark eyes zeroed in on her mouth. "Daron walked me in." He glanced around. "He said you live here, too?"

"Upstairs," Jack said. "We have to go outside to get in. Wanna see?"

Unprepared to take Royce through her meager home, Joy stalled.

"Someday soon," Royce said, saving her from having to come up with an excuse. "Right now your mom is busy, so I figured we'd lend her a hand."

"She doesn't need help. Mom's organized." He looked up at her. "Aren't you, Mom? Everyone says so."

Joy laughed. "I try." She smoothed down Jack's hair. In many ways it reminded her of Daron's. His hair, too, was often un-

ruly. "Why don't you get your picture to show Mr. Nakirk and I'll make coffee for the parents."

As Jack ran off, Royce walked with her to the nook designated as a kitchen area. "Do a lot of adults accompany the kids?"

"More so toward evening, but I always try to be prepared with coffee, regular for afternoons, decaf later on. The kids get juice, and Maris brought over cookies." She went about coffee prep while Jack skidded to a halt with his picture in his hands.

"Let's see." Royce knelt down, took the artwork when Jack shyly offered it, then he fell silent. Joy was just starting to worry when he said, "Wow."

"You like it?" Jack anxiously shifted from one foot to the other. "It's not done yet."

"I… Of course I like it." More silence as he studied the picture.

Curious, Joy set aside foam cups and came to look over Royce's shoulder.

Jack had drawn the big screen of the drive-in, a row of cars and a large man—hands on hips—smiling widely.

"It's terrific, Jack." Joy nudged Royce. "Don't you think so?"

"I think it's better than terrific." He lowered the picture. "How old are you again?"

One hand lifted, fingers spread. "Five, but I'll be six soon."

Royce shook his head in wonder. "This is phenomenal for a kid your age. You've got perspective in here, and the dimensions are good. And I knew it was me." He lowered the paper. "It is me, right?"

Jack nodded, then he, too, looked at the picture. "What's perspect…?"

"Perspective. It means you've shown things in a way that I feel like I'm standing right here, behind the row of cars."

"But you're there." Jack pointed to the figure in the drawing.

"Right. You drew me there, but if someone else was look-

ing on..." He gave up and glanced at Joy. "How do you explain perspective to a kid?"

Joy knelt down beside him. "It's like looking at a photograph. Everything is where it should be and it's all sized right for positioning."

Pursing his mouth, Jack studied the picture once more. "It's not a photograph."

"It's better." Royce dropped to his behind and crossed his ankles, holding the paper against his knees. "Do you think I could keep it?"

A smile beamed across Jack's face. "Sure."

"Will you sign it for me?" Royce glanced back to Joy. "Can he sign his name?"

She nodded. Jack was smart, but more than that, he received loads of attention from her. All that one-on-one helped him to grasp things more quickly. "Jack, try to put it smaller in the bottom corner, okay?" She touched the paper. "Down here."

"Okay." He turned and ran off again.

Royce faced her. "Do you realize how talented he is?"

"He's my son. I think he's brilliant at everything."

Amused, Royce reached out and touched her hair, drifting his fingers from her ear down to the ends that lay against her back. For only a moment, his hand rested there, warm and firm against her, before he withdrew. "That might be, but he's also artistic with natural skill. Few kids would have included that many details, or been able to add depth."

She leaned in, liking this nearness to him. He smelled really nice, sort of dark and spicy, and she could feel the warmth of his body.

So that Jack wouldn't hear, she whispered, "He drew you a little short and thick."

Royce laughed. "He's five." Standing again, he caught her elbow and helped her up, and then didn't let her go. A glance at

Jack showed him hunched over the paper, his lip caught in his teeth as he painstakingly added his name.

When his gaze came back to her, Joy's heart tripped.

Royce looked at her mouth. "Have you thought about it?"

"What?" she asked, knowing exactly what he meant.

"Me, kissing you." He drew closer and his hand slid to her back, his fingers dancing little circles over her spine. "Not here. Not now. But at some point before the afternoon ends, I'll have your mouth."

Her breath thickened and a sweet ache pooled low in her stomach. Such a tease. Well, two could play that game.

She put a hand on his biceps and lowered her voice. "I have." Her attention now snagged on *his* mouth. "A lot. So you should know my expectations are high."

"Good." Coming closer still, he breathed near her ear, "Always demand the best, Joy. Even from me."

Sensation washed over her—and then he stepped away, turning as Jack came up to them.

"All set?"

Paying no attention to adult antics, Jack held up the picture. "I messed up the *J*."

Royce examined it critically. "You know what? I think that gives it character. I wouldn't change a thing." To Joy, he asked, "Is there someplace safe I can put this until I'm ready to go?"

Still a little breathless, Joy indicated the corkboard where a lot of artwork got shared. "You could pin it there."

He looked down at Jack. "What do you think?"

Jack tried to look humble. "If you want to."

They went over to the board together. Royce bent his head to listen as Jack talked. Two males, one under four feet tall, his body narrow, his movements frenetic, and the other more than six feet of calm, carved strength.

It was a dangerous thing, seeing them together, liking how

they looked as they interacted. It'd be so easy to get caught up in the emotions of seeing her son so happy, knowing he enjoyed the attention and praise.

It was dangerous for Jack. Dangerous for her.

Her instinct, always, was to protect Jack from possible hurt and disappointment.

And yes, she wanted to protect herself, as well.

They had a good life right now, and it unnerved her to think of rocking the boat, changing the dynamic of the peaceful, contented existence she'd so carefully created. Yet Jack deserved more.

She did, too.

A kiss, the wild night Maris encouraged or more... Joy didn't know yet, but for now, she was open to all possibilities.

Royce stood back, talking to a man who'd brought three kids—a daughter and two sons—to take part in the fun. Seven other kids were there, too, creating a small, boisterous crowd. Most were rowdier than Jack, definitely louder, but Joy handled them with the skill of a veteran grade school teacher. The noise level alone was enough to make his brain vibrate, yet she took it in stride.

She praised some crazy-looking results, because most of these kids didn't have Jack's artistic bent. She gave directions on others, and assisted with some. Things that should have looked like miniature scarecrows turned out to be the stuff of nightmares.

Even sitting among other kids, Jack managed to be by himself. When it came to art, he was too contained, not at all the animated kid at the camp store the other day. Did Joy notice it, the way he created his own little world? Royce would have loved to see him run around the table once, knock over the glue or shout for attention. Instead, he kept his head down and worked.

Crazy, but at only five, the kid had an artist's soul. Every ounce of concentration was on his task.

Maybe someday he'd show Jack his mother's work. Royce inhaled a deep breath, let it out slowly and accepted that he wasn't ready for that yet. But soon.

At two p.m., Joy wrapped up the activities, promising the kids she had more fun lined up for them after dinner. Parents began to filter in to collect their children, scary scarecrows, falls wreaths and all. Jack looked up, saw things were ending and went back to work with renewed purpose.

Excusing himself from the camper, Royce strolled over to Jack. Around them, chaos ensued...but Jack either didn't notice, or he didn't care. His scarecrow, made from a toilet paper roller, *looked* like a damned scarecrow.

To the side of him, he'd also created a fall wreath. Both were colorful, neat and meticulously assembled.

Royce eyed the small chair, decided it wouldn't hold him and instead leaned over with one hand flat on the table. "Jack."

Brown eyes flashed up. "I'm almost done."

"I wasn't rushing you, but will it bother you for me to watch?"

"I don't care." He was already back to work, gluing a few more pieces of straw around the scarecrow's neck. When he finished, he held it up and scowled. "I got stuff crooked."

"It's a scarecrow. Things are supposed to be crooked." The kid took himself far too seriously. "And actually, it's pretty amazing. See the mouth? You drew on stitches."

"It looks like the one Mom put up there." He pointed to the front of the room where Halloween decorations clustered around the art supplies. Sure enough, a small, smiling scarecrow sat with fake, light-up jack-o'-lanterns.

"But most kids wouldn't have noticed that." On his fall wreath, he'd not only made some lopsided leaves to go on it, but he'd drawn the veins in the leaves. His eye for detail went

well beyond his age, even beyond the average adult's comprehension of art.

"When can we come to the drive-in?" With the scarecrow finished, Jack half crawled up into his seat and tilted toward Royce. "Could we go tonight? Will you play a movie for me? Can I get popcorn?"

Now here was the lively kid he remembered. "Pretty sure your mom wasn't planning any outings tonight." From what he understood of her schedule, they'd overlap; she'd still be working with kids when he'd be at the drive-in, starting the first movie.

"I'll ask her."

"She's been working, right? How about we help her clean up instead, and then when she's ready to visit, she'll let us both know."

It took some doing, but Royce convinced Jack to pitch in. Joy finished saying goodbye to all the guests, reminding them of the next activity planned, and after getting the last kid out, she closed the door. Her gaze sought Royce.

He liked the flush on her cheeks and the anticipation in her eyes. If ever a woman deserved to be thoroughly kissed, she did. Royce banked his smile and asked, "What can I do to help?"

She looked around. "If you don't mind, you could gather up the foam cups and put them in the trash."

"Sure thing."

Going to Jack's seat, she picked up his fall wreath. "Jack, this is wonderful."

Jack shook his head at Royce. "She always says that."

"She's your mom and she loves you. But I don't always say it, right? Heck, I barely know you, and I also think it's terrific."

Laughing, Jack began gathering up crayons.

Joy bent to kiss his cheek. "Thank you for helping, honey." She collected scattered paper scraps and headed to the kitchen.

The quiet, empty kitchen.

While doing his own share of picking up, Royce watched Jack. He was busy sorting crayons by colors, putting them in individual bins. It amused him, because the boy was *such* a little artist, right down to the need for color coordination.

Knowing he wouldn't get a better chance, Royce casually joined Joy in the kitchen. She had her back to him as she emptied the coffee grounds from the maker and rinsed it all in the sink.

After putting his own handful of trash in the bin, Royce came up behind her and nuzzled against her ear. She went perfectly still, her hands remaining in the sink.

With one hand, he moved her hair away from her neck, then brushed his lips over the sensitive skin there. "Jack is busy sorting, so we probably have one minute...and I don't want to waste it." He grazed his teeth over the soft skin along the column of her throat, followed by his tongue.

She melted back into him. "Royce."

Damn, that was a turn-on. He'd missed hearing a woman whisper his name so softly.

He had a few things to discuss with her, parameters that they needed to establish, but first...

When he reached around to gently clasp her chin, she hurriedly dried her hands and turned toward him. Her attention skipped to the door, and when she didn't see Jack, she met his gaze. Voice low and cautious, she said, "He switches gears pretty quickly so we should probably—"

Royce kissed her midsentence. No way in hell would he miss this scant opportunity.

Her lips softened, fitting to his. Keeping things slow and easy, the way a first kiss should be, he tilted his head and traced her bottom lip with his tongue, lightly kissed her upper lip, the corner of her mouth.

God, she tasted good, smelled good—all soft and womanly— and he had to concentrate to keep from moving too fast. More

than anything, he wanted to crush her close, take her mouth with his tongue and press his hips to hers so he could feel every inch of her.

Instead, he forced his hands to stay on neutral ground and reminded himself that her son was nearby.

Joy wasn't quite as restrained. Hands fisting in the material of his shirt, she pulled him closer until her breasts met his chest.

With a low sound of hunger, she opened her lips and deepened the kiss—exactly the way he'd wanted to.

# CHAPTER FOUR

Honest to God, Joy's urgency took Royce off guard—for about two seconds, after which he was right there with her. He tunneled his fingers into her silky brown hair and wondered how a woman this combustible had turned men away.

It had been far too long for him, too, and he couldn't get enough, kissing her deeper, hotter, their tongues stroking, heat spiking. He pressed a hand down her back, urging her hips in, aware of her accelerated breathing.

Whatever the reason, he was damned glad she'd chosen him now that she'd stopped denying herself.

Of course, that reminded him of the here and now. She wasn't only a woman, but a mother, too, and if Jack busted them she might not want to chance it again.

Smoothing his hand over her hair and shoulder, Royce eased up on the kiss by small degrees until he raised his head.

Her amazing eyes were more gold than green now, her cheeks flushed and her long hair mussed. "God, you're beautiful."

She smiled, and given that her lips were damp and full from kissing, it was an especially sexy look.

Because he badly wanted to kiss her again, it seemed prudent to take a step back. As he did so, Royce leaned away and glanced into the other room. Jack was stacking the bins, meaning he'd finish any minute.

"I enjoyed that."

Joy's husky voice drew him back around. "So did I, believe me."

Running his fingers over her hair, he tried to return it to some order. "If Jack wasn't nearby, I wouldn't have stopped."

"I wouldn't have, either," she said. "Thank you for understanding. He's never seen me with a man, other than in a friendly, distant way."

Royce finished with her hair and moved his fingers to her cheek, drawn by her softness. He wanted to touch her all over. Hopefully he'd get a chance soon. "You know I heard you talking to Maris."

Her gaze skittered away. "Yes."

"I'm sorry. I should have left, or walked on in and announced myself, but you took me by surprise. A nice surprise." Tilting up her chin, he brought her gaze back to his. "To say I'm flattered would be the understatement of the year."

Uncertainty sobered her expression. "But?"

"No buts. I just want to make sure we're on the same page."

Stepping out of reach, she leaned back on the counter and waited.

He wished he had more time to work into this conversation, but knowing a five-year-old loomed nearby, he was pressing his luck already. "You said you weren't interested in a relationship."

"I'm not. I have little enough free time as it is."

Nodding, Royce said, "I understand. I suspect I have more

time than you, but I'm still working on the drive-in, and once that's done, I have a ton of renovations to do to my house."

"So we're in the same predicament." With a nod of satisfaction, she clarified, "Interested, but unavailable for anything too time-consuming."

It wasn't the time, as much as the emotional commitment, that concerned Royce. The past few years had drained him to where he felt he had nothing left to give. Not anything meaningful.

Not what Joy and her son deserved.

After being so focused on a single purpose, he'd looked forward to regaining his autonomy, having the power to do what he wanted to do, when he wanted to do it, with no one to answer to. But along with anticipating the future, he'd also grieved and dealt with guilt. Those things combined had compelled him to start over in a new place, away from harsh, sometimes heartrending memories.

He needed to be there for himself again, before he could be there for anyone else.

So he gave Joy a small smile and asked directly, "Does that still work for you?"

"Perfectly." Her chin lifted a notch, but other than that, she showed no reaction. "Where did you buy your house?"

He didn't mind veering off topic, but planned to circle right back. "Next door to the drive-in. It's convenient and the price was right." Right meaning *cheap*.

The house had "good bones," and since he was more than adequate with his hands, he'd eventually enjoy working on it. For now, though, his priority was the drive-in.

"Nice. I know that neighborhood. It's quiet. Most of the people who live there are older."

He hadn't met the neighbors yet, so he couldn't comment on that. "I want to see you, Joy. You and Jack. If things progress to sex, I'm all in. If not, I can handle that, too." He'd still

enjoy her company, even without added benefits—though he was definitely rooting for more. "Like you, I'm not looking for anything too involved."

That pretty smile came again, this time almost mocking. "If I get a vote, things will definitely lead to sex." Her gaze skipped over him. "After all, the idea of sex is what first drew me to you."

Talk about conflicting emotions. What she said, and how she said it, made Royce burn with interest. And yet, it also insulted him. Could she not simply enjoy his company, as well?

"It's been a while since I was attracted to a man that way. The tricky part," she continued, "will be the when and where, but we can work that out later."

Royce rubbed the back of his neck. She might have been discussing her work schedule, for all the emotion she put into saying that. "Good to know." At least she'd agreed to sex. He'd work on the rest when and however he could.

Jack called out, "Mom?"

"Just a second, honey." Joy stared up at Royce. "I think a noncommittal relationship based on convenience works best for both of us. I have no expectations, and you shouldn't, either."

Damn. This blunt acceptance wasn't at all how he'd planned things to go, but since he'd brought it up, all he could do was nod.

"Good. We'll still see you tomorrow?" One eyebrow lifted. "I don't want to tell Jack if we're not getting together."

"We are." Royce studied her face, but whatever she felt, she wasn't showing it. "I could come by and get you both at five, if that works."

"Perfect."

Jack ran into the kitchen, carrying four markers. "These are dried up, and we're running out of red."

Joy said, "Maybe we'll have time to buy some new markers tomorrow, before Mr. Nakirk picks us up."

Eyes widening, the boy spun around to face Royce. "You're picking us up? Where are we going?" He jumped in excitement. "Will I get to see the drive-in?"

Jack had paint-stained fingers, a smudge of marker on his cheek and dried glue on his chin. At least, Royce hoped it was glue. "I'd planned on dinner and a trip to the drive-in. But if you need art supplies, I know the perfect place." He turned to Joy. "I'd be happy to show you both. Maybe make it four instead, to give us time?"

He knew he shouldn't push, definitely not in front of Jack, but the less enthusiastic she seemed, the more determined he felt.

Although she'd been plenty enthusiastic about that kiss.

Because Jack stood there, his gaze ping-ponging back and forth between them, or maybe to make a point, Joy stuck out her hand and said, "Sounds like a deal. Thank you."

Royce had no choice but to shake her hand like a business associate.

Jack whooped. At least *he* was happy about the plans.

Bending down, Royce shook his hand next. With the boy trailing him, a gigantic smile on his face, Royce retrieved the picture Jack had done for him, said his goodbyes and went out the door to make the walk up to the parking area.

From a distance, he watched Joy and Jack leave the lodge, circle around and go up a flight of outside stairs. Seconds later, they disappeared inside.

Wind whistled over the park. It would only get colder, and going up those stairs in snow or ice wouldn't be ideal, especially at night. If he put some thought into it, he might be able to think of a way to enclose them.

That would be overstepping in a big way and Royce didn't want to do that, but...he'd think on it.

On the drive home, he kept glancing at the painting on the passenger seat. Things had ended a little awkwardly, but overall,

he felt good about how the visit had gone. He'd met a few more people from the area, he and Joy had sketched the groundwork of a plan, Jack was happy—and even better, he hadn't thought about his past even once.

He did *now*, of course, but then, he never escaped it for long.

Glancing at the artwork again, Royce smiled. Irony was a son of a bitch. The first woman he'd really wanted in far too long, and her son was a guaranteed kick of nostalgia.

Joy felt a bit like a third wheel.

Several steps ahead of her, Royce listened as Jack exclaimed with enthusiasm over everything at the drive-in. He *loved* the popcorn machine. He especially *loved* the T-shirt Royce gave him, and he was horribly disappointed that the projection room didn't, in fact, have a projector. Instead, everything was computerized.

Her son was a different boy around Royce, and she'd watched him change right before her eyes.

They'd started their "date" with a lot of promise. Since Jack was playing in his room, he hadn't heard Royce knock. The second she'd opened the door, Royce had looked beyond her, saw they had a moment alone and bent to her mouth before she could even finish greeting him.

It was crazy how he affected her, but there at the top of her outdoor stairs where anyone walking by might have seen—and of course someone did—she'd leaned into him, her hands on his shoulders, her lips parted.

At least, that had been her response until the loud "Whoop" interrupted. She'd almost jumped away, but Royce's arm around her kept her from too much movement. With far more calm than she could muster, he'd glanced down, then called, "Hi, Maris."

"My bad. Didn't mean to interrupt." Grinning, she waved to them both, instructed, "Carry on," and strode away.

Snickering, Joy hid her face in his shoulder. "She's going to grill me later."

"Then I better give you something good to talk about." He'd nudged up her face and treated her to a slow, thorough kiss that left her breathing hard and hungry for more.

Lifting his mouth, he whispered, "Damn. Remind me not to start things I can't finish."

"I won't," she said, touching her fingertips to her tingling lips. "That was too nice."

"Nice?" He gave a mock frown. "If Jack wasn't bearing down on us, I'd try to earn higher praise."

Yes, she, too, heard her son's rapidly approaching footsteps, but still managed to say, "Hmm, how about scorching? Bone-melting?"

He leaned down to whisper, "My bone did not melt," and seconds later, as she stifled a laugh, and resisted looking at his lap, Jack joined them.

Chaos reigned as Jack jumped around, asking questions in rapid-fire succession, and thankfully oblivious to the steam in the air.

Joy took that moment to slip away for their jackets, and to calm her racing heart.

The trip to the art supply store was an eye-opener. Yes, she'd known Jack enjoyed drawing, but his face as he looked around at new and unfamiliar medium made her heart swell. Like a kid on Christmas morning, he took it in with wide, awestruck, *hungry* eyes.

Royce clearly had some knowledge of art himself, given how he schooled Jack on various canvases, different types of acrylic paint versus oil, chalks, special textured papers and even self-drying clay with a variety of modeling tools.

In contrast to the rambunctious way Jack had greeted Royce, he moved through the store with near-reverence. Using infinite

care, he'd feathered a touch along the bristles of a paintbrush, studied a set of soft chalks and examined the grain on a canvas.

While he'd been involved looking at the clay, Royce had quietly asked her, "Would you mind if I got him a few basics?"

Knowing she couldn't ask Jack to leave empty-handed, not when this was obviously his world, she said, "That's kind, but I can do it."

"You could," Royce acknowledged, "but I really want to."

Something in his solemn expression swayed her. There was sadness in that dark gaze, and though she couldn't begin to guess why, Joy knew it had something to do with art.

"All right, thank you. Just don't go overboard."

At that point, Royce had looked almost as eager as Jack. Together, the two of them chose a sketchbook, a set of paintbrushes and a very fine box of watercolors with a pallet.

It was a bit much, but she didn't have the heart to deny Jack... or Royce.

Of course her heart lifted at seeing them together. Royce was just so... Damn him, he was perfect. *With Jack.*

Patient, attentive, encouraging. He would make an incredible—

*No,* she firmly told her heart. *No, don't you dare even think it.*

It wasn't what Royce wanted.

It wasn't even what she wanted.

But God, she was such a mom. Royce's affection for her son did more to chip away at her reserve than flowers or gifts ever could.

Dinner had been the unique experience of watching her son and Royce further bond, mostly without her. He'd chosen a kid-friendly place to eat, but in the end, it hadn't mattered. Jack had carried that box of paint tubes in with him, almost like a favorite toy. Instead of playing any of the available games while they waited for their pizza, he'd asked questions. Endless questions.

And Royce had answered.

That is, until she joined in, asking, "Are you an artist, Royce?" He certainly knew a lot about it.

Mysterious shadows stole the easy smile from his face. "My mother was."

*Was?*

Before she could ask anything more, he promptly changed the subject to primary colors, explaining to Jack how to create his own secondary color shades and the impact white or black had on watercolors.

Her takeaway on their scintillating conversation? Don't be afraid of experimenting with color, but always go easy with black because it could muddy hues.

Also: anything too personal was off-limits.

So far, when it came to reengaging with a man, she scored a big fat zero. He preferred her five-year-old son's company to her own.

Oh, Royce was attentive. He kept a hand to her back as they left the restaurant...while Jack ran around to hold his free hand, instead of hers.

He ensured her comfort in his car, a newer Renegade...and then talked cars with Jack, explaining that he also had an ancient Chevy truck.

All in all, she was content to see Jack having such a great time.

As they toured the interior of the drive-in, Royce alternately answered Jack's questions, while also asking her about opportunities for holding events once the season ended. Possibilities included a classic car show, a Christmas bazaar and, as a goodwill gesture, a light show, since the main road brought drivers past the drive-in.

After they finished going through the concession, Royce asked Jack, "You know what's next?"

Still clutching that box of paint, Jack bounced on the balls of his feet and asked, "What?"

"Playground equipment." Around Jack's cheers, he said, "Let's go out and you can try it all while I talk with your mom. Then you can give me some recommendations."

When Jack raced away, Joy warned, "Slow down, please."

Jack reduced his run to a jog, going out the door ahead of them, but it didn't seem important when Royce looped his arm around her and urged her forward.

Near her ear, he said, "Hi."

After spending nearly three hours together, that was so ridiculous she laughed as they stepped into the brisk fall air. At almost seven o'clock, the sun slid low in the sky, prompting some of the security lights to flicker on.

Jack had already reached the gym equipment; he was close enough for her to see, but not for him to overhear.

With their shoes crunching on the gravel lot, the squeaking of Jack's swing cutting the quiet, she and Royce walked together.

It felt...intimate. His hand on her hip. The dusky sky. Her son so happy.

Intimate, like a budding relationship.

But it wasn't and she'd have to keep that foremost in her mind. Royce had made it perfectly clear that he was no more prepared for commitment than she was. Last night, she'd reminded herself that it was for the best. All she really wanted from Royce, all she needed, was the escape of sex. Hot, mind-blowing, satisfying sex.

Today, however, she had some doubts. Royce wasn't acting like a man anxious to get her naked, but he was very natural as a role model to her son.

"Not even a hello, huh?" His hand at her hip squeezed her closer and he lightly nipped her earlobe, touched it with his tongue, then kissed her behind her ear. "I'll have to think of a way to soften you up."

Oh, she was plenty soft. If the breath caressing her skin hadn't

done it, the feel of his mouth and the huskiness of his words would have. She'd gone years not even holding a man's hand, and now Royce had kissed her, touched her, lightly bit her ear...

She stopped and looked up at him. The dim light left secrets in his ebony eyes and that particular tilt to his mouth stirred her need. Thinking back on that earlier kiss... God, she wanted more.

If they were alone, she'd be all over him.

The swing squeaked—not that she'd forgotten Jack. Never that. But with her son so close, what did he want from her?

Ridiculously breathless, she whispered, "Hello, Royce."

"Yeah, that's better." Catching a long lock of her hair, he slowly eased his fingers along the length of it, letting his knuckles brush her shoulder, then her upper chest. "You seem pensive. Did Jack and I bore you today?"

She looked toward her son. He'd scampered off the swing and was climbing the ladder for the slide. "I haven't seen him this excited in a long time. He really enjoys your company." The second she said it, she feared it'd scare Royce off. A boy looking up to him, adoring him, probably reeked of a trap. It was certainly scary in her mind.

What if Jack got too attached? It would be awful to see him hurt when things inevitably ended.

Shaking her head, she said, "I'm sorry, I didn't mean..." Words failed her. How to explain? She was so damn rusty when it came to conversing with interested men.

Hugging her arms around her upper body, Joy warded off the evening chill, and gave it another attempt. "You were wonderful with him today, but I don't want him to get the wrong impression." There. That was frank but not unkind.

For a moment, they stood there in silence.

"Royce?" she whispered. "We were both up front about what this is—what it *will* be." And what it wouldn't.

"Right." He shoved his hands into the pockets of his jacket. "You asked me about my understanding of art."

Something in his tone wrenched at her heart. "It seemed like a difficult topic for you." She knew all about that. There were so many things she didn't discuss with others. "If I overstepped—"

"It's not that." His expression guarded, Royce stared toward Jack. "I don't particularly like talking about it, not yet, but..."

Unwilling to press him, Joy waited.

"I told you my mother was an artist." He popped his neck as if loosening tension. His jaw flexed. "A very successful artist actually. It's how she supported us. Even after she got dementia and would sometimes forget me, she remembered her love of art."

Joy didn't know much about dementia, but for his own mother not to recognize him? That would be wretched for anyone. Had Royce been her caregiver? Did he have siblings who had helped? A father?

He'd made it clear that he didn't want to get into a lengthy discussion, so rather than ask questions, she whispered, "I'm sorry."

Royce nodded his thanks. "To the day she died, she wanted to paint. Anything and everything." His mouth quirked. "She even painted the sheets in her room when she was too sick to get out of bed."

Feeling her heart break for him, Joy lightly pressed her hand to his solid chest, offering comfort. Beneath her palm, his heartbeat thumped steadily. "You feel an affinity to Jack because of that?"

He shrugged. "I recognized his talent." He glanced at her, a quirky smile in place. "I'm sure you did, too."

"I..." Guilt burned Joy's face. "Honestly, before Jack, I knew zip about kids. I wasn't the girl who babysat or wanted to hold other people's babies. I don't think I'd ever held a baby until Jack was born."

The quirk turned into an understanding smile. "Must have been a shocker when you found out you were pregnant."

"That's putting it mildly. I was scared out of my wits." Scared, and entirely alone. She started them walking again. The wind blew and she shivered. "All I know of kids is based on Jack. I've always appreciated his art and thought he was talented, but I didn't realize..."

Royce put his arm around her shoulders, hugging her closer. "Without any comparison, how could you know?"

"I've seen his art compared to other kids' at the camp. I noticed he has a fascination with color, and a singular concentration when he works."

"There's that, yes. Plus he also picks up on details most kids his age would miss. Eyelashes on eyes, four fingers and a thumb on hands. A neck instead of a head just sitting on shoulders." With laughter in his tone, Royce said, "Necks constitute a recall awareness of what he's seen. That's a lot of talent in a five-year-old."

"I'll make sure to carve out more time for him to paint. Unfortunately, I'm not artistic. Crafty, yes, but nothing that's really creative." She got most of her ideas from Pinterest and Facebook.

"What I know," Royce said, "I learned from Mom trying to teach me, and watching her create. Where most people had a dining room, we had an art studio." He glanced down at her. "Windows on two walls gave that room the ideal light."

"Well, you saw my home. We don't have a dining room to convert, or any available space." The eat-in kitchen was just big enough for a table and four chairs. "But I think for Christmas I'll get him an easel, and maybe you could suggest more supplies."

At the mention of the holidays, he grew quiet again. Joy wanted to smack herself. Of course that would be difficult for him if he'd only recently lost his mother.

She was about to overstep again, wondering if he had any other family, when he stopped walking.

His gaze sharpened. "Jack? Where are you going?"

Joy looked up in alarm. Jack had left the lighted area and was peering into the woods that bordered the property between the drive-in and the park. "Jack!" She hurried forward, aware of Royce right behind her.

"Something's in there," Jack said, going to his hands and knees. "I hear it crying."

"Back up," Joy ordered in her most stern, no-nonsense tone that demanded immediate attention. He could be hearing a feral cat, an enraged raccoon or... *"Right this instant."*

Surprised by her vehemence, Jack stood and took a step back—and the brush moved. Just as she and Royce reached him, they heard a whimper.

And something half crawled out.

"It's a dog," Jack yelled as he tried to wiggle free of Joy's hold.

"A puppy," Royce corrected. "You need to be real quiet so we don't scare it, okay?"

In an eager whisper, Jack said, "You gotta get it, Mr. Nakirk."

The light didn't quite carry this far, and all Joy could make out was pale yellow fur and floppy ears framing big dark eyes.

Royce knelt down and held out his hand. "C'mon, boy. I won't hurt you."

The dog limped forward.

"It's hurt," Jack cried, his whole body vibrating with tension and worry.

Joy hugged him closer, saying, "Shh."

"Can we keep him?"

Keep him? In their tiny apartment? Not possible. Jack had been asking for a dog forever, but hopefully she could appease him with art supplies for now.

At least those didn't shed fur, pee in the corner or require walks.

"He's not ours, honey."

"But he could be. *Please*, Mom?"

Joy patted his shoulder and said again, "Shh. You don't want to scare the poor thing."

The dog finally got close enough for Royce to touch it. "That's a good boy," he crooned, his voice soft and low as he stroked the puppy's head and over his back, urging him closer. "What do we have here, huh? Some brambles? Yeah, that's got to hurt, doesn't it, buddy?"

Unfair that Royce was good with her son *and* so incredibly kind to animals. How was she supposed to resist that?

Damn it, obviously she couldn't. "What can I do?" she asked. "Is he hurt?"

"It's too dark out here to tell." Carefully, Royce lifted the animal into his arms. The poor thing licked his chin in a show of gratitude, then looked worriedly at Joy and Jack.

She felt horribly helpless against his appeal, and desperate to somehow assist. "Why don't we take him into the drive-in so we can better see?"

"Good idea. Lead the way," Royce said, and when Jack started to run, he added, "*Calmly*. The little guy is already shaking."

Jack immediately slowed, but still got to the door first. He held it open, his bottom lip caught in his teeth as he watched Royce carry in the dog.

"It's bleeding," Jack breathed, his eyes round with worry.

"Just a little. I think that might be an old wound." Sending Joy a meaningful look, Royce asked, "Would you mind getting a few towels by the dryer, and maybe a wet one so we can see what we're dealing with?"

"I'll be right back." Seconds later, she returned to see both Royce and Jack sitting on the floor across from one another,

legs folded yoga-style. Royce still held the dog, softly whispering to it.

It had its face hidden under Royce's chin, and Jack was carefully pulling burrs from its fur.

"Right here, between us," he said to Joy, and then to Jack, "Remember, slow and quiet, okay?"

Eyes wide and unblinking, Jack nodded.

Joy arranged the towels, but held on to the wet cloth. She saw dirt and brambles in the dog's fur, but also a nasty nick on its front leg, close to its paw, with what looked like both dried and fresh blood.

Royce gently set the dog before him, all the while stroking it and speaking in soft, soothing tones. His large hands moved with care as he untangled pieces of a sticker bush from the dog's scruff and tail. Jack had gotten many of the burrs, but Royce also dislodged a nasty thorn in his hip. The dog whimpered constantly, then snuffled and licked where the thorn had been.

As quietly as she could, Joy gathered up the discarded brambles and burrs and took them to the garbage can, before returning to sit beside Jack.

When Royce glanced at her, she knew without words and handed him the wet hand towel. He tried to swab around the bloody area, to see the source of the wound, but the dog yipped and tried to lurch away, burrowing against Jack.

With tears welling in his eyes, Jack helplessly cuddled the dog.

"Easy, easy now. I know it hurts." For only a second, Royce seemed undecided. Then he let out a breath. "I need to run him to a vet. Do you know anyone?"

Joy shook her head. "Phoenix might, though. She and Coop have Sugar. I'll call her."

Sunday evening, of course, no vets were open. But Phoenix did know of an animal hospital that was open for emergencies

and she shared the number. Fifteen minutes later, they were all ready to go.

Royce wrapped the dog in a towel and stood. "It's getting late. I should probably run you home first—"

"But I want to go, too," Jack said, almost at the same time that Joy said, "We can stay and help."

Searching her gaze, Royce asked, "You're sure?"

"Positive." It wasn't like he could drive while holding the dog, and she wasn't sure the animal would come to her.

Being more familiar with Phoenix's directions, Joy drove and Royce sat in back with Jack, the puppy wrapped in towels on his lap.

Yes, this was definitely the strangest date she could have imagined.

Funny thing, though. As Joy pulled into the hospital, she knew she didn't want to be anywhere else.

# CHAPTER FIVE

Two hours later, Royce unlocked the front door to his small, messy house, reached in to flip on a light switch and then stepped back for Joy and Jack to enter.

Several things went through his mind. It was probably near, maybe even past, Jack's bedtime. He wished he'd tidied up the house more. And apparently he now had a dog.

The pup, which the vet guessed was a three-month-old Lab mix, slept in a box padded with the towels. After meds that made him loopy, his front leg was shaved around the injury, stitched and wrapped, and he'd been treated for several nasty things Royce didn't want to think about.

Stepping around Joy, he headed for the kitchen. "You can leave your coats on the couch. Turn on more lights if you want."

He heard her quietly talking to Jack. Shoes dropped—at least he thought they were shoes—and then Jack slid into the kitchen in his socks.

Royce leaned out of the kitchen to see her laying their jack-

ets over the arm of the couch. The shoes were set neatly by the front door.

At least his couch and chair were new, though the only end table was part of a folding tray set. No rugs. Temporary blinds on the windows. A small TV hanging on the wall.

Not exactly high style.

It wasn't a great first impression, but he hadn't had time for more than the barest necessities for comfort.

When Joy headed toward him, he said, "Sorry it's so barren. I have a lot I need to do yet. Tables, stuff for the windows, rugs... It's just that—"

"You've been busy with the drive-in. It's understandable, Royce. We all have to prioritize." As she walked, she took in the crown molding, the original hardwood floors, the glass doorknobs and the telephone nook. "Besides, your house is really nice. It has a lot of character."

Exactly what he'd thought before making an offer and buying it.

"It's way bigger than our apartment." Jack spotted his picture on the refrigerator and darted forward. "This is mine!"

The pup didn't stir. Royce hoped the poor little thing wouldn't be sick when he woke up. He set the box in the corner, to the side of the refrigerator, before turning to Jack. "I plan to frame it in my office, but haven't had a chance yet."

"You have your own office, too?" Joy smiled. "Now I'm jealous."

"The office is a converted third bedroom, that's all. The second bedroom is empty and I only have a bed in the master." Realizing Joy still held two bags, he took a big step forward and relieved her of them. "Sorry."

"Please, stop apologizing." Tipping her head, she studied him as he put them on the counter. "I'm glad we could help. After all, you've taken on the hardest part of things."

Right. A dog. Definitely not what he'd intended, but what else could he do? Jack had nearly cried when the vet explained the wound on the pup's leg. Somehow, probably on an old fence, the dog had been cut deep enough to cause a lot of pain. Untended, he might have lost the leg—and eventually died.

Joy had looked devastated at the news. Clearly her small apartment couldn't accommodate a puppy that would grow into a large dog.

After assuring Jack that the vet would make it okay, the boy had looked at him like he was Superman. With glassy eyes, Jack had said, "Good thing you got him, huh?"

Yeah. Good thing.

Rubbing the back of his neck, Royce looked at the dog, then at his kitchen. The vet claimed the pup would probably be groggy through the night.

So what would he do with him in the morning? There'd be follow-up appointments, and Royce had entire days where he'd planned to be at the drive-in working.

They were able to buy dog dishes, food, a collar and leash from the hospital, but tomorrow he'd get a real carrier and probably do some repairs to the fence around the backyard.

"What is it?" Joy asked. "Anything I can do?"

He shook his head. "The backyard... I was going to tear down the old chain-link fence, but now, I suppose I should keep it. That is, if it can be made safe." The fence was another thing he hadn't yet tackled.

On his knees next to the dog, Jack whispered, "He sure is pretty." Very lightly, he stroked the dog's ear. "He'll need a name."

Shit. Royce loved animals, but a dog was the very last thing he'd planned—right up there with a kid who tugged at his heart, and a woman who made him forget he *had* plans.

Joy touched his arm. In fact, she touched him often. Re-

cently in commiseration when he explained about his mother, and now, to draw his attention.

Both times that he'd kissed her, she'd clutched at his shoulders as if she felt the same, hotly sexual things he did.

He wanted her. Goddamn, he wanted her bad.

Yet today, much of his attention had gone to Jack. Such an engaging kid. Joy thought her son reminded him of his mother.

Actually, Jack reminded him too much of himself when he was a kid—minus the talent.

Quietly, so her son wouldn't overhear, Joy said, "If you need me to help with the puppy, just let me know." She stared up at him, green eyes tired but still beautiful. "The park is pet-friendly, and once Jack is in school, my mornings are flexible."

The urge to kiss her pulsed inside him. Her upturned face, the sincerity in her eyes, the sweetness in her offer, all drew him. Hell, everything about her drew him, including her dedication to her son.

Of course, accepting her help would only complicate things more and Royce knew he was already in too deep. Enjoying her company was one thing, but the rest of it...

He shook his head, but then heard himself say, "Appreciate it. I'll let you know." Damn it, not a good idea.

Withdrawing, she laced her fingers together and glanced around. "You'll put him here, in the kitchen?"

"Just until I get you and Jack home. Then I'll probably bring him into the bedroom with me. If he wakes up and needs anything, I want to know."

A heart-wrenching softness entered Joy's gaze. "You're a very nice man, Royce Nakirk."

"The nicest," Jack echoed, proving he'd been listening to them.

Hiding a smile, Joy went to the counter and began unload-

ing the bags. "I'll wash the dog dishes for you. Why don't you take the tags off the leash and collar?"

That would make more sense than wallowing in indecision.

It was a unique experience, stepping around a kid in his own kitchen, working together with a sexy woman. He finished before Joy, so he located a few unpacked boxes to block the kitchen in case the dog woke while he drove them home. He wouldn't be more than a few minutes, but still, he didn't want to take any chances.

Once he was done, Royce caught Jack eyeing fruit in the bowl. "You getting hungry again, bud?"

Jack's eyebrows went up and he said candidly, "That apple looks really good."

Grinning, Royce checked with Joy first and got her nod.

By the time they had everything ready to go, including food and water in the dog dishes on the floor, Jack had finished an apple and a banana and was starting to yawn.

"I've kept you too long."

"Actually, I've enjoyed it." She smiled as Jack leaned on the box, watching the dog with that same intent expression he usually reserved for art. "And so has he. Thank you for such a nice day."

"And for the art stuff," Jack added. "I'll paint you another picture when I get home."

"It's your bedtime, Jack. But you can paint him something tomorrow, okay?"

"*Mo-om,*" he complained, making the word into two syllables.

"We need to go, now. Get your jacket and shoes back on, please. And no complaining."

Like a boy sent to the gallows, Jack slowly rose and dragged across the kitchen to the living room.

It was all Royce could do not to laugh—until he realized he had her alone again.

He drew her against him. "Today didn't go quite as planned."

"Fair warning, Royce. Things that involve kids never do."

Her hair, light brown, long and silky, always drew his fingers. "Today was nice, but will I ever get to see you alone?" They had arrangements to make, and sooner would be preferable to later. He cupped his hand around her neck, using his thumb to tip up her chin. "I want to do more than sneak a kiss or two."

She drew in a shuddering breath and nodded. "Me, too." Her tongue licked over her lips; she took a peek at her son, then went on tiptoes to kiss him firm and quick. "Text me your upcoming schedule. We'll work it out."

Before he could register that heated promise, she slipped away. When he came out of the kitchen, he saw why. Jack was slumped on the couch, all but asleep, one shoe on and the other in his hand.

While she tended to Jack, Royce finished blocking the kitchen doorway. Tomorrow they'd compare schedules.

After sealing away his feelings for so long, there were now many things he wanted, many things he craved—all with her. Only her.

With any luck, they'd finally be able to make it happen.


"Nothing has worked out."

At that sorrowful voice, Daron looked up from his phone to where Maris and Joy were whispering at the counter.

Sitting toward the back of the camp store, Daron gave the women their privacy. Or at least he'd tried to. Joy sat with an elbow on the counter, her head propped on one hand. Maris, as usual, bustled around. Busy. Always busy.

The woman never slowed down—not for anyone or anything.

Although…she did pause now and then to whisper with Joy.

He studied her high ponytail and sun-kissed cheekbones, those soft, full lips that always flattened when he got too close. Her

long-sleeved T-shirt and well-worn jeans shouldn't have been sexy, yet the way they fit kept his gaze glued to her, imagining the body underneath.

That is, until Maris slanted suspicious brown eyes his way.

Quickly, Daron pretended to text, even smiled as if he'd read something amusing.

Truthfully, he had zero amusement right now. None.

Instead, he had frustration, with a capital *F*.

Aware of Maris, always aware of her, he knew when she shifted closer to Joy. "What does that mean? Haven't you two... sealed the deal yet?"

"Not even close," Joy lamented.

Sealed the deal? Knowing that had to be a euphemism for sex, Daron went still, his gaze blindly on his phone screen.

"You've been over to see Royce a lot this week."

"It's that puppy," Joy said.

"Uh-huh. So a big gorgeous guy has nothing to do with it?"

Joy laughed. "Well, that's a bonus, sure. But I'm worried that Jack is getting too attached."

"To Royce or the dog?"

"Both," Joy lamented.

"And you, hon? Are you getting a little attached, too?"

Daron blinked. Maris had never used such a sweet, understanding voice with him.

"Don't be silly." And even to him, Joy sounded defensive. "I've only been seeing him a little more than a week."

"That's long enough," Maris argued. "Definitely long enough to get better acquainted. Like *naked* acquainted."

It was all Daron could do not to frown at her. Far as he knew, Maris didn't have sex, most especially not with him. He was pretty sure...not with *anyone*.

He'd have noticed something like that, right? Another guy

hanging around, making moves? Or Maris wearing that look—
the look of a woman satisfied?

No, Maris worked from sunup to sundown, leaving no time
for *naked* acquaintances.

If she'd let him, Daron could work around her schedule. Instead, she was pushing Joy to have all the fun?

Maris continued, saying, "I thought the whole plan here was
to enjoy Royce."

Laughing, Joy replied, "So you could live vicariously, yes, I
remember."

Scowling, Daron wondered why Maris wouldn't just sign on
for the real deal. Give him a sign, any encouragement at all, and
he'd be there in a heartbeat.

"It's just that things haven't worked out. Royce has to be at
the drive-in every Friday and Saturday, and I need to be here
doing crafts. During the week would be better, but then Jack
missed school two days for his cold, and Royce had one catas-
trophe after another with the pup. Did I tell you he named that
sweet little dog Chaos?"

With a grin, Maris asked, "Should I ask why?"

"You can probably guess. After surviving outside, the dog is
used to going anywhere he wants. Royce is trying to house-
train him, but Chaos isn't catching on too quickly to the concept. Worse, he likes eating shoes. Royce thought he had it
covered by closing the closet, but while he was in the shower
the dog figured out how to slide it open. Royce lost a favorite
pair of sneakers."

Maris's husky laugh made Daron draw a shaky breath. Before
he accidentally sent a gibberish text to some unsuspecting contact, he deleted the meaningless letters he'd put on the screen
and opened Facebook instead.

"Sounds to me like you both deserve to get laid," Maris stated.
"Sort of as a reward for surviving all that."

Daron stared blindly at his newsfeed. Ha! Like *Maris* was a proponent of sexual activity? Not likely, not when she happily said no to his every suggestion. Every damn time he tried to get closer, she pushed him farther away.

He'd tried just spending time with her, being helpful, chatting as she did now with Joy—but she rejected that, too. Hell, she rejected that *more*, as if letting him close would be worse than casual sex.

And yet, he couldn't stop trying. Sure, he covered it now by joking more about sex, but if she'd only give him a little leeway, he felt sure they'd be a good fit.

In more ways than one.

Really, he'd turned into a masochist, trying to sweet-talk her even as she insulted him with a scathing look. Other women didn't disdain him.

But unfortunately, he didn't want other women. Not anymore.

Not for a while now.

"Tell you what," Maris said. "Sundays are my slower days, and those work for you and Royce, right? Let me watch Jack for you then. He likes hanging out here and he's never any trouble—"

"Maris." Joy touched her forearm, momentarily keeping her in place. "I couldn't do that. If you get any time to relax, you should take it for yourself."

"Pfft." Maris slipped away to remove cookies from the oven. The woman was forever baking.

Speaking louder from the kitchen, she said, "Jack can visit while I do a few chores. He has a favorite coloring spot, you know, right by a window so he can see the lake. I'll even print out some neat coloring pages for him." She came back around the corner, a slight frown in place. "That is…unless you're uncomfortable leaving him with me?"

"Of course not!" Joy protested. "You're always terrific with Jack."

"Well, I know you're protective," Maris said, without her usual conviction, "so I'll understand if you'd rather find someone else."

"It's not that, I promise." Joy drew a finger around the top of her coffee cup. "You and I have gotten closer lately." She hesitated. "We're better friends now, right?"

"Good friends, definitely. I wouldn't live vicariously through just anyone."

When Joy laughed, Maris glanced at Daron again, almost like a dare.

Daron didn't look away. He held her gaze until she frowned. Teasing her, he slowly smiled…and got to his feet.

"So," Maris said quickly. "I'll watch Jack on Sunday."

"But I don't want to take advantage of our new friendship, and what would we do with the dog? If Royce leaves him alone, he might destroy the whole house."

Before Maris could speak, Daron plopped down next to Joy and said, "How about I contribute to the cause?"

As if she'd just remembered him, Joy jumped. She looked at him with caution, maybe trying to decide how much he'd heard. "How would you do that?"

"I'll stick around Sunday, too, and keep an eye on Chaos. I'm good with animals," he added, before Maris could refuse him. "Better than good actually. My uncle used to train dogs, and when I was a kid, I sometimes helped."

"That sounds like fun," Joy said. "I love animals, but my family never had pets when I was growing up, and then I had Jack and, considering where I live, up a flight of stairs, a dog never seemed like a good idea. Jack adores that puppy, though, so I'm sure he'd enjoy visiting with you both." She turned back to Maris. "If you're positive you don't mind?"

Put on the spot, Maris said, somewhat through her teeth, "I'm already looking forward to it."

"Me, too." Daron couldn't quite remove the triumph from his tone. For once, he'd managed to outmaneuver her, and it was for a good cause. "I'll check out the dog's temperament and then teach Jack some simple commands to practice with him."

"I think Royce would appreciate the pointers, too. Right now, he can't leave Chaos alone for a minute. The dog goes with him everywhere, even the grocery store."

"Then that's decided." To keep from pushing his luck, Daron stood again. "In fact, I was heading out to see Royce. I'll talk to him about the dog."

Maris folded her arms and gave him a look. "Why are you seeing him?"

"What's that?" Damn it, he hadn't expected her to ask.

"You and Royce. What's up with that?" After a meaningful glance at the clock, she tucked in her chin to make her expression stern. "It's Friday. You're usually finishing up work so you can be on your way to a hot date."

Not as true as she might think, but then, he'd allowed her to go on believing it rather than have her know that he spent most of his free nights thinking about her.

After a second of mental scrambling, Daron came up with a truth. "With the campers thinning out, I have less to do so I already finished." And like a glutton for punishment, he'd gravitated to Maris, though he hadn't realized that she and Joy would have such a fascinating conversation.

It struck him funny then.

He'd known Joy as long as he'd known Maris. Both women had been off-limits, in part because he worked with them, but mostly because they both made it clear they weren't interested.

No problem with Joy. He'd been more than happy to go the platonic route with her.

But Maris? Everything she did and said sizzled with underlying emotions and he wanted her. Maris wanted him, too—he felt it in his bones—but for whatever reason she *did* refuse him.

And he would never pressure any woman, so he'd turned his attention to joking instead—and annoyed her in the process.

Getting back to her question, Daron rolled a shoulder. "Royce had asked about a few tools to borrow. I'll go through the maintenance building to see what I can find, then take the stuff over to him."

"I need to get going, too." Joy slid off the stool and gathered up her purse. "It's time for me to get Jack from school." She paused, smiling at Maris, then at him. "Thank you both. Really. If I can ever return the favor, please let me know."

She already had, by giving him the opportunity to spend time with Maris under different, better circumstances. With Jack around, Maris couldn't give him hell—and he couldn't come on to her. Not overtly, anyway.

They'd be forced into neutral ground, and that had to be a good thing. "You're welcome, hon. Anytime."

The second Joy walked through the doorway, Daron felt it. A ratcheting up of awareness. Throbbing sexual tension.

His own heavier heartbeat.

He was now alone with Maris.

Neither of them spoke. He still stared at the door, giving himself a moment to think.

After he managed to plaster on a smile, he turned to her.

Ugh…not good. Her crossed arms tightened and her eyes narrowed. Over the years he'd learned to read Maris's many moods, and this one proclaimed he was in the doghouse.

"Problem?" Maybe if he played dumb…

"You *know* what the problem is."

Yeah, he did. Pretending an exaggerated wince, he leaned on the counter. "Well, two things can be true, right? Yes, I manip-

ulated that situation just a bit so I could visit with you." Prefer-
ably without her scowling at him the entire time.

"Daron…" She made his name an exasperated groan.

"*But.*" He let that sink in, because he did have a caveat. "I like
Joy, too, you know. You don't have exclusive interest in seeing
her loosen up a little."

Miraculously, her expression softened. She even dropped her
arms as she sighed. "Okay, so you're also her friend."

"And you know Joy, so you know that took some doing.
Friendly, yes. She always is. But accepting me as a real friend?
She's…cautious." That seemed like as good a word as any.

"Same," Maris said. "She's only recently opened up to me."

"About sex." Daron nodded as if that made perfect sense.
"Maybe we should be thanking Royce for creating the change
in circumstances."

Her lips lifted into a grin. "Maybe."

"I like seeing her happier. Plus Royce is a great guy. Jack sure
adores him."

"Whoa." Leaning down, Maris crossed her arms on the counter. "Don't get ahead of yourself."

The words hit his brain but he didn't quite follow, not with
Maris that much closer to him, her breasts sitting on her crossed
arms, plumped up in an impossible-to-ignore way. What his
brain did was conjure an image of her in that exact posture, but
maybe with a low-cut sweater on instead of her usual, no-nonsense crew neck top. Something that would show some cleavage.

Or more.

Naked would be good, too. If he ever got her to say yes, he'd
reenact this exact scenario, just to feed his muse.

God, he had it bad when his imagination with Maris was better than reality with anyone else.

To cover for his male-brain deficiency, he said, "What does
that mean?"

"Joy doesn't want to get locked down with anyone, and from what she's said, neither does Royce. She just wants to live a little again."

Of all the... Daron snorted. "Yeah, right."

"She deserves to enjoy herself," Maris stated with conviction. "Not only as a mother, but as a woman."

"Couldn't agree more. Every woman deserves that." He knew she'd caught his point when her gaze shifted away. "But I also overheard the two of you talking."

In clear complaint, Maris muttered, "There's an awful lot of that going on lately."

Daron grinned. "Maybe if there weren't so many fascinating discussions happening to catch our attention, the men wouldn't stop to listen."

She gave him that one, saying, "It has been fascinating, hasn't it? The change in Joy is incredible. I nudged her, yes, but she was already headed in the right direction."

From what he'd heard, Maris was doing more than nudging, but Joy didn't seem to mind. "They're already involved. If they're saying they aren't, they're just fooling themselves."

Maris rolled her eyes. "I know you're the expert on detached relationships—"

"Wait, what?" Daron was far from detached when it came to her.

"But you can't speak for Joy or Royce."

He let the first part of that go and said instead, "Have you *seen* them together?"

She shrugged. "You know, women can..." Her mouth closed.

Oh, but he knew what she'd been about to say, so he finished for her. "Women can enjoy sex for the sake of sex. I'm aware."

"Of course you are."

The fact that she laughed after saying it didn't take the sting

from the words. "More importantly," he asked, "are *you* aware of it? Because from what I can tell, you haven't—"

She smashed her fingers over his mouth, then lowered her voice in another warning. "Don't pretend you know me, Daron."

Yeah...so. Her hand on his lips smelled like fresh sugar cookies, and just the fact that she touched him, touched his *mouth*, caused his balls to clench. He considered options for all of a split second, then for another second he tried to talk himself out of it—to no avail. He gave in and prodded the seam of her first two fingers with the tip of his tongue.

Her eyes flared, warmed, and she snatched her hand away. "Did you just *lick* me?"

That kind of talk wasn't helping his balls to relax. "Yeah." Shit. That sounded like a feral growl so he cleared his throat and tried again, striving for indifference. "You touched, I reacted."

For the first time in forever, deep pink washed her face.

A blush. On Maris? Oh, now that was interesting.

She looked him over, calculating...something. "So you're saying if I touch you again—" she reached out one finger to lightly prod his shoulder "—I can expect...what?" Proving she had a torturous mean streak, she whispered, "Another lick?"

Full. Blown. Boner.

That's what she could expect. He resisted the urge to clear his throat again. "I aim to please."

"Wonderful. Then please be on your way so I can get back to work."

Such a cruel, cruel woman. Daron caught her hand before she'd completely straightened. "Maris."

She gave him a look so sultry he felt singed. "Daron?"

Of its own accord, his thumb drifted over the smooth, sugar-scented skin of her wrist. "Gotta admit, I like it when you tease me."

She gave a playful shrug. "It's payback, because you're always teasing me."

"Flirting, more than teasing. It's a habit now."

"A bad habit," she pointed out.

"Oh, I dunno." She wasn't pulling away, so Daron slid his hand up her forearm in a featherlight caress, until he reached her upper arm just above her elbow. The cotton T-shirt was soft, but not like her skin. "I can't believe anything with you is bad, although I know I'd enjoy it more if you were just a little more receptive."

"But then, would I enjoy it?"

*Such a loaded question.* He looked into her eyes and made a heated promise. "I'd make damn sure you did."

Her lips parted. Better still, her gaze dropped to his mouth. Daron held his breath.

"You're younger than me."

Not at all what he'd expected. "A couple years," he said, dismissing the age difference. "It's nothing."

"Six years," she countered. "With a decade of conflicting perspective added in."

"Perspective?" He'd rather talk about licking, but since she brought it up... "What do you mean?"

"Outlook. Attitude." She came closer, her words going breathless. "Priorities."

What did she know of his priorities? He was about to ask when she closed the space between them, putting her mouth to his.

Oh, hell, yeah. Daron nearly groaned aloud. After wanting her so long, a single kiss equaled a massive accomplishment. She wanted to talk about priorities? She'd been a priority to him for longer than he wanted to remember.

Now that she finally wanted him, too, he wasn't about to let her get away.

Catching the back of her neck under the fall of her ponytail, Daron kept her close while they fell into a hot, openmouthed, hungry kiss.

God, she tasted good, even better than he'd ever imagined. And this close, various scents filled his head. Sugar, yes. Maris was forever baking for the camp store customers and the employees. Feminine warmth, too, because damn it all, that warmth had a fragrance and it intoxicated him.

In contrast, he picked up the scents of lemons from her shampoo, and something floral in her lotion. All combined, it equaled Maris, a fantasy come to life.

He wanted closer. He wanted every part of her against every part of him.

Damn the counter between them.

And damn the open front door that meant anyone could walk in.

Knowing he had to do this right, that he had to consider Maris and all the things that mattered most to her, Daron lightly cupped her shoulders and started a slow retreat.

A nip to her bottom lip. A lick to her upper. A kiss to the corner of her mouth and then her chin.

She wouldn't want to be caught making out over the counter where she served customers. More than anyone he knew, Maris lived and breathed her work. She had a reputation and never, not in a million years, would he want it to feel tarnished because she got busted fooling around with him at work.

It was one of the harder things he'd done in the last decade, but he gradually ended the kiss.

"Mmm," she murmured, eyes still closed, body slightly swaying and her breath heavy. "That was perfect."

*Perfect.* Yeah, exactly the description he would use, because *she* was perfect. "We should try this again," he suggested, his

voice low and deep. "Maybe in a place where we're guaranteed some privacy."

Smiling, she slowly opened her heavy eyes. Through kiss-dampened lips, she whispered, "Maybe."

He needed no more encouragement than that. "Maris—"

"But not tonight." She licked her lips, and managed to clear her gaze. "Not even this weekend."

Well, hell. How long did he have to wait? "What are we talking here?"

Drifting her fingertips through his hair—something she'd never done before—she wore a look of barely banked curiosity.

Daron had the urge to smooth his hair back down. He rarely did more than a quick combing of his unruly mop, followed by smashing on a ball cap.

Given her touch, he was glad he'd skipped the hat today.

"A few things, Daron."

*Anything.* Trying not to sound that anxious, he replied, "Yeah?"

"You're tempting."

*Hell, yeah.* He lifted his brows, waiting.

"But I've been focused on…other things for most of my life. I have a set of rules I follow, and they don't include getting involved with someone like you."

He wasn't cut out for too many rules. "What do you mean, someone like me?" Was she still hung up on the age thing? Ridiculous. He was twenty-five, not eighteen.

She glanced toward the open door, making him aware of voices approaching. "Customers are coming."

"Now wait a minute! You can't leave me hanging." Were they going to happen or not?

"I'm sorry. Really." She touched his hand in a gesture of sincerity. "Rule number one is never ignore the job, and I'm about to have customers."

For a woman like Maris, would he ever come first?

"Let me think about things and I'll get back to you." After patting his hand, she retreated to put Joy's coffee cup away and wipe off the counter.

Was he really going to feel insulted? He'd been aware of her for years. He'd wanted her forever. She knew that, and damn it, she wanted him, too.

And yet, after that kiss, she needed more time to think?

Yes, apparently he felt insulted. Straightening away, Daron waited until she got close again, then said, "You do that."

His indignation only made her grin. "Relax. We'll both still be here Monday. We'll talk then."

Why did he have his doubts? "If you say so."

Now she outright laughed. As two campers strolled in, she leaned closer to say, "We promised Joy we'd watch Jack on Sunday, along with a rowdy puppy, so whatever you're thinking or feeling, put a lid on it for now."

Call him easy, but he liked this new casual vibe on her. "How am I supposed to do that?"

She winked. "Let the anticipation build. That's what I plan to do."

With that parting remark, she greeted the campers, and happily took their orders for hamburgers.

She seemed unaffected, while he was anything but.

Walking out, Daron had to wonder how his ingenious plan to infiltrate her space with a kid and a dog as allies had somehow morphed into one more way for Maris to torture him.

# CHAPTER SIX

It was awkward, Joy thought, having others know her intentions for Royce. Maris was one thing; she'd enjoyed having a woman to talk to, to share her most intimate thoughts.

But Daron? He was everything she wasn't—carefree, openly sexual, free.

Even thinking it gave her a twinge, because it seemed like she resented Jack when nothing could be further from the truth. It gave her pangs to think of leaving him with Maris even for an evening. An early evening. She'd literally only be gone a few hours.

Stolen time with Royce... Did *he* know what she intended?

Joy hoped so, because she intended sex, *tonight*, while the opportunity presented itself.

If she had to wait any longer, she just might go nuts.

Skipping ahead of her, Jack occasionally stopped to pick up rocks that caught his eye. One streaked with pink, another smooth as a robin's egg, another coal black.

How had she never noticed his artistic eye?

"Look at this one, Mom!" He held up a dirt-streaked hand with the small rock displayed on his palm.

Joy looked, but to her, it was just a rock, like all the others in the gravel lanes. "Very nice."

He lifted it toward the sun to study it, and then asked, "How far do you think I can throw it?"

She grinned. Being a little boy took precedence over art, apparently. "We'll go down on the shore and see. But we have to make it quick."

When he started to run ahead, she cautioned, "Don't get your feet wet!"

At a slower pace, Joy followed, enjoying the feel of the sun on her face and the scent of fall in the air. It was a day for new experiences, fresh excitement, and she couldn't keep the smile off her face.

She'd arrived a few minutes early so she'd have a chance to talk to Maris before Royce got there with Chaos. Maris had her number, and Joy trusted her to call if she needed to, but... for her own peace of mind, she wanted to go over things again.

A dark sedan caught her eye. Sleek, shiny, obviously expensive and parked where it shouldn't be, blocking in the golf carts used only by employees.

As a single mom living off an RV resort's employment, pricey transportation had no relevance to her.

But she'd come from money, and she knew money when she saw it.

The new model Bentley would cost more than most people made in an entire year. More than some people's houses.

Dread throbbed like a live thing inside her, making her mouth dry and her stomach churn.

Daron, who'd been standing in the camp store doorway, spotted her and strode out. He looked grim and that bothered her even more.

She knew. Of course she did. Time away hadn't made her dumb, but God, it had numbed her to the hurt—a hurt that came washing back with the force of a tsunami.

Jack. She sought him out on the shore, watching him use all his might to throw that rock out into the cold lake. He was her world and she wouldn't let anyone, *anyone*, hurt him.

When Daron reached her, she grasped his hands. "Jack. Can you watch him for me? I don't want him..." *To face whatever I'm about to face. To meet the people who don't love him.*

The people who didn't want him.

Daron nodded. "You got it, hon." He hesitated. "You know who it is?"

"No." She inhaled deeply through her nose, drawing in calming purpose. "Not specifically." But she had a good guess, and she knew whoever it was would only bring heartache.

Daron worriedly searched her gaze. "She says she's your mother."

Worst suspicions confirmed.

For a second, Joy had to close her eyes. What could have brought her here now? How had her mother even found her? No, Joy didn't keep her location a secret, but neither had she been in touch with her family, not in six long years.

Not since they'd disowned her.

What if her father had died? He was ten years older than her mother, but last she knew he'd been in good health.

He'd allowed her mother's decision, but Joy couldn't say that he'd actively participated in it. He never really did. All her life, her father had been busy. Busy with work, busy with socializing. Busy managing his fortune.

He was kind to her, and he'd sometimes enjoyed showing her off. She couldn't recall him ever forgetting a birthday...and yet, they hadn't been close. After the last big blowup with her mother, she'd seen sympathy in her dad's eyes.

Well. There'd be no sympathy from her mother, so she may as well quit stalling. Joy worked up a strained smile. "Guess I should see what she wants."

He didn't let her go. Instead, he drew her into a tight hug, surprising her with the unfamiliar gesture. It took her a second, and then Joy returned the embrace, drawing strength from his friendship.

"Thank you," she whispered as she pulled back.

He nodded. "It's what friends do. Remember that, okay?" With one last reassuring look, he headed off for Jack.

Grateful, so very, very grateful, Joy got her feet moving and walked, as gracefully and unhurried as she could manage, into Summer's End.

Maris caught her eye the second she entered. She, too, wore a false smile. "There you are." Circling out from behind the counter, she said, "Your mother has come to visit."

Joy nodded, not yet looking in that direction. Unable to make herself do it.

"Coffee? A cola?" Maris got closer and whispered, "What can I do?"

How? Joy wondered. How did these amazing people know this was difficult for her? Was it intuition, her mother's cold persona or did they simply know her well enough, despite her lack of sharing in the past, to see it for what it was?

Honestly, the tension in the air was as thick as soup.

Maybe it was just that hard to miss.

"A cola," she said to Maris, meeting her eyes and managing a wan smile to let her know it was okay. "Thank you."

"You bet." Maris's long ponytail bounced as she headed off to get the drink.

Girding herself, Joy turned and there in a booth was her mother. The set of Cara Vivien Reed's mouth showed her disdain. Back ramrod straight, she sat slightly forward as if afraid

that resting against the plastic seat might somehow infest her. She looked the same as she had so long ago, the same disapproving manner and impeccable appearance. She'd be sixty now, but she hadn't aged a day.

That was a perk of the wealthy: the best dieticians and cooks, yoga instructors, personal cosmetologists and stylists to provide an ever youthful appearance.

The one thing that had changed? Her mother looked...tired. It only showed a little, but Joy saw it just the same.

Standing in the aisle, just behind Cara's shoulder, was a suited man who likely served as driver and bodyguard. He was new to Joy, yet the position was familiar. Her mother had always traveled with security.

So pretentious.

Never in her entire life had Joy known her mother to actually *need* protection. So much of what she did was for effect, from the house with more rooms than they could ever use, to the designer clothing that didn't look at all comfortable and the jewelry specifically created for her, to the fake friends she chose and the family she...thrust aside.

A fatherless grandson, regardless of how passé that thinking might be, didn't fit the illusion of perfection through privileged wealth.

Feeling contrary, Joy smiled at the driver and asked, "Would you like something to drink? Maris makes the best coffee ever. Or a cola?"

Startled that she would speak to him, the man shifted his alert stance. "No, ma'am. Thank you."

Ignoring that, Joy turned and said to Maris, "Another cola, okay? It had to have been a long drive to get here. Just put it on my tab."

Her mother tipped her chin. "Are you deliberately wasting my time?"

Joy replied, "Yes?" and then accepted two drinks from Maris.

"Mrs. Reed," Maris said with absurd deference, "are you sure you wouldn't like something?"

She eyed the plain glass and plastic straw. "No, thank you."

To Joy, Maris whispered darkly, "Maybe I should go get one of the guys?"

"I'm fine, I'm promise. This is nothing new." She hesitated, then admitted, "I'm glad you're here, though. That's enough."

With a crooked smirk, Maris said, "It's my place. I'm *always* here, and just so you know, I've thrown out bigger guys than that dude."

Joy chuckled at the visual that leaped to mind. "I believe it."

"You, however, would have to tangle with your mother." Leaning in closer, Maris whispered, "I'm not getting anywhere near that one."

Understanding that sentiment only too well, Joy nodded. "Let's hope it doesn't come to that."

Maris winked and headed back to the counter, which meant Joy couldn't stall any longer. Drawing a breath, she approached the booth, again without haste, and handed the cola to the driver. He had no choice except to take it, his gaze skirting down to her mother.

Cara gave him a small nod and dismissed him.

How had she ever belonged to that world? Joy shook her head with a small laugh and took the liberty of sitting across from her mother. Elbows on the table, her chin in her hands, she said, "You've caught me at a bad time. I have an appointment in just a few minutes." *An appointment with a big, gorgeous, kind man who will hopefully take me to bed today.* "Is there a reason you've called?"

"Your grandmother Reed passed away."

Shock swept away Joy's feigned indifference. She searched her mother's stern expression. "You're serious?"

"Your father's mother. And of course I'm serious. It's hardly a joking matter."

*Grams.* Throat going tight, Joy thought of the bold, irreverent and sometimes silly grandma she'd adored. Not long after she'd gotten pregnant with Jack, Grams had suffered a severe stroke and it changed everything. Joy had still visited her, but it wasn't easy, not with nurses always around her and the acrimony in her family. Grams was just as smart, just as caring, but she had so much difficulty expressing herself that visits almost seemed to frustrate her. After her family disowned her... Joy never went back.

Oh, she'd wanted to. She'd thought about her grandmother many times, but she'd been too busy surviving, too determined to find a way to support herself and her baby. Too busy putting distance between herself and her mother.

Suddenly those excuses didn't suffice.

Guilt was a terrible thing, but Joy swallowed it back, determined not to let her mother see her pain. "When?"

"A few months ago."

Her mouth nearly dropped open. *Months?* And no one had cared enough to tell her? That said a lot. Too much, really— none of it a surprise.

As if her mother had read her mind, she gave a slight, defensive shrug. "Since you walked away from your family, I wouldn't be here now except that it appears your grandmother left you an inheritance."

Joy reacted to the first part of that statement with a gasp of outrage. "You *told* me to leave. You said I wasn't your daughter anymore."

"Well, you didn't exactly fight to stay, did you?"

Of all the... Had her mother wanted her to beg? Why would she bother when she knew her mother so well? Cara Reed never retreated.

Arching one carefully drawn brow in censure, her mother pushed a crisp business card forward. "There are papers to sign, of course. You need to meet us at the attorney's office Monday morning. The date and time are noted, as a reminder."

Staring at the linen card without touching it, Joy's thoughts scrambled. Jack had school on Monday. Any attorney her grandmother used would be at least two hours from here, closer to where her parents lived.

They'd have to reschedule.

However, she'd discuss that with the lawyer, not her mother. The real dilemma was figuring out what timing would work for her. She'd need the better part of the day just for traveling back and forth. And if the meeting took too long? She wouldn't be back in time to get Jack. Yet taking Jack with her was not an option.

She didn't know how she'd work it out, but she wasn't about to share the difficulty of her circumstances with her mother. Even now, after delivering that awful news, she knew Cara watched her for signs of weakness.

"Have your...*circumstances* changed?"

Stumped by the abrupt question, Joy lifted her gaze to her mother. Her circumstances seemed pretty clear. After all, her mother had found where she lived. "What do you mean?"

Brows beetling, Cara clarified, "The child."

Dear God. Her mother didn't even know that she'd birthed a son—*her grandson*. Yet she thought...what? That Joy had at some point changed her mind about having him? That she'd left her family and everything familiar just to be difficult?

No, she'd done that for Jack, and she'd do it all again in a heartbeat.

"If you count being a mother a change of circumstances, then yes."

Her mother sucked in a breath, her expression unreadable.

"You knew that's what I always intended." Joy's hands tightened of their own accord, now fisted on the booth top. How dare her mother come here and disrupt her peace? Rage pressed against her composure. Resentment boiled up, churning with hurt.

And then Joy felt it, felt *him*, and she shifted in her seat to see the door.

Royce stood there, taking up a lot of space, his direct gaze calmly evaluating the situation.

Joy saw the moment he made up his mind. The intent showed clearly in his dark shark eyes, in his purposeful stride as he came to her.

Was this good or bad?

She frantically tried to decide. Yes, his presence helped to order her emotions, but as Joy hurriedly stood to greet him, she badly wished him away from the venom her mother would spew.

"Royce," she said, trying to keep her tone light despite her anxiety. "I can join you in just a—"

"Who," her mother's sharp voice demanded, "is this?"

Joy closed her eyes. She wasn't in time. Keeping her back to her mother, she tried to think. "No," she whispered, telling herself not to engage.

Undeterred, her mother stood, too. "Is this the man you allowed to use you? The one who ruined your life?" Each question cut a little deeper. "The one who left you saddled with a—"

Whirling to face her, Joy snapped, "*Don't say it.* Don't you *dare* say it." Nostrils burning with her fast breaths, her eyes glazing with furious tears, she pointed at her mother. Her hand shook as scalding rage burned through her.

She would not allow *anyone* to insult her son.

Joy had gladly stayed away from all of them to protect Jack. To insulate him from their poison. She would not tolerate her

mother showing up so many years later with the same hateful agenda.

Royce moved closer. She felt the heat of his body along her back. Not a bodyguard, certainly.

But something so much better.

Royce offered silent support, and the generous gesture meant the world to her.

Drawing a slow breath, Joy lowered her arm…and lifted her chin. "No one ruined my life. To the contrary, I love the life I have now."

"So." Her mother breathed harder, too, her narrowed gaze going over Royce. "Is he the father, or just another mistake about to happen?"

Royce shifted—and released a short, soft laugh of pure amusement.

Laughing? He was laughing at her mother's taunt?

True, it was absurd, but…he wasn't insulted?

He laughed again, more a snicker that he couldn't control, and that somehow zapped the tension from Joy's body.

Somewhere behind her, Joy heard Maris's not-so-subtle "Ha!" and suddenly everything was easier.

She could relax her shoulders. She could draw a deep, smooth breath.

These fun, quirky, supportive people were in her life. People who accepted her, faults and all, instead of judging her.

Blinking back tears of appreciation, Joy picked up the card from the tabletop. While her mother glared, she said, "Thank you for bringing this to me. I'll get in touch with the attorney."

The dismissal hung there in the air.

There'd been no polite greeting for her. No introductions to her friends. Joy wasn't about to gift Cara with a nice farewell.

Her mother left no room for anything nice.

Like a bad actor in an absurd performance, Cara overplayed

her lines, ruining the impact of the delivery. Now if Joy could just get her away from the park before she met Jack, the visit could be chalked up as a blip in her otherwise wonderful day.

Not really tragic.

Not *too* devastating.

It felt good to know she'd grown beyond her mother's realm.

After grabbing her clutch purse, her mother glanced around the room. "This is exactly what I warned you about. I told you this is where you'd end up, but you didn't listen." Her attention went over Joy, and she shook her head. "I should have known better than to think you'd changed."

With a gentle smile, Joy said, "I certainly knew you hadn't."

The dig hit home, and Cara reacted as if she'd been slapped. For only a single heartbeat, Joy saw hurt in her eyes.

Then, with a lot of indignant fanfare, her mother departed, the poor bodyguard hurrying ahead to lead the way as if he feared some heinous danger lurked between the camp store and the lakeshore.

No, the only thing out there was...

Crap. Joy pushed past Royce and rushed to ensure her son wasn't anywhere near. She wouldn't allow her mother to see him, to possibly slight him in some way.

She paused in the doorway, frantically searching, but she didn't see Jack anywhere.

Royce put his hand to her back. "Daron took him over to the scuba shack with Chaos. They're playing."

Ah, so Daron had known there was trouble and he'd been a true friend by removing her son from the scene. Relief and gratitude made her knees weak.

Suddenly depleted, Joy dropped a shoulder against the door frame and released an exhausted breath. "She still knows how to suck the oxygen out of a room."

His hand smoothed up and down her spine. "You held your own."

Barely, and now of course Royce would want an explanation. An explanation beyond what he'd just witnessed.

What could she say? That after nearly six years of separation, her mother wanted to reinforce her disappointment in her only daughter? Clearly, she could have called. She could have sent someone else to give her the news of her grandmother's passing.

But no, then she would have lost the opportunity to spit her scorn one more time.

Joy felt...not disappointment. That had died a few years back. But embarrassment? Yes, she felt that in spades.

Most people had normal families that were a little quirky sometimes. They had a member or two with eccentricities, a relative who tended to say the wrong thing, another who arrived late to every event.

Hers was more in the range of abnormally detached, superficial and spiteful.

Trying to push through her humiliation, Joy spun to face Royce. The concern in his dark eyes tested her resolve. It invited her to confide in him, lean on him.

But that would be a breach of their agreement.

Companionship, with hopefully some side benefits of a sexual nature. That's what they each wanted. Despite the scene he'd happened into, emotional support wasn't part of the deal. He was not her rock.

And she stood on her own now, damn it.

"Well." Shoulders back and a painful smile in place, Joy asked, "I hope you're not in a hurry. I need to talk to Jack before we go—" she badly needed to hug him "—but I'll only be a minute."

With his gaze unnervingly intense, Royce searched her face. "You're okay?"

"Of course." She tried a carefree laugh, and succeeded more than otherwise. "That nonsense with my mother is nothing new, believe me. It's fine." I'm *fine*.

"Joy," he said in soft exasperation, as if he knew she lied not only to him but herself, as well.

"Really, Royce. It's nothing at all—"

He bent and touched his mouth to hers in the sweetest, least demanding kiss ever. His warm lips lightly caressed, reassured. Lingered, but only for a moment, lasting just long enough to silence her. Still very close, his tone rough but gentle, he asked, "That was your mother, right?"

Unfortunately. "Yes."

With a hand cupped to her neck, he stroked his thumb over the line of her jaw. "She thought I might be Jack's father?"

"She was fishing. Or maybe she just wanted to be nasty and found an excuse." Joy shrugged to show that it didn't matter. "I hope you weren't offended."

"It caught me off guard." His fingers tunneled into her hair at the back of her head in a brief massage. "Sorry I laughed."

"Don't be. I'm not." His amusement had saved her from escalating the scene. "It was exactly the right response to her nonsense."

His touch and tone gentled even more. "I thought your mother knew Jack's father and disapproved of him."

Joy understood how he'd gotten that impression. "Mother knew *of* him." To keep this as short and succinct as possible, Joy said, "Vaughn had a rather colorful reputation and my parents learned of it through their friends. Everyone was scandalized that Joy Reed, the princess of Cara and Wallace Reed, would lower herself to associating with a bartender." Her mouth twisted. "That was his job when I hooked up with him, but he never kept any job long. My parents were furious when I refused to stop dating him, and doubly so when I married him. They were

certain he was only after my money, and in hindsight, that was probably true."

Royce frowned slightly. "Despite him being their son-in-law, they refused to ever meet him in person?"

Joy shrugged. "We got married at a justice of the peace. The whole relationship was doomed from the beginning. My parents continued to ensure I had money, but they didn't subsidize anything Vaughn wanted." Remembering his reaction when she told him no money would be coming for his extravagant indulgences, she huffed a short laugh. "Rightfully so, as it turns out. When Vaughn didn't have unlimited funds, he tired of me pretty quickly."

"He sounds like a prick."

Joy stole her own small kiss this time. "Rest assured, Royce, you're not like him in any way."

"I take it you and your mother are still at odds?"

Covering her mouth, Joy laughed and shook her head. "Truthfully, Mother despises me."

"That can't be true."

"I disappointed her one time too many." Glancing at the door to ensure Jack remained out of hearing range, Joy added, "Marrying Vaughn was bad enough, but when he left me pregnant, she wanted me to wash my hands of…well, everything that had to do with him."

Royce went still as understanding dawned. "She didn't want you to have Jack?"

"She was quite clear that if I wanted my family's support after the divorce, if I planned to stay with them while I regrouped, I had to do so without any connection to Vaughn."

"That wasn't her decision to make."

Oh, how Joy agreed. "When I refused, she disowned me and I moved out." That massive blowup felt like an eon ago. She'd changed a lot since making her own way.

She liked the person she was now much more than she liked who she used to be. At least for that, she could thank her mother.

"They've never met Jack, and I'd prefer to keep it that way."

"Got it." After a brief hug, Royce stepped away. "I'll go get him for you. I need to check on Chaos, anyway."

"Thank you."

The second he was gone, Joy's gaze skipped over to Maris. She bustled around as always, refilling napkins and straws in their dispensers, but she met Joy's gaze.

"That was wild," Maris remarked casually.

Putting a hand to her throbbing temple, Joy said, "I'm sorry that happened here."

Abruptly she stopped, her gaze direct. "I'm sorry it happened at all. It shouldn't have."

"No, but that's never stopped my mother." She came up to the counter, but didn't sit. Instead, she picked up a stack of paper napkins and helped to fill another dispenser. "My mother and I aren't close."

"No shit."

How amazing that Maris could make her laugh even now. Truly a blessing in a friendship. Smiling, Joy explained, "She doesn't like it when anyone goes against her wishes."

"And you did?"

A hard truth to share, but with Maris, sharing seemed easy. "I had Jack, so yes."

Maris scowled, dropping the box of straws and jamming her hands on her hips. "That's why she was so hateful? Seriously? She resents her own grandson?"

"He's not her grandson." The denial came out harsher than Joy meant it to. Rubbing her temples, she said, "I'm sorry."

"Hey, I get it. You probably wish it was true."

Joy dropped her hands, knowing there was no way to escape the tension, or the embarrassment. "Jack is mine, so by blood

he's also related to my parents, but they've never met him, have never even asked about him." *They don't care about him any more than they care about me.*

Maris shrugged. "Their loss."

It amazed Joy that Maris could always be so pragmatic. It *was* their loss. If she thought about it long enough, she could almost feel sorry for them.

*Almost.*

"After my divorce, I stupidly wanted to go home." It dawned on her that her apartment with Vaughn had never felt like home, not really. "I thought I could stay with my parents awhile, figure out what I wanted to do." It wasn't easy, but Joy met Maris's gaze—and was glad she had when she saw only the usual acceptance. No judgment, no pity. "It seemed the easy way out of my predicament, you know? Suddenly single, no job and a baby on the way."

"That's what family is supposed to do, lend a hand when you need it."

Maybe for family who hadn't burned bridges, but Joy had. Looking back, she knew she'd torched that bridge completely. "I was spoiled rotten without realizing it. I'd never worked. Even while married to Vaughn, we'd lived out of accounts my parents had set up for me." When she'd returned to them, her pride damaged and fear of the future a live thing inside her, she'd wanted more than a hand. She'd wanted them to make it okay for her.

Their solution had been...unacceptable.

It still hurt Joy's heart to remember. "We had a big argument about me being pregnant...and it ended with my mother disowning me. I left and I haven't been back."

Maris thought about that while finishing a chore. "Striking out on your own must've taken a lot of guts."

Leave it to Maris to see the best in her. It's how she treated

everyone. "Honestly, it was the best decision I've ever made," Joy said. "If I hadn't left, I never would have learned to take care of myself. I'd still be dependent on them." She wouldn't have Jack, wouldn't be at the park...

"And we wouldn't be friends," Maris said, almost as if she'd read Joy's mind.

"Another upside," Joy agreed with a smile...that quickly dimmed. "Apparently Mother hasn't kept up with my life at all. She didn't know if I'd had a son or daughter."

Picking up the now-empty cardboard containers, Maris took them to the recycle can. "So basically, she disowned you and her grandchild?" She shook her head. "You might have been a little spoiled, but what she did seems downright mean."

It *felt* mean, especially for her mother to seek her out only to continue the antagonism.

She and Maris settled onto stools, knees touching. It wasn't planned, but it just happened. Sort of like their growing friendship. "I'm glad she's not a part of my life anymore, because that means she's not a part of Jack's life, either, and as you just saw, that's a good thing."

Rather than remark on that, Maris asked, "Was it horrible growing up with her for your mother?"

"Not at all. In fact, I was pampered. I had stuff before I even thought to ask for it." More stuff than she ever needed. More than she could even use. The truth of that shamed her. "Everything except love."

"Are you *sure* they don't love you?"

"Did that look like love to you?"

Maris shrugged. "When someone doesn't care, they rarely show strong emotion. She found out where you live, right? She could have sent a letter. Or even just called the park and left a message."

Huh. Maris had a valid point. Had Joy misread the situation? "If they loved me, they didn't tell me so very often."

"Saying it doesn't always mean much." A crooked smile put a dimple in Maris's cheek. It wasn't her usual smile, full of wit, warmth or sarcasm, depending on where she aimed it. Combined with her downcast eyes, this expression was...poignant. "My parents told me all the time how much they loved me, but they didn't do much else."

Confused by what that meant, Joy put her hand over Maris's, giving her fingers a squeeze. "I'm sorry."

"Not sure which is worse, you know? An empty belly or an empty heart."

An empty belly? Dear God, what had Maris gone through? Her expression closed off, keeping Joy from asking too many questions, but she didn't release Maris's hand. Not because Joy needed it, but because, for once, she sensed that Maris did. "I think being hungry would be a terrible thing."

"It was." Deliberately lightening her expression, Maris nodded at the tray of fresh cookies. "Maybe that's why I enjoy baking so much."

"Maybe." In that moment, Joy saw Maris in a whole new way. Possibilities opened up, reasons for her workaholic attitude and stringent lifestyle. She was a strong woman, a survivor and a valuable friend.

For so many reasons, Joy considered her a good influence in Jack's life. Daron was, too—as well as Coop and Baxter, Phoenix and her sister, Ridley...

The park sign took on new meaning for her: Cooper's Charm: A Good Place to Get Away. It should also say *The best people in the world work here.*

"So." Pulling her hand free, Maris said, "What I want to know is, how did you turn out to be such a sweet person? Because seriously, Joy, you were way too nice to her."

Just that easily, Maris broke the melancholy and returned to her usual self. In one respect, Joy was relieved. It hurt her to see her friend hurting.

But in another...well, she hoped that one day Maris would trust her enough to share everything—the good, the bad and the unfortunate, past disappointments and future goals.

For now, Joy had one little secret she could share. Hopefully Maris wouldn't see it as an unwelcome obligation.

There was only one way to find out. "You're on Jack's emergency contact list," she blurted.

Blinking, Maris leaned back, eyes widening. "Come again?"

"I don't expect there to be an emergency," Joy rushed to say, "but I felt that if something happened to me, if Jack got sick and they couldn't reach me, or...or whatever."

"You named *me*?"

Joy rather liked the astonished look on Maris's face. It reflected surprise, but not in an unpleasant way. More like she'd been given a gift. "The school needed a contact. You're it."

"You... I mean, I..." Laughing, Maris shook her head and started over. "Okay, first, wow, I'm flattered."

"You are?" Relieved, Joy let out a breath and smiled.

"Seriously, insanely flattered. I thought you might not want to leave the squirt with me, since I don't have kids of my own."

"You're good with him," Joy promised. "He treats you like an aunt."

"An aunt, huh? Hey, I like that." Boasting, Maris said, "I'm an honorary aunt," she said, tasting the words and then nodding. "Cool beans."

Laughter bubbled up. "You don't mind? Being on the emergency list, I mean?"

"I'm seriously honored, but when did that happen?"

With a wince, Joy admitted, "The beginning of the school year." Joy rushed into explanations. "I should have told you, I

know that, but it never seemed like a good time and then I guess I just put it out of my mind. Even without discussing it, I knew if the school ever called you, you would go. I've always..." Joy shrugged. "I've always trusted you—whether I told you so or not."

Pleasure put color in Maris's face. Softly, without humor to detract from the sincerity, she whispered, "Thank you." She even leaned in for a brisk hug before setting Joy away from her. "Really. That means a lot."

"Thank *you*," Joy laughed. "I hope nothing comes of it, but I feel better knowing there's backup for Jack."

"Hey, we're part of a club now, right? I'm here for you."

Well, then... "I want to be here for you, too. If you ever need me to help, or to fill in for you, I'm a quick learner. You'd just need to tell me what to do."

Appearing bemused by the offer, Maris nodded. "I might take you up on that someday."

Joy grinned. Who knew being needed could feel so good?

On some level, she realized now why Maris was so happy about being her backup. They'd just forged a new bond in their friendship, something far more substantial than compliments and conversation, and it filled her with warmth.

Right now, though, she had other things to discuss. "My mother said that one of my grandmothers had passed and left something to me, so I need to make arrangements to sort that out."

"That's why she tracked you down today?"

"So she says, but to be honest, I don't trust her." Knowing her grandmother, the inheritance could be anything from family photos to substantial funds. Whatever it was, her mother probably knew all about it. "I don't think she'll return, but if you see her again, or my father or a lawyer—anyone other than our friends here in the park—"

Proving she understood, Maris said, "I won't let them any-where near Jack. Daron or I will have eyes on him every second." The added reassurance helped. "Thank you."

A clatter had both women swiveling toward the door. Jack stormed in, laughing silly, with Chaos hot on his heels. The dog still had bandages around one leg, but he already looked health-ier, his pale yellow fur silkier now that it was free of burrs, his ribs no longer visible.

"I won," Jack said, dropping onto his butt on the floor, legs out, for Chaos to scramble over him. The pup frantically licked his face while Jack laughed some more and attempted to dodge him. In a quick turnabout, Chaos shifted and tried to chew on Jack's sneaker.

Jack found that hilarious, too. His carefree laughter proved contagious and soon Joy and Maris were chuckling, as well.

Royce and Daron came in right behind Jack. Even amid all the hilarity, they couldn't disguise their concern. It wasn't Joy's intent to ever make Royce worry over her. She'd need to ex-plain that to him, but she put that on hold as she pulled Jack aside and gave him a list of rules.

"I want you to listen to Maris and Daron."

He nodded, anxious to rejoin the dog.

"Stay right with them," she emphasized. Better than any single person, Joy understood how quickly a boy his age could run off. "And don't get too rowdy in the camp store, especially when customers come in."

"Okay, Mom."

"Remember to be polite."

Grinning, he said, "I *know*, Mom. Don't worry," with all the drama of a little boy who just wanted to play.

"Most of all," she added, pretending to be stern, "have fun."

When Jack threw his small, strong arms around her waist, she

drew him closer, one hand in his fair, silky hair. She clutched him a little too tightly. A little too desperately.

Until that day the doctor had placed Jack in her arms, she hadn't known real love, couldn't even have comprehended the scope of an emotion so powerful and deep.

Leading up to his birth, she'd fretted over so many things, and she'd felt sorry for herself.

But the second she'd held her baby boy, her focus had narrowed to razor-sharp intent. She'd both wept and smiled, felt vulnerable and yet infused with iron determination. She'd stopped thinking of Vaughn, because she knew Jack was better off without him in his life. And she quit grieving the separation from her parents, determined instead that she'd pour all the love she had on Jack so that he'd never, ever feel unwanted or unworthy.

Motherhood, she'd learned, was a constant battle of emotions. Today was no exception.

"I love you." Joy smoothed down his hair.

"Me, too," he said by rote, grinning up at her. "Daron's going to teach Chaos and me some dog tricks."

Daron clipped the leash onto Chaos's collar and lifted the squirming bundle into his arms. "We'll be right here, Joy. No reason to fret."

"I know." She did. Truly. Otherwise, she wouldn't go, but already Jack was excited and she...well, she knew they each deserved the fun planned for today.

Royce stood back, giving her all the time she needed. If it hadn't been for her mother's visit, she wouldn't feel so edgy about going. Trust, she reminded herself. She trusted these people completely.

Hoping she looked confident, Joy smiled at Royce. "Ready?"

# CHAPTER SEVEN

They were only in the car two minutes when Royce said, "You don't have to do this, you know."

Lost in thoughts of her mother, the attorney and the idea of an inheritance, Joy replied, "Hmm?" And then it occurred to her, and her eyes widened.

*What if Royce had changed his mind about wanting her?*

No, she told herself. That couldn't be it. He was here, so that said something. Yet she still sounded cautious as she asked, "What, exactly, don't I have to do?"

He shot her a look. "Pretend none of that happened."

"None of what?"

"Your mother, her attitude. The way you reacted to her." He lifted one shoulder. "All of it."

"Actually, I can." When he gave her another look, she clarified. "I can pretend it didn't happen. You should do the same." After all, she'd gotten pretty darned good at pretending she didn't have a family, that they hadn't hurt her, that she was just fine and dandy on her own.

Actually, she *was* fine on her own, no pretending there.

Unfortunately, Royce didn't let it go. "You don't want to talk about it?"

She already had, with Maris.

Maris was a friend. She made a good confidante, was supportive without being sappy, funny without being dismissive. Most importantly, Maris hadn't stressed up front that there were boundaries—as Royce had.

To be considerate, though, she'd be careful about unloading on Maris too many times. She didn't want to be a buzzkill, not when she and Maris could have so much fun just visiting. And once she found out more about Maris's upbringing, she'd be better able to return the favors if, when, Maris needed anything.

So far, though, Maris was a rock of independence.

"Joy?" Royce prompted.

He missed the turn toward his house. In fact, they should have been there already. Surprised, she finally took note of their surroundings. The road he remained on would take them into town. "Where are we going?"

"Dinner. It's a quiet place, so we'll have some privacy."

Joy stared at him. That had to be a joke. For what *she* wanted, no restaurant could provide enough privacy. "I thought we'd go to your house?"

He slowly inhaled, as if bracing himself. "We can go there if that's what you want."

"Good."

A muscle ticked in his jaw and his hands flexed on the steering wheel, gripping, releasing. Gripping again. Following a few seconds of silence, he stated, "After dinner."

Of all the... Here she was, giving herself a pep talk, all prepared to forge ahead, and he wanted to spend their time on food? Well, he wasn't the only one here, and what she wanted mat-

tered, too. He wasn't the inconsiderate sort, so maybe he didn't know her preference.

Should she tell him? How exactly should she word that request? *I'd rather we go to your house, get naked and have sex until we're both exhausted.*

No, she couldn't say that. She'd never been overly outspoken and here, now, didn't feel like the right time to start.

But in her head, she could almost hear Maris telling her to speak up. Unfortunately, she wasn't Maris, not by a long shot. Maris wouldn't need someone prodding her to take a stand.

In honor of her new friendship, Joy decided the least she could do was give it a try.

"So… I'm not hungry." Oh great. That was miles away from bold. She quickly added, "I mean, are you actually hungry?"

Rather than answer, he said, "You can admit you're upset, honey. I'll understand."

Joy blinked at him. He would understand.

Okay, sure, that was nice of him. But nice wasn't what she wanted right now.

She wanted him. As a man.

Why had she assumed this would be easy? Actually, she knew why. She thought Royce would jump at the chance to get physical, that he'd somehow take charge of the situation and all she'd have to do was go along.

It wasn't working out that way, so apparently she had to steer things in the right direction. "I appreciate the concern. I really do. But the situation with my mother isn't new and I'd rather not dwell on it."

He shot her an appraising look. "Are you sure?"

Frustration sharpened her tongue and she asked, "Should I remind you what this—" Joy gestured back and forth between them "—is about?"

He was silent a moment as he drove, and then he nodded. "Yeah. Why don't you?"

Huh. Joy hadn't expected that. "Well…" She screwed up her nerve, tamped down her modesty and stated, "Today, it's about sex."

"What?" He shot another look, this one almost comical because he looked so surprised. Oh, he kept driving, but he didn't blink; he even took a few seconds to inhale. "You said sex?"

Did he have to sound so unsure? "Us. Today. At least, that's what I'm hoping." Embarrassment put her tongue on the fast track, and she started rambling. "I realize things went off the rails a little bit today. I was surprised that my mother dropped in so unexpectedly." Mild definition of her reaction. "I'll have plenty of time to think about it later, I promise, but right now we have a limited opportunity. Who knows how many times Maris and Daron will work together to make this happen?"

"Wait." He lifted a hand. "You're saying…?"

"Sex." She repeated again, and it was easier this time. "Us. Today."

"Right. Believe me, I'm with you on that part. But did you say that Maris and Daron know that's what you have on the agenda?"

After Joy explained, Royce gave a short, gruff laugh. "It makes sense now, the way Daron offered to watch the dog, how insistent he was about it." Pulling up to a stop sign, Royce turned toward her. His gaze had warmed, and his mouth curled in the slightest smile. "So you made these arrangements, huh?"

*Do not blush. Do not blush.* "Yes." She'd even bought condoms, though she was hoping he had his own. She'd taken extra care with her appearance, too. "So what do you think? Could we skip food for now?" If they delayed, she had the awful feeling they'd miss the opportunity.

Royce glanced in the rearview mirror, drove forward and made a U-turn. "I'm thirty."

Unsure what that meant, but relieved that he'd turned around, Joy said, "We're the same age, then."

"I had a bitch of a year before coming here. Actually, more than a year, though the last year was the worst. It wore on me, to the point I feel fifty most of the time."

Again, she didn't know why he mentioned it, but she also felt older than thirty, mostly because she'd been in permanent mom-mode with her sexuality on ice. "I understand." She just hoped this wasn't his way of edging out of a sexual relationship.

"The thing is, around you, I feel like a horny high school kid."

A big grin of relief made her "Oh good" sound silly. She laughed, only a little embarrassed. "I mean, because I feel the same."

"Good to know."

Briefly, she wondered what had happened in his life to make the past so difficult. Because he'd been clear about those damned boundaries, she didn't ask.

Royce reached for her hand and held it on his thigh. "Don't ever think I'm disinterested, okay? If it ever seems that way, check me on it."

"Same here." Before meeting Royce, she might have thought about sex every now and then, in an abstract, peripheral way featuring blurry, imaginary men.

With Royce, her thoughts were very specific, very direct and detailed. All about him.

"We both have a lot going on right now, and honestly, I'm out of practice. But for the immediate future, consider me an automatic *yes* anytime there's opportunity, okay?"

That "immediate future" qualifier didn't bother her in the least—because it went both ways. "Same from me."

"Yeah?" Grinning, he pulled into a deli. "How much time do we have?"

Joy didn't know what to think. "I told Maris I'd be back by eight."

"Perfect." He parked and removed his seat belt. "Give me two minutes to grab some ready-made sandwiches—for *later*." Leaning across the seat he took her mouth in a firm, warm kiss that held loads of sensual promise. "Be right back."

Holding the bag of food in one arm, Royce unlocked the front door, then stepped back for Joy to enter.

With her expression a mix of shyness and anticipation, she silently stepped over the threshold.

Joy might be thirty years old, but this was new for her.

Hell, it was new for him, too—because it was Joy, and he not only wanted her, he admired everything about her. It was a different combo for him.

Prior to his mom's illness, he'd enjoyed bachelorhood and the freedom from commitments. He'd set his own hours, leaving plenty of room for travel. His mother's illness had altered his life drastically and there'd been no room to cultivate relationships with women. Never had he even been tempted to try.

It had been easier and less complicated to just get through each day, to do what had to be done, focus on the necessary stuff and keep his mind free of anything else.

Now here was Joy, and she drew him in in ways no one else had—before or after his move. If ever a woman deserved patience and finesse, she did, but the urge to rush her straight to the bedroom punched a wild beat in his heart. He wanted to touch and taste her everywhere.

Hell, he'd been thinking about it since he met her.

She was here in his house with him now because she wanted him, too, enough that she'd taken the initiative and arranged it with her friends.

Knowing that created lust so powerful he had trouble breathing as he closed the door again behind them.

"I'm amazed at everything you've accomplished."

Flipping on a few lights, Royce asked, "How's that?"

"All the remodeling at the drive-in, getting to know the community, and you're even unpacked and organized here. When I moved in at the park with Jack, I lived out of boxes for a long time. I think he was a year old before I finally got everything set up the way I wanted."

"You were younger and had a baby to take care of." He couldn't imagine what that must have been like for her, especially after seeing her mother firsthand. "This place…" Royce glanced around at the very underwhelming interior of his home. "It's orderly, but it's not even close to what it'll be after I put in some work. I have ideas—a ton of them—but they'll have to happen later."

She stripped off her coat and put it with her purse on the sofa. "Jack and I have distracted you."

Royce gave a low laugh. "Jack's entertaining. But you?" He let his gaze skim over her. Joy had a way of making a plain skirt and sweater ultrafeminine yet still professional. He'd love to see her in jeans.

Naked would be even better. Soon. Very soon.

"You are most definitely distracting," he managed to say. "In all the best ways."

She smiled and smoothed her hands down her skirt. "Good."

Reminding himself that he couldn't rush her, Royce said, "I'll put this stuff away," and headed for the kitchen.

Joy followed, but paused in the wide doorway, still looking around at his house, specifically his bare walls. "Do you own any of your mother's art?"

He had everything his mother had completed after she became ill, as well as gifts she'd given him throughout the years.

It added up to a sizable collection. "Some," he said noncommittally. For now he kept the art in storage, where it would stay until he could emotionally tackle it.

"You said she was...ill?" She wasn't sure how to categorize dementia.

Royce inhaled and held a breath. Right, they were both out of practice, but Joy couldn't seriously expect him to talk about his deceased mother right now?

Given her concerned gaze, she did.

Aware of her tracking his every movement, Royce took his time storing the food in the fridge. "The dementia came with a lot of complications," he said, in a way that didn't invite more questions.

"I'm sorry."

Nodding, Royce killed time by carefully arranging the sandwiches on the middle shelf, the colas on the bottom, the potato salad on top.

But to what end? Not like he'd start wanting Joy less. Not like they had all night.

"Did Chaos do this?"

Closing the fridge, he looked at the bottom of the kitchen door frame where deep gouges in the white paint exposed the wood. "Yeah, first time I tried to leave him behind." To keep his hands off her, Royce braced them behind him on the counter. "Poor dog went nuts. I think he felt abandoned all over again."

When he'd found Chaos loose in the house, two different shoes destroyed and a screen knocked out of a window, he'd been both exasperated and apologetic. The dog couldn't help his fear, and Royce hadn't meant to add to his anxiety.

For the next hour he'd played with Chaos in the yard, hoping his attention would reassure the dog, and that the play would help to wind him down. He'd also vowed not to leave Chaos behind again—not if he could help it.

Nodding at the scratched-up linoleum, Royce said, "He tried to dig his way out, I guess. Once I was here, he went crazy loving on me, then wouldn't leave my side."

"Poor baby," she said, full of sympathy.

To lighten the mood, Royce grinned and asked, "Me or the dog?"

Her smile matched his. "Both?"

He accepted that with a laugh. "Even while I showered, Chaos kept his nose stuck in past the curtain. At least when I can see him, he's not getting into trouble."

"I'm glad he has you." Moving closer, her gaze on his chest, Joy said, "Someone else might have given up on him already, especially when he does so much damage."

"It's not that bad. I think by the time I start remodeling here he'll be more secure." The house felt strangely quiet without Chaos racing around from one end to another, yapping at shadows and sliding across the hardwood floors, or sometimes just chasing his own tail. "It'd be great if Daron could teach him some commands before then."

Smiling, she turned those beautiful eyes up to him.

And there went the last of his restraint. She was close enough now that he couldn't keep his hands off her. Catching her shoulders, he drew her into his body. God, she was soft, and curved just right. With her height, she fit against him perfectly.

His voice rasped as he said, "I don't want to talk about the dog—" or my mother "—anymore."

Her palms settled against his chest. "Okay."

"Joy." He looked from her eyes, now heavy with need, to her slightly parted lips. "I'm about to implode here."

Nodding, she inhaled a deep breath. "Me, too."

"Good." Perfect, even. Sliding his hands down her back, he paused here and there to stroke, to absorb the shape of her—the

dip of her waist, the rise of her hip. When his hands opened on her backside, she pressed her face into his neck.

*Patience*, he told himself again…but he was already too far gone. "If I start this here, we won't make it to the bedroom."

"Honestly, here works for me."

He choked on a laugh. His first time with her would *not* be up against a counter. "Let's be a little more conventional this first time, okay?" Stepping her back, he caught her hand and headed down the hall to his bedroom.

Unfortunately, he hadn't even come close to making his bed. Chaos had pulled one corner of the blanket off on the floor. Royce's pillow still wore the indent of his head, and the other pillow…well, it was pretty obvious Chaos had slept curled up on it.

Shit.

"The dog fur—" he started to explain.

"I don't care."

He turned to see her stripping off her long cardigan and stepping out of her shoes. She didn't wear nylons or tights, and her bare feet looked so cute that it stalled his brain for a second until it registered that she was undressing.

His cock thickened. Soon, very soon, he'd have this woman and he didn't quite know how he'd managed it. Beauty, brains, compassion—and she wanted him enough to make arrangements. Despite him being obtuse. Despite the obviously painful visit from her mother.

All together, that said a lot. Joy claimed she wanted this and nothing more. Well, then, he'd make *this* as good as he could.

That meant he had to lay some groundwork to ensure her pleasure. If she got her clothes off first, he was a goner.

"Slow," he murmured, hauling her close and taking her mouth in a deep, thorough kiss. Her lips immediately opened, an invitation to his tongue. No finesse, but she didn't seem to mind,

not with the way she pushed closer, how she clutched at him and sucked on his tongue.

God, there was so much he wanted, *needed*, to do with her, but he felt her hands on the hem of his sweatshirt and knew he couldn't wait. "Let me." He moved back far enough to jerk it off over his head.

Joy inhaled, her gaze stroking every inch of his upper body. The way she whispered, *"Wow,"* so breathlessly made him even harder.

Wearing an expression of fascination, she reached out to touch him, molding her palm across the front of his shoulder, then trailing her fingertips down to his pec, over his left nipple, down to his waist—and the snap of his jeans.

She really was in a hurry, and much as he wanted to accommodate her, he knew she needed to catch up.

Lifting her hand away, Royce kissed her fingers. "Your turn." He finished easing her cardigan down her arms and tossed it toward a chair. With both hands, he brushed her long hair behind her shoulders—and then had to linger on it a moment. Thick, silky, golden brown, her hair had factored into his fantasies a lot lately.

None of those fantasies were as stirring as the reality of having her here, in his bedroom, hearing the quickness of her breath and seeing the thrust of her nipples through her shirt and bra.

He skimmed his hands down her narrow waist and hips, then up again. She held herself so still he thought conversation might help and asked, "Do you always wear skirts?"

She swallowed, nodded. "Usually."

Slowly, he pulled up the shirt, revealing first the smooth skin of her midriff, then the lacy edging on her bra, and finally the fullness of her breasts.

Right there, with the shirt held under her chin, the material bunched in his hands, Royce paused to soak up the sight

of her. Until this moment, he hadn't realized that she'd be so lushly built. Her white bra was both sturdy and pretty, supporting breasts that would fill his large hands.

Joy didn't play up her figure in any way. Hell, she probably played it down in an effort to shore up that persona of a mother, only a mother.

Before he took her home, she'd have no doubts about being a woman.

"Royce," she whispered, her hands fluttering at her sides.

His gaze sought hers. The flush in her cheeks and the trembling of her lips showed equal parts embarrassment and urgency. "You're incredible."

She gave a slight shake of her head. "I'm just...me."

Pressing a gentle kiss to her lips, he said, "There's no 'just' to it." Slowly, he eased the shirt up and over her head, while reminding himself that she hadn't undressed in front of a man in a very long time. Much as he wanted to visually devour her, he'd have to save that for later.

As he tackled the side zipper of her long tan skirt, he kissed her, along the column of her neck, the sensitive spot where it joined her shoulder, up to her jaw and ear.

The skirt dropped to her feet. Before he could steal a look at her, she stepped out of it and against him, her hands on his chest again, her mouth on his.

Now when he held her bottom, only silky material separated his hands from her warm, pliable flesh. He didn't mean to rush. In fact, he was telling himself not to do that when he pressed one hand inside her panties, the other into her bra. She sure as hell wasn't complaining—and so he stopped thinking.

Just stopped.

Instead, he gave in to instinct, touching and tasting, licking and fondling. Like a man starved, and maybe he was, he greedily explored every inch of her available to him.

The softness of her combined with the scents of her hair, her sex, her excitement, made him hard enough to hurt.

He loved the way she lightly dragged the tips of her nails over his back with just enough pressure for him to feel it, to know she was turned on. He didn't think she was aware of it, that she did it deliberately to turn him on. No, she was wrapped up in her own innate response, soft, mewling moans escaping her. When he opened her bra to free both breasts and bent to draw one stiffened nipple into his mouth, she speared her fingers into his hair and held him close.

"Royce," she whispered on a shuddering breath.

Suddenly they were both busy, him stripping away her bra and panties, her attacking the zipper on his jeans.

Again, he took over. It was that or risk injury, a thought that pushed him even more. Joy wanted him, probably not as much as he wanted her, but close. It was there in the heat of her mouth on his skin, the broken way she breathed.

He kicked off his shoes and shucked his jeans and boxers in record time. For a single heartbeat they looked at each other, and what he saw in her gaze, the same sharp hunger he felt, had him reaching for her, then tumbling with her to the bed.

He kissed her hard, each of his hands filled with her breasts, his erection burning against her belly.

Protection. Belatedly, it sank into his head and he levered up to his forearms. Her eyes were heavy, her lips wet and her hair tumbled around his pillow. Damn, he didn't want to leave her, not even for a second, but... "I need to get a rubber."

She licked puffy lips, swollen from his kiss. "I brought some, but I forgot my purse in the other room."

God love her. "You bought rubbers," he repeated, a little awed that someone so sweet, so sexy, could also be so practical.

"Are you laughing at me?"

"No, I'm—" *Loving you.* Shit. He shook his head.

"What?" she whispered, her hand to his jaw.

True, he loved things *about* her, but it couldn't go any farther than that. He wouldn't let it.

"You impress me, that's all." Another kiss, because he couldn't resist her mouth. "Thank you, but I have it covered."

He left her long enough to snag the box from the closet. He fished out a condom and tossed the rest of the box on Chaos's pillow.

"You bought them, too?"

He grinned, wondering if she'd gotten hers from the same small, family-run pharmacy. If so, he imagined a little speculation going around.

"As soon as I knew I wanted you. Seriously, I wasn't making assumptions, but neither would I ever take chances."

She tucked back her hair. "So that whole box...is for me?"

Deadpan, teasing, he said, "I don't think we'll use them all today."

She grinned. "Well, if we do, I also have a box, but I only brought three with me."

Three? She had more faith in his stamina than he did.

Joy watched him intently as he ripped the packet open with his teeth, then rolled it on.

The short interruption returned a modicum of control to him, so when he came back down beside her, he took the time to touch her again, to leisurely lick her nipples until she squirmed.

He trapped her legs with one of his own, and then drifted his fingers up the inside of her knee, along the warm velvet length of her thigh.

Just as he reached the slick softness between her legs, she arched her back, silently asking for more. Drawing in her nipple, he caught it with his teeth and lightly tugged...as he pressed the tip of his finger into her.

*Wet.* And so damned hot.

Tight, too, tight enough to make him ache.

He worked his finger deeper, loving the rough groan she gave, the impatient shifting of her hips. To make it easier on her, he slid his finger out, and worked two back in, stretching her a little, preparing her, all while reveling in the new rush of wetness.

"Now," she demanded, suddenly tangling her fingers in his hair and drawing his mouth up to hers. "Right now."

Not a problem. Royce kneed her slender thighs apart and settled into the cradle of her body. As her legs went around him, he positioned himself, and entered her with one firm, steady thrust.

Her head back, her eyes staring into his, Joy gasped…and the gasp turned into a vibrating moan of pleasure.

Thank God. Knowing he wouldn't last, Royce braced on one elbow and concentrated on her, on what she needed, how she reacted to what he did, if she liked it easier.

Or harder.

Her hair tangled around her and she strained against him, matching the roll of his hips, reaching desperately for a climax.

Scooping his free arm under her hips, he levered her up so he could go deeper, so that with each thrust and withdraw he slid against her clit—and it was enough.

Her teeth clenched and her eyes squeezed tight.

The climax came on her so quickly it stunned him. Her pleasure was raw and real, and so fucking hot he felt his own release gathering in unstoppable force.

She clenched around him, her hold on him tight.

And perfect.

Tucking his face into her throat, he struggled to hold back until he felt her begin to soften, the tension easing from her limbs.

And then he let himself go, one hand clasping her ass to keep the contact just *there*, driving hard and fast while looking at her, her bouncing breasts, yes, but also her face, her slight smile,

those amazing green eyes and the complete satisfaction in her expression.

He put his head back and gave in with a guttural growl as he pumped into her. It had been so long since he'd felt this bone-melting pleasure.

Actually, he was pretty sure he'd never felt anything like this.

Great sex, yes. But...more. So much more.

Dodging the thought of that, Royce rested against her a moment, both of them spent, both struggling for breath.

"Wow," she whispered again, making him smile.

Smiling, he moved to his side. For a heartbeat they were separated and he didn't like it, so he slung an exhausted arm around her and dragged her close.

She snuggled in, draping one slim leg over his and resting a hand over his heartbeat. Long before him, she recovered and began toying with his chest hair. Normally that might have tickled, but at the moment he wasn't feeling much.

Except satisfaction.

Maybe a little confusion.

With a bit of alarm creeping in.

If he had any sense, if he was half as dedicated to his plans as he professed, he'd be running as fast as he could. Instead, he put a kiss to the top of her head and wondered where they went from here.

He had jackola to offer a woman like her. A struggling business under rehab? He had faith in the drive-in, but since he'd bought it just as the season was closing, he wouldn't be able to measure its success until the spring. His house was in desperate need of repairs. Eventually it'd be nice, but now? He ran a hand over his face, knowing it was underwhelming at best.

His bank account was strained from his mother's illness, and he'd recently taken in a troubled pooch who wouldn't let him out of his sight, and enjoyed eating shoes.

A man his age should have had more to recommend him.

Almost as if she'd read his thoughts, Joy opened her hand over his sweaty shoulder. "That was pretty amazing."

Right. Good sex. That was enough to build on, right? Did he *want* to build more? He wasn't yet sure.

Not yet opening his eyes, still trying to reground himself, he teased, "Braggart."

Laughing, she lightly swatted his chest…and went back to exploring him. "I meant you. Or maybe us." She nuzzled her nose to his throat. "Together."

His cock stirred. So did his heart.

He couldn't deny it, this wasn't just great sex.

It could be more…if he let it.

And if Joy wanted it.

He got one eye open. "Are you hinting that we should do this again?"

"Would you be up for it?"

The slow smile crept in on him. "Joy Lee, is that a double entendre?"

She quirked a supercilious brow. "Yes?"

This playful mood of hers could be his undoing. She made it too damn easy to be comfortable with her—before sex, during and after. If he said that to her, she might see it as an insult. She couldn't know that comfort had long been missing in his life.

Yes, she turned him on, more than any other woman he'd known, and if it was just the chemistry, he could get past that. Explore it, enjoy it and move on.

It'd be a hell of a lot harder to dismiss everything else she made him feel.

Taking her to her back, he said, "For your information, I'm half-up already, and—" leaning around her, he glanced at the clock "—we have plenty of time yet."

"Plus we have all those condoms." Grinning, she looped her

arms around his neck. "So my vote is that we make the most of it. Who knows when we'll get a chance to be alone like this again?"

It was a strange thing to be turned on, wary and regretful all at once. Here he was thinking about the future, and she wasn't even sure they'd have a next time.

He wanted her. Again. Now and tomorrow, too.

But even if he managed to remember that he was supposed to get his act together, to reestablish who he was and what he wanted before committing to anyone else, after today *she* might not think it was worth the trouble to align their schedules.

Then what?

She didn't exactly sound ready to jump through hoops for him. *Who knows when we'll get a chance to be alone like this again?*

She could make it happen. *They* could make it happen—if it mattered enough. But did it?

God knew Joy had more than her fair share of responsibilities already, one of them a five-year-old boy who she would never shortchange.

So where did that leave him?

"Royce?" She turned somber, concerned, as she traced a fingertip over his chin. "Is something wrong?"

He didn't know how to answer that, so instead he kissed her, thoroughly and lazily, enjoying the way she curled into *him*, how she wanted *him*.

For now, that'd have to be enough.

"I need to get rid of the spent condom," he said against her lips before sitting up. "And I heard your stomach growl. Think I can convince you to eat before you have your way with me again?"

Green eyes glimmering, she smiled. "Depends. Can we eat here in bed?"

With the dog hair? If she didn't mind, he didn't, either. "I'll be back in three. Stay naked."

Stretching out, she said, "I will if you do."

To Royce, to a man who'd mapped out his future with specific details, that sounded like one hell of a plan.

# CHAPTER EIGHT

It surprised Daron how much fun he had. Sure, he always knew he liked kids and animals, but it was different enjoying them with Maris.

How had he overlooked her maternal streak?

The endless cookies, the quick effort to serve—not only her guests but her friends... Actually, anyone and everyone who came within her realm. Maris lived to make others comfortable.

Did anyone do the same for her?

He wouldn't exactly call her a homebody. Overall, he'd describe her as goal-oriented, a planner and sharp businessperson who understood how to continually advance her own personal agenda, whatever that might be.

Financial security, sure. But it was more than that. She'd taken Summer's End from a place to get a few necessities or a cup of coffee, to the central hangout for everyone who worked at or visited the park.

It frustrated Daron that Maris's mantra was all about hard work. Back to work.

Stuff to get done.

Things to do.

*Work.*

She always sang the same refrain.

Yet yesterday, during major lulls in business, she'd joined in during his not-so-successful attempts at showing the dog a few commands.

Chaos was aptly named because the frisky little pooch couldn't seem to focus on any one thing for more than a heartbeat. The puppy raced, full speed, from Jack to Daron, occasionally tripping over his own feet, playfully tugging at shoelaces, demanding attention, turning circles, chasing his tail, attacking a rogue leaf that dared blow past him, barking at the shoreline and so on.

The little dude seemed hell-bent on soaking up as much attention as he could, while he could get it. It'd take time, patience and consistency to train the dog, and it'd be easier after a long walk that wore him down a little.

But during his efforts to accomplish that, Daron had heard Maris laugh. Repeatedly. Like, *real* laughs. Robust and rich. Free-spirited.

Damn, it was sexy.

*She* was sexy.

Clever, too, because once Royce and Joy showed up, both of them pretty damn mellow and smiling, Maris closed up shop and left with them, thwarting Daron's plan to see her alone.

He'd wanted to get another kiss—actually, he wanted much more than a kiss, but he liked to keep his expectations reasonable.

Regardless of how she'd ended the night, he'd had a great time.

Chaos had, too. The dog had finally worn down a little right before Royce returned. Royce might not have known the fun they had, given the way the pup carried on when reunited.

Clearly, Chaos loved Royce, and once he saw him, he remembered it, going berserk with happiness, his barks high-pitched, fast and frantic.

Until Royce cuddled the squirming little furball up close and spoke softly to him. Then finally Chaos had quieted down.

Maybe Chaos thought he'd been abandoned. Again.

He was a heartbreaker for sure.

Much like Maris.

One way or another, Daron knew he'd get the dog to trust him enough for basic training.

And as for Maris…well, if she just trusted enough to give him another kiss, he'd count it as a win.

For now.

Poking her head around the camp store door the next morning, Joy spotted Maris behind the counter, a cup of steaming coffee held in both hands close to her face. Eyes closed, she inhaled the steam.

"Knock, knock."

Cocking one eye open, Maris saw her and quickly took a big gulp. "Come in and tell me everything!"

Broom in hand, Joy moved the doorstop out to keep the door open. "I refuse to sit and gab when I know you have a routine. So I'm going to pitch in—" it was the only thing she could think of to show Maris how much she appreciated her "—and we can talk while we both stay busy."

Maris eyed her, eyed her coffee cup and asked, "Do I look like I'm busy?"

"I know you." Joy began sweeping away the fallen leaves from the stoop. "You might slow down long enough to inhale that coffee, but it'll be a short-lived pause. Once I get these leaves cleared up, I'll get them in the trash and then you can tell me what to do inside."

Maris laughed. "Got it all planned out, huh?"

Putting her nose in the air, Joy teased, "You're not the only hard worker."

"Fine. Knock yourself out. But at least give me the big scoop. How'd it go last night?"

Joy couldn't hold back the smile that felt like it came from the inside out. She'd never really had anyone to talk to about stuff like…well, anything, really. But definitely not sex.

Since she hadn't had sex in forever, that one was easy to skip. But even back when she had been sexually active, there'd been no one close enough to share with.

She wanted to dish now. She wanted to somehow explain everything Royce had made her feel, but was that done between grown women? She didn't know.

"Uh-oh," Maris said. "Are you hesitating because he let you down?"

"No! Definitely not." In fact, the opposite was true. Royce had exceeded her wildest expectations.

"My God, you're blushing!" Maris said. "Stop teasing and tell me, did you get lucky or not?"

Laughing, Joy gave up on her uncertainty. If there was a standard decorum on the issue, Maris clearly didn't follow it, or care about it. "Oh, indeed I did. Very, very lucky." Grinning, Joy lowered her voice when she admitted, "Three times!"

Maris gave a long whistle. *"Three?"*

"Well, three for me, two for him."

Laughing, Maris hurried around the counter and grabbed her up for a big hug, even danced around with her in a circle, then she thrust her back the length of her arms. "He was good?"

"Oh, Maris." Leaning her weight on the broom, Joy sighed. "He was absolutely *perfect*. Honest to God, I didn't even know it could be that…"

"Orgasmic?"

"Yes." He'd pushed her over the edge *three* times. It didn't get much more orgasmic than that.

"Explosive?"

So explosive. Joy happily nodded.

"Made your toes tingle, huh?"

The giddy laugh erupted. "He made *everything* tingle."

Maris grinned with her. "And how about you? Did you rock his world?"

Ugh, a sobering thought. Joy covered her face with one hand. "Sad to say, I have no idea."

"Are you telling me he was a quiet comer?"

"What?" Quickly Joy peered around to make sure no one else was around to hear that. Her face went hot when she said, "I don't mean that at all. He, ah, he…"

"Got his?"

Joy hadn't laughed this much in forever. "Yes, he did. And he seemed really satisfied. But what do I know? I haven't been with anyone since I got pregnant with Jack."

Maris whistled again, this time with surprise.

Joy gave her a playful shove. "How about you? When was the last time you—?"

"You know those triple chocolate cookies I make?"

Unsure what that had to do with anything, Joy nodded. "What about them?"

"I call them 'chocolate orgasms,' because that's as close as I've gotten in forever."

Joy started snickering, and when Maris joined her, the humor escalated and they ended up roaring together like two loons.

Coop poked his head in the door, said, "Um…never mind," and started to leave again.

"Wait!" Wiping her eyes, Maris called him back. "What did you need? Coffee? Danish?"

He looked back and forth between them. "Did you spike the coffee?"

"Nope."

"Then I'll take two to go." Propping a shoulder in the doorway, he asked, "You have any cookies this morning?"

And Joy absolutely choked on her hilarity.

Doing some snickering of her own, Maris brought him the coffees in foam cups, along with a plastic bag of oatmeal cookies.

Coop took it all, but paused to smile at them. "Whatever's up with you two, I like it." His gaze strayed to Joy's face. "It's nice to see you laughing. Both of you." He lifted one coffee in a toast. "Thanks, hon."

"Anytime. Give Phoenix my love."

"Will do."

After he left, they both drew some deep breaths to regain control.

"Ah." Maris slid into a booth and beckoned for Joy to join her. "My face hurts now from laughing."

"Mine, too. And I've ruined my makeup."

Grabbing a napkin, Maris leaned over the booth and carefully touched it to the corner of her right eye. "There. Good as new."

They looked at each other and grinned.

"I read *Cosmo*," Joy admitted. "You know, to see if I could bring myself up to speed."

"Yeah? How'd that work out for you?"

Joy wrinkled her nose. "I think I'm thirty going on fifty or something, because none of it sounded right to me. Nothing that would happen naturally, and I'm not up for forcing a situation just to make it erotic."

Maris agreed. "I read this magazine article once that talked about all the ways to drive your boyfriend insane with lust. It pissed me off." Wearing a frown, she said, "If I ever get around to having sex, he's the one who'll be working at it, not me."

"Last night," Joy said, "it was mutual."

"Mutual work, mutual payoff?"

"There was no work." Joy knew she could have been happy exploring Royce's body for an entire day. An entire week.

Maybe longer?

She shook her head, dismissing thoughts of the future and concentrating instead on what they'd experienced.

It fascinated her, the things that made Royce grit his teeth. The touch that caused a groan. How his eyes blazed dark fire when he watched her come.

"It was more than I'd ever expected." Leaning in, Joy confessed, "We laughed a lot. Isn't that nuts?"

"Depends on your timing, I guess."

"We joked around and ate cold sandwiches in bed, and then had sex again." Joy remembered something important, and grabbed Maris's hand. "Did you know he lets Chaos sleep with him? Isn't that the sweetest?"

Mouth twitching, Maris nodded. "He's a good guy, but now I'm glad Daron butted in and insisted on keeping the dog. Otherwise, I might not be getting this fascinating report right now."

Two more customers came in, and while Maris tended to them, Joy finished clearing the walkway. She really hadn't meant to sit down on the job.

She was just about done when the campers left.

Maris looked at her face, at the smile Joy couldn't suppress, and she shook her head. "So tell me this. Was he good enough to make you start thinking about more than just the horizontal mambo?"

Joy caught a golden leaf tipped in red that rolled in on the breeze and swept it back outside with a few insistent brushes of the broom. Phoenix, the park's groundskeeper and Coop's wife, had her hands full with all the leaves this time of year.

Leaning on the broom again, Joy decided to be honest. "You

know, I could. It'd be so, so easy. But it's not my decision to make. Not alone, anyway. Royce was pretty up front about things. Whatever he had going on before he moved here, he's not looking to get tied down again."

"You're not a rope, Joy. He'd be lucky to have you."

Having such a loyal friend was a real ego boost, but when it came down to it, a single mother of a rambunctious little boy screamed commitment, and Royce didn't want that. "Thanks. I don't want to get ahead of myself, though. I'd rather just enjoy the moment."

"I know what you mean since I'm not looking for commitment, either." Maris put her nose in the air and said, "I'm married to this store."

Joy laughed at that sentiment. She couldn't seem to stop laughing, or thinking about Royce, or wanting him. Again.

But how would that work?

"So did you two make any new plans?" Maris asked.

Joy shook her head, and since she didn't see anything else to sweep, she headed into the kitchen. "No new plans."

"Well, why not?" Maris followed after her.

The kitchen was disgustingly pristine, not a single pan out of place, the sink scrubbed clean. "Yesterday, Royce wanted to take me to dinner."

"So?"

"He didn't realize that I preferred to go to his house, get him naked and have my way with him."

Maris grinned. "Had to explain it to him, huh?"

"I brazenly laid out my intentions once. Shouldn't I give him a chance to do the same? I mean, if he wants to see me again?"

"He'll want to see you again."

Joy wished she could be as confident about that as Maris seemed to be. "Until he says so, we can't know that for sure." Though they had joked about all the condoms and how they

shouldn't go to waste, so she was hopeful. "Now give me something to do."

Giving in with a toss of her hands, Maris opened a few cabinets, found cleaning supplies and led the way back to the seating area. "The napkin holders need to be polished."

Joy jumped on it. This, at least, was something she could do for Maris.

They collected all the metal holders and sat at a booth together again. Maris poured her a coffee, and refilled her own.

A few minutes into it, Joy said, "This morning I made arrangements to meet the attorney. My appointment is on the Monday after Halloween here at the park." They celebrated separately from the night of the community, using the entire weekend for decorations and parties, and letting the kids "trick or treat" on Saturday evening.

"So not this week, but next?"

Joy nodded, feeling pretty damn anxious about it. "It's going to be awful."

Worried, Maris set aside her cloth. "Why don't I go with you?"

This time, Joy's smile was of appreciation. Under no circumstances would she subject a friend to her family's scrutiny. She adored Maris for her casual vibe, her workaholic manner and indifference to impressions, yet those things would make Maris a prime target for Joy's mother.

"Thank you, really, but it's something I should do alone."

Maris snorted, but kept her gaze on the polishing cloth. "I met your mother, remember? You should *not* face her again by yourself." She seemed to give that another thought and added, "No offense."

"None taken."

Glancing up, Maris said, "If you won't let me be your wing-

man—or wingsister or whatever—maybe you should take Royce."

Wingsister. Now, didn't that sound amazing? She'd never had a sibling to share the good times and the bad. If someone had offered her a choice, she'd have happily taken Maris as her sister.

But the suggestion of Royce around her family... Good God, no. Joy couldn't imagine anything that'd scare Royce off quicker than being invited into her mother's drama. "I'll be fine, I promise. I'll drive straight there after I drop Jack off to school, and I should be home before he finishes for the day." She dusted off her hands. "Done."

She could tell that Maris didn't buy her nonchalance, but being a true friend, she didn't pressure her.

"It's so quiet here this time of year." Maris peered out the window. "I love the bustle of the summer, the work that keeps me jumping."

Joy nodded. "Then we roll into fall and it gets so chilly." Through the window she saw little foamy caps on the lake, stirred by a brisk breeze. The waves repeatedly lapped at the shoreline, leaving a darker line in the sand. The blue sky was easily visible through now-barren trees. All together, Joy thought it was beautiful.

"And quiet." Propping her chin on a fist, Maris sighed.

"Not a fan of the quiet?" Joy guessed.

"You have to feel it, too. The big...lulls. Too much time to think."

"Keeping busy is better," Joy agreed. Another idea hit her. "Will you shop with me? I mean, for clothes and stuff. Girl shopping. We could have lunch and each buy a cute new top."

"That might be fun." Gesturing at her own body, Maris asked, "But do you ever see me wearing *cute?*"

No, she didn't. "You could totally pull it off."

"No, *you* pull it off." Maris grinned. "But hey, I could use a new coat and maybe some boots, so let's do this."

"Today?" Joy asked.

"How about tomorrow instead. *But,*" she said with emphasis, "if anything comes up with Royce, he gets priority, and I want your word that you won't hesitate to let me know if you want me to watch the squirt again."

Joy thought of the times she'd had to take Jack out when he was sick because he needed medicine, and she had no one to watch over him. All the times she'd gone without sleep so she could get things done around Jack's schedule, and the times she'd been running late for work because Jack had skinned his knee and needed coddling.

She wouldn't overly impose on Maris, but the idea that she could rely on someone else almost overwhelmed her.

It felt good, not being alone. So damn good.

"Hey," Maris said. "Don't go getting weepy on me. Jack isn't any trouble, I've told you that, and it's not like I have anything else going on."

Words weren't sufficient, but for now, they were all Joy had. "Thank you."

"It's my pleasure."

"But speaking of your lack of a social life…"

Maris groaned.

Ignoring those theatrics, Joy asked, "How'd it go with you and Daron?"

"Nothing *goes* with us."

"You keep doing that," Joy accused.

"Doing what?"

"Putting emphasis on different words." Usually in a way to play down the truth. Maris thought she wasn't *cute*, when in fact she was extremely pretty—and yes, with her ponytail and

smile, very cute. She thought there was nothing between her and Daron, when anyone with eyes could see the truth.

They were totally into each other.

"I only do that when it's *necessary*," Maris said with a cheeky grin, letting Joy know she'd done it again on purpose.

"Know what?" Joy sat back and folded her arms. She'd gladly accepted advice from Maris, but it was time for her to share some of her own. "I think you're trying to convince yourself that you don't like Daron, and it's a lost cause because you and Daron—"

"Joy—"

"Set off sparks. I think you know it, and what's more, I think you *like* it."

"Joy," Maris said again, this time a little more urgently.

"I think you like him. A lot." Judging by the look on Maris's face, Joy knew she'd hit the nail on the head. "Admit it."

Instead, Maris said, "Now who's doing all the emphasizing?"

"You want him. And you know what? I think you should give it a shot."

"Hell, yeah," Daron said from right behind her, making her jump. "I second that."

Glancing back, Joy saw that Daron had his arms folded on the back of the booth, meaning he'd been there long enough to get comfortable.

Feeling her face heat, Joy asked, "What is it with all the eaves-dropping going on around here?"

"Not my fault if you two get so busy talking you don't notice anything, even the sound of the tractor pulling up out front."

"The tractor?" Joy asked.

"Yeah, weather is supposed to turn nasty so Phoenix and I are putting in double time to get the leaves up first." He turned puppy-dog eyes on Maris. "I was hoping for a few cookies to sustain me for a long morning of work."

Given the way Daron grinned, and how Maris glared at him,

Joy decided she'd done enough for one day. She mouthed a silent, *Sorry*, to Maris, then said, "See if she has any chocolate—"

"Joy!" Maris's face went red.

Brows up, Daron studied each of them in turn. "Chocolate... what?"

"Maris will explain—or not," Joy said with a wink before sidling out the door.

From outside, she heard Daron say in a low, sexy voice, "I'm intrigued, Maris."

Whatever Maris replied was lost on Joy, but still she started grinning again, and by the time she reached the lodge, she was laughing. Her life had taken many twists and turns, not always for the better.

This, though, having friends, laughing over coffee, teasing the resident stud, was definitely an improvement over isolating herself. Especially since, for the time being at least, she had a stud of her own.

She hoped Royce would call.

And if he didn't? Well, she just might chase him down again.

Maris wasn't sure what to say to Daron with him giving her that particular look, a look that said too many things, showed too many things—like interest and humor and...hope?

Was it possible he really wanted her? Or, as one of the few women to turn him down, was she just a challenge? It didn't feel that way. It felt...genuine. And scary.

God, she was a coward. But what did she know of relationships with men? Especially a man like Daron, a guy who could have his selection of women.

And yet, he seemed to want her.

He watched her with complete attention, his gaze fixed on hers. "You skipped out on me last night."

Yup, she had—but she wouldn't admit it. "How could I skip

out on you, when I wasn't with you in the first place?" She headed around him for the kitchen. Putting a half wall and a counter between them made sense to her self-preservation. "I have brownies, oatmeal cookies, cranberry scones or shortbread."

"One of each would be great."

Jumping, Maris turned—and there he was, right behind her, standing too close and looking far too tempting. What was it about his disheveled appearance that turned heads, including her own? He hadn't shaved today and the light brown scruff made her fingertips twitch with the urge to feel his jaw. Brisk wind had tossed around his always-unruly hair. His sweatshirt looked older than him, fitting over his broad shoulders and then dropping loosely around his torso.

And yet, all together, it equaled some seriously hot appeal.

"I like when you look at me like that," he murmured.

A rude sound escaped before she could stop it. "You like when any woman looks at you."

"Well…" He rubbed the back of his neck as if the truth made him uneasy. "Yeah, sure. I mean, being noticed is nice. But no one else is you."

Barely resisting an eye roll, Maris made to step around him.

He stepped, too, blocking her, and when she glared he immediately held up his hands. "I get it," he said. "Tell me to get lost and quit trying, and I'll respect that, I swear." In a rush, as if he feared she might take him up on it, he added, "But there's something between us. You know it. That kiss the other day proved it."

"Pfft. That kiss was an experiment," Maris lied.

He looked insulted, and maybe a little hurt. "The results were so bad you don't want to try it again?"

Damn it, now she felt guilty for giving him that impression. "That's not what I said."

"No, you didn't. You said to let the anticipation build, and I have. I'm about to combust with anticipation."

Damn it, so was she, but she had to stick to her guns.

Didn't she?

Determined, Maris stared up at him. "I also said I had rules." So many rules. It was past time she remembered them.

Daron nodded. "Right, rules that we'd discuss—but then you dodged out instead." He held out his arms, which raised the hem of his baggy sweatshirt, giving her a peek at his low-hanging jeans, and a downy line of hair leading from his navel into the top waistband of colorful boxers.

Her mouth went a little dry.

Daron Hardy was young, sexy, playful, fit...and he wanted her. Wouldn't she be nuts to pass that up?

With emphasis, he stated, "So here I am. More than anxious to know what I'm up against. Should I take notes? I have a good memory if we're talking a list of one to ten, but if it's, like, one hundred rules long or anything—"

She smashed her fingers to his mouth, and damn it, that was the exact move that led her to kissing him last time. In contrast to his firm bod and sharp wit, his lips were soft.

The contact sizzled, jolting through her fingertips, her arm and straight to her core. A *starving* core. She had it bad.

So maybe she should just give in.

He probably read the indecision in her eyes because he caught her wrist and carried her hand to his chest. "Come to my place. I'll cook dinner."

It was an old habit, using sarcasm as a defense mechanism. First she said, "By cook, do you mean you'll order a pizza?" and as if that weren't bad enough, she tacked on, "Could be like a step back in time, right? I bet your apartment is decorated with band posters and black lights. Will I find another woman's underwear beneath the bed?"

His hold on her wrist loosened, then fell away. He even took a step back, his expression masked. "Actually, I'd thought about making fried chicken. And my *house* might not be up to your standards, but I left posters behind in college."

Her jaw loosened. "You have a house?" That absolutely was not envy squeezing her heart, but...she'd longed for a house forever. Then the rest of what he'd said hit. "I didn't know you went to college."

His mouth firmed and his chin jutted. "Yeah, some colleges let anyone in as long as they pay tuition."

God, she'd been insulting. Protecting herself at his expense... well, that made her a not-very-nice person. "I didn't mean it that way. I just didn't realize—"

"I have an associate degree in business," Daron explained, his brows still pulled tight. "Nothing too fancy, but it's useful now and then."

"But...you've been working here for so long—"

He shrugged. "I was in college when Coop hired me. This is a full-time job, so it put me behind a little, but I eventually finished up."

Maris remembered telling him that he didn't know her, and that was true, but did she know him any better? Curious, she offered him a cookie, took one for herself, then leaned on the counter. "Business, huh?"

He smirked. "Yeah, not like I'll use a degree here, right?"

"I didn't mean that. A business degree would probably come in handy lots of places." Heck, she wished she had one, but education hadn't been high on her list. Independence had been her basic goal.

"I could put it to use somewhere else. That was actually the original plan. But I like it here. Actually, I *love* it here. The park suits me."

Yes, it did. Would Cooper's Charm even seem the same without Daron?

No, it would not.

Enjoying this new insight into him as a man, Maris said, "And you have a house?"

"It's small. Three bedrooms, one and a half baths, quarter-acre lot."

He called that small? To her, it was an unattainable dream.

"I figured it was an investment, right?" he continued. "Rent doesn't earn equity, but property does."

She nibbled at the edge of her cookie, feeling pretty low, before admitting, "I'd love to get a house. Right now I'm dumping everything into savings. Well, that and making improvements to this place. Eventually, I hope to buy my own home. It's just not in the cards yet." There were days, sometimes weeks, when it felt like it'd never happen.

Daron reached past her—bringing the heat of his nearness and the scent of the fresh outdoors—right past her nose as he pilfered another cookie. "You run a good business."

The *but* hung loud in the air. She felt defensive, but said, "I'm open to advice."

"No," he stated firmly, "you aren't. Not ever. Especially not from me."

True enough. Before this minute, she might have bit his face off if he'd offered an opinion, because she would have taken it as criticism.

The truth didn't set well with her, but she faced it all the same. She'd been terrible.

It would be best to start over, and that could more easily begin with another kiss. When he started to take another bite of his cookie, she stopped him, blocking his hand, then stepped into his space, close enough that her body pressed all along his.

His mellow brown eyes widened and he went very still. "Maris?"

An actual apology stuck in her throat, but she managed to ask, "Is the dinner offer still open? Maybe tomorrow night around seven?"

With his gaze on her mouth, he nodded, followed with a fast, "Yes."

Bless the man, he was far more forgiving and flexible than she'd ever been. "Perfect. Rule number one, my work comes first." When he started to speak, she touched his chest. "Rule number two, never underestimate me—and going forward, I'll give you the same respect, I promise."

His arms looped around the small of her back. "Rule number three, always be yourself, because I like you, Maris. A lot."

She was starting to believe that he did. "These are my rules," she reminded him with a smile.

"Well, that one should be included." Without waiting, he turned his head and fit his mouth to hers in a cookie-sweet kiss that left her crowded against him, and a little carried away.

As she caught her breath, she said, "Rule number four, no sex on a first date."

His slow grin did crazy things to her insides. "I think you just made that up because you're tempted."

"Daron—" she tried to object…even if he was right.

"Hey, as long as there's a second date, I can live with number four."

Well, damn. He could live with it.

But could she?

# CHAPTER NINE

Joy shivered as she cut construction paper into shapes inside the lodge. Glancing toward the window, she saw the flurries coming down, just as Daron had predicted. Ohio weather was nothing if not unpredictable. Too many times, over too many years, snow fouled up Halloween, then went away again.

She hoped this wouldn't be one of those years.

Not long after she'd picked Jack up from school the day had turned gray and gloomy. She wondered if Phoenix and Daron had finished their work.

Just then the lodge door opened and before she'd even finished turning, Chaos bolted in. Jack looked up from his task and squealed. Together, he and Chaos made a fair ruckus, reuniting like friends long separated.

Royce stomped his feet a few times, then stepped in and shut the door. His cheeks were ruddy from the cold, his dark hair mussed, and he wore a coat rather than a jacket.

He looked good enough to eat.

While Jack and Chaos greeted each other, Joy went to him. "I didn't expect you."

"Hope you don't mind us dropping in. I returned a tool to Daron and since I was here—"

"Of course I don't mind." She reached up to smooth his hair into place. "Coffee?"

He shook his head. "I just had hot chocolate at the camp store. I wanted to see if you two were free for dinner."

Her heart jumped but she tried to suppress any outward reaction. No, it wasn't alone time with him, but it was terribly sweet of him to include Jack again.

She thought of the chops she had marinating, but they'd keep. Turning to Jack, she asked, "Would you like to go to dinner with Mr. Nakirk?"

Jack cheered, and that got Chaos running in circles.

Grinning, Royce said, "Obviously, it'll be at my house since I can't leave Chaos alone. I'd planned on steaks off the grill, but it might be too cold for you."

Steaks sounded amazing. "I'll bundle up," she promised.

He stuffed his hands in his pockets, and said low, "Do you know how hard it is not to touch you?"

Warmth spread through her. "Oh, I have a guess, since I so badly want you to."

"When can we get together again?"

Thrilled that he'd sought her out to ask, she said, "It depends on how together you want to be." Before Royce could take that the wrong way, she explained, "I can eke out an hour or two most afternoons, while Jack is in school, especially now with things so slow. Any more marathons, though, I'd need to arrange for Maris to watch him again."

His mouth quirked. "It was a marathon, wasn't it? Should have tided me over for a day or two, but I swear the minute I got home, I wanted you again." With a warm smile, he mur-

mured, "Your scent was on my sheets, but then, so was a lot of dog hair, so I had to wash them."

Joy laughed. "I think it's sweet that you let Chaos sleep with you."

"I didn't really have a choice. That first night, he damn near slept on my head. I didn't have the heart to put him out of the bed."

He'd probably cuddled the dog, she thought, knowing how good he was to Chaos. "I'm glad."

At the sound of laughter, they both looked over to see Jack darting around a table, Chaos hot on his heels.

"Good news, though. Daron suggested that I get him a dog-house, with his own cushy bed in it. It's an indoor thing that almost looks like furniture. I put it in the corner of the bedroom and added a few of his favorite toys. He seems to like it. Last night he started out with me, but middle of the night he went to his own bed."

While Jack was occupied, Joy stepped up against Royce. "So we might not need a dog sitter next time?"

"Next time," he whispered. "I like the sound of that." He, too, glanced at Jack, then stole a quick kiss. "Chaos isn't there yet, so yeah, I might still ask Daron to lend a hand. He agreed to help train Chaos, but he'll still know why I'm asking."

Joy gave that quick thought, and decided it didn't matter. Not to her, anyway. "Will it bother you for others to know?"

"Not if you're okay with it."

Always so considerate. "Thank you."

"I just remembered. The school called and they want to do a field trip to the drive-in sometime after the season ends."

"I suggested it, but I didn't know they'd made a decision." Her brain started to buzz with ideas. "I'll volunteer as a chaperone, and maybe we could do some activity for the kids while

they're there. A short animated movie inside so they could see how it works."

Royce nodded. "I like it. I figured I'd give each kid a little bag of popcorn, but I don't know about drinks."

"We'll take care of it. The school and I, I mean. Let me think on it and I'll get some ideas together."

Jack skidded up next to them, and Chaos tumbled right over Joy's feet. Laughing, she bent down to stroke the dog's downy ears, and then gave her attention to Jack.

"Can me and Chaos go outside?"

The correction for his grammar was on the tip of her tongue when a memory from the past hit her. She hadn't been much older than Jack when she asked about going to the school's haunted house. Suddenly she could see her mother's face, the disapproval pinching her features. Yes, she'd gone to the school function, and the next day she had a speech tutor.

"Mom?" Jack asked, a little more uncertain.

Royce was looking at her, too, so she smiled. Actually, she had so much to smile about it was easy to do.

"I need to clean up this mess—"

"I'll help," Royce offered.

"Awww," Jack complained, clearly disappointed by a delay. "Chaos has to go."

They all turned to see the dog actively sniffing the floor. Royce quickly scooped him up. "How about I take these hoodlums outside, and you can join us as soon as you're done?"

Jack cheered, taking her agreement for granted, and ran off to grab his coat.

"Hat, too," she called to her son, pleased to see his excitement, and then to Royce, she said, "I'll only be five minutes."

"If you're done here, we could go to my place straightaway."

She looked around at her half-finished project, but there wasn't anything critical that had to be done. Actually, it felt

nice to concentrate on something besides work, to have a reason to put it aside.

The dog did more squirming, so she said, "That sounds perfect. I'll finish up here, grab a warmer coat upstairs and be out before either of you can get too cold."

Two hours later, as Royce put the last few dishes in the dishwasher, Joy stood nearby drinking hot chocolate. Her nose and cheeks were no longer pink from the cold, but either way, she looked beautiful to him.

The snow had fallen steadily, accumulating two or three inches, but Joy and Jack had both stuck with him in the yard, bundled up in hats and scarves, boots and mittens, while he'd grilled steaks and potatoes.

As the weather conditions had worsened, he'd tried to talk her into going inside, especially when she started shivering. Instead, she'd scooted closer to him, soaking up the warmth of the grill. In between turning steaks, Royce had hugged her—and Jack didn't even seem to notice.

As if impervious to the cold, he and Chaos had raced the perimeter of the fenced yard, slipping and sliding in the snow.

Everything about that had felt intrinsically *right*: small talk with Joy, her nearness, the sounds of Jack's happiness and Chaos's excitement.

For once, his run-down little house had felt like a home.

A happy home.

Had he been craving that without even knowing it?

Of course they'd eaten inside, and though she'd worn knee-high boots outside, Joy had them off now so that he could see her thick socks. She'd also removed Jack's snow-caked boots, and even dusted off Chaos's paws.

Going by what Daron suggested, Royce fed Chaos a cup of doggy chow while they ate at his small table.

Apparently the dog and Jack had worn each other out, because once they'd both finished, they crashed in the living room to watch a TV-edited version of *Toy Story*. Side by side on the floor, Jack, with his elbows bent, braced his head on his hands, and Chaos rolled to his back against Jack's side, occasionally snuffling against him.

"They'll both be out shortly," Joy predicted.

"Jack, maybe." Royce had his doubts about the dog. "Daron thinks Chaos needs more exercise to burn off energy."

Smiling, Joy said, "Why do you think I take Jack to the playground almost every day?"

Ha. So it worked for kids and animals alike, huh? "I'll try some walks in the morning and evening." Royce looked out the window. "That is, when the weather cooperates."

Joy bit her bottom lip, glanced in at Jack and then set her empty mug in the sink and pulled him to the side.

He saw it in her eyes, what she wanted, what she would do, and damned if he didn't react to it. As her hands slid up his chest to his shoulders, he clasped her waist and drew her body flush to his. He bent down as she tilted her face up, and they met in the middle with a kiss that started slow and easy and advanced from there. Twice they stopped, only to come right back for more. He threaded his fingers into her hair close to her scalp and fit their mouths together for a deeper, hotter taste.

His forehead to hers, Royce said, "Soon, Joy. I don't think I can last much longer."

She gazed at his mouth and nodded. "I'm sorry. I shouldn't have let that get out of hand."

He tipped her face up again. "That's not on you, babe. Not even close."

"I started things."

And she'd quickly melted against him, so Royce quirked a

smile. "Okay, so it's partly your fault. If you weren't so damned sexy—"

She gave a strangled laugh.

"And so irresistible, I might be able to keep it together."

"I could say the same for you." She touched his mouth with her fingertips and sighed. "I think about you, about being with you again, far too often."

"Good to know." He smiled.

"I had no idea a fling would be so difficult to maneuver."

A fling. Well, hell, that was a sobering thought. She stared up at him with those incredible green-gold eyes full of sincerity, and called this, their time together, a fling.

It's what he'd told her he wanted. Just because he'd *maybe* changed his mind didn't mean she felt any differently.

He needed to get his thoughts in order. One thing at a time, he decided, and the first thing was a softer, gentler kiss. "I don't mean to complicate your life."

The smile came quickly, followed by a quiet laugh. "Hot sex, a night out, a friend—trust me, those are not complications."

Still relegated as a friend? Shit. He tried not to let that bother him. "No?"

"I'd call them improvements."

For him, definitely. "Let's see what we can do about repeat performances, okay?"

"We'll make it happen," she promised. "If you find yourself with time while Jack is in school, let me know. If I have ten minutes' notice, I can be ready."

He didn't know if he could find someone—or at least someone he knew well enough to trust—to watch Chaos during the day, but he'd give it a try. Daron's time with the dog would be more toward evening, so it wouldn't interrupt his own work at the park.

Just then Jack appeared in the kitchen doorway, Chaos at his

"My son," Joy said. "The master manipulator."

"Tell you what." Royce knelt down beside him, Chaos still held close with one thick arm. "Each time you come to dinner, you have to agree to try something new. Deal?" He held out a hand.

Rolling to his bottom, Jack sat facing him, ready agreement tripping off his tongue. "Deal."

They shook hands.

"If you decide you like fish, we could try catching our own in the spring."

In the spring? Around Jack's enthusiastic response, which included jumping up and down, Joy wondered where they'd be in the spring. A fling couldn't extend that long, could it?

When it eventually ended, as she assumed it had to, would they remain friends? Would Royce still be a part of her son's life? Jack might be satisfied with that arrangement, but Joy couldn't imagine a time when she'd see Royce and not want him. Like now.

Royce, Jack and Chaos all tumbled around the floor, wrestling and laughing, with Royce alternately hefting Jack into the air over his head, and playfully pinning him down so Chaos could lick his face. It was an irresistible scene, hearing her son's hilarity and seeing how comfortable he was with Royce.

One that made her long for more.

It would be so easy to fall in love with Royce.

Heck, she was already halfway there.

"Wow." Maris looked in the mirror, turning her head this way and that. "Trimming off that tiny bit made a big difference."

"The conditioner helped, too." As did the way Joy blew out her hair for her, using a round brush to add some volume. "You have gorgeous hair. I know women who would pay big bucks to get those summer highlights, and yours are natural."

For now, though, Royce continued to watch her, so she tucked away her phone and picked up Jack's coat. Leaning toward him, speaking in a stage whisper, she stated, "Maris is going to Daron's for dinner."

The surprise she expected never came. Instead, Royce tipped back his head and groaned. "Guess that means tomorrow is out for us." When he looked at her again, he wore a lopsided grin. "Good for Daron, though."

Smiling, Joy handed Jack's coat to him and sat down on the couch to pull on her boots. "Remember, call anytime."

Jack, not understanding the significance of that, said, "Yeah, call us. We can come over to dinner again." He held Chaos's face. "You'd like that, wouldn't you, boy?"

Chaos gave an enthusiastic *yes*.

"Well, now," Royce said. "Your mom will have to let me know your favorite foods."

Jack's face lit up. "I'll eat anything!"

With a roll of her eyes, Joy said, "If only he felt that way at home."

Turning on her, Jack said, "But you cook fish."

She grabbed for him, but he squealed and ducked behind Royce, which got Chaos superpumped for a game.

Laughing, Joy said, "I *try* fish. Occasionally." With a mock frown aimed at Jack, she added, "Someone says it smells bad."

Falling to his back and sprawling out like a starfish, Jack groaned. "It's terrible!"

"Personally, I love fish." Royce scooped up Chaos before he could accidentally scratch Jack's face. The pup's paws were oversized for his body, which meant he had a lot of growing to do yet. "When fish is raw, it smells, but once it's cooked... Mmm. Delicious."

Cracking open one eye, Jack peered up at him. "I could try your fish."

"You know what I'm talking about. He makes everything a joke."

Gently, Joy said, "It's called being happy."

Two pulse beats of time passed, then Maris muttered, "Shit."

"It's true," Joy offered, "that he teases you more than anyone else. Always has. We all realize it's because he has a thing for you, and you…well, you seem to like everyone except him."

Sounding hurt and defensive, Maris whispered, "I like him."

"But you're afraid of liking him too much?"

"I already said *shit*, right?" She groaned loudly, then said it again, a little louder. "Shit."

Joy grinned. "It'll be fine. You two will talk over dinner and work out any misunderstandings. I'll get to the camp store early tomorrow so we can make plans."

"Maybe I could have him pick me up at your place? That way you could help me spiff up and I won't have a chance to ruin it?"

"Love that idea. Consider it a date!" Smiling, she disconnected— and found Royce standing there, Chaos sitting on his foot, Jack leaning against his thigh. The three of them watched her.

Royce asked mildly, "Date?"

Though he tried to seem relaxed, resting one hand on Jack's shoulder, wariness had crept into his expression.

Silly man.

Joy could barely work out a time to see him, so he shouldn't think she'd have time—and definitely not interest—to see anyone else.

"With Maris," she specified. "For some girl stuff." Even saying it made Joy want to laugh in giddy excitement. Maris might expect big changes, but they weren't necessary. With her dark blond hair and naturally dark lashes and brows, any more than the barest makeup would be too much. Joy knew exactly what she wanted to do, the top she wanted to loan Maris and the advice she'd give before she left.

feel good about herself and boosted her confidence. "We'll enhance things a bit. Do you have scissors?"

"Um…scissors?"

"We'll trim an inch off your hair. Only an inch, I promise." Joy didn't know if Maris had ever cut her hair, but a trim to tidy up the ends always worked wonders. "And I have a fabulous conditioner that you're going to love."

"Oh wow." Maris sounded a little dumbfounded. "Am I really doing this?"

"Having a date with Daron? About time, if you ask me."

"I told him no sex."

Joy huffed a laugh. "What? *Why?* You insisted it was good for me, but now you—"

"He's six years younger than me."

"Big deal. You're both young and healthy and that's what counts."

With a long sigh, Maris said, "I don't feel young."

"Well, you are, because you're only a year older than me and I'm young." No way could Maris argue with that logic.

"He has a *house*, Joy. Did you know that?"

Of course she did, but Maris sounded so surprised Joy asked with caution, "Didn't you?"

"No! He comes off all… I don't know. Irresponsible."

"Daron? Daron Hardy?" Joy repeated with disbelief. "We're talking about the same guy, right?" Yes, Daron liked to joke and God knew he had his fair share of female admirers, but Joy could never fault him on his sense of responsibility. "The same man who pitches in to help anyone who needs it, who keeps everything in the park working, who stays late or comes in early when something goes wrong? The same Daron who always answers his phone, smiles at everyone while working his behind off, who—"

"Ugh, enough already." Maris sucked in an audible breath.

Oh, the workings of a five-year-old mind. Royce laughed. "Sure, if your mom's okay with it."

That seemed to solve everything, at least for Jack.

For Royce, it wasn't quite that easy.

Joy could hear the low hum of voices in the kitchen as she returned Maris's call. What did Jack think, seeing them together?

She didn't have long to ponder it because Maris answered on the first ring.

"Hey, it's Joy. Sorry I didn't get to the phone in time."

"I need your help tomorrow," Maris blurted.

"Okay." Maris didn't sound upset, like there was a problem, but something in her voice made Joy go on alert. "Whatever you need."

"I'm going to Daron's house, for dinner. And...well, it's dumb, but I want to look pretty."

"Oh my gosh!" A hundred questions buzzed through Joy's brain, but she said only, "You're *always* pretty."

"Prettier, then. Like...hair, makeup. A cute shirt?" Maris groaned. "We won't have time to shop and I don't own anything! Not even mascara. How pathetic is that?"

"It's not pathetic at all, but don't worry, I have it covered." Catching on to the excitement, Joy paced the living room. "I have everything we need, and I can stop at the store tomorrow after I drop Jack off at school."

"I don't want to put you to any trouble."

"Are you kidding? I'm already excited!" This was something Joy could do for Maris, and she could barely wait.

"I can't look like you, hon. I mean, no skirts or—"

"You look terrific in denim! I wouldn't think of changing anything like that." She could imagine a pretty shirt and softer hairstyle. "You don't need to go heavy on the makeup, either." Joy knew that sometimes a little makeup just made a woman

side. The boy looked first at his mom, then at Royce, who slowly stepped away so he wouldn't appear too guilty.

Curiosity had Jack's brows twitching, but all he said was, "Your phone's buzzing, Mom."

"Oh, thank you, sweetie." She brushed a hand over Jack's hair as she hurried past him, heading to the couch where she'd left her purse.

Jack stood there still studying Royce. He rubbed his nose, his mouth shifted to the side and he stared some more.

The kid was smart, no two ways around that.

"Blast," Joy said, poking her head back into the kitchen. "It was a call from Maris and I missed it. Do you mind if I take a minute to call her back?"

"No problem." Royce gestured at the table. "Jack and I will grab some dessert."

"Thanks." Joy disappeared back into the living room.

Coming forward and climbing into a chair, Jack said, "You were hugging my mom."

Yup, not much got past the kid. "Hugged her outside, too, because it was cold." Royce poured a cup of milk and got a packaged cookie from the cabinet, setting both in front of Jack.

"It's not cold in here."

Unsure what else to say, Royce shrugged. "Guess not."

"I think you just like hugging her."

Very true. Royce enjoyed talking with her, touching her, hugging her—and so much more. "You like hugging her, too, right?"

Jack said, "Yeah, but she's my mom," like maybe Royce had forgotten.

He tried a different approach. "Do you mind that I hugged her?"

"No." Then, being a sly little boy, he asked, "Does that mean I can come here and play with Chaos again?"

# CHAPTER TEN

Daron knew he needed to stop staring, but…damn. He'd been half-hard ever since he laid eyes on Maris tonight. She'd greeted him in Joy's apartment with a discernible chip on her shoulder. Her beautiful, almost bare shoulder…which led into the creamy skin of her chest and down into mouthwatering cleavage.

Maris as her usual self was tempting enough.

This was just overkill.

"How far to your house?" she asked.

"Almost there." He tried to keep it together because tonight was to show her he respected her rules, that he was a grown-ass man, and that they had more in common than she thought. "You warm enough?"

"Yes."

That curt answer didn't reassure him, especially with the way she sat huddled in the seat, her arms folded around her, her shoulders up. Since he'd picked her up, his truck hadn't completely lost the heat, but the wind outside sent tree branches dipping and dried leaves tumbling. In the space of a few hours, a cold

front had moved in and it felt more like winter than fall. If they got the precipitation that the dark clouds predicted, there'd be problems at the park tomorrow.

Last he'd noticed, a few couples were in the cabins, one young man was in a tent and three RVs remained on the property. He didn't expect any of them to last much longer, especially with the weather changing.

"Here we are." His headlights danced over the front windows as he turned into the driveway. He hit the garage door opener and pulled into the single car space.

As Maris opened her seat belt, she checked out the shelving and the tools placed precisely on pegboards. "So tidy."

For some reason, it made him feel self-conscious. "Yeah, well, being organized is a necessity at the park so naturally it carries over." He got out and circled the car, but she didn't wait for him and was already out, hugging herself again, before he reached her.

"Come on." He took her elbow and led her to the two steps up into the kitchen. This was his favorite room of the house, with the bright white Shaker cabinets and black granite tops.

She looked around in something close to awe. "It's so warm."

"The slate floor is heated. Same in the bathroom. When I'm home, I prefer to go barefoot." And he was often in just his boxers. "When I remodeled things, I tried to figure out all the modern gadgets, you know?" Like a kid showing off his first car, Daron stepped over to the sink to point out the faucet. "I agonized over this beauty the most, but..." It suddenly hit him that he was being rude. "Here, let me take your coat."

"Thank you." She stripped it off and handed it to him.

As if it didn't leave her standing there looking like his hottest fantasy.

While he soaked in the sight of her, she pushed up her sleeves

side. The boy looked first at his mom, then at Royce, who slowly stepped away so he wouldn't appear too guilty.

Curiosity had Jack's brows twitching, but all he said was, "Your phone's buzzing, Mom."

"Oh, thank you, sweetie." She brushed a hand over Jack's hair as she hurried past him, heading to the couch where she'd left her purse.

Jack stood there still studying Royce. He rubbed his nose, his mouth shifted to the side and he stared some more.

The kid was smart, no two ways around that.

"Blast," Joy said, poking her head back into the kitchen. "It was a call from Maris and I missed it. Do you mind if I take a minute to call her back?"

"No problem." Royce gestured at the table. "Jack and I will grab some dessert."

"Thanks." Joy disappeared back into the living room.

Coming forward and climbing into a chair, Jack said, "You were hugging my mom."

Yup, not much got past the kid. "Hugged her outside, too, because it was cold." Royce poured a cup of milk and got a packaged cookie from the cabinet, setting both in front of Jack.

"It's not cold in here."

Unsure what else to say, Royce shrugged. "Guess not."

"I think you just like hugging her."

Very true. Royce enjoyed talking with her, touching her, hugging her—and so much more. "You like hugging her, too, right?"

Jack said, "Yeah, but she's my mom," like maybe Royce had forgotten.

He tried a different approach. "Do you mind that I hugged her?"

"No." Then, being a sly little boy, he asked, "Does that mean I can come here and play with Chaos again?"

Oh, the workings of a five-year-old mind. Royce laughed. "Sure, if your mom's okay with it."

That seemed to solve everything, at least for Jack.

For Royce, it wasn't quite that easy.


Joy could hear the low hum of voices in the kitchen as she returned Maris's call. What did Jack think, seeing them together?

She didn't have long to ponder it because Maris answered on the first ring.

"Hey, it's Joy. Sorry I didn't get to the phone in time."

"I need your help tomorrow," Maris blurted.

"Okay." Maris didn't sound upset, like there was a problem, but something in her voice made Joy go on alert. "Whatever you need."

"I'm going to Daron's house, for dinner. And...well, it's dumb, but I want to look pretty."

"Oh my gosh!" A hundred questions buzzed through Joy's brain, but she said only, "You're *always* pretty."

"Prettier, then. Like...hair, makeup. A cute shirt?" Maris groaned. "We won't have time to shop and I don't own anything! Not even mascara. How pathetic is that?"

"It's not pathetic at all, but don't worry, I have it covered." Catching on to the excitement, Joy paced the living room. "I have everything we need, and I can stop at the store tomorrow after I drop Jack off at school."

"I don't want to put you to any trouble."

"Are you kidding? I'm already excited!" This was something Joy could do for Maris, and she could barely wait.

"I can't look like you, hon. I mean, no skirts or—"

"You look terrific in denim! I wouldn't think of changing anything like that." She could imagine a pretty shirt and softer hairstyle. "You don't need to go heavy on the makeup, either." Joy knew that sometimes a little makeup just made a woman

feel good about herself and boosted her confidence. "We'll enhance things a bit. Do you have scissors?"

"Um…scissors?"

"We'll trim an inch off your hair. Only an inch, I promise."
Joy didn't know if Maris had ever cut her hair, but a trim to
tidy up the ends always worked wonders. "And I have a fabulous conditioner that you're going to love."

"Oh wow." Maris sounded a little dumbfounded. "Am I really doing this?"

"Having a date with Daron? About time, if you ask me."

"I told him no sex."

Joy huffed a laugh. "What? *Why?* You insisted it was good
for me, but now you—"

"He's six years younger than me."

"Big deal. You're both young and healthy and that's what
counts."

With a long sigh, Maris said, "I don't feel young."

"Well, you are, because you're only a year older than me and
I'm young." No way could Maris argue with that logic.

"He has a *house*, Joy. Did you know that?"

Of course she did, but Maris sounded so surprised Joy asked
with caution, "Didn't you?"

"No! He comes off all… I don't know. Irresponsible."

"Daron? Daron Hardy?" Joy repeated with disbelief. "We're
talking about the same guy, right?" Yes, Daron liked to joke
and God knew he had his fair share of female admirers, but Joy
could never fault him on his sense of responsibility. "The same
man who pitches in to help anyone who needs it, who keeps
everything in the park working, who stays late or comes in
early when something goes wrong? The same Daron who always answers his phone, smiles at everyone while working his
behind off, who—"

"Ugh, enough already." Maris sucked in an audible breath.

"You know what I'm talking about. He makes everything a joke."

Gently, Joy said, "It's called being happy."

Two pulse beats of time passed, then Maris muttered, "Shit."

"It's true," Joy offered, "that he teases you more than anyone else. Always has. We all realize it's because he has a thing for you, and you…well, you seem to like everyone except him."

Sounding hurt and defensive, Maris whispered, "I like him."

"But you're afraid of liking him too much?"

"I already said *shit*, right?" She groaned loudly, then said it again, a little louder. "Shit."

Joy grinned. "It'll be fine. You two will talk over dinner and work out any misunderstandings. I'll get to the camp store early tomorrow so we can make plans."

"Maybe I could have him pick me up at your place? That way you could help me spiff up and I won't have a chance to ruin it?"

"Love that idea. Consider it a date!" Smiling, she disconnected— and found Royce standing there, Chaos sitting on his foot, Jack leaning against his thigh. The three of them watched her.

Royce asked mildly, "Date?"

Though he tried to seem relaxed, resting one hand on Jack's shoulder, wariness had crept into his expression.

Silly man.

Joy could barely work out a time to see him, so he shouldn't think she'd have time—and definitely not interest—to see anyone else.

"With Maris," she specified. "For some girl stuff." Even saying it made Joy want to laugh in giddy excitement. Maris might expect big changes, but they weren't necessary. With her dark blond hair and naturally dark lashes and brows, any more than the barest makeup would be too much. Joy knew exactly what she wanted to do, the top she wanted to loan Maris and the advice she'd give before she left.

For now, though, Royce continued to watch her, so she tucked away her phone and picked up Jack's coat. Leaning toward him, speaking in a stage whisper, she stated, "Maris is going to Daron's for dinner."

The surprise she expected never came. Instead, Royce tipped back his head and groaned. "Guess that means tomorrow is out for us." When he looked at her again, he wore a lopsided grin. "Good for Daron, though."

Smiling, Joy handed Jack's coat to him and sat down on the couch to pull on her boots. "Remember, call anytime."

Jack, not understanding the significance of that, said, "Yeah, call us. We can come over to dinner again." He held Chaos's face. "You'd like that, wouldn't you, boy?"

Chaos gave an enthusiastic *yes*.

"Well, now," Royce said. "Your mom will have to let me know your favorite foods."

Jack's face lit up. "I'll eat anything!"

With a roll of her eyes, Joy said, "If only he felt that way at home."

Turning on her, Jack said, "But you cook fish."

She grabbed for him, but he squealed and ducked behind Royce, which got Chaos superpumped for a game.

Laughing, Joy said, "I *try* fish. Occasionally." With a mock frown aimed at Jack, she added, "Someone says it smells bad."

Falling to his back and sprawling out like a starfish, Jack groaned. "It's terrible!"

"Personally, I love fish." Royce scooped up Chaos before he could accidentally scratch Jack's face. The pup's paws were oversized for his body, which meant he had a lot of growing to do yet. "When fish is raw, it smells, but once it's cooked… Mmm. Delicious."

Cracking open one eye, Jack peered up at him. "I could try your fish."

"My son," Joy said. "The master manipulator."

"Tell you what." Royce knelt down beside him, Chaos still held close with one thick arm. "Each time you come to dinner, you have to agree to try something new. Deal?" He held out a hand.

Rolling to his bottom, Jack sat facing him, ready agreement tripping off his tongue. "Deal."

They shook hands.

"If you decide you like fish, we could try catching our own in the spring."

In the spring? Around Jack's enthusiastic response, which included jumping up and down, Joy wondered where they'd be in the spring. A fling couldn't extend that long, could it?

When it eventually ended, as she assumed it had to, would they remain friends? Would Royce still be a part of her son's life? Jack might be satisfied with that arrangement, but Joy couldn't imagine a time when she'd see Royce and not want him. Like now.

Royce, Jack and Chaos all tumbled around the floor, wrestling and laughing, with Royce alternately hefting Jack into the air over his head, and playfully pinning him down so Chaos could lick his face. It was an irresistible scene, hearing her son's hilarity and seeing how comfortable he was with Royce.

One that made her long for more.

It would be so easy to fall in love with Royce.

Heck, she was already halfway there.

"Wow." Maris looked in the mirror, turning her head this way and that. "Trimming off that tiny bit made a big difference."

"The conditioner helped, too." As did the way Joy blew out her hair for her, using a round brush to add some volume. "You have gorgeous hair. I know women who would pay big bucks to get those summer highlights, and yours are natural."

"Life in a sunny park," Maris said, peering closer to see her eyes. "The mascara is nice, too. It's just enough that I look like me, but better."

Joy grinned, pleased with the results. "And the sweater?" She'd borrowed from her own closet, choosing a black, criss-cross sweater with a wide V-neck. She'd bought it on clearance, then regretted the purchase when, the one time she'd worn it, it had felt too revealing, like she might actually fall out. Because Maris had a smaller bust, it fit her perfectly.

She was also shorter than Joy, so it crossed at exactly the right spot. Luckily, Maris had worn a black bra.

Paired with trim-fitting faded jeans and black boots, Maris looked amazing.

She slanted Joy a look. "Now I have boobs."

That made Joy laugh out loud. "You've always had them. You just wear boxy T-shirts and sweatshirts that make them harder to notice." She glanced at Jack, saw he was involved painting with the kit Royce had bought him. Knowing he wasn't listening, she said low, "That never slowed Daron down, though, which is why he was always teasing you."

"Yeah, well, he can't miss 'em tonight, can he?" Maris shook her head, making her hair drift back and forth over her shoulders. "It feels so different. I keep it in a ponytail so it's not in my way, but this is more feminine."

"Most women like changing up their look every now and then."

"And those boxy shirts? They're comfortable for working."

Joy turned Maris to face her. "You're not working tonight, and I'm going to give you the same advice you gave me, but maybe tempered a little. Have fun."

"Yeah, we'll see."

Joy didn't like that lack of confidence. It wasn't Maris's way. "You really do look terrific."

She nodded. "Thanks. You do great work. It's just... I'm wondering if this is all too obvious?"

"What do you mean?"

"Is Daron going to think I want to impress him? Because I *don't*. I'm doing this for me, not him."

It was a novel thing, seeing Maris struggle with uncertainty. In a way, it made her even more likable. "I vote you do it for both of you."

There was a knock at the door, and Maris blanched.

"I'll get it," Jack said, already scrambling out of his chair.

"Look out the window first," Joy reminded him. They'd arranged for Daron to meet Maris here so they could ride together to his house. Still, she wanted Jack to always be careful.

Hand to her stomach, Maris whispered, "This is a mistake."

Joy lifted her brows. Wow, Maris really was nervous. How crazy was that? Grabbing her up in a hug, Joy said, "This is *amazing*. Now put on your game face and get ready to have a well-deserved good time."

# CHAPTER TEN

Daron knew he needed to stop staring, but…damn. He'd been half-hard ever since he laid eyes on Maris tonight. She'd greeted him in Joy's apartment with a discernible chip on her shoulder. Her beautiful, almost bare shoulder…which led into the creamy skin of her chest and down into mouthwatering cleavage.

Maris as her usual self was tempting enough.

This was just overkill.

"How far to your house?" she asked.

"Almost there." He tried to keep it together because tonight was to show her he respected her rules, that he was a grown-ass man, and that they had more in common than she thought. "You warm enough?"

"Yes."

That curt answer didn't reassure him, especially with the way she sat huddled in the seat, her arms folded around her, her shoulders up. Since he'd picked her up, his truck hadn't completely lost the heat, but the wind outside sent tree branches dipping and dried leaves tumbling. In the space of a few hours, a cold

front had moved in an...
got the precipitation that ...inter than fall. If they
problems at the park tomorr... ...redicted, there'd be

Last he'd noticed, a few coup...
man was in a tent and three RVs ... ...abins, one ...ung
didn't expect any of them to last m... ...he propert... He
the weather changing. ...especially ...ith

"Here we are." His headlights danced o...
as he turned into the driveway. He hit the ...nt w...dows
and pulled into the single car space. ...or o...her

As Maris opened her seat belt, she checked out ...shelvin...
and the tools placed precisely on pegboards. "So tidy.

For some reason, it made him feel self-conscious. "Yeah, ...ell,
being organized is a necessity at the park so naturally it ...r-
ries over." He got out and circled the car, but she didn't w...t
for him and was already out, hugging herself again, before ...e
reached her.

"Come on." He took her elbow and led her to the two steps
up into the kitchen. This was his favorite room of the house,
with the bright white Shaker cabinets and black granite tops.

She looked around in something close to awe. "It's so warm."

"The slate floor is heated. Same in the bathroom. When I'm
home, I prefer to go barefoot." And he was often in just his
boxers. "When I remodeled things, I tried to figure out all the
modern gadgets, you know?" Like a kid showing off his first
car, Daron stepped over to the sink to point out the faucet. "I
agonized over this beauty the most, but..." It suddenly hit him
that he was being rude. "Here, let me take your coat."

"Thank you." She stripped it off and handed it to him.

As if it didn't leave her standing there looking like his hottest fantasy.

While he soaked in the sight of her, she pushed up her sleeves

and tested the hands-free faucet. "Huh. That's pretty neat." She dried her hands. "Will you show me the rest?"

"Sure." It might not matter, but he wanted her to see that he was settled, that he had as much yearning for home and hearth as the next person.

A tour through the house that should have taken three minutes took twenty with Maris admiring every small detail and giving lots of oohs and aahs.

Showing her the bedrooms tested Daron. The smallest, which was *really* small, was still mostly empty. The guest room was sort of an office with a foldout bed on one wall and a desk and chair on the other, and his room…well, his room made him think about getting her on the king-size bed. Naked.

But by God he'd follow her rules if it killed him, and to that end, he led her back to the kitchen. "Something to drink? Beer, wine?"

She shrugged one shoulder. "Tea?"

"I have bottled but not fresh. Is that okay?"

"Yes." She slid her sexy behind into one of the chairs along the island bar. "So you're going to have a chicken dinner sometime tonight?"

"It's mostly done, smart-ass." He grinned as he set her drink on the counter with a paper napkin. Turning, he opened the oven and showed her the fried chicken, already cooked and keeping warm, with an oven-safe bowl of mashed potatoes beside it. "I fixed everything before I left to get you."

"Good, because I'm hungry." She closed her eyes and took a deep breath. "Mmm. Smells delicious."

For a second, Daron couldn't pull his gaze away, caught by that soft, somehow sensual expression on her face. When her lashes lifted, it jolted him back to reality and he grabbed up a pot holder to get out the food.

His hands shook. *Crazy.*

But yeah, he wanted her that much, had wanted her for too long, and now he had her here and his main goal was *not* sex.

Somehow he'd survive, but he suspected the evening would be both pleasure and torture.

Using tongs, he put the chicken on a platter. With a serving spoon he stirred the potatoes. Glancing over his shoulder at her, he said, "I had two tomatoes left on the vine. Just picked them yesterday. Give me five minutes and I'll have it on the table."

She turned to see the small four-seat table in his connected dining room. "You already set the table, too."

"For you." And only for her. "I usually eat here at the bar or on the couch watching TV."

She went quiet, too quiet, as he cut the tomatoes into thick slices. Nothing fancy, but then he wasn't a fancy cook. Yeah, he could read a cookbook and follow directions, but his tastes ran more toward down-home cooking.

"Where do you sit with your dates?"

He paused on his way to the table. Maris stayed half turned away, only her eyes slanted toward him, almost like she didn't want to face him head-on.

It pissed him off a little, her mentioning other dates. He was here with her, and no one else mattered. He didn't think saying that would score him any points, though, so he tried to be honest. "I don't generally cook dinner for other women."

"Don't bother feeding them, huh?"

Yeah, she was out for battle. Was this another of her defensive moves? A way to make him lose interest?

No way to tell for sure, but he'd gotten her this far so he wouldn't give up easily.

"If I do," he said as he put the dishes on the table, "it's pizza or something like that." There, let her stew on that.

He walked past her, trying his damnedest not to scowl, and

adjusted the playlist on his phone so muted music filled the air. "Tea okay with your dinner, or did you want something else?"

She lifted the glass like a toast. "This works."

At the table, he pulled out a chair for her and waited.

"Such a gentleman."

He locked his teeth at the way she said it, which didn't sound anywhere close to a compliment. "I have my moments."

"I like your music."

Well, that was something. "I prefer country," he told her, "but if you have another preference—"

"I don't." She listened as she chose a chicken breast. "Who is that?"

"Keith Urban, 'Parallel Line.'" He chose two legs, a heap of potatoes, then asked, "You like it?"

"It's sexy." She swayed a little in her seat. "That's what you listen to?"

Usually his music was a little rowdier, but these lyrics were perfect for their first date. "I have a variety. A little of this, a little of that. George Strait, Brad Paisley, Sam Hunt, Chuck Wicks, Carrie Underwood—"

Her head shot up, a forkful of mashed potatoes held just before her mouth. "You listen to Carrie Underwood?"

"Course." What, did she think he singled out male singers? "Some of hers are my favorites." He gave it quick thought, then said, "I'll make you a playlist. When you have a little quiet time, you can give it a listen."

Her gaze softened even more. "Okay, I'd like that. Thanks."

Daron made a mental note to get the music together right away. It'd give him a good excuse to see her again.

They managed a few peaceful minutes while they each ate. Every couple of bites, Maris made one of those sexy "Mmm" sounds that he somehow felt everywhere, most especially in inappropriate places.

"Good?" he asked, just to make conversation.

"Delicious."

At least he could do something right. "I'm glad you like it."

"I had no idea you cooked."

So she thought he sustained himself…how? On cold cereal and her cookies? "There are probably a lot of things about me you don't know."

"No kidding. Like this amazing house? I love it. When you said it was small, I wasn't sure what to expect." She got another helping of potatoes. "But there's enough room here for a whole family."

Daron almost choked on his bite of tomato. He swallowed, cleared his throat and said without thinking, "It's our first date, so let's not get ahead of ourselves."

The second she froze, he knew he'd blundered. Damn it, he wanted to relax, to be natural, *to be himself*, able to joke, but she had him on pins and needles, worrying about how to act and what to say.

So of course he said the wrong thing.

The slight narrowing of her eyes gave fair warning to her mood. "Probably our first and only date, so you have nothing to worry about, believe me." Her hand fisted in her napkin. "I shouldn't have wasted my breath on the compliments. I should have known someone like you would take them wrong."

Carefully, Daron set his fork aside. She'd been tossing barbs left and right and he'd done his best to ignore them.

No one could ignore a direct hit like that, though.

"Someone like me?" he repeated. "Tell me, Maris, what the hell does that even mean?"

Her mouth pinched, she breathed through her nose—and then she deflated with disgust. Sitting back in her seat, she muttered, "I have no idea."

"What's that?"

She gestured at him. "You're so full of charm and so...well, the opposite of serious. No matter what you're doing, it seems like you have a good time. You're...free."

That last word emerged as a whisper, diluting some of his annoyance. "Yeah, well, as you can see, I'm not the drunken frat boy you paint me to be."

"I know." Her frown seemed self-directed. "I think that bugs me most of all."

Meaning he couldn't win for losing?

Sitting back in his seat, Daron studied her, the averted gaze, the downturned mouth. Hell, he hadn't invited her here tonight to make her miserable. "I like you, Maris." That felt inadequate, so he corrected, "I *more* than like you."

Her startled gaze latched on to his. Was that fear he saw?

Yeah, he thought it might be. So did Maris fear what she felt for him? It would explain a few things.

With his heart punching against his ribs, he asked, "So what would it take?"

Her tongue slipped over her lower lip, and she asked, "What do you mean?"

"What would it take for you to give me a shot?" He saw her breath stall, her gaze dart away.

*Talk to me. Tell me the problem and we can work through it.*

For the longest time she looked down before picking up her fork and scooping up a bite of potatoes. "You really are a good cook. No reason to let the rest of my meal go to waste."

Of all the... Daron struggled with his frustration, but he felt like he was on to something here and he instinctively knew pushing Maris would never work. She was too independent to be verbally strong-armed, while at the same time he sensed her vulnerability. Giving her time, he followed her lead and finished eating.

When her plate was clean, she set aside her cutlery and folded

her hands in her lap. Her nervous swallow seemed to signal something.

Daron gave her his complete attention.

"I grew up pretty poor." Her gaze darted to his, and away. It took her a few more seconds, and she added, "Embarrassingly poor actually."

Embarrassingly? The way she tensed, as if waiting for a reaction, put him on the spot. If he knew what she needed, he'd give it to her, but he wasn't a mind reader so he said, "I grew up middle class. Dad worked at a car plant and Mom taught grade school."

After a deep breath that seemed to ease her a little, she smiled. "That sounds really nice."

He rubbed the back of his neck. Hell, her tension had become his own. "What did your folks do?"

"Well..." Color painted her cheeks and chest.

Maris didn't do anything half-assed, not even blushing. It intrigued him, seeing that wash of color over the tops of her breasts, her neck and cheeks.

"Mama mostly read the Bible." She rushed on, anxious to explain. "She loved me a lot, she really did, but she also enjoyed praying. I think because Daddy tended to drink too much in between jobs, and he was usually in between...because of the drinking."

Hoping to acknowledge that without any overt reaction showing, Daron gave a very slight nod.

"He wasn't a drunk. I mean, not like a mean drunk who abused anyone." Using both hands, she tucked her hair behind her ears and hunched her shoulders. "Mama said he was a functioning alcoholic, and that his own parents had been mean, is why he drank so much, but..."

This was the first time Maris had ever opened up to him and

as awful as the subject matter was, he considered it a step in the right direction.

The direction that would bring her closer to him.

"That's why you were poor?"

She nodded. "Mama spent most of her time in a rocking chair, sometimes reading the Bible aloud, sometimes reading it silently. My parents relied heavily on assistance, but they didn't always ask for it, so there were times that we did without dinner. All my clothes were donated hand-me-downs."

Damn. Maris deserved better. *Every* kid deserved better. Doing his utmost to keep any judgment from showing, Daron asked, "Donated from the church?"

She nodded. "And some neighbors. I used to wonder what it would be like to go to a store and just...buy what I wanted."

Daron barely kept his jaw from clenching. He saw nothing wrong with people getting help when they needed it. Hell, it was as nice for the one helping as it was for the one who got the help. But it sounded like her parents could have done a lot better.

In his mind, there was all kinds of abuse, some worse than others, and what her parents had done to her counted. A child should be cared for in *all* ways, and obviously she hadn't been.

"So, anyway," Maris said, switching tracks. "From the time I was thirteen I knew I'd be different, because I decided it."

"Different from them?" Or did she mean different from... him?

She answered in a roundabout way, saying, "I wanted to be my own boss."

"Mission accomplished," he said with a smile. "You have a hell of a business."

She nodded. "I never wanted to...to rely on anyone for anything."

"But you do so much for others." Maris was one of the most generous people he'd ever met.

She snorted. "Cookies and coffee? Big deal. I wanted to support myself, to never ask anyone for anything important."

That's why she worked so hard? Was it also why she shied away from getting involved with him? She didn't want to rely on him? "Determination is a powerful incentive."

His observation earned him a bitter laugh. "Maybe. I screwed up, though, diving straight into a job instead of getting an education." She peeked up at him. "I wanted to do that shopping, you know? And I did, but even then I was frugal. I've never bought music. We didn't have it growing up, and there's a radio in my car, so…" She shrugged. "I've *always* been frugal. I don't how to be any other way. Heck, even this sweater is Joy's, not mine."

Is that why she'd asked him to pick her up there?

Or was it that she didn't want him anywhere near her apartment? It seemed every answer with Maris led him to two more questions.

He'd be willing to bet Joy had done something with her hair, too, and all in all, it relieved him, because that meant Maris *would* accept help.

But maybe only from certain people.

Wishing he could hold her, wishing he could say a lot more but not wanting to bash her parents, Daron remarked, "College isn't for everyone."

"Maybe. But for several years it felt like I was just spinning my wheels, barely able to save any money, definitely not enough to get ahead." She looked across the table at him. "Stability is important to me."

"I can imagine." He had a few bites left on his plate, but his appetite was gone. "Where are your parents now?"

"They've both passed, died in a house fire from smoke inhalation. I gave them the best funeral I could, but it wasn't much."

No way did he want to blow this by misspeaking or interrupting, so Daron only said, "I understand."

"When I got the job at the park, I thought it'd be a part-time gig, a way to make some extra money. Then I took over Summer's End, and things kept changing, the situation grew and now…" She pressed a fist to her chest. "Summer's End is mine."

And that meant it mattered, even more than he'd ever realized. Cautiously, going for honesty and hoping it was right, Daron said, "You know everyone likes you. A lot. But the foundation of that like is a ton of respect and admiration." From him more than anyone.

"I think I resented you." She winced. "I've been an awful date and I know it, but seeing everything you've done, it just reminds me what I haven't been able to do yet."

"Our experiences are night and day." He was glad for the explanation, and the semiapologetic tone, but she needed to understand the advantages he'd had. "I'm close with my parents, always have been. They've given me things—" guidance, encouragement and, yes, the occasional loan when he was first starting out "—that your parents couldn't give you. It makes a huge difference."

"Still—"

"You might not realize it, but you're special." He meant that with all his heart. "The park wouldn't be the same without you."

Smiling a little, she played with the ends of her hair. "Are you trying to get laid?"

Grinning with her, he held up his hands. "I'm being honest, I swear." That feminine gesture with her hair was something he'd never seen her do before because she always wore it in a pony-tail. Now that he'd seen it loose, the dark blond waves trailing over her shoulders and chest, he'd always know what she looked like with it down. It'd probably plague him, but in a good way.

Maris said, "It feels like we're all important to the park. We work together like a family, don't you think?"

"Yes." Though Daron didn't want her thinking of him that

way, not when he wanted a more intimate relationship. "I have this vision of me as a cranky old seventy-year-old unclogging the showers, tweaking the pump on the pool and tuning up the mowers." Folding his arms on the table, he studied her. "What about you? Do you see yourself retiring from the park?"

"That wasn't my plan in the beginning, but now, yeah, I can't imagine ever leaving." Making another topic switch, she patted her stomach. "I'd ask if you have dessert, but I'm stuffed."

"Give it a few minutes and I can get us ice cream." He hesitated, but couldn't hold back. "I'm glad you plan to stay at the park. Whatever happens with us—"

"Nothing is happening with us."

"I'm glad you'll be there."

After speaking at almost the same time, they stared at each other.

Her gaze dropped to his mouth.

It was like she'd cast out a fishing line and reeled him in. He found himself pushing back his chair, which prompted her to quickly do the same. As he circled the table, she licked her lips, her eyes tracking him—until he stopped right in front of her.

"Maris." Her name sounded like a groan, but he was dying a little here, especially with the hungry way she looked at him. "Something *is* happening. You know that, right?"

Emotion seemed to coil within her, and Daron didn't know if it was anger, or...

She grabbed him, her hands sliding over his shoulders to lock behind his neck, her body crashing against his, her mouth on his mouth, her tongue slipping past his startled lips.

*Lust.* That emotion was lust and he wanted to rejoice. He turned his head for a better fit, softening the onslaught so his tongue could twine with hers, so he could taste her deeply. One hand settled low on her back, the other tangled in her silky hair.

God, he could kiss her all day and it wouldn't be enough.

Suddenly she pulled back, breathing hard, staring up at him as if dazed. "This is nuts."

"Then let's be nuts." He started to pull her close again... No, wait. Rule number four. No sex on the first date. He shook his head, hoping to clear it of the pounding need. "I mean—" He cleared his throat. "Let's be nuts enough to make out."

Maris searched his face. "Make out?"

"Yeah, you know. Neck a little. Maybe go to second base." He bobbed his eyebrows playfully, needing to lighten the sexual tension. "I can take it if you can."

She blinked once, twice—then shoved him back and turned, one hand pressed to her forehead. "No, I don't know that I can take it. I don't feel like me. I don't even look like me."

He eased up behind her the same way he would with a fractious animal. "You look amazing, but you always do." He kept his voice gentle. "Have to admit, I like seeing more of you."

"You mean my boobs."

Standing behind her, he rested his hands carefully on her rigid shoulders, his thumbs moving in slow circles over the base of her neck. "I'm always a fan of more skin, but the biggest difference is this." He nuzzled against her hair. "You have fucking amazing hair."

She turned with a purpose. "Okay, I'm convinced. I want you. You clearly want me. Let's do this."

*Let's do this?*

She wasn't much for romance. Or maybe that was just what she wanted him to think. He tried to sort out the ramifications of scooping her up and taking her down the hall to his bedroom.

Her cursed list of rules danced through his brain. Tonight was supposed to be about getting closer to her, period.

"Well?" she demanded.

"Um..." Damned if he did, damned if he didn't, so he opted for the long haul and said, "Rule number four, remember?"

Her eyes flared. "*You* are citing rule number four?"

"It seemed important to you."

"Rule number four," she repeated, musing. "Rule number four..."

Did she even remember the fucking rule? His shoulders bunched. "That's the one where you stated no sex."

"Thank you for reminding me." Stepping around him, she snatched up her plate and empty bottle of tea, and headed for the kitchen.

Goddammit, this was not good. "What are you doing?"

"My share of cleanup."

He grabbed his own plate and hustled after her. "You don't have to do that. Let's...talk. Maybe watch TV. I'll clean up later."

"Nope. It's time for me to go." She opened the cabinet under his sink, didn't find what she was looking for and opened another cabinet.

"Maris." He set his dishes on the counter. "Don't go."

"Where the hell is your garbage?"

Shit. Was it too late for him to agree to sex? One look at her face and he knew it most definitely was. "Son of a bitch."

Startled, she drew back. "Are you *cussing* at me?"

"No, because I would never do that—just like I wouldn't ignore *your* damn rules that said no sex." He snapped open the dishwasher and practically threw in the dishes. "Frustration is the son of a bitch. Do you know, I never walk on eggshells? I'm just me, and if that's not good enough for someone, that's their problem. But for you, I tried." He jammed in a pan, making the stupid thing fit, without even rinsing it.

"You know that's not going to come clean."

"Shows what you know. It has a pot scrubber feature." He closed the dishwasher and turned to her, arms folded. "I want to spend time with you, Maris. A quick fuck would be great—"

"I was hoping it wouldn't be all that quick."

*"If that was all I wanted."* She had an answer for everything. In other circumstances, he'd admire that about her. Now, it just infuriated him.

By small degrees, her features softened. "What is it you want?"

"Sex, for sure." She needed to understand how much he wanted her. "But more than that, too—and all you do is fight me." He smoothed a hand over her hair, then tipped up her chin. "It was *your* rule, honey. I'm just trying to make sure you don't regret coming here."

Her lips twitched, then bloomed into a self-deprecating smile. She snuggled in against him, not with lust this time, but with something even better, more like affection. "Can you forgive me?"

He rested his jaw against the top of her silky head and breathed in the scent of floral shampoo. He had her in his house. She was hugging him.

How could he not forgive her? "Consider it done."

"Thank you for being the reasonable one."

Not a trait she normally applied to him. "I have my moments, when something really matters." If Maris caught on that *she* mattered, she didn't say so.

"Date one, in the books." She looked up at him. "Really, Daron, I'm sorry. I don't usually unload my family history on people."

"I know and I'm honored that you told me." It made him feel a little special, too.

"I don't usually run from hot to cold in a heartbeat, either."

"It keeps me on my toes." He was so glad she wasn't slamming out, hell, he'd forgive just about anything.

"I didn't mean for any of that to happen, it just... I'm not used to being sexually frustrated, I guess. It's made me both whiny and bitchy."

He grinned at her roundabout way of admitting she wanted

him. "You are not either of those things, I swear. But hey, I could tell you about sexual frustration."

Maris snorted. "Like you've ever done without."

"I've done without you, and that counts for a lot." He kissed her hard and fast, before she could protest. "Truce?"

"All right. Truce." She glanced around the kitchen. "Where do you keep your bowls? I think I want ice cream, after all."

Joy woke to the sounds of hushed voices outside her apartment, which was really odd since she lived up a flight of outside stairs. The glow of the digital clock showed it to be 6:15. Too early for visitors.

Slipping from the bed, she peeked out the window, but the angle was wrong and she couldn't see the landing from where the low voices came.

More curious than alarmed, she darted into her son's room and found him sound asleep, sprawled sideways across his bed. Jack often ended up in that position, which made sleep tough on the nights that he had a bad dream or when he'd been sick and wanted to sleep with her.

Feet in the face, or a head in her ribs, was the norm whenever they shared a bed.

Quietly pulling Jack's door shut, she peeked into the living room. Through the curtain she saw shadows moving beneath the security light outside her door. She glanced down and saw that the door was still locked.

Should she call Coop? No, not yet. It might be a camper at the wrong door, or it could even be Coop, waiting for her to wake up because...of an emergency?

Moving more quickly now, Joy hurried into the bathroom, took a few seconds to take care of business, then pulled on a thick chenille housecoat and stepped into fuzzy slippers. She didn't dare look in the mirror as she tied the belt around her

waist. If she did, she'd probably find the need to comb her hair or rinse her face...

Vanity was a stupid reason to keep anyone waiting.

Creeping now, she went back into the living room and carefully pulled aside the curtain on the window.

There on her landing, both of them bundled up in winter coats, were Royce and Daron. What in the...? Dropping the curtain, she turned the lock and pulled open the door.

Startled, they both looked at her.

Then Royce looked all over her while Daron grinned and turned his back. "I'll wait at the bottom with Coop." Holding tight to the handrail and moving cautiously, he went back down the stairs.

With Coop? Joy leaned out the door, and sure enough, Coop stood at the base of the stairs with Chaos and his own dog, Sugar. The two animals were busy sniffing each other in impolite places and wagging their tails.

"Morning," Coop called up to her.

"Good morning." Gaze back on Royce, Joy asked, "Is something wrong?"

"No, and I'm sorry that we woke you." He pressed forward, which caused her to step back and into the apartment. Royce followed, quietly closed the door, looked past her and then at her mouth.

Knowing that look oh too well, Joy backpedaled. "Nope." She put a hand to her mouth. "I haven't even brushed my teeth yet."

Smiling, Royce caught her, anyway. "Just a quick kiss," he murmured as he bent to press his chilled lips to hers, gradually tugging her into full-body contact.

Still not fully awake, she had no defenses and melted against him.

With small pecks he kissed her jaw, her neck, and nuzzled

right below her ear, before he breathed, "Damn, you look incredibly hot straight from your bed."

Joy touched her hair and felt her face heating. "So...what's going on?"

"Ice storm last night." He put one more kiss to her temple and stepped back. "I found out when Chaos wanted out at the butt-crack of dawn, and I knew you'd be using those steps to get Jack to school. They're treacherous." His gaze went down her body. "By the way, the schools are on a two-hour delay."

"It's that bad?" She returned to the window to look out again. Sure enough, the outside light glinted over a layer of ice coating the front half of each step. "There's salt in the maintenance building."

"Yeah. Daron was here when I arrived, already salting the parking lot and all around the camp store."

Because he'd been worried about Maris. *Aww*, Joy thought with a small smile. She couldn't wait to hear how their evening had gone. She'd waited up as late as she could, but her car was still in the lot when she finally went to bed.

Daron's diligence this morning was more proof that he wasn't the negligent, immature person Maris wanted to believe him to be.

Royce cocked a brow. "Want to tell me what that secret little smile means?"

The smile widened into a grin as she headed into her kitchen. "Just wondering how he and Maris did last night."

"Daron's in a good mood, if that helps."

"Daron's always in a good mood." Joy got down the coffee can and filters from an upper cabinet. This time of year, Maris wouldn't arrive at the park for another hour, but Joy was willing to bet all the men would appreciate coffee since they were already up and working. While filling the carafe with water, she asked, "So why is Coop here?"

"Same as me—he was up with Sugar and realized the park would be a mess. He came out to help Daron."

"And now you're all here because of my steps?" She shook her head, touched by their consideration but feeling bad that they'd gone to so much trouble. "I would have seen the ice and been careful."

"Sure." He leaned against the cabinet beside her and pulled off his gloves. "But it's still dangerous, and you have a five-year-old to think about, plus his school bag and your purse."

She didn't admit that she'd slipped on those steps more than once. "If you guys leave the salt, I can—"

"Joy." He traced a still-cold finger over her jaw. "How about you let us take care of it? I'm already here, Coop and Daron are already up, and we don't mind doing it. In fact, Coop has a rubber mat he's going to put at the camp store and we're thinking of running into town to buy some treads for the stairs, at least until I can do something about keeping the snow and ice off them in the first place."

Her mouth dropped open. He planned to do *what*?

Joy knew there was something she should say, some denial she could make, but her brain drew a blank.

Finally she managed, "Let the guys know I'll have coffee in five. I'll be right back," and she rushed away before Royce could reply.

# CHAPTER ELEVEN

In her bedroom, Joy closed the door and, still racing, went into the bathroom to clean her teeth, brush her hair and wash her face. She looked in her closet, but everything seemed too complicated with three men waiting, so she pulled out a thick, tunic-length sweatshirt and lined tights, which she usually wore only when doing yoga...which sadly, didn't happen often enough. She pulled on socks and stepped into low boots. No makeup, but it was the best she could do on very short notice.

When she reached the kitchen again, she found Royce filling three mugs. He glanced up—and his gaze snagged on her all over again.

That particular heat in his eyes could be lethal. Feeling as if he'd just physically stroked her, she held her breath and waited.

Voice rough, he growled, "I need to be with you again, Joy. Soon. Right this second wouldn't be soon enough."

Joy flushed with reciprocal heat. Yeah, she needed that, too. Unfortunately, it wasn't meant to be. At least, not in the next few hours.

"I… That is, Jack…" She lifted a hand toward the hall behind her. "He's sleeping, but—"

"What I need," Royce stressed, giving her a fond smile of understanding, "and what I think should happen are two different things. It's almost guaranteed that every time I see you, I'm going to want you, but you shouldn't worry that I'd take a chance on Jack walking in on us. You have my word right now that I'd never do anything to hurt that little boy."

His ebony eyes, which looked a little tired to her, shone with sincerity. "Thank you."

"Ah, honey. Don't thank me for *not* being a selfish ass, okay?"

Smiling, Joy nodded. "So, what brought that on? The sudden interest, I mean."

"You're kidding, right? Nothing sudden about it, but seeing you like that—" his gaze went over her again, his nostrils flaring slightly with a deep breath "—is enough to make me half-hard."

Of course her gaze dropped to his lap, but his coat covered his fly. She swallowed in equal parts relief and disappointment. A little self-conscious, she tugged on the thick sweatshirt. "People don't usually see me all sloppy."

"Your version of sloppy is hot." After getting down a fourth cup, Royce said, "Hope you don't mind that I made myself at home."

"I'm glad you did." When he carried two cups outside, she used the opportunity to doctor hers with a liberal amount of sugar and creamer. She needed both caffeine and a sugar jolt this morning. Her heart thumped from the exchanges with him.

He wanted her as much as she wanted him.

Better still, he truly cared about Jack's feelings. That, more than anything else, endeared Royce to her.

Endeared him and made her question her intent with this entire affair.

A few seconds later, her door opened again and, after clean-

ing his feet on the entry rug, Royce strolled back in. Ice crystals clung to his hair and shoulders, telling her it had started to sleet again.

If the winter weather held, it'd throw off her Halloween plans for the park—and would also negatively impact Royce's business since Halloween at the drive-in almost guaranteed a packed lot.

But not under these conditions.

She was used to the crazy Ohio weather and had adjusted plans too many times to count when snow arrived on the worst possible day. Things could flip again just as quickly, so for now, she'd hold out hope for milder weather.

Stuffing his gloves into his coat pockets, Royce went first to the coffee, took a few drinks, then turned to her. "I told you I'm handy with my hands, right?"

Oh, the things that statement brought to mind. She knew well what he could accomplish with those hands.

His grin told her he'd read her thoughts. "Besides that," he said, one brow arrogantly cocked as he approached, stopping right in front of her. "I'm good with building and repairs."

"Yes?" Joy had no idea where he was going with this, and it wasn't easy for her to think with him so near, the brisk scent of the winter storm mixing with his own delicious aroma.

He dropped his head for a moment, and when he raised it, he snared her gaze with his own. Looking far too serious, he said, "Your stairs are solid, but still dangerous. The treads and salt will help for now, but there's a better long-term solution."

"The stairs are fine," she said, already knowing her budget didn't allow for "long-term solutions."

As if she hadn't spoken, he continued. "Covering the stairs so the snow and ice never reach them is the way to go."

"Royce." She didn't like the idea of imposing on him. "You have enough to do with your own repairs."

He ignored that, too. "By the way, Coop told me to let you

know he'll cover the cost. Said he should have done something about the steps ages ago, but you'd never complained so he hadn't thought about it."

*Until Royce pointed it out?* Joy gulped down the rest of her coffee, letting it warm her from the inside out, hoping it'd clear out the cobwebs.

Setting aside the cup, she took a step forward, until she and Royce almost touched. "Royce."

He brushed his knuckles over her cheek. "Hmm?"

"I appreciate what you're doing. I really do."

The problem was that their relationship didn't make allowances for him to do things like this. It crossed the bounds of a friend with benefits into something very different.

Didn't it?

Joy shook her head. "You shouldn't be here now, bothering with this stuff when your hands are already full."

He held out his muscular arms, palms up, fingers spread. "Do I look like I've taxed myself?"

No, he looked like a sensual offering. His coat parted, showing her a thermal shirt fitted over a broad chest.

*Stay on track.*

Joy cleared her throat and worked up a slight frown. "That's not the point."

"The point is that those stairs should be covered to make them safe."

Deciding to be blunt, Joy said, "I don't need you to take care of me. I've managed on my own for years now."

There was something in his eyes, something she didn't understand, before he turned away and retrieved his coffee from the counter. He kept his back to her as he sipped. "The thing is…" The words trailed away. He set the coffee aside and braced both hands on the edge of the counter.

Concerned, Joy edged closer to him. "What?" She'd never

seen Royce like this, so pensive and obviously troubled. "What is it?"

Dropping his head, he laughed, but it wasn't a happy sound. "Royce?"

Wearing a smile of irony, he turned to face her. "When I moved here, I had this grand idea of being..." He visually searched for a word. "Unencumbered."

Joy didn't know what that meant, but surely if he wanted less on his plate, he shouldn't be here this morning, offering to take on more work. "I see," she said, because it seemed like the appropriate response. "Well, then, taking on my responsibilities isn't—"

"I'm not. I *couldn't*." He ran a hand through his hair, pushing the inky strands back, then letting them fall forward again.

Could a man be any sexier? She honestly didn't think so.

"Look," he said, "I can't imagine a bigger responsibility than a child, right? That's a lifetime commitment and the bulk of it is going to fall on you no matter what. Doesn't mean others can't help a little, especially when the help is easily given."

"Caring for Jack isn't a hardship," Joy countered, "because I love him so much."

"I know, and full disclosure, it's damned appealing."

"It is?" Joy didn't entirely understand that, either. She started to say that all moms loved their children—and then she thought of her own mother and bit her lip instead. No, all mothers most definitely did not feel the same love and devotion that she had for her son. She'd cross heaven or hell, and everywhere in between, to care for Jack.

That didn't mean she wanted to take advantage of Royce.

Folding her arms, she studied him. "The thing is, our... arrangement doesn't allow for such an imposition."

As if that description of their relationship offended him, his brows twitched down.

Joy didn't know what else to call it. "Royce—"

"The last few years were nonstop. I guess I got used to staying busy."

"You're still busy."

He shook his head. "The drive-in doesn't take nearly as much time as I thought it would, and we'll be off-season in another week. I'll work on the house, but still, I feel like I'm at loose ends, like things aren't quite as I imagined them. Or maybe…" He let out a breath and said lower, "Like maybe I don't even know what the hell I want anymore."

She understood that feeling. Lately, she'd been uncertain, as well, not just for herself but for Jack, too. Any decisions she made would ultimately affect him.

Keep things as they were, and lavish all her attention on her son?

Or consider the idea of a stronger male influence, a unique bond with another person who cared for him?

That person could, or could not, be Royce. His indecisiveness now didn't necessarily mean he was looking for a more meaningful relationship with her. If she took his words at face value, he simply wanted to help because he could—as any *friend* might.

Joy tried to think of the right thing to say, something that wasn't too heavy. "You have Chaos."

His laugh this time sounded just right, making her smile with relief.

"He's a frisky little pup, but not exactly a time-sink, and not at all what I meant." Royce caught her waist and hauled her in.

Oh, how she liked that, the familiarity of his body, the comfort of their interactions.

Much, much nicer than wading through emotional questions she had no answers to.

"The point," Royce stressed, "is that I'm adjusting my ex-

pectations, and I *want* to help with your stairs. Do me a solid and say yes."

That was so ludicrous Joy stared at him. "It's doing you a favor for me to…let you help?"

He put his forehead to hers. "Yeah, something like that." Warmth filled eyes as dark as pitch, the brawny hands on her waist gave a slight squeeze and his mouth brushed hers. Close, so very close, he murmured, "Now agree, because Daron and Coop are waiting for me."

That statement hit her like a dousing of ice water. "Oh my God." How had she forgotten about them standing outside in the freezing sleet? Pushing Royce back and shooing him with her hands, she said, "Go, go. But please be careful."

"The same to you. If you decide you and Jack need to leave, text me first, okay?"

Her independent pride bristled. "For what reason?"

"So I can make sure the stairs are clear."

Umbrage lifted her chin. "You think I can't do that?"

His mouth curled. "I'm pretty sure you can do anything you set your mind to, but I meant I'd move any tools we're using."

"Oh." And…now she felt foolish. It had been a very long time since she'd checked in with anyone, but she had little resistance left so she nodded. From someone else the request might have felt intrusive, but with Royce it felt caring. "Will you also let me know if you need anything?"

"Sure." His gaze moved to the hall that led to their small bedrooms. "Will it wake Jack if we start working?"

"A Mack truck driving through here probably wouldn't wake him."

Royce grinned. "Perfect." Hesitating at the door, he looked at her over his shoulder. "Maybe if I finish in time, and Jack is still in school, Coop would keep an eye on Chaos."

His gaze was so intense, so probing, it thrilled her. "That would be perfect."

A slow appreciative smile promised heated things. "Then I can guarantee we'll finish in time."

For once, Maris wasn't working. It felt oddly right, sitting in a booth with her feet propped on the opposite seat, a hot coffee in hand as she waited for Joy to arrive. She used the YouTube app on her phone to listen to more country music, now that Daron had turned her on to it.

She liked it. She couldn't see herself purchasing music, not when she could put the money to something she deemed more important, but if Daron did as promised and made her a playlist, she wouldn't need to, anyway.

Why had she never thought about music before? Sometimes in her car she turned on a radio station, but not out of any deep preference. Mostly she needed to break the quiet. Being still had always been a problem for her, but there was no way to bustle around when behind the wheel. That stillness, combined with the silence, always drew her into the past.

It was never a friendly visit.

Now, thanks to Daron, she might actually find a new way to ease her troubled thoughts.

She'd made some crazy assumptions about him, like the idea that he'd gravitate to death-metal music or something equally loud and jarring. It was dumb, because that didn't really jive with his overall persona of a happy-go-lucky guy.

Pegging him as a carefree, too-young bachelor who spent every additional minute in the sack with a variety of young women who would idolize his fit bod and sexy smile was equally dumb.

Oh, she wasn't under any illusions. She figured Daron had more than his fair share of sexcapades, but it couldn't be to the

degree she'd assumed, not with all the work he'd put into his house.

And the man had a garden. Before he'd driven her home, he'd shown her the rectangle of yard that, over the summer, had yielded tomatoes, green beans, squash, zucchini and carrots. He'd also shown her the coop he'd recently started building so in the spring he could get some chicks.

*A stud who wanted to raise chickens and grow his own produce?*

How the hell could she have ever envisioned that? It was like he'd dragged together her version of the perfect guy—short a few years of age—and rolled it all up into the perfect package.

Just for her.

He'd set down roots. He'd focused on his future.

He'd be practically self-sustaining!

When she closed her eyes, Maris could almost see him in his yard, bare feet in the lush, neatly trimmed grass, a bucket of corn in hand as he strolled along, feeding chickens in his usual summer garb of loose board shorts and a raggy tee.

The image made her mouth go dry and accelerated her pulse.

It was a nice visual, calming and peaceful, but it also sent a frisson of heat racing through her.

What would it be like to have that life?

*He didn't propose marriage*, she reminded herself.

*If you want that life, you have to get it for yourself.*

Another good one.

Maris looked out the window at the rippling surface of the lake.

There'd be no more leaving the camp store door open in welcome, not with frost everywhere. This time of year usually made her a little melancholy. She needed the liveliness of the season, the nonstop frenzy, to keep her thoughts focused away from her past, away from the feelings of hunger, of people looking down on her with pity.

This year was a little different. She felt such an incredible bond to Joy that she actually anticipated the quiet so they could visit more. Instead of her thoughts going inward to sadder times, they bloomed out, thinking of Joy's reaction to different things, wondering what her suggestions might be.

Wondering, too, how she and Royce were getting along. That made her smile. Daron had been right. Joy was falling for Royce fast and hard. She only hoped Royce felt the same.

But then, if he didn't, Joy would get through it. Her girl was a fighter clear down to her soul. A quiet, unassuming woman with a will of iron.

Damn, but Maris loved Joy's spirit.

She was busy searching for a new song when the door opened and a gust of wintery air blew in. Thinking it'd be Joy, she smiled as she looked up—and the smile froze when she found Joy's mother in the doorway instead.

Whoa. The wintery storm had nothing on that lady.

Suddenly being in the shop alone didn't feel quite so cozy.

Without standing, Maris asked, "Can I help you?"

"Where is my daughter?"

Other than a slightly red nose, the woman seemed impervious to the cold, thanks to her fur-trimmed leather coat with matching gloves.

"Who's your daughter?"

Maris's question, deliberately absurd, caused her mother's mouth to tighten. "Young lady, you know exactly who I mean. Where is she?"

Maris made a point of looking around the store. "Not here."

"I can see that."

She hadn't moved from the doorway, which Maris considered a good thing—except that she kept the door wide open. When the furnace kicked on, Maris mentally tabulated the additional cost to her electric bill.

Lazily, she dropped her feet to the floor and stood, coffee cup in hand as she headed around to the serving side of the counter. Less chance of frostbite with a little space between her and Joy's mother. "If you want to leave your name and a number, I'll tell Joy that you dropped in. But it might not be for a while." Actually, it could be any minute now. "Or not at all today."

"I demand that you give me her address."

*Demand?* Maris didn't mean to exacerbate the situation, but her snort of laughter probably did just that. "Go ahead," she said, full of challenge. "Demand."

Footsteps carried in, and then Daron pushed past the woman, his gaze seeking out Maris, and filling with relief when he spotted her. Keeping his gaze resolutely on her, he said, "Ah, there you are."

Maris couldn't help but smile. "Yes, here I am." It amused her how he deliberately ignored the other woman.

Pulling the stocking cap from his head, he lifted his brows in question. "Everything okay?"

Praying Daron would understand, Maris said, "This lady is looking for Joy, but I told her Joy isn't here and we don't know when to expect her. Probably not for a while, right?"

"Right," he said, quickly putting a thermos on the counter. "Fill her up and I'll be on my way."

Hoping that meant he'd warn Joy, Maris took thirty seconds to do as asked. Daron screwed the lid back on, nodded at her, said, "Ma'am," to the mother and stepped back out—thankfully pulling the door closed behind him.

Releasing a breath, Maris smiled. Daron would warn Joy and it'd be up to her if she wanted to see her mother or not.

Maris voted for not.

The driver from the previous visit stuck his head in the door. "Are we staying?" he asked. "I'll need to park if we—"

"Wait outside," Mrs. Reed snapped, and pushed the door shut

in his face. Eyes narrowed on Maris, she said, "You may give my daughter a message."

"Okay, sure." Maris refilled her own coffee, and no way in hell would she offer any to the old bat. "Shoot."

"Tell Joy that…" As if lost for the right words, she hesitated, and for only a single moment she looked almost human.

Then her narrow chin shot up. "Tell her we need to talk before she visits the attorney. It's important."

"I'll pass it along. When I see her, I mean."

"See that you do."

Because…she was an errand boy? Pretending nonchalance, Maris blew on her coffee to cool it.

There was another moment of indecisiveness, and the woman said a brisk, "Thank you."

Huh. Maris summoned a smile. "You're welcome."

Nodding, the woman turned to leave.

Wow. The second the door closed, Maris set down the coffee and slumped on the counter. Good God, how had Joy survived being raised by that churlish, rude witch? Here she'd thought her own mother was bad with her constant rocking and praying. At least she'd prayed for Maris; she'd hugged her often and always told her she loved her.

No, her mama hadn't shown that love in conventional ways, but she'd never made Maris feel *unloved*.

Pulling out her phone, Maris texted Joy. Your mother just swept out of here. Stay low for a bit.

An immediate reply showed. I'm so sorry!

It seemed clear to Maris that while her parents' lack of initiative had made her überdriven, the cold demeanor of Joy's parents made her sympathetic.

And apologetic.

Don't be, Maris texted. *Not with me.* Want to gab soon? I have coffee to share & updates to give.

Be there in ten!

Ten minutes. Crazy how much she valued that time with Joy. She'd grown up without anyone to really talk to, to confide in. Like music, she hadn't known what she was missing.

But now she did, and she'd never take it for granted.

Not when she was dying to unload on everything that had happened last night with Daron. Being this confused wasn't a usual occurrence for Maris. Throughout her life she'd set goals, and then worked her ass off for them. The situation with Daron was a challenge she couldn't figure out, because she couldn't decide if she wanted it—wanted *him*—or not. It would be such an enormous change, and yet—

The door opened again and he strode in, his expression uneasy. "Hey, you okay?"

Now why the hell wouldn't she be? Maris was coming up with a snarky reply, just to be contrary, but he hadn't stopped walking and it struck her that he was coming right around the counter and that he apparently planned to—

Lips on lips, firm, two seconds... His warm breath caressed her cheek. Three, four, five...

He straightened and his hand went to her face. "I hated leaving you alone like that, but I figured you wanted me to warn Joy."

Maris didn't mean to, but she licked her tingling lips. "I..."

Daron took her mouth again, deeper this time, more thoroughly. As he gradually eased back, he groaned, then murmured, "Sorry. You were saying?"

Who the hell knew? Maris sure didn't.

"You're okay?"

Right. He'd come in like a hero to save her. Unacceptable.

After clearing her throat and standing a little straighter, Maris said, "I'm fine. Sharp words have never done me any damage."

"They can hurt all the same." He wrapped his hand lightly

around her ponytail and slow-stroked it to the end. "I found Joy in the maintenance shed with Royce. She was worried about you, all hell-bent on charging down here to take the heat off you." He leaned down, and this time his mouth trailed over her neck. The damp heat of his lips, the touch of his tongue on sensitive skin, made her belly flip-flop in a delicious way. "I told Joy you had it under control."

See, now *that*, his confidence in her, mattered more than his macho need to protect.

"It took some convincing, because Joy feels responsible for her mother's behavior. When Royce told her he'd come along with her, she gave in and stayed put. Guess she didn't want Royce dealing with the woman, either."

"Cheers to Royce."

"Yeah. I came as soon as I saw the car. I swear when I stepped in, the store was ten degrees colder than outside. That lady is like an arctic wind, freezing everything around her."

No kidding. Maris still chilled. "If Joy had come straight here, instead of flirting with Royce, she'd have walked into that unpleasant surprise." Maris patted his shoulder and tried not to think about the rock-solid body beneath his coat and sweatshirt. "Thanks for heading her off."

"Not a problem." He grinned. "Still surprises me to see Joy with someone. She's always been…"

"Distant, I know. Having met her mother, I can understand why."

"Royce told me all about her. Sounds like a nightmare."

"That covers it." Maris tried to be casual, but having a man touch her, kiss her, didn't fall into the norm for her daily routine. "I should get back to work." Not that she actually had any work to do. Thanks to the morning ice storm, there'd been a rush on the coffee when the sun first rose, but now the few re-

maining campers had departed. Many promised to be back for Halloween, weather permitting.

"Yeah, me, too. With the sun out, the ice will start to melt and things can get back to normal. Weather in Ohio, right? Mild one day, winter storm the next, and right back to a typical fall."

Damn it, he could be so engaging with his casual small talk and friendly smiles. Moments like this only made her want him more.

"I'm making chili for lunch," she blurted, before the intent fully processed in her brain. *Do I have the ingredients for chili? Hope so.* "If you're hungry later—"

"Count me in." He gave her a boyish grin, then scooped her in for a hot, passionate, openmouthed kiss that made every female part of her stand up and beg for more.

When he released her, he said, "I better go before I remember that we're past rule number four now. Does chili count as a date? No, don't answer that. Let me dream a little." He kissed the tip of her nose and strode away, all sexy swagger and teasing charm.

Maris was still standing there, dazed and too warm, when Joy arrived. As she rushed in, stripping off her coat and hat, she said, "I'm so damn sorry about my mother. I owe you for helping me dodge her. Now tell me all about your date."

That effervescent enthusiasm was just what Maris needed right now, and she laughed. "Your mother wants you to call her. She's insistent that you two need to talk before you see the attorney. I say screw that, but I felt compelled to pass it along."

Nodding, Joy came behind the counter and helped herself to coffee. "Message received. Your duty is done. Now, do we need to work as we talk? Or do you have a few minutes?"

"Actually, I have all kinds of time. Let's sit."

The surprise that widened Joy's eyes and parted her lips had Maris laughing again.

Damn it, she felt pretty good today...and she knew it was because of Daron.

How scary was *that*?


Ten minutes later, Joy sat back in disbelief. Based on Maris's cheerfulness, she thought for sure she misunderstood. "So, you're saying you *didn't* sleep with him?"

"No thanks to me. I practically jumped the poor guy's body."

Joy would never have described Daron as a "poor guy," but... had Daron turned Maris down? That didn't make any sense, either. "What happened?"

"I made a giant assumption that he'd be all on board with some extracurricular activity. Not so."

"Baloney. If Daron held out, he must have had a reason. I just don't..." Joy couldn't imagine what that reason might be. "He's chased you *forever*, it seems."

Maris pinched her mouth to the side, then sighed. "Okay, here's the worst part."

Oh no, there was a worst part? Worse than being turned down? Sympathy drew Joy closer. "Go on."

"Before I agreed to go to his house for dinner, I laid out these stupid rules—and one of them was no sex on the first date."

Oh my. When the whole point had seemed to be extracurricular activity, Joy couldn't imagine why Maris had done that... well, except that Maris had some skewed perceptions of Daron. Maybe she'd been trying to protect herself?

If so, Joy completely got it. More and more, she felt the same way. "You said one of them? There were other rules?"

"Yup. Whole stupid list. Made up on the spot." Maris slumped back. "Most idiotic thing I've ever done."

"Let me see if I'm following. You made up these rules so he wouldn't expect sex, but then you got there and *you* wanted sex, and he...still said no?"

"He reminded me of the rule." Maris rubbed her face. "Didn't expect that one, you know? But lo and behold, the man has scruples, at least where I'm concerned. He said he was afraid I'd regret coming there and he didn't want that."

Ah. Seeing a method to Daron's madness, Joy asked softly, "What does he want?"

"More?" Maris rolled a shoulder. "At least that's what he said."

"That's so sweet." To Joy's mind, Daron's restraint showed that he cared.

"Not exactly how I'd describe it."

"You and Daron. After all this time, it's hard to believe nothing happened."

"I didn't exactly say that." As if to fortify herself, Maris finished off her coffee, plunked down the cup and stared Joy in the eyes. "We played around."

"Oh goody." Leaning forward again, Joy said, "Describe 'play around.' I need details."

Maris bit her lip in an effort to hold back her laughter, but it did no good. "He's an amazing kisser. I hadn't realized it could be like that—it's been so long since I've done anything."

"Same here, and yes, what an eye-opener, right?"

"I had no idea what I'd been missing."

Joy tipped her head, curiosity dawning. "You've never dated as far as I know, and I've known you a little more than five years. So how long are we talking?"

"Basically..." Maris winced. "Ever?"

"*Ever?*" Joy quickly tried to hide her shock. "Ever as in... you've never...?"

"Made out? Nope. There were a few kisses behind the bleachers at school, but they were pretty underwhelming, so they don't count." Maris dismissed the shocking confession by asking, "How could I, when I didn't date?"

"Why not?"

Rolling her shoulder, Maris said, "I didn't want anyone inside our house, and I definitely didn't want anyone meeting my parents. Heck, from one hour to the next, I was never sure if my dad would be drunk or sober, and whichever it was, you can bet the house would be full of prayers."

Sympathy nearly smothered Joy. "But...what about school dances? Parties?"

"When I only owned worn hand-me-downs? It was easier just to skip that stuff."

Joy couldn't hide her devastation.

And that prompted Maris to say, "Hey, it wasn't all that."

Sadly, Joy thought maybe it was, and in her usual way Maris chose to shrug it off.

Rather than make her more uncomfortable, Joy forced a smile. "Now I'm doubly glad you got together with Daron and had a nice time."

"It was *so* nice," Maris agreed. "Daron was pretty intense, but funny, too, and..." She glanced down at her now-empty cup.

"Hey, we're in a club, right? No secrets in the club, so spill."

Maris's gaze shifted around, ensuring no one had snuck in without her knowing. Leaning over the booth table, her hushed voice giddy with excitement, she said, "Daron Hardy looks incredibly sexy when he's turned on. Like off-the-charts sexy."

Joy grinned. "You're just now noticing how attractive he is?"

"No, I'm serious, Joy. We have lots of attractive guys around here. It's like this park is a testosterone factory and it's made me immune to man-candy. But after a lot of smooching on Daron's couch—"

"And some touching?" Joy interjected. "Please, Maris, tell me there was touching!"

"Nothing to write home about or anything, but it was a real learning experience for me." She blew out a breath. "Holy cow,

he looked hot. It was all I could do not to strip naked and dare him to resist."

Joy burst out laughing. "I think it's safe to say that would've pushed him right over the edge. But hey, if you ever try it, I'll want the nitty-gritty on that, too."

"Today, back in my real life, I don't know if I should be glad nothing else happened, or if I should arrange another date and ensure that it does."

Hand in the air, Joy said, "The answer is…second date."

"Daron's sowed his wild oats, right? But I haven't. With zip for experience, it's possible I could be a major letdown in the sack." She made a face. "Then what?"

Maris's concern struck a chord with Joy and she went still. Had Royce sowed his wild oats before moving here? Or maybe that had been part of the plan he wasn't so certain about anymore. What if he needed that freedom to get it out of his system, but she'd edged in—little boy in tow—and interrupted?

Royce was the type of kind, responsible, caring person who would think of her and Jack instead of himself when it came right down to it. But was that fair?

No, it wasn't.

Clearly, she had a lot to think about. For now, though, reassuring Maris took precedence.

Reaching over the tabletop, she took Maris's hand. "You'll have to trust me on this. Daron will *not* be disappointed. I promise."

Maris didn't seem convinced. "How do you know?"

"Because I have a little experience—granted, until very recently it was six years old, but men and women haven't changed that much. When you and Daron get together, and you will, just be honest with him. Tell him what you like and what you don't. Ask what he likes—" she bobbed her eyebrows "—or ex-

periment around and find that out for yourself. Try not to be shy, but if you are, say so."

"Me, shy?" Maris gave her patented snort. "As if."

"You big faker." Joy folded her arms on the booth in a way that matched Maris's posture. They were close together, speaking in near-whispers even though they were in the camp store alone.

The subject seemed to require it.

"You say you're not shy," Joy accused, "and in most things I'd agree one hundred percent. But when it comes to Daron, everything is different." Saying it as a question instead of a statement, Joy added, "Maybe because how you feel about Daron is different?"

"I'm not shy, not ever," Maris insisted. "It's just that… Daron scares me a little. If I sleep with him, I know I'll be a goner." Putting her face in her hands, she groaned. "God, Joy, I'm already half in love with him."

Since Maris couldn't see her, Joy gave in to a smile. "I think that's wonderful."

Parting her fingers, Maris peeked out. "Do you, now? Well if that's true, why won't you admit you're falling in love yourself?"

Joy started to scoff, but paused as sensations thrummed to life. *Love.*

Was she?

No, she couldn't be. *Shouldn't* be. And yet…

"See what I mean?" Dropping her hands, Maris nodded. "Shakes your foundation, doesn't it? I don't know about you, but I can admit the idea makes my stomach hurt."

Yeah, Joy's stomach was starting to ache a little, too. "A fling was different enough for me."

"Tell me about it. I keep thinking of everything that could go wrong."

Automatically, before she could apply the logic to herself, Joy said, "But think of everything that could go right."

"Uh-huh." Skeptical, Maris asked, "Is that what you're doing?"

No. She was trying to reconcile herself to the fact that she wasn't suave enough, or practical enough, to have an affair without getting emotionally involved.

But hey, this was Maris's time, so screw her own misgivings. She was here to boost her friend. "My situation is entirely different. I haven't known Royce that long, but you've been around Daron for years."

"Right. And you think that makes this any easier?" She fell silent, her eyes rounding and her jaw loosening. In an agonized whisper, she said, "Jesus, Joy, I've *watched him grow up.*"

"You did not!" That was too absurd not to laugh. "Daron came to the park as a legal and mature adult. You've watched him age a few years, but he was already a grown man." Joy laughed again at the silly argument.

"Stop that." Maris thunked her head on the tabletop. Twice. "He's only twenty-five."

"And you're only thirty-one, so stop groaning and get over the age thing already."

Ignoring that advice, Maris groaned. "I always thought he was just a handyman, that he'd eventually move on. Now I know he won't, and I don't plan to go anywhere—"

"Well, I would hope not," Joy said, startled by the idea that she could lose Maris. Or Daron for that matter. "We need to make a club rule right now—no quitters."

"Don't you get it, Joy? If I sleep with him and things don't work out, I'll still be looking at him, and probably lusting after him, for the rest of my life. We work together, for crying out loud. A day doesn't go by without us speaking to each other."

"Hmm. I see your point." At least in her own case, she and Royce didn't work together. Granted, it was a small enough town that they'd probably bump into each other now and then,

but it'd be happenstance instead of a guaranteed daily occurrence. "That could definitely be uncomfortable, but I'm a big believer in honesty." *Yeah, right, then be honest about your feelings for Royce.* Joy shook that off. "I suggest you tell Daron about your concerns. Maybe he's more than ready to settle down."

"It's tragic irony that he's more settled than I am. Have you seen his house?"

Joy shook her head. She was friendly with Daron, but she'd never had any reason to see him away from the park.

"It's incredible. He's done all this work to update it and it's so...cozy. Like a real home should be. Clean and organized, but still friendly, you know?"

Knowing Daron, Joy could almost picture it. "A place to live, and a place to love?"

"It's not just a wall and floors under a roof. The man has a garden! And he's going to get chickens. And I'm..." Maris looked around at the camp store. "I'm just here, craving the security of my own home while saving every dime I can because houses cost money and debt terrifies me."

"Avoiding debt is smart." Before her emancipation from her family's wealth, Joy hadn't concerned herself with a budget of any kind. Once alone, though, that budget had taken up rent in her head and she'd fretted about it around the clock. How would she live, eat, care for the baby...?

Getting a job at Cooper's Charm that included use of the small apartment over the lodge had been a true godsend. Otherwise, where would she be? How would she and Jack have made it? She would never, ever take financial security for granted. For her, and for most other people, it was a constant concern.

Oddly pleased that she could relate to Maris's money worries, Joy prompted, "Will you tell me more about your childhood?"

"Why?"

Joy had one simple answer. "Because you're my friend and I care."

After giving it some thought, Maris shrugged. "Sure, why not?"

For the next half hour, she told Joy all about her mother's obsession with prayer for things rather than going after them herself, about her father's penchant for drinking up any money they got, the usual lack of clothes, heat and sometimes even food.

And she talked about her shame at being the neighborhood charity case, always looked at with scorn, pity or both.

"I left there as soon as I could and I haven't been back except to bury my parents." Pensive, Maris traced her fingertip around the top of her empty coffee cup. "You know what?"

The words were so softly spoken Joy worried. "What?"

"You can run away from a place, but not from what it made you feel."

Tears burned Joy's eyes. She hated that Maris was hurting, and that she was so strong she didn't lightly share that burden. "Will you promise me something?" Joy asked just as softly.

"Sure." Maris's smile flickered. "If it's something I can do, consider it done."

"Will you pretty please give Daron a chance? I know you told him about your background, but tell him how you feel about everything, okay?" In her heart, Joy knew they were right for each other. Maris just needed a nudge to let it happen.

"Hmm." Pursing her lips, Maris considered the request. And considered some more. Finally, looking Joy in the eyes, she said, "Tell you what." She stuck out her hand, as if to make a deal. "I will if you will."

# CHAPTER TWELVE

*I will if you will.*

Her promise to Maris kept replaying, over and over, in Joy's head. She had another two hours before she needed to leave to get Jack. Royce and Daron, now done with the treads, carried the tools and leftover supplies to the golf cart wagon so Daron could return them to the maintenance shed.

Knowing Royce would join her any minute, and why, had her pulse leaping and her skin tingling. She'd missed his touch. She'd especially missed his mouth.

Coop had a meeting, but Daron had volunteered to keep an eye on Chaos, and the dog now sat on the golf cart seat, panting in exuberance. From the top of her stairwell, Joy watched Royce walk around to the dog, give him a few strokes down his back, then cup his head and bend to say something to him.

Joy couldn't hear, but from the way Daron smiled the whole time, whatever Royce said must have been amusing. The dog certainly liked it; his whole furry body wiggled with his butt going opposite of his head and shoulders. He licked at Royce's

face—and Royce allowed it, still speaking softly, still petting until the dog calmed again.

In such a short time Chaos looked prettier, with thicker fur, the wrap on his leg gone, and his belly full.

You could tell a lot about a man by the way he treated a stray dog. Royce's dedication to the animal was admirable.

What would he say if he knew much of her attraction to him had to do with how he'd interacted with her son and Chaos?

Joy grinned. Yes, Royce's appearance had first snagged her interest, and there was no denying he offered a very fine visual, but a troll's personality would have taken care of that in no time.

Royce was the total package, inside and out.

He spoke to Daron one last time, clapped him on the shoulder and then watched as Chaos rode away. The dog didn't look back, which seemed to satisfy Royce because he turned and headed up the stairs.

Stopping one step below her so that they were eye level, he leaned in and took her mouth in a quick kiss. "I need fifteen minutes to run home and shower, and get back here."

No way would she let him go. Joy caught a handful of his coat and said, "Or you could just shower here."

He stilled, his gaze suddenly intense, as if he saw things she hadn't said.

*I will, if you will.*

*This one is for you, Maris.* "Stay." Joy slid her hand inside his coat, feeling the warmth of his body beneath the thermal shirt. "Stay and I'll shower with you."

"Damn." Ever so lightly, his fingertips grazed her cheek. "Can't miss that, now can I?"

Until Joy heard his agreement, she hadn't acknowledged how much his answer meant to her. They both knew it was a step forward for him to be invited for a lengthier visit into her home.

Others in the park would see them together and make assumptions. Daron for sure knew what they were about.

Joy didn't care, and apparently Royce didn't, either.

When he took her hand in his, it felt right. So very, very right.

He led her into the apartment. As Joy went about locking the door, she said, "It'll have to be a quick shower, because I'll need to pick up Jack at—"

His hands came around her, one open low on her stomach, the other cupping a breast while he nuzzled against the side of her neck.

"It's...it's a small shower," she whispered, barely able to speak with the way his thumb taunted her nipple through her sweatshirt.

"I'll fit." He nudged a solid erection against her backside, making her think he meant something other than the shower. "We'll just have to get really close."

They *were* getting closer, in more ways than one.

Leaning back against him, Joy gave herself over to his touch, closing her eyes and breathing deeply.

"Mmm," he murmured. "Maybe you can't wait." The hand on her stomach worked under her sweatshirt, and then into her leggings, pressing down over her mound.

Even though he'd just come in from the cold, his hand was warm, a little rough, his fingers firm as they moved over her, and then *in* her, wringing a soft moan from her throat.

So many sensations conspired against her: his mouth on her neck finding the most sensitive places to lick and suck, his big hand still kneading her breast and plying her nipple.

Lightly penetrating her, one fingertip gathered a rush of wet excitement and used it to tease her clit.

She bit her lip, braced her hands on his steely thighs and gasped for each and every breath.

"That's it," Royce murmured minutes later when she felt the

release swelling within her. He readjusted his hold, wrapping his arm around her under her breasts for support.

His breath was soft near her ear, his tongue licking her skin, his fingers moving faster—

When she cried out, it embarrassed her but she couldn't do anything about it. He gathered her closer, crooning to her, encouraging her, until her legs trembled and she thought she might sink to the floor if he let her go.

"I've got you."

The soft words seemed to promise more beyond the current moment.

Or maybe that was just her being wishful.

She *did* want more. So much more. Going forward, she'd have to be careful not to pressure him.

Turning in his arms, Joy slumped against his broad chest, vaguely aware of him carrying his fingers to his mouth. Looking up, she saw his eyes close as he tasted her off his own hand.

Heart thundering, legs like noodles, she whispered his name.

His eyes opened, liquid black with desire, and he kissed her, not just any kiss but one that felt powerful and possessive.

Reaching between their bodies, Joy found his erection through his jeans. Abruptly he ended the kiss, stepping back to strip off his coat while staring at her. Next he removed his lace-up boots.

Coming to her senses, she hastened out of her coat, as well, and toed off her boots.

Royce grabbed her hand, and in no time at all, they were in the small shower, warm water cascading over them, Royce on his knees in front of her, until she came again.

By the time they got to the bed, she really was limp, sated from the fast back-to-back climaxes.

It was nice, because this time she didn't get lost in her own quest for release, which made it possible for her to watch his.

The powerful way his shoulders bunched as he held himself over her, the flex of his upper body when he entered her.

The rich, almost painful pleasure that tightened his features when she gripped his ass and matched his thrusts.

No man could be more beautifully masculine than him, and watching him build to the pinnacle brought her there again, too. He drove into her one last time, pressed hard and deep and stayed that way, head tipped back, eyes squeezed closed, while he shuddered and growled out his release.

Joy kept moving against him, getting that last bit of stimulation that she needed for her final orgasm. Heaven. That's what it was.

Heaven with Royce.

Could it be that way for a lifetime?

Royce couldn't think of a time when he'd been this relaxed with, or this hyperaware of, a woman, of his own wants and needs, of the *rareness* in a moment.

Joy did that to him, draining away tensions, annihilating his plans...or more like realigning them to include her. Every moment with her felt special so that his instinct was to hold on to her, to not let go.

So far he'd been successful in fighting that inclination, but every time with her made it more difficult. And now, he didn't think he wanted to fight it. Not anymore.

He glanced at the clock, saw they only had half an hour left before she'd need to leave to pick up Jack, and he silently resented the narrow timeframe while also kissing her temple.

He should have been spent, but having Joy warm and soft against his side, one bare thigh over his, her hand toying with his chest hair, stirred him all over again.

Her mother's visit intruded on his thoughts, and he recalled how it had shaken her.

In so many ways he wanted to protect her.

Without a doubt he knew she'd reject that idea.

To him, to anyone who looked, she'd already proven herself to be a strong, resourceful, capable woman who could handle the world on her own terms.

Royce also knew that dealing with the outside world didn't take the same emotional toll that dealing with family did. Trying to inch his way into her confidences, he asked, "Have you called your mother yet?"

"Hmm?" Tracing idle circles on his chest, she whispered, "No. I'm not even sure that I will."

Avoidance? That didn't seem like Joy, which meant dealing with her mother was even harder for her than he'd imagined. "You don't think it's anything important?"

"She didn't call me to let me know Grams had passed. What could be more important than that?"

Good point. Her mother presented a rare form of insufferable detachment, and he should know since he'd lived with detachment for years.

But *nothing* like what Joy had suffered.

His mother had merely had other interests that took precedence. She hadn't deliberately snubbed him.

"Royce?" Joy twisted to look up at him, then tucked close again. "Do you have plans for dinner?"

"Not yet." Touched that she, too, wanted to spend more time together, he gave her a one-arm hug. "You and Jack want to go out for something? We haven't tried the pizza parlor yet, but I hear it's good."

"It is. They have incredible bread sticks." She flattened her hand against his abdomen. "But I was thinking you could eat here. With us."

As if kick-starting, his heart gave a hard thump before breaking into a gallop. How Joy posed the request was as important

as the request itself. The timid way she hid against him proved that she was inviting him into her *life*, not just her home.

"Nothing fancy," she added, keeping her face down, "but I have enough pork chops, and I can easily make extra mashed potatoes."

"Thank you." To make sure she didn't retract the offer, he tugged her up on top of him and accepted. "I'd enjoy that."

Sprawled over him, her hair pouring over his shoulders, Joy smiled. "Really?"

He had to draw a slow breath before he could nod.

Her smile faded. "Is something wrong?"

"No, nothing," he promised quickly. God, she was beautiful, inside and out. Gentle, loving. Sometimes apprehensive. This had to be as unusual for her as it was for him.

One way to find out.

He threaded his fingers through the fall of her hair, letting it sift free in silky waves. "I feel like this means something." Waiting for a reaction, he cupped a hand over her cheek and watched her, wondering if she'd deny it or pretend she didn't understand.

Expression softening, Joy touched her nose to his, then gave him a sweet kiss. "Does that scare you?"

So, she didn't deny her intent to deepen their relationship. He liked that Joy was up front with him, and he understood why.

She had a lot at stake, most importantly Jack's well-being, which left no room for misunderstandings. Having dinner out, or even at his house, was different. Jack was away from his home. By inviting Royce to stay *here* for dinner, she took a risk on letting him further into their lives.

"Scare me? No." Actually, it felt like one hell of a gift. "A few days ago it might have." He coasted his hands down her back to her rounded bottom. He could die happy like this, Joy resting over him, his hands cuddling her sexy ass, her long hair tickling his chest. "You realize I'll have Chaos with me, right?" Joy

kept her home neat and organized—and Chaos was anything but that. "You sure that's okay?"

Her smile twitched. "Chaos is also invited. Jack will be thrilled." But she wouldn't let him sideline her. "A few days ago, I wouldn't have invited you over because I was worried about Jack getting too close to you."

"I know."

"You do?"

"Sure." The care she gave Jack was an intrinsic part of her. "I was raised by a single mom, sort of."

Curious, she tilted her head. "What do you mean, sort of?"

Good question. "Mom wasn't like you."

"Like me how?" She folded her arms on his chest, clearly getting comfortable in her current position. "You said she was an artist?"

"Right, and she was wholly invested in her artwork. You know the distraction and disruption a boy can cause. Nana said I was well behaved, but I didn't have Jack's talent and it plagued my mother." He gave a short laugh. *Plagued*, now that he thought about it, was an apt word to articulate his mother's struggle. "She couldn't understand why I didn't see what she saw, how I overlooked details—details that Jack sees, by the way. That's how I recognized the artist in him."

"Not because you were an artist—but because your mother pointed out that you weren't?" She shook her head. "That's a little confusing."

It had been more so for him as a boy. He wanted to please his mother, but he could never remember all the little things she thought were obvious. Things like fingers on a hand, or branches on a tree.

Like many kids, he'd drawn people as stick figures. If he got two arms and two legs on a torso, he thought he'd done pretty darn good. Nana had agreed, but his mother had not.

"I think Mom assumed I'd be her little prodigy. Unfortunately, when she gave me paints, I stacked the tubes to build a fort. She gave me chalk and I rolled them across the floor, racing the red against the blue." Those memories both amused him and still made him a little sad. "She couldn't believe that her son would rather climb a tree than paint it."

"Where was your father?"

"He was never part of the picture. According to my mother, they had a brief fling that resulted in me. She never gave me his name, or any details beyond that. I assume he was an artist, as well, and honestly, one disappointed parent was enough."

Sympathy and understanding pinched Joy's brows, and the gold in her eyes eclipsed the green.

Royce loved her eyes. His mother would have loved them, too. No doubt they would have inspired her, they were so unique. If he had his mother's talent, he'd certainly paint them.

"Your mother told you she was disappointed?"

Joy probably couldn't imagine such a thing since she was, as he'd said, a different type of mother. "Not outright, but I could tell." Kids could *always* tell. "I didn't share her talent, and she didn't share my interests."

"Your interests?" Her curiosity sharpened. "Like what?"

"I did sports all through school." He rolled one shoulder. "Mom had no use for anything too physical, so that's where Nana came in. She rarely missed a game."

"Then I'm grateful that you had your grandmother." Joy pressed a lingering kiss to his chest, right where his heart would be. "You and your mother had a good relationship otherwise?"

"She wasn't cruel or anything, if that's what you mean. She was a dramatic, emotional, creative person...who got pregnant and had me, and did the best she could with her artist's soul." He smiled. "I remember sitting cross-legged on the floor in her studio when I was probably a year or so younger than Jack.

She'd put a painting tarp beneath me so I could eat my cold cereal where she could see me. She knew I needed to be watched, but her painting was 'calling to her.'"

"Were *you* calling to her?"

"I don't remember, but if I was, I was probably asking to go outside." He looked up at the ceiling, remembering their small yard, the birds that visited one of their biggest trees, the dog two doors down that often barked... "God, she tried so hard to get me to paint, or work in clay, or even to color with crayons. I tried hard, too, but I mostly made a mess. My mother would look at my work, put the back of her hand to her forehead and lament my lack of talent. She did that a lot." He grinned, remembering. "Hell, she did everything with theatrical flair."

Joy touched the edge of his smile. "That's actually horribly sad."

Maybe. Royce didn't want to ruin their quiet time together, so he explained an upside to his youth. "Nana would step in and carry on as if I'd created a masterpiece."

"Go Nana."

Royce gave a short laugh. "She kept damn near everything I made."

"Like you kept Jack's picture?"

Yes, he'd remembered how good it felt to have his effort appreciated, but with Jack it was different, since the kid *did* have talent. "One day Jack will sell his art. I was just getting a leg up on other buyers."

Joy laughed softly, then asked, "How often did you see your grandmother?"

"She moved in with us when I was a baby. Nana said that my mother loved me too much to have me away from her, but that artists were flighty and not ideal for parenting. The 'flighty' part, she said, was our secret." Everything he remembered of his

grandmother filled him with warmth. "She pretty much raised me, though my mother paid the bills."

"Your mother must have been very successful."

Royce nodded. "I used to be bitter about it. I loved her, but I resented her talent like she probably resented my lack. Still, we made it work and then...then she got sick and required around-the-clock care."

"You put your own life on hold?"

Exactly how it had seemed. "There was no one else, definitely no one who would have understood her artistic bent. Now she's gone and..."

Laying her cheek against his chest, Joy whispered, "And you came here to be unencumbered?"

Wishing he'd never said that to her, Royce rubbed his mouth. How could Joy ever be a burden? Wasn't possible. She brought laughter into his life, warmth and direction. All good emotions, with lots of sizzling physical need, too. Around her, he felt completely alive.

Somehow, without obvious effort, Joy had drawn him from his sad, burdened past and focused him squarely in the positive present.

When he didn't answer, she tentatively asked, "How long did she have dementia?"

"Years, with the last few being the worst. It's a disease that steadily steals from a person—memories, thoughts...the ability to function." God, he still hated thinking about it. "She started falling, each time causing more damage, until she ended up in a wheelchair—and hated it." He should have stopped there. He meant to, but the words flowed seemingly against his will. "Sometimes she hated me."

"Royce." Scooting up so she could look him in the eyes, Joy cupped her small soft hand to his jaw. "That can't be true."

"Honestly, I have no idea if it's true or not. The doctors told

me that people with dementia react in different ways, some with rage, some going completely passive."

"Your mother raged?"

"I think she was understandably miserable." Saying it aloud helped Royce believe it, to maybe start to understand it. "She had me late in life, and got the disease early. Before that, she'd been a strong person, doing as she pleased, when she pleased. Celebrated for her talent. Physically healthy, but steadily losing her independence and dignity."

Putting himself in her shoes, Royce could only imagine how he'd react. Anger might be the least of the emotions.

"I'm so sorry."

He lifted her palm to his mouth and pressed a kiss there. "She got to where she wouldn't eat, then to where she couldn't drink." His voice softened to a rasp. "She cursed me daily, but there wasn't anyone else. No other relatives. So I cared for her the best that I could."

"Because you're a good, kind person. And you were a good son." With her eyes growing misty, she said, "I'm sure it was the disease, not your mother, who said unkind things."

It wasn't easy to let Joy see him like this, a grown man baring his fucking hurt. He only told her now to explain the stupid way he'd started this relationship, the absurd boundaries he'd set.

Because now he wanted more. From her. *With* her.

It relieved him when Joy settled down against his chest again, no longer looking at him, quiet but still very much with him.

"Mom never forgot her painting." For some reason, stroking Joy's hair made it easier to talk. "I changed jobs so I could be with her more, and I made sure she always had her art supplies at hand."

"What did you do for a living?"

"Mobile sawmiller." He briefly explained that to her, and doing so made him miss it. He'd always enjoyed working with

his hands, being outdoors and later repurposing the wood. "I took only the jobs I wanted, and since I worked on my own timetable I could arrange for the occasional caretaker to stay with Mom while I was away."

"Did she do well with the caretaker?"

He gave a short laugh. "She despised anyone I hired, no matter how kind or qualified, so before leaving for a job, I'd set her up in her studio, getting her wheelchair arranged just right with a canvas in front of her. It was best for the caregivers to be there in case of an emergency, but otherwise they'd leave her be and let her paint." He thought about that, again seeing his frail mother, lost to her own little world where only her painting existed. "There were times she could barely hold a brush, but her eye for color and light never faded. Her talent was a fundamental part of her, or so the doctor said. One day I'd like to show her work to Jack. It might inspire him."

"That would be nice," Joy replied softly, "but I thought she sold her art."

"She did. There were several galleries who bought her, and toward the end, before the disease worsened, her paintings had tripled in value." Even now, gallery owners asked about his personal collection. "Through the years she gave me different pieces for my birthday, Christmas. Sometimes just because." He couldn't bear to look at them right now, but neither would he part with them. Not ever.

"Really?" Excitement brought Joy to her elbows again. "What a special gift that would be. Can you tell me about some of the paintings?"

Why not? As the minutes ticked past, talking about his mother and her obsession became easier. "The tree I most enjoyed climbing? She painted me in it." A memory rekindled and he laughed. "Mother told me every day not to climb that tree, that I'd fall and break something, but I always did, anyway. I'd sit on this

big branch and let my feet dangle. Sometimes I'd find a cater-pillar in the leaves, or a bird would land nearby and I'd sit real still so I wouldn't scare it. That's what she painted. Me in torn jeans straddling a branch, my bare dirty feet dangling and a blue bird looking at me from a different branch."

Joy smiled. "I can't wait to see it."

He let out a breath. "Honestly, it's an amazing piece. You can almost feel the heat of the summer day when you look at it."

"What else?" Joy asked, and there was something in her eyes, a spark that turned them more gold than green.

Thinking about it, Royce said, "She did a massive painting of me at eight years old, sleeping on top of my covers. Another of my toy race cars lined up on a shelf. All you can see of me is my forearm, and a grubby little hand arranging the cars."

"Royce," Joy whispered, holding his face in both her hands. "Can't you see that your mother was trying to show you her love?"

Joy's tone arrested him, making him still. "What do you mean?"

"Your mother sounds very unique, but she noticed the same things about you that I see in Jack. His favorite toys mean more to me, because I know what they mean to him. When he's sleeping, he's so peaceful and sweet, my heart melts. And you in your favorite tree? The forbidden place you so often snuck off to?" Joy sniffed, her eyes glassy with emotion. "That's how she pictured you, happy and free, following your heart, doing what you enjoyed most."

The truth started to sink in. "Since I couldn't do what she enjoyed?"

Smile trembling, she nodded. "Yes."

Jesus. Suddenly he knew Joy was right. *How the hell had he missed it?*

His heart seemed to fill his chest and he ran a hand through

his hair, giving it a slight tug. "That painting of me in the tree was one of the last she completed. Hell, I was a grown man when she did it, but it was still crazy accurate..."

"Right down to the dirty feet?"

Emotion squeezed a laugh from his constricted throat. "Yes. Being barefoot gave me better traction to climb."

Even ill and struggling, his mother had painted *him* when he was happiest. Why hadn't he realized it before?

No, she might not have shown her love in conventional ways, but she'd shared it in the way that was best known to her.

Through her art.

"You know," Royce said, ready to unearth the work, "I think I'll get out some of her smaller pieces to show Jack. Do you think he'd like that?"

"I know he would." Joy sat up and this time there was no hiding the tears in her eyes.

It sent emotion welling in him, too. He teased his fingers lightly up her arm, enjoying the warmth and silk of her skin. "Don't cry, babe."

Swallowing heavily, Joy dashed a hand over her eyes. "I'm not."

He sat up beside her. Voice a little too gruff, he said, "Thank you for listening." He kissed her shoulder. "And for seeing things I didn't."

"Sometimes when we're too close to a situation, the obvious is out of reach." She leaned into him, but only for a second, and then she stood, beautifully bare.

Too bad they were out of time.

As she reached for her panties, she shared a wobbly smile. "Dinner is at six."


A week passed as quickly as a single day when you enjoyed every moment as much as Royce did.

With Chaos repeatedly tugging on his boot laces, pulling them loose as he growled and shook his head, Royce looked around at the park. After closing out the drive-in late last night, he should have been tired. Yet here he stood, just outside the supply building with Coop and Baxter, his shoulder braced against the metal wall.

He couldn't seem to stay away.

Being closer to Joy for any reason was worth less sleep. And besides, he enjoyed helping out the guys.

Over the past several days, the weather had decided to co-operate, warming up for the Halloween weekend. The temps had gradually climbed each day so that now, by late afternoon, they reached the lower sixties. The mornings were still cold, but with all the sunshine it wasn't too uncomfortable. No rain or sleet in the forecast.

Perfect, beautiful fall weather, at a perfect, beautiful location.

"The cover you made for the stairs looks great." Coop stacked a few more things on a wagon, then bent to scratch at Chaos's ear.

The dog reared back, wiggling butt in the air, and pounced on Coop's hand, grabbing his sleeve and tugging. Laughing, Coop freed his coat and stood again.

"I should have it finished up soon," Royce said. He'd worked on it nearly every day, and with Daron's help, they'd completed the majority of the project. Joy wouldn't have to worry about the elements causing problems on the steps this winter. A slanted roof protected the stairs from precipitation, and partially enclosed sides kept snow or sleet from blowing in.

"Speaking of Daron," Baxter said, "is he with Maris again?"

"That's where he's spent every free minute for the past week," Coop said with a grin. "Looks like he's finally worn her down."

"I'm happy for him," Baxter said. "But am I the only one to notice she's offering fewer cookies these days?"

Royce laughed. Either Maris was too busy to bake, or Daron ate her offerings before anyone else could get to them.

"Speaking of new developments…" Baxter lifted his brows at Royce.

Yeah, he'd spent some part of each day visiting Joy. It warmed him, remembering Jack's excitement the first night he'd shared their dinner.

Joy was a terrific cook, the atmosphere was relaxed and Jack had repeatedly beamed at him. Guests in the apartment, for any reason, rarely happened.

"No denials from me," Royce said. "You can probably expect to see me often."

"We appreciate you pitching in." Coop looked around at the busy park. "Halloween weekend is always huge."

"My pleasure." Literally. "Like Daron, I'm happy to have a reason to hang around."

"As if you need an excuse," Coop said.

Everyone knew Joy was enticement enough.

"And to think," Baxter said, "we all warned you off, saying she wouldn't be interested."

"Whatever you did, I approve." Coop stared out toward the lake. "She smiles more now."

Royce felt honored to be the first man Joy had shown interest in since having Jack. After that first dinner in her apartment, they'd just naturally fallen into a pattern.

On the first sunny day they'd hung out at the playground after school with Royce pushing Jack on the swing or standing ready to catch him while he climbed on the jungle gym. Joy stayed bundled up on the bench, drinking hot chocolate and taking lots of pictures with her phone.

Another day, he'd brought the food to them and they'd made use of the picnic table and the warmth of the sunshine down by the beach. They'd all worn coats and stocking hats, and they'd

laughed a lot watching Chaos chase the water along the shore-line. After the meal, Jack had predictably used a stick to draw in the wet sand.

An artist, Royce well knew, utilized every opportunity.

When Chaos ruined it with his paw prints, Jack just laughed and had an impromptu game of chase with the dog.

What really warmed Royce was the way Joy praised every-thing her son did, from how fast he ran, to questions he asked, to his gentleness with Chaos. She was just the most amazing mother, and though he'd never thought about that as an asset for a woman he dated, he had to admit he liked it a lot.

Twice that week, he and Joy had slipped away in the after-noon for some horizontal alone time. Royce would have been happier with twice *a day*, but he understood and accepted the limitations.

She'd already made numerous allowances for him, and based off what everyone had told him, that was an aberration of the best sort.

It felt good to be accepted, not at all the burden he'd thought a relationship would be. Total opposite, in fact.

"There's Daron now." Baxter nodded toward Maris's store.

From where they stood on a slight rise, they could just make out Daron's progress. It looked like he planned to jog past the pond, the lodge, numerous campsites and the playground.

If the trees were green instead of bare, they wouldn't have had such a clear view. On this particular Saturday, the park was already packed with RVs and fifth-wheel campers ready to cel-ebrate Halloween. Women and men went all out decorating their areas with Halloween lights, signs, animated characters and more. Joy was already in the lodge, setting up the kid-friendly haunted house.

"Huh," Royce said, seeing Maris call out to Daron, which had him turning back. "Guess he forgot something."

They all grinned.

When Daron reached Maris, she spoke to him, then he grabbed her up and twirled her in a circle before kissing her with enthusiasm.

Baxter laughed. "He's relentless."

Coop grinned. "I'd say he's getting encouragement in that regard."

"Shame on you guys," said a female voice. "Clucking like a bunch of hens."

Royce turned to see Coop's wife, Phoenix, coming to them arm in arm with her pregnant sister, Ridley.

The two women had similar blue eyes, but very different personalities. Even while obviously pregnant, Ridley came off as innately sensual whereas Phoenix was all understated sweetness.

"Maybe they're jealous," Ridley said, giving Baxter a lazy smile. "Because they're old married men now."

"Who are you calling old?" Baxter scooped her up, which made her squawk, and disappeared with her into the supply building.

Phoenix rolled her eyes. "Every time she provokes him, he uses it as an excuse to act like a newlywed."

Royce had a feeling that's why Ridley did it.

Sliding an arm around his wife, Coop asked, "Now who's jealous?"

Phoenix's cheeks warmed and her smile bloomed. "I have you, Cooper, so I have no reason, ever, to be jealous of anyone."

So in love, Royce thought, seeing the way Coop and Phoenix looked at each other, how openly they shared their affection.

Damn it, *he* might be the jealous one.

Then Phoenix said to him, "Ridley and I are going down to help Joy decorate."

"Looks like a big job. I'm sure she'll appreciate it."

"Maris wanted to help, too, but she can barely keep the cof-feepots full, plus she's trying to stock up on cookies."

"Maris and Joy are close now," Royce said. "Almost like you and Ridley."

"They do act very sisterly," Phoenix agreed. "Except they get along better than Ridley and I do." She raised her voice. "Since my sister is always sneaking off to dark places with her husband."

"Mind your own business," Ridley shouted back.

They all heard Baxter laughing.

Wearing a grin, Phoenix shook her head. "I might as well head on down. See you guys later."

Coop gave her a quick kiss and hug, and seconds later Ridley came scurrying out, her hair a little mussed, one hand pressed to the small of her back, grouching as she hustled toward her sister, "Wait up, already. Pregnant lady waddling through."

Baxter reemerged, a smug smile in place. He yelled to his wife, "You don't waddle."

"Bite me!" she called back, making Baxter's smile widen.

Just then Daron joined them. He was more windblown than usual, his hat on crooked, his grin stretched from ear to ear. Whatever Maris had told him, Daron liked it. "Did I miss any-thing?"

Royce laughed. The three men were really nothing alike, except that they were each so obviously in love. Pretty sure he was headed in the same direction.

Kneeling, Royce wrestled his leather lace from the dog and noticed it was considerably shorter now. Apparently Chaos had won that particular battle.

He handed the dog a small rawhide chew from his pocket, and tied the laces the best he could.

Glad that he'd come by to help with the Halloween setup, Royce said, "There's never a dull moment here at the park." He lifted Chaos. "I like it."

"We know what you like," Baxter drawled. "And it isn't the fine scenery."

"True enough." Royce shrugged. "But the scenery is nice, too."

# CHAPTER THIRTEEN

Joy was surprised when shortly before the haunted house would open Maris burst in. All around her, black lights blinked and gray gauze hung in atmospheric tatters.

As Maris made a beeline for Joy, darting around the yarn-web obstacle course, the hanging pool noodle maze and the table-ful of creepy cupcakes, she did her best to hold a smile at bay.

The second their gazes met, Maris gave up. Grinning hugely, she grabbed Joy and pulled her toward the kitchen. "I need two minutes."

"I'll give you twenty." Which was exactly how long she had before she'd need to open the doors and welcome in the kids. Luckily, she had everything ready to go. "What's up? Why are you smiling like that?"

Furtive, Maris glanced around to ensure they were alone.

"No one's here," Joy assured her. "Ridley and Phoenix left a few minutes ago to get dressed in their costumes." The two women would help hand out snacks and supervise activities. "Jack is busy making a glow-in-the-dark ghoul." Joy had warned

him not to make it too scary, but given the gleam in his eyes, she wasn't sure what to expect.

Maris sucked in a big breath, then blurted, "I've decided it's time for me to hold up my end of the bargain."

Joy didn't follow. "Your bargain for…?"

Flagging a hand between them, Maris reminded, "I will, if you will? Do you recall that promise? Well, you and Royce have been living it up all week—and don't deny it!"

"I wouldn't," Joy said, allowing her own smile. Normally she'd have given Maris a daily update, but with them both now in relationships, and all the activity at the park, they'd barely had time for chatting. "It's been wonderful. *He's* wonderful."

"I'm glad for you. And see? You've inspired me." Nodding to emphasize that, Maris said, "Tonight's the night. For Daron and me, I mean. Oh God, did I just say that out loud?" Bouncing on the balls of her feet, she shook her hands, her nervousness palpable. "Joy, I'm so anxious I'm about to go nuts."

Laughing, Joy said, "What? Why?"

"Daron is a terrible tease. He's had me on pins and needles all week. The man is diabolical with the way he kisses me, knowing it'll obliterate my concentration. How could I keep holding him off?"

"I'm surprised you've managed this long." Joy shook her head. She hadn't understood Maris's restraint, so how could Daron? "It's going to be wonderful, you'll see."

"But what if I suck?" Maris went still, her eyes widening. "Wait. Let me rephrase that. What if I'm lousy at this? I'm…" She threw up her hands. "I'm *worse* than a virgin, because I'm *thirty-one*."

"Let's put that on T-shirts," Joy said, holding up her fingers to make a square, as if to frame the saying. "'Worse Than a Virgin.' I like it. It's catchy."

Maris shoved her shoulder. "Be serious, will you?"

Laughing, Joy said, "Okay, okay. Here I am, dead serious." She tempered her smile, but only a little. "You, Maris Kennedy, are one of the strongest, most capable people I know. I admire that about you. So you aren't superexperienced? So what?"

"Daron *is* superexperienced."

"That doesn't mean he won't be nervous. Know what he's probably worried about? Disappointing you. After he's spent all this time winning you over, the stakes are higher than ever for him." Joy halted Maris's automatic denial with a raised palm. "I know what you're doing, Maris. You're used to attacking problems, but, hon, Daron isn't a problem."

"God," she groaned, covering her eyes. "He's the worst problem ever."

"Only because you care so much about him." When Maris lowered her hands, Joy cocked a brow. "You do, right?"

"I don't want to," Maris grumbled.

"But you do, anyway. Be brave and admit it."

"Only to you." Dropping back against the wall, eyes closed, Maris deliberately clunked her head. Twice.

Joy waited.

Peeking one eye open, Maris asked, "Any advice?" Her mouth twisted. "I mean, since you appear to be happily burning up the sheets with Royce and all that."

"As a matter of fact…" Joy leaned into the doorway to make sure Jack was still in his seat.

He wasn't, and her heart almost stopped, especially when she saw the open door. "Jack!" Already striding out of the kitchen, she called his name again. *"Jack."*

He stepped into the doorway. "Mr. Nakirk is here, Mom."

Joy strode over to him, each step echoed by the hammering of her heart. "Jack Lee, you know better than to open that door without me."

Royce stepped in. "My fault. I poked my head in, saw you

were, um—" he glanced at Maris, who had stepped up to her side "—busy talking and decided to wait a few minutes more. But Jack saw me."

That didn't matter. "Under *no* circumstances," Joy stressed, "is he to open that door without asking me first." Strangers filled the park. That was bad enough, but add in the visits from her mother and her worry was totally legit.

Embarrassed, Jack cast a glance at Royce, then at Maris, before ducking his face in shame. Voice small, he whispered, "Sorry, Mom."

Damn it, now she'd hurt her son's feelings. Hand to her forehead, she turned to Maris. "I need—"

"Totally get it. I need to head back to the diner, anyway."

"No!" She didn't want to let Maris down. "I only need one minute. Wait. Please."

As if to console her, Maris patted her shoulder. "Okay, sure."

With a hundred awful scenarios winging through her head, Joy knelt down. "Jack, honey. I need you to know how dangerous it could be to—"

"I saw Mr. Nakirk, Mom," he said, his voice subdued but stubborn. "I knew it was him."

"I know. And I understand why that seemed perfectly fine to you. Can you also understand why I would worry? I didn't see you, so I didn't know you were with him. All I knew was that my son wasn't where he should be." Her heart continued to gallop.

"I answered soon as you called me."

Mouth firming, Joy drew back. "We've talked about this before, Jack. With so many people coming and going, I need to know where you are. *Always.* No exceptions. No excuses."

Shoulders hunched, he nodded.

Joy stroked back his hair. "Tell me you understand, Jack."

"I understand."

"Jack." She lifted his chin. "I need your promise, honey."

He cast another look toward Royce.

Royce surprised her by putting his hand on Jack's shoulder. "I don't want your mom to worry, so I'm going to promise, too."

Wide-eyed, Jack looked up at him. "You are?"

"Absolutely. I should have told her right away that you were with me. I was thoughtless and for that I'm sorry." His gaze shifted to Joy. "I promise, in the future, I will always let you know."

Awed, Jack nodded. "Me, too. I promise, Mom."

Royce patted his shoulder. "We don't want to upset her, do we?"

Slipping his arms around her neck, Jack squeezed her. "Sorry, Mom. I promise I won't worry you again."

A lump of emotion clogged her throat. Joy seriously doubted Jack could keep that promise, but for now, it was good enough. She returned his hug while smiling at Royce. She silently mouthed, *Thank you.*

He nodded, then helped her up. "How about Jack shows me around the haunted house while you and Maris finish your conversation?"

Without waiting for her permission, Jack slipped his hand into Royce's. "We have peeled grapes in gelatin," he said in excitement. "They feel like eyeballs! And gummy worms in crushed cookies that look like dirt, and…"

His chattering voice faded as he dragged Royce to the food section.

Joy stared after them, seeing more than just her son with Royce. She saw a future, she saw a family. She saw…love.

Until Maris slipped her arm around her. Dry with irony, Maris said, "Yeah, no one will ever guess how you feel."

Oh Lord. She'd been gazing after them like a lovesick fool.

"Come on," Maris said, urging her along. "I need to get back

to the diner, and you need to get it together because a slew of costumed kids are arriving in three, two, one…"

"I'm sorry," Joy said. "I just—"

"Panicked. Big-time. I know. Totally understandable." In the kitchen, Maris grabbed a cup of punch and pressed it into Joy's hand. "I don't suppose you have anything good to slip in that?"

Joy laughed, knowing neither of them would spike a drink while responsible for entertaining children. "Sadly, no." She sipped, then set the cup aside. "I'm fine now, so let's get back to you and Daron."

"Advice. Right." Maris braced herself. "Quick, lay it on me."

"I already told you this once. Trust Daron. Tell him your concerns and everything will be fine."

"Yeah, sure." Maris scrunched up her face. "How would that conversation go? *Sorry, Daron, but I'm clueless so you have to do all the work.*" She rolled her eyes. "I don't want to look that dumb."

"You mean inferior, and that's just silly because you won't." Knowing she was out of time, Joy took her hands. "I can promise you, Daron won't be judging you, and you won't be judging him. Just enjoy yourself."

"Okay." Maris puffed up. "Enjoyment. Should be a piece of cake."

It would be, if Maris stopped overanalyzing it. That wasn't likely to happen, unless… "Best advice? Get Daron naked first."

Maris's eyes flared wide. "Okay, I'm with you so far."

"Once he's naked, you'll have the upper hand, right? Start with that and then improvise as you go along."

"See, this is why I came to you." Maris offered her a high five. "I think I'll nominate you as prez of our club."

"Only if we get to wear the Worse Than a Virgin shirts."

They were both still laughing when Phoenix and Ridley slipped in. Phoenix made a beautiful fairy, and Ridley made a nicely rounded jack-o'-lantern.

Royce ducked and darted through the hanging pool noodles, a laughing Jack slung over his shoulder.

These people, Joy thought, looking at each of them. Oh, these wonderful, friendly, warm people.

She adored them all so much.

As she headed in to get the party started, she said to Maris, "Soon as you can tomorrow, I want to know how it went."

"Guaranteed." Maris shrugged. "You're the only one I have to tell."

If things progressed as Joy suspected they would, Maris would soon have Daron as a confidant, too. But for now, Joy relished that singular closeness.

She faced the room, and announced, "Let them in. We're ready!"

Maris paused in his kitchen, looking uncharacteristically timid. Daron wondered at it—and then an awesome, incredible, boner-inspiring thought occurred.

Maybe she was ready to put him out of his misery.

The second he thought it, he couldn't unthink it, and it probably showed in the hot way he looked at her. It felt like he'd wanted her forever, and in fact, it had been years.

Earlier at the park she'd initiated their public display, which indicated she was ready to accept their relationship, instead of still denying him. He'd been plenty pleased by that, but this? The chance for more?

His heart started pumping hard. "Maris?"

She took off her corduroy coat—a coat that had to be a decade old—and laid it over a stool at the island. "One of these days Joy and I are going to shop together and grab lunch. I'll probably get a new coat." She wrinkled her nose. "The thing is, I've never been shopping with another woman. Never turned it into an adventure, you know? Joy assures me it'll be fun."

"I'm sure she's right." Daron did his utmost to look casual, while fighting the urge to kiss her.

After shoving her phone into the back pocket of her jeans, Maris put her purse on top. Nothing unusual in that since the stool had become her unofficial coat and purse tree over the past week.

Shifting, she asked, "Do you feel bad that we're not at the drive-in supporting Royce on his last night?"

"Not even a little." Not if it meant he'd finally get to have Maris. He took a few steps toward her, unable to pull his gaze from her eyes. "You seem different." He cleared the gravelly lust from his throat. "Want to tell me what's up?"

"Besides you?" she asked, nodding at the erection behind the zipper of his jeans.

Without hesitation, he said, "Yeah, besides me." He wouldn't deny wanting her, wouldn't deny he reacted strongly to her.

She'd moved near enough to touch, so Daron drifted his fingertips over her cheek. Because she still looked nervous, he teased, "Want to make out?"

Maris nodded. "Yes." Yet when he reached for her, she held him off and said, "Get naked."

Trying to reconcile what she'd said and what she really wanted, Daron blinked. He rubbed his mouth, at a loss, then looked around at his house. They stood halfway between the kitchen and the dining room. "Here?"

Her mouth twitched. "Just like that? I ask and you'll do it?"

"Pretty sure there isn't anything I wouldn't do for you, Maris."

She sucked in a breath. "Wow. Way to make me feel powerful."

He couldn't stop touching her skin. Maris was so soft and warm he was dying to feel her all over. "I'd rather make you feel hot."

"Yeah, okay." She snagged his hand and dragged him down

the hallway to his bedroom. "You can strip in here." She put her phone on the nightstand, sat down on the side of the mattress and gestured. "Go ahead."

It was all Daron could do not to laugh. No one would accuse him of being modest, but he'd never stripped on command before.

"Whatever the lady wants." Toeing off his shoes, he pushed them aside, then bent and tugged off his socks. Probably going a little too fast—which he'd blame on burning lust—he straightened and peeled his sweatshirt off over his head.

Licking her lips, Maris nodded her approval. "You're gorgeous."

"You've seen me without my shirt before."

"Often," she replied. "You like to flaunt your bod all over the place."

"Er..." That sounded like a complaint. "You realize we work at a casual resort and it gets hot in the summer, right?"

She snorted. "You wouldn't pare down so often if you didn't look so damn good."

He looked *so damn good*? Nice.

Appreciating her assessment, Daron brought his hands to the snap of his jeans.

"Wait!"

If he didn't let his dick free soon, it'd break the zipper.

Maris pretended to grasp the air with her hands. "Lemme."

"You want to open my pants?"

She nodded fast. "Yup. Bring your sexy self over here."

"Yeah, all right." Crazy that *he* now felt uncertain. "Go easy, though, okay? I don't want to—" Her small hand squeezed him through the denim and he sucked in a breath...that ended with a broken groan as her small, strong hand worked over him. Through his teeth, he said, "That's probably not a good idea."

"Let's find out." By slow degrees, she eased down the zip-

per, making it a form of torturous foreplay. Once the jeans were opened, she wedged her hand inside to stroke him again, this time with only his boxers in the way.

Every muscle in his body clenched. "You're killing me, babe."

"Killing myself a little, too," she murmured, then she surprised him by leaning in and brushing her nose over the line of hair leading down from his navel. "Mmm, you smell good."

Daron put his head back and concentrated on control. Wasn't easy, not with Maris's breath on his stomach, her lips on his hip, all while her fingers toyed with his erection.

Abruptly releasing him, she said, "Off with the rest."

The husky note in her voice pleased him. Hoping to get things going, Daron shoved out of his jeans and boxers as fast as he could, all the while watching Maris.

Her delicate nostrils flared and color bloomed on her cheeks. "You're big."

"Average actually."

"No," Maris whispered, the words strained. "There's nothing average about you."

"Tell you what." He leaned in to take her elbows and gently tugged her to her feet. "Let's even things up a bit, okay?"

Swallowing audibly, she nodded. "Fair warning—I haven't done this in a really long time."

Daron wondered *how* long. Since he'd known her, Maris had never dated or even hinted interest in a guy. She'd broken that long dry spell with him and he was determined to ensure she enjoyed every second.

"It'll be fine," he promised, while dipping down to her throat, trailing his lips over her skin, up to her jaw and to the delicate shell of her ear. In the barest-there whisper, he breathed, "Leave everything to me."

"Joy was right," she gasped.

Um… Daron paused, pulling back to see her. "Right about what?"

"This is easier with you naked. She promised it would be."

Yeah, that didn't make a bit of sense, but at the moment Daron didn't care enough to ask her to explain. Instead, he returned to her throat again, opening his mouth against her just the way he knew she liked it. On her own, she stepped up against him, her hands going to his bare back.

Within a single minute, she frantically touched him everywhere, up to his shoulders, down his spine to his ass. Taking that as an invitation, Daron reciprocated, and soon they were both breathing hard and fast.

He fingered the hem of her thick sweatshirt. "Let's get this off, okay?"

Nodding, she tried to wrestle out of it, but got it twisted up with the T-shirt she wore underneath.

"Let me help." He eased each arm out first, then pulled it and her T-shirt up and over her head, leaving her with frazzled hair, a deep blush and a plain bra.

He was busy taking her in, loving the curves of her body, when Maris thrust up her chin. "I don't own any lingerie."

Pulling his gaze from her sweet body to her face, he smiled. "If you think this—" he gestured at her bare skin "—isn't sexy as hell, you're wrong."

She looked down at her beige bra and quirked a disbelieving brow.

"It's you, Maris." Clearly she didn't get how madly in love he was. "I don't care what your bra looks like, as long as you're willing to take it off."

Humor, and relief, curved her mouth. "You're the hot shot. You get it off me."

"Yes, ma'am." Reaching out, he opened the front closure with a flick of his fingers.

"Wow." She blinked down at her bra. "You are good."

He wanted to give a joking reply, but couldn't manage it. Gently, he parted the cups and revealed her bare breasts.

Beautiful. He'd always assumed the tawny glow of her skin was sunshine, but now he knew she carried that subtle glow everywhere.

And it made him nuts.

He brushed the bra straps off her shoulders and pulled her up against him for a kiss meant to rattle her as much as she'd rattled him. He coaxed her lips to part, licked over the edge of her teeth, then deeper into her mouth, feeling both possessive and starved for more.

When she tangled her fingers in his hair, Daron slipped his hands down to open the snap of her hip-hugging jeans. He pushed them down to her knees at the same time he eased her onto the bed. His heart thundered and any finesse he possessed abandoned him.

This was Maris, and he'd finally have her.

Even while she struggled to kick her jeans off the rest of the way, he couldn't stop kissing her. Her tongue played against his, her breasts pressed to his chest as she wiggled and contorted— and then finally they were both naked.

Daron was so hard that he actually hurt with need, but he also wanted to taste her all over—and did.

Encouraging him with little gasps and mewls and soft moans, Maris relished his mouth on her breasts, arching when he drew on her nipples. When he slipped his fingers between her thighs, over her sex, then in her, she clutched at him and rocked her hips.

"Daron," she gasped.

She was so tight, as tight as a virgin, and he nearly lost it.

Against her stomach, he murmured, "I have a rubber."

"Good." Her hold on his hair was almost painful.

He left her long enough to grab the protection from the night-stand drawer and roll it on. Maris hadn't moved a muscle, but her dark eyes tracked him.

The second he finished, she held out her arms to him.

He went to her, and she feasted on his mouth as Daron struggled to rein himself in. When she hooked a leg over his hips, he lost the battle and reached down between them to guide himself in.

Eyes heavy and hair tangled, Maris bit her lip.

"Easy," Daron whispered, pressing into her in slow degrees.

She breathed harder, hooked her other leg around him and lifted her hips to take all of him.

They both groaned. Undone by her urgency, Daron put his forehead to hers. "Christ, you're tight."

"And you're big."

He choked on a laugh. If she wanted to think that, he wouldn't debate it with her. No, he was too busy concentrating on giving her a few moments to adjust.

"Daron?"

At her husky whisper, he lifted his head and met her smoldering gaze.

She kissed him and said, *"Move."*

God, he loved her bossy ways. "Yes, ma'am." He stared into her eyes as he began slowly thrusting.

Her heels pressed into his back, her fingertips dug into his shoulders and she squeezed his cock while making those low, sexy sounds.

They moved together, the rhythm accelerating, him going deeper, her squeezing harder.

When he knew he was losing the battle to hold back, he scooped a hand under her bottom, tilted her up—and she cried out a long, charged, ragged release.

Yup, that did him in.

Daron let himself go, loving the moment, loving *her*.

And hoping like hell he could turn it into forever.


Maris shifted on the bed, her skin finally cooling, her heart-beat slowing.

The tingling sensations remained, almost as if little sparks continued to ignite in select places.

She was pretty sure that was as good as sex could get, because she didn't think she could survive anything more intense.

Daron had rolled to her side, but kept her close, one leg resting over hers, his fingers idly combing through her hair.

*What now?* She should probably open her eyes.

Should she also ask him to take her home?

"Stay with me," he whispered.

Startled that he seemed to have read her mind, Maris turned her head and whispered back, "What?"

"Stay the night." His hand coasted down to cup around her breast, his thumb idly playing over her nipple—and making her squirm. "Stay."

Coming up on an elbow, she looked around. Their clothes were scattered over the floor and the blankets were off the foot of the bed.

Daron was wonderfully naked, and every inch of him was enough to fill a lifetime of fantasies.

"Do you need to do something with that?" She nodded at his now flagging penis and the spent rubber.

"Yeah, I do." He stared into her eyes, his gaze probing. "Will you stay?"

The thought of getting dressed and going back out in the cold didn't appeal to her at all, whereas the idea of sleeping with Daron...yeah, that definitely enticed. "I've never stayed the night with anyone."

"Then show me I'm special and stay."

He *was* special. Why was she still fighting it? Stubbornness, probably.

"What if I snore?"

"It'll be adorable."

Snorting over that nonsense, she warned, "I'll need to be at the store early."

A wide grin made him even more handsome. "No problem." He bounded up from the bed, gave her a firm, quick kiss and headed for the bathroom.

"I don't have a toothbrush," she called after him, a little flustered at how quickly they'd moved from sex to an overnight visit.

Bare-assed and not the least bit reticent, he said, "Feel free to use mine."

Dropping back to the mattress, Maris laughed. A second later she decided she wanted a quick shower.

It turned into a long shower...because Daron joined her.

Then they were both hungry so they ate PB&J sandwiches on the couch while watching an old horror movie. She did use his toothbrush, and he helped her straighten the blankets before they both got into the bed.

Before Daron could reach for her, Maris grabbed her phone.

Brows lifting, Daron asked, "Everything okay?"

"Yup. I just need a second." Pulling up Joy in her contacts, she texted, He sealed the deal.

She knew Joy was at the drive-in still, so she didn't expect a reply—

What deal are we talking about?

Grinning, Maris replied, Followed your advice & I'm officially hooked.

Yay! Knew you would be. ☺

Yes, Joy had been quite certain. Staying the night but will let you know when I'm home. ☺ Details tomorrow.

Joy replied with Whoo hoo! Can't wait.

Funny, because Maris couldn't wait, either. It was such a novel thing to have someone close to share her excitement, to celebrate with her, to talk about the most private parts of her life.

She hesitated, swallowed nervously…but it felt right, so she texted, Luv ya.

There was a pause, then three hearts came across the screen, followed by, Luv u, too!

When Maris grinned, Daron asked, "Should I be jealous?"

"If you want to be jealous of Joy, sure. Knock yourself out."

"You're texting Joy…now?"

She set the phone on the nightstand and turned toward him. Oh, but he looked incredibly delicious. How had she resisted him for so long?

Teasing, Maris said, "We tell each other *everything*."

"Is that right?" Tugging the blankets away again, Daron loomed over her. "Guess I better make sure it's all bragging without any complaints."

Maris was about to assure him—but then his mouth was on hers, his hands on her body, and she decided to let him have his way.

After the back-to-back Halloween kid movies ended, Royce breathed a sigh of…relief? They'd wrapped up with a bang, a full lot and a great many happy customers. He'd lost track of the popcorns and hot dogs they'd sold, and the candy counter was now almost empty.

He had big plans for the off-season, and for reopening in the spring, but for now, he'd get some downtime—which meant more opportunity to further his relationship with Joy.

He was in the back, wrapping up a few things, when through the open doorway he saw them come into the concession stand.

Jack slumped against his mother's hip, looking more asleep than awake. Two nights of movies was clearly throwing him off his schedule, especially after the earlier Halloween festivities in the park.

Jack and Joy, along with most of the families, had segued directly to his drive-in. More than a few of the kids still wore their costumes.

Jack had changed into sweats; Royce suspected he'd be sleeping in them. He thought of Joy trying to get a sluggish five-year-old up the outside steps and to his bed, and more than anything, Royce wished he could be there to help. He liked the idea of carrying Jack up and tucking him in.

He especially liked the idea of being alone with Joy afterward.

"I'll be right there," he told her.

"We were just going to say goodbye." She steered Jack one step toward the door.

"Hold up. I only need a minute."

Joy smiled. "All right, if you're sure we're not interrupting."

"Never." Even while Royce had fought it, even while *she'd* fought it, both Joy and Jack had become priorities for him in a very short time.

Earlier today, when he'd slung Jack over his shoulder and the kid had called him Mr. Nakirk...that was the moment Royce knew he needed the formalities to end.

Jack was more important to him than that, and he wanted to be more important to him, too.

Since he hoped Joy would take down the barriers, he'd start encouraging her tonight.

Headlights repeatedly flashed against the windows of the concession as cars pulled away from the theater. Only one of

his employees remained. Cindi, who'd just turned twenty, had proven herself more than capable of locking down the premises.

Giving her a set of keys for the cases, Royce said, "I'll be right back."

"Take your time. I can handle this."

"Thanks." Royce walked over to where Joy and Jack waited by the door. Joy had to be tired, too, and here he was, keeping her out. "Thanks for coming in." He lifted Jack so the little boy could rest against his shoulder, then took Joy's hand. "Come on."

"Where are we going?"

"I want to tell you something." *And I'm dying to kiss you.*

Her smile flickered with curiosity. "Okay, but it will have to be quick. Jack needs his bed."

Around a huge yawn, Jack said, "I'm not tired."

"Well," Joy teased, "I am."

As he led them to the back room, Royce asked, "The haunted house was a success?"

"Some girl spilled the food," Jack voluntarily mumbled. "Then a boy fell and ripped his costume and cried for, like, *forever.*"

Joy smoothed his hair. "Ridley got a headache and Phoenix walked her home early, but it was fun."

Royce laughed. "Sounds like a rockin' good time."

"Yeah," Jack said, his head lolling.

He knew the second Jack nodded off, his little body going boneless against him.

"Uh-oh," Joy said. "He's out. Now you'll have to carry him to my car."

"Not a problem." Royce leaned his cheek against Jack's crown, giving him a small hug. How would Joy get him up to bed? Hopefully she wouldn't try to carry him.

"You're good with him," she said, her voice softer than he'd ever heard it.

Leaning forward, Royce pressed his mouth to hers in a brief

but tender caress. As he drew back, he said, "About Jack..." Unsure how to lead into the topic, he hesitated.

The gentleness left her, and her eyes turned wary. "What about him?"

Disliking that look, the one that said she still didn't completely trust him, Royce stated, "I'd like Jack to call me by name."

"You—" Joy blinked, the wariness replaced by surprise. "You want him to call you Royce?"

"He talks about Coop and Baxter, Phoenix and Ridley, Daron and Maris... I'm the only *Mr.* in the group and—" he sounded like a kid himself, complaining about being left out. But what the hell? Left out was exactly how he felt "—I want to be part of that group. His group. I am, right? So the Mr. thing has to go."

He saw it in her expression, the knowledge that this was another big step, a signal that they were getting serious.

He was here for the long haul.

"This area is now my home," Royce explained. "I don't want to feel like an outsider." Shit, that sounded lame. "Especially not with you or Jack."

A smile flickered over her lips, one of happiness, maybe understanding. "You're right, of course. I'm sorry I hadn't thought of it before now."

Jack surprised them both by mumbling, "I wanna call him Royce, too. He's my friend."

They both looked at him, at his angelic little face that showed no signs of being awake.

"Are you faking?" Royce asked, rubbing his hand up and down Jack's narrow back.

No answer. Jack just snuggled in and let out a sigh.

The grin caught Royce by surprise, and without thinking about it, he gave Jack another slight hug. "Will you be able to get him up to bed?"

"He cooperates." Joy watched him with a soft expression he

couldn't quite read, but enjoyed all the same. "Like a little sleep-walker, he puts one foot in front of the other and I just steer. Brushing his teeth is out, though. He cleaned them the best he could in the car with a bottle of water and a travel toothbrush."

Damn. Again, she surprised him. "You planned for every-thing, didn't you?" And here he'd thought he had a lot of de-tails on his mind.

"I've been bringing Jack to the drive-in for Halloween since he was two. We've learned a few shortcuts."

Royce tangled his free hand in her hair. "You should win Mom of the Year."

With a husky laugh, she said, "Right along with every other mother who's doing the best she can." She stepped into him, tilting up to kiss him one more time before saying, "It's past time for us to go."

Royce would have a few minutes more before he could lock up the drive-in, but he carried Jack out and got him buckled in his booster seat in the back. By then, everyone else had left the lot and the screen was dark.

A cool breeze stirred the night air.

Tonight, with Joy, it felt like possibilities.

"Want to get together tomorrow?" So that she wouldn't think he meant only for sex—though he'd certainly be there in a hot minute if she wanted him to—Royce added, "I'm free whenever. We could do dinner again. My house or yours, or I could take you and Jack out." He wanted time with her. Hell, he needed it.

Joy touched his arm. "Hopefully we'll all sleep in a little, and then I need to take down the haunted house and get the rec center in order. I'm free after that, though. Oh, and Monday I have...errands. So after tomorrow, it'll probably be Tuesday before I'm available again."

It hit Royce that he didn't know what Joy did in the off-

season. He'd been so wrapped up in his own business, his own needs, he hadn't thought to ask.

"Tuesday," he said. "When Jack's in school, you and I should talk."

Solemn, she nodded. "Agreed."

"Tomorrow, though, I'll help you with the cleanup."

"Royce—"

He touched a fingertip to her mouth. "I want to." He wanted to be with her, regardless of what they did.

For a moment, she simply stared at him, those green-gold eyes hiding all sorts of secrets. Then she smiled and nodded.

Accepting him. Accepting *them*.

Another step forward. At this rate, he'd have their relationship settled in no time.

# CHAPTER FOURTEEN

Tinted floor-to-ceiling windows softened the afternoon sunshine of a blustery but bright Monday. Inside the conference room, the overall mood was edgy and grim. Joy didn't care. She wouldn't allow herself to care.

Spine straight, shoulders back, she sat in a leather chair facing the attorney at the end of a long teakwood table. Her mother and father flanked her, her father's posture guarded but not unfriendly. Her mother's, however, screamed of disapproval.

*I expected nothing else,* Joy reminded herself. *What she thinks no longer matters. It hasn't mattered for six. Long. Years.*

Ms. Barbara Wickham, a very nice woman in her midsixties, went over details about little divisions of property, photos, jewelry and furnishings. The bulk, of course, went to Joy's father as Grams's only child, but she did bequeath respectable settlements to dear friends, her caretaker and her house staff. A few keepsakes would go to Joy, and the kindness of the gesture touched her. One of the items was a whimsical glass elephant

that Joy had often admired as a child. That Grams remembered meant the world to her.

Unfortunately, since her grandmother's estate was sizable, it took quite a bit of time to cover everything and Joy began watching the clock. At this rate, she'd be cutting it close to get back on time to get Jack from school.

Before the attorney could finish going over a few other details, her mother's clipped voice interrupted. "I want to know your intentions."

Ms. Wickham paused and glanced at her, a frown in place.

But of course Cara Reed wasn't speaking to the attorney. Her icy gaze was leveled on Joy.

Sighing, Joy pretended her mother wasn't there. *Not an easy feat.* She had a limited amount of time to get this done and still get back in time to pick up Jack from school. Arguing with, debating or even acknowledging her mother's eternal animosity wasn't worth the effort, or the wasted time.

Cara Vivien Reed wasn't easily deterred. Never had been. Once, so very long ago, Joy had admired that about her mother, how she would stick to her principles no matter what.

Now Joy had a difficult time even thinking of the stubbornness as a principle of any sort.

Flattening a hand on the table, her mother said low, "What do you plan to do, Joy? And who was that man with you at the trailer park?"

"RV resort," Joy corrected, before she could stop herself. Damn it, why did she let her mother provoke her? But even as she thought it, she added, "You disowned me, remember? My plans, my life, are my own."

Her mother straightened in a snap, creases forming at either side of her mouth. "Disowned means you don't inherit."

Joy nodded at the attorney. "If that's so, I have no idea why I'm here." Honestly, she was more curious than anything else.

She'd already heard the phenomenal assets bequeathed to her parents, who were already wealthy. Now they were more so. The numbers hadn't fazed them, and they meant absolutely nothing to Joy.

"Family dissension," Ms. Wickham stated, "may or may not be an influence. So if I may continue?"

Whoa. Score one for strong women. Joy barely suppressed a smile at the attorney's calm and professional tone. "Yes, please do."

"Wait." Her father shifted.

Joy felt him staring at her, and though she didn't trust her own judgment, she thought his gaze felt…concerned.

For her mother, or for Joy?

It was impossible to tell.

Her father had always deferred to her mother. No, he'd never been unkind to her. Just the opposite.

But she remembered him as often busy, involved in travel, and for the most part he'd left the parenting decisions to her mother. Joy loved him, yet she'd never shared a special bond of any sort.

Voice gruff, he said, "I have a question, if I may."

After a brief hesitation, the attorney deferred to Joy. "Ms. Lee?"

She really wanted to get this over with, but couldn't remain immune to the expression on her father's face and in his eyes.

Eyes that, she realized, had aged a lot in the years she'd been gone.

"If you have the time, Ms. Wickham, then I can also spare an extra minute or two." Joy almost winced; she'd sounded as cutting as her mother. Softening her tone, she said, "Go on, Daddy."

Her father's mouth firmed, not in anger but almost as if he was suppressing strong emotion. "How are you?"

Oh. Oh, that's what he wanted to ask? The inquiry sounded

so genuine Joy's heart began to thaw. Not a good thing under the circumstances. She needed to keep up her guard.

She needed to end this bitter reunion as quickly as possible, before she crumpled.

Leaning forward, her father said, "Tell me, honey. How have you been? Are you well?"

"I am, yes," she said slowly, touched by the warmth in his gaze. "I'm doing quite well."

He studied her face for only a moment, and his mouth softened. Sitting back, he said, "Good. I so often wondered..."

Her mother cleared her throat. Loudly. *"Wallace—"*

With a single look he shut her down. "We're here for a reason, Cara. Allow me to get to it."

*For a reason?* An inheritance, only that and nothing more, Joy reminded herself.

So why did it suddenly feel like more?

The urge to run had her breathing faster, yet pride kept her in her seat.

He smiled at Joy. Toying with a pen on the table, he asked, "How did you...?" He clutched the pen. "Joy, honey, how did you...?" Again he faded out. "I see your necklace is gone."

The necklace? Joy's fingers automatically reached to her throat, then fell away because there was nothing there to touch. Not for years had she thought about the gift given to her on her thirteenth birthday. A gift she'd cherished for so very long.

All of the jewelry she'd parted with had gone to a greater cause than sentiment. Namely: survival. "I sold it, along with the rest of my jewelry. Is that what you're asking?"

"Sold?" he repeated with a stricken expression.

"Pawned actually." Talking about it dredged up the desperation she'd felt back then. It shored up her resolve...and sharpened her tone. "I learned all about pawning jewelry for cash."

"Dear God," her mother whispered, equal parts horrified and dismayed.

Her dad looked so old suddenly, older than his seventy years.

On the other side of her, her mother remained silent...and almost worried?

Why not tell them? She could sum up her life in only a few short sentences. "If you recall, I left with my clothes, my jewelry and a few of my personal possessions." Fortunately, that included a limited savings account, though it hadn't taken her very far. "Without a job, I knew I'd run out of funds pretty quickly, so I sold the jewelry and then looked for work that would allow me to be both a mother and an employee. The park was perfect for me because..." Did she really want her mother to know where she lived, as well as where she worked?

Yes. Because it no longer mattered. Never again would she allow her mother to intimidate or bully her.

"My job at the park came with a modest apartment. That's where I've raised Jack."

"You sold...everything."

The disbelief in her mother's tone had her turning to face her head-on. "What exactly did you think I would do?"

Cara's head snapped up and her eyes glinted. "I thought you would *return*."

Without Jack. That's what she meant, whether she said it or not, and it infuriated Joy. She felt her temper unwinding, control slipping away—

"Jack," her father repeated, savoring the name and interrupting the flare of hostility. "My grandson."

Reluctantly, Joy broke her gaze from her mother's and turned back to her dad. "Yes, you have a grandson. He's an absolutely beautiful, brilliant, *kind* little boy." Love for Jack blocked all other emotions, allowing her an authentic smile. "He's also a talented artist."

"Did he get that from his *father?*" her mother asked.

Joy laughed. "No. I'm pretty sure Vaughn wasn't into painting." How absurd. Vaughn had been into sex, cars and parties—in that order.

Her father sat forward. "Is Vaughn out of the picture?"

"Completely." At her father's questioning frown, Joy assured him, "He made it clear before Jack was ever born that he had zero interest in a child." Much as her mother had. "I haven't seen him since the divorce."

"Hmm." Wallace Reed looked at the attorney, then back to Joy. "We should legally ensure it stays that way."

"No," Joy said gently. "I'm sorry, but there is no *we. I* care for Jack. *I* ensure his safety. And *I* alone make the decisions that are best for him." She'd keep it that way, come hell or high water.

It was odd, but something like pride curved her father's mouth, lifting the lines that age had carved into his features. "You always were strong-willed."

"Me?" Joy said, unsure how that description applied to her.

Her mother snorted. It was such a rude sound, so uncouth, that it not only startled Joy and her father, it startled her mother, too. The hilarious look on Cara's face caused another laugh to escape Joy. The laugh might have been part nerves, but was largely hilarity.

Her father tried and failed to suppress his own chuckle.

Cara cleared her throat and murmured haughtily, "Excuse me." Then, with a frown, she asked, "Could we get down to business now, instead of all the idle chatter?"

Her father checked his watch, and tried for a compromise. "Maybe we should finish this on another day."

For him, that would be no problem. For Joy, it'd be a major inconvenience. She thought of her life, of the changes she'd made, not only since her parents had made their preferences known, but lately.

With Maris as a sister of her heart.

With Royce as a lover *and* a friend.

With a home at the park where she cared for people, and they cared for her.

She said to her father, "Today is good for me." To the attorney, she asked, "Do they need to be here for the rest?"

"Actually... I've already explained the details to them, so there's no reason for them to remain. I can update them on the decision later."

Joy wasn't sure what that meant. What decision? *Whose* decision?

Whatever the explanation, Joy preferred that her parents go. Not because of the heart pangs caused by proximity to them. Not because hurt ruled her. No, she realized her life was currently so full she had new defenses, new emotions, to counter the old.

Happiness to repel the sadness.

She'd already had that with Jack. Never, ever would she regret the choices she'd made. But now the contentment was bigger, richer, brighter.

She'd gone from a flashlight in the dark, carefully picking her way toward the future, to the full illuminating scope of the sun.

Now, thanks to those additional changes, she had the ability to forgive. Not that either of her parents had asked for forgiveness; it was just that, for her own sake, it made sense to shrug off the depressing weight of resentment.

"We're not leaving."

Joy tipped her head at her mother's militant stance. Clearly, she wouldn't budge. Was it worth a debate? No, not really.

"Fine." Standing, Joy moved down the table, aware of her mother's gaze burning against her. She took the seat to the immediate right of Ms. Wickham. "If you would continue?"

"It's easy," her mother stated. "Reconcile with your family, and you inherit."

Ah, so it was as she'd suspected. There were strings attached… and that meant her business here was done.

To Ms. Wickham, Joy said, "In that case, I should be going. Thank you for your time."

"You will not leave yet." Cara cleared her throat. "Not until I've finished."

Joy tried to keep her back to her mother, but it proved impossible. No matter what, she was her mother and deserved some respect. Inhaling a deep, bracing breath, Joy swiveled on the seat and lifted one brow.

Hands clasped before her, chin elevated, her mother said, "If you return to your family, we'll…double the inheritance."

Double her… *"What?"* A slap couldn't have confounded Joy more.

Her father seemed equally surprised. "Cara—"

"It's time for you to return home," her mother said. "End the rebellion. Move away from the trailer park—"

"It's an RV park!" Without thinking it through, Joy found herself on her feet again. "But FYI, Mom, there is nothing wrong with living in a trailer park. They're good, close communities for kids. Small homes are wonderful, too. Even an *apartment* is terrific when the people who live there make it a home." Since Joy lived in an apartment, she felt compelled to make the point. "There's nothing wrong with working for a living, and staying within your means." Arms out, she said, "There's nothing wrong with my life."

"Except that you have no family."

"You're wrong. The people I work with are my family."

Slashing a hand through the air, Cara said, "But you don't have to work."

Fist to her heart, Joy assured her, "I *enjoy* my work. I enjoy

where I live and I enjoy the people there, too." How dare her mother try to buy her? Did she honestly think it'd be that easy? That Joy would throw away everything that mattered to her just to have a pampered life? "Actually, I love each and every one of them." She lifted her chin to match her mother's expression. "And I especially love my son."

Shooting to her feet, Cara stepped forward, her tone nearly shrill, to insist, "Since you kept him, we have a right to know him!"

Ice ran through Joy's veins. "You have *no* rights, not when it comes to Jack." Somehow they were now toe-to-toe. "Not since you discarded us both."

Oh damn. That just sort of dropped out there, hostile and filled with hurt. It gave away far too much, things Joy would prefer her mother never know.

They stared at each other.

As if this particular battle had taken all their strength, they each breathed heavily.

Slowly, her mother pulled her dignity around her like a cloak. "You were a spoiled, ungrateful child, refusing our advice, and for all your bragging about the wonders of your new life, I can see that hasn't changed." With that parting remark her mother turned and left the room, closing the door quietly behind her.

Joy was still troubled a half hour later when Ms. Wickham finished explaining the details of her inheritance. It was…well, she refused to call it life-altering, because she refused to alter her life.

Her grandmother, in her misguided way, had hoped to put them all back together by offering two choices. Joy could have a nice inheritance, enough to upgrade to a newer car, or add a comfortable cushion to her bank account, no strings attached.

Or, *with* strings—maybe more like chains—she would be

given enough to purchase a house with cash, to ensure a higher education for Jack, to never again have to worry over a budget.

All she needed to do was make amends with her parents.

Easy to say, not so easy to do.

With the second choice, she'd be able to give Jack things she couldn't before. But at what risk?

Her son was a sweet, caring child in part because she hadn't spoiled him.

*He's an artist, and art supplies cost money. I could give him an art tutor, or send him to classes...*

Again, Joy mentally shook her head. Jack was still only five, for crying out loud. Despite Royce's assurances and Jack's obvious inclinations, no one knew who they were at such a young age. Why, Jack could turn to a sport, or music. Favorites changed as people matured.

*And those things cost money, too.*

While Joy struggled with the stipulations of the inheritance, her father remained silent at the end of the table. He hadn't joined her mother in the outer area and Joy wondered if they'd decided together that one of them would remain with her. Maybe her father wanted to give Cara time to cool down.

Or maybe he wanted to spend more time with Joy.

Feeling very uncertain, she glanced at him.

The second their eyes met he smiled, the same warm, indulgent smile she remembered as a little girl, a teenager and a young woman. She'd missed it.

Ms. Wickham stood. "I have a phone conference in a few minutes. This room is free for another hour, so take your time deciding."

Joy shook her hand and thanked her.

Once the attorney had gone, her father stood, as well. "I can't tell, honey." He didn't yet approach her. "Are you pleased with the money, or upset?"

Good question. "I'm…numb?" She truly couldn't decipher her own mood. "I don't know what to do." If she had Royce here, or Maris, or *both*, they could help her decide.

*No*, she corrected herself, *this is not their problem.* But it'd be nice to have a sounding board at least. Someone she truly trusted.

Gruff, trying to give her a nudge, her father said, "It should be an easy choice."

"It's not." Seeing the hurt on his face caused her to hurt, as well. "Try to understand, Daddy. Jack and I have a nice, comfortable life. That kind of money…it could change everything."

"It's not such a staggering amount as all that."

Not to him. Not to a man who had never lived on an inflexible budget.

Very seriously, he said, "Your mother meant it, you know. We will happily double that amount."

Joy twisted her mouth. "Until she said it, you knew nothing about it."

He nodded. "That happens a lot actually. But I don't disagree with the idea. Just think, you could buy a house for you and Jack." He held up a hand. "I know you said you like your apartment. I wasn't suggesting you leave it. Only offering ideas for your future. For Jack's future."

Hearing her father say Jack's name brought home all the ramifications. "I can't drag my son into that life."

"That life?" He looked down at the table, and when he lifted his gaze, she saw a touch of anger in his eyes. "I tried to give you everything you needed or wanted. Did I spoil you? Yes. Not because I didn't care, but because I did. Were we the best parents?" He shook his head. "I'm not sure perfect parents exist."

"You disowned me, Daddy." She loved him, yes. God help her, she loved her mother, too—if she didn't, none of this would be so difficult—but she wouldn't let him delude himself. "I never

asked for perfection, but to be told to toe the line or else? That if I had my child, I would no longer be *your* child?"

His mouth firmed and he looked away.

No, her father hadn't said those words, but neither had he gone against her mother's wishes. "You sent me away, alone and pregnant, very unprepared to deal with life. How can you call that love?"

"It was misguided, I agree, but we were so worried for you. Vaughn was never a good person, certainly never good enough for you. We feared how he might destroy you."

"And instead it was my parents who almost did that."

He flinched, his breath catching before he regained control. "Your mother thought it would shake you up, that you'd come to your senses and return to her."

"Minus my baby?" Joy could barely get those words out of her constricting throat. All of this—rehashing the past, seeing her parents, having to defend her position all over again—wore on her.

"As I said, it was misguided. Worse than misguided, it was wrong, but it *was* a decision made from love. How could a future child who we didn't know ever compare with what we felt for you?"

More importantly, Joy wondered, how could they make her feel so all alone if they really did care?

"You think you won't make mistakes but you will." Hands in his pockets, her father gave her a sad smile. "Different mistakes, sure. But would you want them to damage your relationship with your child for life? Or would you hope that your son would forgive you, that he'd understand you meant well."

Had her mother meant well? It was hard to imagine.

Before Joy could reply, he added with heartfelt emotion, "Would you want Jack to understand that you were doing the

best you could with what you knew of life, and your own experiences?"

Was this his way of saying her mother hadn't known any other way to deal with the situation? Did that make it excusable? "She tried to control me," Joy stated, tears burning her eyes. "It was my decision, and she tried to insist on making it for me."

"Yes, she did." With the briefest of smiles, her father whispered, "But instead of giving in, you countered Cara's bluff and managed just fine on your own."

Had she? Joy recalled that day, how devastated she'd felt, how scared. With her voice emerging small and wounded, Joy said, "It didn't feel like a bluff."

"I'm sure it didn't. Cara might not have realized it was when she spoke it. She was so relieved that Vaughn was out of the picture. We both were. But a baby could have caused long-term ties—" His jaw worked as he sought more explanations. "Honestly, we were afraid if Vaughn stuck around he'd drag you down with him."

"If I'd let him, yes." Joy couldn't deny that. "If only you'd trusted me."

"You chose Vaughn," he reminded her, his own eyes suspiciously red. "How was I supposed to trust you when I still don't understand why you hooked up with that bum in the first place?"

Because Joy didn't understand it, either, she couldn't explain. She couldn't recall ever feeling a great love for Vaughn.

Not like the things she felt for Royce.

She closed her eyes. With Royce, everything was bigger, stronger, richer and deeper than any emotion that had driven her to Vaughn. Mostly, she'd gone to Vaughn because...

Her eyes popped open with the realization. "He was the first thing you denied me."

Her father's bushy, graying brows scrunched together. "What?"

"You gave me everything, no matter how extravagant. Then I wanted Vaughn, and you and Mother both flatly denied me." Oh God, this didn't speak well of her decision making at all. With a self-deprecating laugh, she admitted, "It's just this second occurred to me that I never learned how to cope with *no*."

He blinked at her, and then scowled. "Should we have given our blessing to that bum?"

"Of course not." What an amazing, *awful* realization. "You're right that I was spoiled."

"Your mother said that, not me."

"But you were thinking it, too," she pointed out, her heart starting to lighten a little, "and neither of you were wrong. I was also horribly immature. The truth is, I really could have ruined my life."

"You didn't," he insisted, belatedly affronted on her behalf.

"No. My life only expanded, showing me new challenges and teaching me things about myself that I never knew." She was a stronger person now, her priorities in proper alignment. "Jack is a blessing. In every conceivable way, he's made my life wonderful."

"I can see that." He edged toward her, that slight smile in place again. "You might have been slow to mature, but you've made up for it."

"Having a baby will do that for you, teach you what's really important and show you what you can do, instead of what you can't." Because it was necessary. Because Jack depended on her. Her throat tightened. "With Jack, I've learned who I truly am."

His tone softened, went husky. "I'm proud of you, Joy."

Hearing it felt wonderful, she could admit that now, but was the sentiment too little, too late? Could she and her parents ever repair all the damage? She glanced at her mother outside the office, and it didn't seem possible.

"If you think about it," her father said, "if you go over ev-

erything we've discussed here today, you'll see that we were all a little to blame for this current situation."

Yes, Joy acknowledged that she did have blame, at least as much as her parents. "That's fair—though I'm not sure it can change anything."

Her father stopped before her. He looked so solemn, so grave, it surprised her when he said, "You're as beautiful as I remember."

"Daddy." She shook her head. "I was never beautiful."

"You are." He clasped her shoulder for a gentle squeeze. "Regardless of whatever decision you make here today, if you find it in your heart, I'd like to meet my grandson."

Joy had gotten so used to the idea of them not being in Jack's life, she almost gave an automatic *no*.

At the last second, she caught herself. Something this important deserved more than a gut reaction. She needed to consider everything. And she'd also talk with Maris and Royce before she came to a decision. Not so they could make the choices for her, but because they cared and could possibly help her weigh possibilities.

Through her friendship with Maris she'd learned the value of talking out a problem. She'd never again underestimate the value of caring friends.

Her father prompted her, asking, "What do you think?"

Gently, she replied, "I need some time."

Disappointed, he nodded. "On your terms, okay? No pressure at all."

"Mother might not agree with that."

"Your mother might surprise you."

Feeling a bit like she'd landed in an alternate universe, Joy struggled with saying goodbye. "Before you go, can I ask you something?"

Her father nodded. "Anything, always."

*Except for while I was disowned?* No, she wouldn't allow herself to keep harping on that. As they'd both concluded, there was plenty of blame to go around. "Why now? Jack is five—he'll be six before too much longer. Why reach out to me now? Why start caring about him now? Is this new concern really only spurred by Grams's death?"

It was her father's turn to take his time mulling over his answer. Finally he sighed. "I'm seventy, Joy, ten years older than your mother. Not a young man." His smile faltered. "My mother lived to the ripe old age of ninety-two, but look how incapacitated she was. From one day to the next, everything changed. It's made me think about life. Pretty sure it's done the same for your mother. We've wasted too many years already. I don't want to waste a single minute more." He took both her shoulders in his hands. "None of us are guaranteed tomorrow, and regrets are a son of a bitch. I know, because I have plenty of them."

Going on instinct, Joy embraced him.

After a second of surprise, he hugged her back, his arms folding tight around her just the way she remembered before the years of animosity had pulled them apart.

He seemed in no hurry to let her go, and honestly, other than the tears clinging to her lashes, she enjoyed the embrace.

In her ear, he whispered, "Your mother is a stubborn woman, but you're more so."

Taking that as an insult, she stiffened, but still he hugged her, and she didn't like the idea of forcing him away. "Daddy—"

"All I'm saying is that you're stubborn enough, *strong* enough, to keep her in line. That is, if you decide to come around." He patted her shoulder and finally let some space between them. "She's not a young woman anymore, either. Think about that."

Joy saw the sheen of tears in his eyes, and it broke her heart. "Okay," she promised. "I will."

He touched her face. "What I said about regrets is true, and

no one, not even you, gets to avoid them." He kissed her fore-head and walked out to join his wife.

Leaving Joy alone with her confusion…and new regrets.

Through the open door she saw her mother glance at her, her posture and bearing just as unforgiving, yet there was some-thing else in her eyes.

Did she dare believe it was…hope?

Joy had yet to decide when her parents left.

It was a relief when the attorney returned because it gave her a new focus.

When she explained that she wanted to wait until she had time to consider things, Ms. Wickham was very understanding.

"Give me a call when you've made up your mind and I'll fit you in."

Glad that at least the attorney didn't press her, Joy said, "Thank you."

"No thanks needed." In an impetuous move, Wickham reached out to pat Joy's hand. "It's what your grandmother wanted, for you to be treated with care, respect and patience. I was with her a long time, so I would never dishonor her wishes."

Bless Grams. Though Joy hadn't seen her for years, she missed her now that she was gone. Regrets…yes, she had them. Al-ready too many to tally.

With a glance at the clock—and a swift kick of panic—Joy realized she'd waited too long. Bidding Ms. Wickham goodbye, she hustled out of the building without an ounce of decorum.

Gray clouds covered the sun and it felt as though winter had returned once again. Shivering, Joy pulled her coat around her, unlocked her car and slid behind the wheel.

As long as she didn't hit any traffic, she'd make it home just in time.

All went well for the first hour of her drive, and that freed up her mind to dwell on her parents.

A mistake apparently, because as she drove through a more rural area where pine trees lined the road, a deer jumped in front of her and she reacted...badly.

Swerving and braking, her heart in her throat, Joy narrowly missed the beautiful animal, but the action sent her car in a slight spin. With a white-knuckle grip on the wheel, she felt the rear of the car punt hard against a rock on the side of the road with teeth-jarring impact.

Thank God her airbags didn't deploy.

Finally stopped, her heart punching like mad, she struggled to catch her breath.

Turning her head to the side she spotted the white tail of the deer—probably a buck, judging by his impressive rack—as he disappeared into the woods.

She dropped her head to the steering wheel.

Too much, all of it. Overwhelmed, buried in tension, she nearly let the tears free. A slow, deep breath brought them under control, but didn't stop the shaking in her hands. At least she was more off the road than on it.

After checking that no one else was around, she opened her door and stepped out. The car seemed intact...until she circled the back and found a shredded tire.

Gentle snowflakes began to float on the brisk air, the clouds thickening.

Numb, Joy got back in the car, locked the doors and turned on her blinkers.

Then she sat there, trying to decide what to do. She definitely wouldn't make it home in time, so her first priority was Jack.

When she dug out her cell phone, she saw that, being here on the long stretch of wooded road, she had only a few bars.

Worse, her battery was nearly dead.

She didn't have a way to recharge. That awful realization lev-

eled her after she dug through her purse and found that she'd somehow left the cord behind.

Frustrated, despondent and more than a little panicked, she called Maris before the damn thing died completely. It took several heart-stopping tries before she finally got reception.

On the first ring, thank God, Maris said, "Hey, how'd it go?"

With no time to waste, Joy said, "Maris, I have to rush through this. I'm so sorry but can you get Jack? I have a flat and there's no way I'll—"

"Whoa. Slow down."

"I can't! My phone is about to die."

"Yes," Maris affirmed, "I'll get Jack. Don't worry about that. Are you near an exit?"

"No, I'm in the middle of nowhere." She stated the highway and the last exit she'd passed.

"Do you know how to change a tire?" Maris asked.

Squeezing her eyes shut, Joy shook her head, and admitted, "No."

"Well, I do," Maris informed her, "so just stay put. I'll grab the squirt and come to you, okay?"

"I can't ask you to do that."

"Actually, you're right. I have a better idea." Maris drew a breath. "This is a call for Royce."

*"No."* Calling Royce would make her a burden, after all.

*"Yes.* Please. Let me call him for you."

Since her phone was dying, Joy rushed to say, "Could you just call a garage or something instead?"

"Sorry, but no garage is going to drive out to you."

The battery icon on her phone turned red. Danger zone. Dying any second. "My phone is almost gone!"

"I got this," Maris said fast. "Sit tight! Help is on its way."

"Maris—"

"Thanks, hon. You just gave me an excuse to get hold of Daron."

For a single heartbeat, that gave Joy pause. "You need an excuse?"

"Well, I can't let him know how much I'm starting to care, now can I?"

Before Joy could reply, the phone blinked off.

Gone. Kaput. Never before had she realized what a lifeline her phone could be. The tall trees left her in shadows and she shivered, both from the cold and a bone-deep dread. She was at least forty minutes from home.

Carefully, going very slowly, she put the car in Drive and rolled farther off the road in case it started to get icy. The last thing she needed was to get sideswiped by an out of control driver.

Like herself.

Groaning, Joy dropped her head back against the seat. Should she attempt to change the tire herself? One peek out the window at the glistening sleet and the trees casting long shadows, and she opted against it.

First thing tomorrow she'd buy an extra cord for her phone and leave it in the car. The second thing she'd do is order Triple A.

And the third...? She'd have to make a decision about the inheritance.

Honestly, she'd rather learn to change a tire.

# CHAPTER FIFTEEN

Royce and Chaos arrived at Summer's End in time to see Daron stomping snow from his feet on the stoop. He noticed Daron's scowl and wondered at it. Usually Daron personified a happy-go-lucky guy. These days, especially, he was all smiles.

His new romance with Maris had done that to him.

"Hey," Royce said, wondering what had turned Daron's mood.

Glancing up, Daron saw him and asked, "You on camp store duty, too?"

Having no idea what that meant, Royce shook his head. "I was just going to grab a coffee while I wait for Joy to get home."

After a long pause, Daron chuckled and bent to give Chaos some attention. "I have a feeling your master is in the dark."

As if he understood, Chaos barked and turned a circle, getting wrapped in his leash.

"In the dark about what?" Royce asked.

Opening the door with a flourish, Daron gestured for them to go in. "Let's talk inside."

They brought in with them a gust of cold air that sprinkled snow over the floor. It worried Royce that Joy was driving in the nasty weather, even just to the school and back, but he held that concern in check. She'd gotten along just fine without his input for a very long time.

"Maris?" Daron called.

She poked her head out from the back. "Oh good, you're here." Then her gaze went to Royce and Chaos, and she frowned, too. "You called him?"

Daron crossed his heart. "Nope. He just showed up."

"Oh." Speculative, Maris bounced her gaze back and forth, then said, "I guess you should clue him in while I get these cookies on a plate. Then I need to roll."

"Yes, ma'am. Whatever you say, ma'am."

Maris shot him another look, but didn't say anything before disappearing around back.

Holding the dog to check his feet for snow, Royce asked, "What the hell's going on?"

Daron went behind the counter to pour two coffees. "Long story short, Joy left town to meet with her grandmother's lawyer after dropping Jack off at school. Apparently the place is better than a few hours away. She had a mishap coming back and she needs Maris to pick up Jack."

Royce's heart slammed against his ribs. "She's all right?"

He must have hugged Chaos a little too tightly because the dog wiggled.

"She's fine." Daron slid a coffee over to him.

Royce drew a breath, unleashed Chaos and set him on his feet.

The dog immediately attacked Royce's shoelaces, and he was worried enough that he didn't even mind. "So what's up, then? What mishap?" Had something gone wrong at the meeting? Had Joy's mother shown up and upset her?

"Joy's on the side of the road with a flat. Relax," he said when

Royce tensed again. "She dodged a deer and must've hit something that damaged the tire. Maris will pick up Jack and then head out to help Joy."

Royce didn't even realize that Joy was going out of town. The meeting was today? He remembered her saying she'd be busy... but he'd decided to try his luck, anyway. He could always find an excuse for being at the park. "Why the hell didn't she call me?"

"That's between you and Joy," Daron said with a roll of a shoulder. "All I know is that when I offered to go after Joy instead, Maris almost bit my head off. Said she could damn well change a tire without my help, and that, besides, I couldn't get the squirt. So..." He spread his hands. "Here I am, ready to watch an empty store."

Fuming inside, Royce jerked out his phone and called Joy. No answer. What the hell did that mean?

"Er, Maris mentioned that Joy's phone had died in midconversation."

*Son of a bitch.* So she was stranded on the side of the road, in the cold and snow, with no way to call anyone? What if something else happened?

Bothered in part by the fact that Joy hadn't called *him* instead of Maris, Royce rounded the counter and headed toward the back. Chaos barked and charged after him.

Startled, Daron followed, too. "Royce—"

He found Maris pulling on her coat, fragrant cookies cooling on a rack beside her. "Where is she?"

When Chaos started sniffing the air, Maris broke off a piece and offered it to the dog. "Who?"

"Don't do that," Royce said, doing his best to keep his tone calm and noncombative.

"Cookies will hurt Chaos?"

Yeah, a sugary diet wasn't what the dog needed, but it wasn't

what he meant. "Don't act like you have no idea who I'm talking about." With emphasis, he asked, "Where is Joy?"

Maris glanced behind Royce at Daron, then back again. "For some reason, Joy didn't want to bother you."

He took that on the chin. Yes, he'd told her he wanted to stay unencumbered, but come on. They'd talked about it, he'd explained—and they were supposed to be well past that now.

Why the hell hadn't he told her that he wanted a more committed relationship? He couldn't remember. "Tell me where she is and I'll go get her while you get Jack."

"I'm not sure that's what Joy wants."

"It is," Royce assured her. "She just thinks it's not what I want."

Arms crossed and hip jutting out, Maris asked, "But you do?"

"Yes." He wanted to take care of her and Jack, to be there for her—and he wanted her care and attention in return.

"Think maybe you ought to tell Joy that?"

"We were going to talk on Tuesday, but tonight will be better."

"Nah," Maris said, relaxing enough to get a purse off a hook. "Stick with tomorrow. I have a feeling she did enough talking today. She'll need time to chill."

"Tell me where she is. You can get Jack, I'll go get her, and I'll let her do all the chilling she needs."

Daron backed him up, saying, "I'll watch Chaos for you. Jack will love seeing him."

Royce nodded. "Thanks." In his mind, it made perfect sense.

"I don't know," Maris said, hedging.

"Come on," Daron urged. "Cut the man a break."

She frowned at him. "Because I never cut *you* any?"

Typical of Daron, he grinned, and sidled over to loop his arms around her. "I'm spending time with you, so I'm not in a complaining mood."

"It could be a win-win," Royce said, hoping Maris would agree. "You'll save Jack from the drive in the cold. You know he'd rather hang here and play with Chaos and Daron."

"Fine." Disengaging from Daron, Maris explained where Joy's car was, going into extra detail since Royce wasn't from the area. "It's going to take you more than a half hour to get to her, but I'll feel better knowing you'll reach her sooner than I could, since I need to get Jack first."

Royce pulled her into a hug of his own. "Thanks. Tell Jack not to worry."

"Do you have a phone cord with you?"

"Yup. Keep one in my car."

"Great. Have Joy let me know when she's on her way back."

"Will do." Royce knelt to give Chaos some extra attention. "Stay here with Daron."

Chaos turned a circle, barked and tried to get at his laces again.

Smiling, Royce handed the dog a chew that would hopefully keep him and his puppy teeth busy for a while. "Be good."

When he started away, Maris stayed him with a hand on his coat. "You do know how to change a tire, don't you?"

Daron started laughing, then couldn't stop, even when Maris gave him a push.

On his way out, Royce assured her, "Piece of cake."

And just before he got out of range, he heard Daron say, "You do love busting balls, don't you?"

Royce grinned as he jogged to his car. Maris and Daron made a fun pair. He had a feeling they'd be teasing each other fifty years from now.

It was a nice thought.

His humor ended when he thought about Joy alone on the road with a steady snowfall. There wasn't much accumulation

yet, the flurries mostly a nuisance, but the longer he drove, the more slick spots he found on the road.

Forty minutes later, after fearing he'd missed her, he finally spotted her car, blinkers on, at the opposite side of the old highway.

Soon as he could, he made a U-turn and came back to her. She recognized him and stepped out before he'd gotten into Park.

Collar and shoulders up, snow collecting on her hair, she greeted him with an apology. "Royce, I'm so sorry. I told Maris not to call you! I wanted her to try a garage or something."

He met her with a kiss...and a pounding heart full of realization.

Damn it, he wasn't falling in love.

*He was already there.*

Her chilled lips softened under his and Royce fought not to deepen the kiss, to pull away instead. Touching his nose to hers, he growled, "I want to be number one on your list."

She blinked up at him. "Number one?"

Yeah, throwing that out there hadn't been the smoothest move. He didn't want her to think he placed himself above Jack, so he clarified. "When something comes up. When you need someone." He brushed snowflakes away from her hair. "Especially when you need a helping hand. I want to be the person you think to call first."

It crushed him when her eyes went glassy and she swallowed heavily. "I'm sorry—"

"Please stop saying that, honey." Royce kissed her again, light and easy. "Please."

That earned a choked laugh and a shaky nod. "Okay. May I say thank you?"

"Not for this." It dawned on him that her nose was cherry

red and her car wasn't running. "You turned it off?" She had to be freezing.

"On top of causing a flat and forgetting my phone cord, I didn't think to fill her up before leaving."

He hated the embarrassed, guilty note in her tone. God knew she'd carried an emotional burden when it came to her mother. It was enough to throw off anyone. "Deer take everyone by surprise, so the flat isn't on you."

"I still should have been better prepared."

"Pretty sure you had other things on your mind. Come on." He led her to his car and got her inside. "Stay warm in here while I get the tire changed, okay? Then I'll see if you have enough gas to make it to the next station."

"I think I will. That's why I turned off the engine, to conserve fuel."

"Good thinking." He moved his mouth over hers one last time before saying, "Maris wants to hear from you, so feel free to use my charger." He pointed out the white cord dangling from his dash.

She jumped on it like it was salvation. "Thank goodness. It's crazy how lost I felt without my phone."

He never wanted her to feel that way again, not if he could help it. "Sit tight. This won't take too long."

While Royce changed the tire, Joy texted Maris. You got Jack okay?

Yup. Playing with Daron & Chaos.

Thank you for doing this.

You're not mad about Royce? 😊

Joy laughed at the smiley face that somehow managed to look hopeful. Not mad. Grateful, she texted back.

::High five::

So...you & Daron?

I'm flippin' addicted.

Joy could almost hear Maris's voice. Yay!

Catch up when you get here. Don't worry!

Joy replied with a thumbs-up emoji.

No, she wouldn't worry about Jack...but she couldn't keep her thoughts from veering to the big decisions that loomed ahead.

What she needed was a distraction, so she leaned forward to watch Royce. In the headlight beams from his car, she saw him working the jack. A minute later he sat back on his haunches, frowned, then stood and went to the back of his own car.

He returned carrying a funny-looking tool. If she had any lady-balls at all, she'd get out there with him to observe the whole process.

But seriously, why should they both get cold and snow-covered?

Not that he looked cold. He just looked very masculine and actually...sexy.

One day when it wasn't snowing and freezing cold, she'd ask him to teach her how to change a tire, so she could truly be self-sufficient. Didn't have to be today, though.

Not when she'd already learned more than she'd expected.

Joy's emergency spare was a joke and he didn't trust it, so Royce followed close behind her as she drove to the next exit

where they found a gas station and she filled the tank. Luckily, the gas attendant also knew a nearby place to get a tire.

Once they arrived there a few minutes later, he'd tried to convince Joy to get a complimentary cup of hot chocolate while he dealt with everything.

Apparently allowing him to change the tire was as far as she'd go in relying on him.

At least for now.

He watched her as she ordered the tire for her car, saw her nod at the technician and ask how long it would take.

Royce wanted to know how the meeting with her parents had gone, but didn't want to ask her in the tire station, not when she already looked so very fragile.

Whatever had happened, it had taken its toll on her.

Getting each of them a hot chocolate, they went to a small waiting room with a plastic-covered couch and a television turned low.

Joy first used her phone, talking quickly with Maris, explaining their progress and giving a guess on when they'd return before sinking into the seat. She smiled when he handed her the chocolate. "Mmm, thank you."

Royce watched her sip, and saw that her hands were shaking. "Have you eaten?"

"Not since breakfast, but Maris says food will be waiting when we get to the camp store. Coop and Phoenix dropped in, too, so Chaos is playing with their dog, Sugar, and Jack is..."

Her voice faded off.

"Jack is what?" he asked gently.

"Having the time of his life." Her smile trembled, and she swallowed heavily. "They really are family to him, you know? I don't think I totally grasped it before, but a lot of things are clearer to me now."

What she felt for him—was that clear, too? Royce hoped so.

She sipped the cocoa again, holding the foam cup in both hands. "I know you don't want to hear it, but I'm grateful for you, for this." She gestured at the station. "Thank you for coming out in this weather, for changing my tire and...and waiting here with me."

"Here with you is where I want to be. I mean that. You and Jack are both important to me."

She gave him another heartbreaking smile. "Maris said that Phoenix and Coop brought down a big pot of stew. They thought Baxter and Ridley would be joining them, but Ridley is miserable with a cold so she stayed home with Baxter pampering her."

Royce let her switch topics without complaint. There'd be plenty of time for him to tell her how much she meant to him. "My guess is that Baxter is good at pampering."

"He adores Ridley, so I'm sure you're right. With her pregnant, he's especially attentive—too much so, Ridley sometimes complains, but I can tell she loves it."

"Because she loves him."

Eyes averted, Joy nodded. "Maris baked bread to go with the stew while Daron looked over the dogs and Jack." Her next smile was a little more carefree. "She said that Jack tried to sketch Daron with the dogs, but the dogs didn't cooperate."

"That's where a photograph can come in handy." Royce wouldn't mind showing Jack how to use photography to help him capture a moving object. Because his mother had done her best to train him, Royce could even explain the technique of showing motion. He couldn't execute it, but he could describe it.

"Maris said Daron tried to corral them—and lost, and it was so funny she heard Jack laughing all the way in the kitchen."

Royce was enjoying the intimate chat so much he almost regretted it when the technician came into the waiting room a while later to let Joy know her car was done.

By the time they got out of there and drove the rest of the way to Cooper's Charm, the sun had set and the security lights were on. Joy parked in her usual spot near her apartment, so Royce parked beside her.

Hand in hand, each of them silent, they walked down to Summer's End. The wind off the lake was extra chilly, but it also felt clean and crisp.

"I want to talk," Joy whispered.

His gut clenched at the way she said that with such dark foreboding. "All right."

Briefly resting her head on his shoulder, she added, "I want to see Jack first, though. Are you in a rush?"

He'd sit up all night with her if that's what she needed. "I'm here as long as you want me." If she wanted him for the rest of her life, he wouldn't mind at all.

The second they stepped inside, Jack looked up from his seat on the floor with the dogs. "Mom!" He ran to greet Joy with an enthusiastic hug, both dogs chasing and yapping at his heels. Talking ninety miles a minute, Jack told her about his awesome day, which, typical of little kids, didn't include any worry for his mother who'd been stuck on the side of the road with a flat.

While Jack chattered on, Royce scooped up Chaos and accepted his adoration, including lots of tongue swipes and wiggling.

Because Sugar was caught up in Chaos's enthusiasm, Royce gave Coop's dog some attention, too.

Even while stroking the dogs, Royce noticed that Joy clutched Jack a little tighter, a little longer, than usual.

He met Coop's gaze and knew others had noticed, as well.

These people cared about Joy. As she'd said, they were family, closer family than her own could currently claim.

As casual as he could, Coop said, "Glad you're both back. No problems?"

Knowing Maris had surely updated everyone, Royce said only, "None at all, except we're both hungry." The stew did sound good, but it was Joy he worried about. She needed to eat and she wouldn't appreciate being singled out.

Maris, who'd been sitting with Phoenix and Coop, her gaze fixed on Joy, stood with her empty bowl. "Grab seats and get comfortable. I'll bring it out to you."

Daron called Jack over, saying, "Now that Sugar knows a few tricks, let's see if we can teach Chaos."

Excited by the prospect, Jack squirmed out of his mother's arms and was off again in a flash. Sugar followed, which meant Chaos was frantic to do the same. Smiling, Royce put the dog back on his feet and watched him scamper away.

"It's nice," Joy whispered, "seeing Jack so animated."

"He's a happy, healthy, well-adjusted boy." Because she was such an amazing mom.

Her breath shuddered in. "Yes. He really is."

Sensing there were emotions at play that he didn't understand, Royce put his arm around her. "Let's grab a seat."

It spoke volumes to her exhaustion that she allowed him to lead her away. Before she slid into a booth, he helped her out of her coat, and removed his own. While watching Jack, she rubbed her cold hands together. They were in the seating area with her son, Daron and Maris, Coop and Phoenix, but because they'd sat apart they had a touch of privacy.

With his pinky, Royce eased back a tendril of hair, tucking it behind her ear. Her cheeks and nose were pink from the cold, her lips chapped, her mascara a little smudged. And she was the most beautiful woman he'd ever seen. "You okay?"

She nodded, but then murmured, "My grandmother left me a sizable inheritance."

It was more her inflection than the words that gave him pause. "Oh?"

Maris coasted in with a tray holding two bowls of stew, hot slices of bread with a bowl of butter and glasses of tea. She kept her gaze trained on Joy. Probably for the same reason Royce had difficulty looking away.

She saw Joy's vulnerability.

"Dig in while it's hot," Maris said with false brightness. "There's more if you want it."

Joy had already picked up her spoon when she said, "I'm famished, but I didn't mean to have you waiting on me."

"Don't piss me off, Joy." Maris gave her a brief but fierce hug. "If our situations were reversed, you'd do the same."

"I would try," Joy said, "but you're really good at making people feel pampered."

Maris preened comically. "It's my calling. Now eat."

"It smells delicious." Louder so that Phoenix would hear, Joy said, "Thank you for the stew. I didn't have time to eat today and this will be perfect."

Phoenix turned in her seat to see her. "My pleasure. Hope you enjoy it."

Joy took a bite, and said, "Mmm. Nirvana."

With a smile, Phoenix nodded and turned back to her husband.

Holding the now-empty tray, Maris hesitated. "Everything go okay?"

"Overall, yes." Joy sighed. "I had a few surprises at the meeting. Good ones, I guess."

"You aren't sure?" Maris asked.

Joy shook her head. "Want to get together in the morning? Right now I'm beat, but I can update you then."

"Club meetings start directly after school drop-off."

Royce had no idea what that meant, but Joy laughed. "I'll be there." She reached out to take her friend's hand. "Everything went okay with you?"

"Jack is a doll."

"Uh-huh," Joy said knowingly. "But I meant with Daron. We haven't talked much this week, not since...you know."

Royce was starting to feel like an interloper, but he liked seeing Joy like this, teasing a friend. "Maybe I should—"

Maris waved him back into his seat, then glanced at Daron. "He's good with Jack. And animals. And people in general, so yeah, other than him being too freaking perfect, everything is great." Her gaze went to Royce, which prompted him to show a lot of interest in his stew. He couldn't quite suppress his smile, though.

"Tomorrow," Maris said. "We have a lot of catching up to do."

"Or," Royce offered, "I could find somewhere else to be for a few minutes."

Maris patted his shoulder. "If we got started, it'd take longer than that and you two need to eat." She winked at Joy and rejoined Phoenix and Coop.

Royce waited, but when Joy didn't say anything, he prompted, "You got an inheritance?"

"With a stipulation." Holding a warm hunk of fresh buttered bread, she added with a strange detachment, "All I'd need to do is reunite with my family."

A bribe? Was that the reason for her upset? "By sizable, you mean...?"

"Half a mil." Her mouth pinched as she stated that astronomical sum. "My mother said she'd double it if I moved back."

His lungs seemed to empty of air. Royce couldn't take it in. Joy would be financially set? And her mother wanted her to move back, as in...*leave the park*?

Well, obviously a million dollars would give her better options than being a recreation director at an RV resort.

Where did that leave them?

Misunderstanding his expression, Joy shook her head. "Believe me, that's chump change for my family. I have no idea why my grandmother decided to use it as a lure, though I'm certain she meant well."

"Joy..." Tension gathered at the base of his skull. He wanted to hold her tight and ask her not to go, but had he missed his chance? Would it even be right to put her in that spot now?

"If I return to them," Joy said, "they'd probably expect me to live by their standards, their rules."

That would make her miserable. Royce tried to sound neutral when he asked, "Can you do that?"

"No. Definitely not."

He didn't feel relief, because regardless of what Joy said, he sensed her indecision. He couldn't remark on it, so instead he sat quietly, his thoughts in turmoil as they ate.

Would he really lose her—on the very day he realized that he loved her?

Joy literally devoured the food. Few people knew it, but she ate more when stressed, and tonight she felt more stressed than she had since before Jack was born.

No, she couldn't live with her parents' expectations. But was it fair to keep them from Jack? Was her father right? Could she control the situation to somehow have the best of both worlds?

If she reconciled with them—and honestly, she already had with her father—she could offer Jack the best of schools. He'd receive, in moderation, all the luxuries she'd grown up with, the things she'd been accustomed to and had taken for granted.

The things she better understood now.

Yet they were poor replacements for love and affection, attention and guidance.

Would Jack grow to resent her later in life when he learned what he could have had, what she'd deliberately kept from him?

Worse, would access to those things change him?

Joy shook her head, more to shake off the old disturbing memories of who she used to be, more than in any type of denial.

Royce sat back, and it felt like a retreat, as if he'd pulled away. "What will you do?"

There was something in his low voice, something she didn't understand. "I'm going to refuse."

"Are you sure that's wise?"

The gruff sound she made was part hurt, more disbelief. Speaking in a hushed whisper, she asked, "You think I should expose Jack to people who would hand him the world while not caring about him, about who he is as a person? Without any love?"

"Is that what it would be?"

"*Yes*." She hadn't meant to raise her voice, and now the others looked at her with concern. Joy swallowed, trying to clear the anger and hurt from her throat. Anger directed not at Royce, but at the situation. "I'm sorry."

"Don't be."

Of course he said that. He was so damn nice all the time, and she was...a mess. One little hiccup in her life and she was ready to fall apart.

Yeah, she was such an independent woman.

She wasn't fooling anyone, least of all her mother.

Her eyes grew damp, forcing her to blink fast and take deep breaths. Her lips trembled, and no matter how she tried to control herself, Joy knew she was losing the battle with her emotions.

On a gulping breath, she choked, "I can't cry here. Not where Jack will see me."

"Come on." Royce stood, gently catching her elbow and drawing her up.

If he hugged her now, she'd lose it. She'd already fought it

off for so long any sign of sympathy would turn her into a sobbing mess in seconds.

"Outside," he whispered. "We'll walk along the shore."

She nodded, hating herself for relying on him again, but also immeasurably grateful that he'd save her from humiliating herself.

He said to Jack, "We'll be right back."

Jack was so busy teaching Chaos to sit he didn't even reply.

Royce snagged their coats, and she was aware of him passing a significant look with Maris. By now she knew what that meant. Her friend would keep an eye on Jack, probably with help from Daron, who didn't seem in any hurry to leave.

Damn it. The tears welled over and slid down her face.

As they stepped outside, she slapped them away, her breath catching, her throat squeezing tight.

Gruff, as if he did a little struggling of his own, Royce said, "It's cold. Let me help you with your coat." As she buttoned it up, he pulled on his own, and then steered her well away from the camp store.

Frosty air, prickly with sleet, pelted her face, making the tears sting.

Near a tree, Royce turned her and pulled up her collar, then wrapped her muffler around her throat. While she pulled on her gloves, he glanced out at the stars twinkling on the rough surface of the lake.

"I'm sorry," Joy said, knowing it was a weak refrain. "It's been such a long day."

Shielding her body from the wind with his own, he cupped her face with hands somehow still warm. His thumbs brushed away the tears she couldn't seem to stop, and then he kissed them away, his mouth gentle as it touched each cheek, her forehead and her lips.

She thought she might be able to get it together...until he

folded her close, those big, strong arms secure around her, holding her tight, rocking slightly.

Emotion pounded against her restraint and the dam burst. The first sob was horrible, a wounded animal sound that should have embarrassed her more than it did, but God, she hurt too much to care.

"Joy," he whispered.

"I'm sorry," she sobbed again, unable to hold back as six years of grief overflowed, prompting his arms to tighten even more.

He tucked his face close to her, saying softly, "It's okay, sweetheart." His hand petted her hair, then his fingers tunneled in and he held her close.

Giving her permission to cry.

How had she gotten so lucky to meet this amazing man? To have him in her life, as either a lover or a friend, was a true blessing.

Yards away, she heard the camp store door open as conversation spilled out. The soft glow of light barely reached them before it all faded away again.

"Just Coop and Phoenix," Royce told her. "Maris and Daron are still with Jack."

Horrified by the idea of what her face must look like, she hiccupped a breath. "I don't have a tissue."

She felt his mouth warm against her temple. "Want to use the hem of my shirt?"

"God, no." She probably had mascara everywhere, and she didn't even want to think about her nose.

"How about this?" He offered her a knit glove, then retracted it. "Oh wait. Napkins. I grabbed them for Chaos's paws the other day, but then didn't need them."

Joy took one, mopped her eyes, blew her nose and stuffed it into her pocket. "I forgot about Chaos."

"The dog is fine."

"But I'm keeping you out here in the cold..."

"Joy." He brought her back against his chest. "As long as you're warm enough, I'm happy to be with you. Take all the time you need."

*This man.* He was the finest, nicest, most caring person she'd ever met.

Today she'd been offered a huge sum of money, but she didn't want it. Her parents offered her reconciliation, but she wasn't sure she could accept it.

What she wanted was Royce. On a more permanent basis. Was that fair, to project her neediness on him?

No, most definitely not.

"I shouldn't be unloading on you."

His thumb brushed her face just under her eye, maybe removing a tear. "I want to be that person for you, remember? You can trust me, Joy. With whatever you're feeling or thinking."

Damn it, she almost welled up again. To hold it at bay, she related everything that had happened at the attorney's office, including her father's revelations.

"He thinks it was a big misunderstanding?"

Royce asked it with honest curiosity and no accusation. "No, but he says we were all to blame—and he's right. I never should have been with Vaughn in the first place."

"If you hadn't gone against their wishes, you wouldn't have Jack now. That means it wasn't a mistake, right? Not in any way."

So very true. Why couldn't her parents see it that way? "I can't imagine my life without Jack, so obviously I wouldn't change a thing, but Vaughn *was* a terrible person."

"In the scheme of things, it's a blip on the radar."

Joy almost laughed. See, *this* was why she'd wanted to talk with him and Maris. She'd known they could add perspective that would lighten her load, make her feel less like a spoiled screwup and more like a regularly flawed human. "A blip, huh?"

He nodded. "I'd like to see anyone who gets through life without tripping a few times."

"Including my parents?"

"There's a blip, and then there's a deliberate explosion."

Joy managed a small wobbly smile. "They are incredibly outrageous, especially my mother."

He smoothed her hair. "And no matter what, she's still your mom."

Joy nodded. "I see their side of it now. They thought having Vaughn's child would keep Vaughn hanging around and they... Dad said they were afraid for me."

"And yet they let you go?"

"Thinking I'd relent." She shook her head hard. "It doesn't excuse them. Disowning me financially would have been one thing, but they cut me out entirely. Mom said I wasn't her daughter anymore and my father didn't correct her. Nothing excuses that."

"Or makes up for all the hurt?"

So, so much hurt. "Is it fair to keep Jack from them?" Before Royce could reply, she said, "My father thinks I can take charge and allow the relationship on my terms."

"He's right there," Royce agreed. "You're an incredibly strong woman, and the love you have for Jack would always protect him."

His faith buoyed her. "I don't feel strong."

"You are. I see it, and so does everyone else who cares about you." He tipped up her chin. "We're always our own worst enemies. Try not to be so hard on yourself."

Because she wanted it to be true, Joy nodded. "I think... I *hope* you're right. I'd always do my best for Jack." The problem was *how* to protect him—or would she actually hurt him by forbidding contact with his grandparents? "If I only reconciled

with my parents, I would inherit from my grandmother and I wouldn't be obliged to them."

Royce loosened his hold on her. "It's a lot of money to pass up."

"Yes, but I have zero interest in being manipulated." More than most people, Joy knew the insignificance of money when compared to things of real value. "I don't know what to do. The inheritance would be nice obviously." Even if she only put in the bank, it would be security for the future. For *Jack's* future. "It's been so long since I heard from them, I easily convinced myself that it was the right thing, that they didn't care about him, anyway. Now my dad says I was wrong and that they care very much. Have I been selfish by not seeking them out?"

"It's not selfish to do the best you can for your child, especially since your best was pretty damn good. No one could ever doubt your devotion to Jack."

She appreciated the sentiment, but devotion didn't always equal wise decisions. A gust of wind blew her hair into her face and she shivered. She'd kept Royce outside in the cold long enough. "Thank you for listening, for understanding, and for the pep talk."

He took another step back and his smile seemed strained. "So you'll get in touch with your folks and call a truce?"

What an assumption he'd made! It was such a big decision she didn't plan to rush it. "I didn't say that." The sleet increased, stinging in intensity. "It's getting late. I should get Jack home. It's past time for his bath."

Nodding, Royce asked, "You feel better now?"

Her smile went crooked and she swiped her gloves under her eyes. "People talk about a 'good cry' and how you should let it out. For me, though, crying always stuffs up my nose and makes my eyes swell so bad I look like a miserable troll."

"You're beautiful."

That made her laugh it was so absurd. "Maybe the darkness helps hide me."

"I see you just fine."

Oh, what that husky voice did to her. She hugged his arm, loving his strength, needing his sense of humor. "I do feel better, not as pent-up, but I regret sobbing all over you."

"Hey, no regrets." He closed his hand over hers when she held his arm. "Not with me."

Joy wondered about their relationship. Everything had changed recently—too many things, really—and she needed to sort it out one emotion at a time.

Royce walked with her the few yards to the camp store. "I meant what I said. If you need me for anything, I'll be there."

Something in the way he said that made her think she'd have to reach out to him...because he wouldn't be in touch? No, she was just emotional and too tired to think straight.

Leaning into his shoulder, so big and solid, she nodded. "One more favor?" Scrunching her nose, she said, "I'm such a mess... I don't want to step in there for Daron and Maris to see. Will you get Jack for me?"

"You want to stand out here in the cold?"

Actually, the cold was preferable to the embarrassment she'd feel. "Do you mind?"

Royce kissed her ever so gently, and said, "We'll be back out in one minute."

# CHAPTER SIXTEEN

After Jack had a lingering, playful bubble bath, a bedtime snack and had brushed his teeth, Joy lounged in his bed to read him a story. She wanted, *needed*, her usual routine with her son to ground her after all the surreal happenings of the day.

Few things could calm her turbulent thoughts and fill her with peace like cuddling with Jack.

With her shoulders propped against the headboard, only the bedside lamp on, he rested beside her, smelling little-boy-sweet.

Beneath her fingers, his hair was soft and cool. He listened intently while she finished reading aloud *Hecate the Bandicoot*, by Janet Little. It was one of Jack's favorites, in part because the illustrations fascinated him, but he always felt sorry for the bandicoot.

Honestly, so did Joy.

"If I had a bandicoot," Jack said, "I wouldn't make it take a bath."

Joy grinned. "Most people wouldn't bathe a bandicoot, and

from what I understand, most bandicoots are too small to want to eat a human. They're more like a big mouse."

He tipped up his face, his eyes filled with curiosity. "Can you show me?"

"All right." Joy picked up her phone and did a search.

For a long time, Jack studied the images she found, then peeked up at her again and asked, "Could I get a bandicoot?"

"They're wild animals, honey. Not pets."

"Could I get a mouse, then?"

How in the world had they gone from reading to requests for a mouse? "Do you think Chaos would like that?" She stroked his hair again, comforted by the warmth of him. "He might get jealous."

Giving that some thought, Jack shrugged. "Yeah, probably." Abruptly he sat up and crossed his legs on the bed. "Maybe Chaos would like a friend, though."

Joy gave a silent groan. She knew this particular look on Jack's face. He wouldn't give up easily. "You're his friend," Joy pointed out.

One eye narrowed in calculation. "Bet he'd like a dog friend, though."

"Jack…" They'd been through this before, and she'd repeatedly pointed out how difficult it would be to have a pet in the apartment. Every time she had to refuse him, she felt guilty.

"I know," he mumbled, his tone melancholy. "We don't have enough room."

No, they didn't—but now she might have the opportunity to change that. Maybe this was the perfect time to see what Jack thought about moving.

Joy reached for his small hand, tangling her fingers with his. "You know, I was thinking…" She needed to word this just right so that she didn't worry him.

His earnest little face scrunched up. "Something wrong, Mom?"

"No, sweetie. No." She tugged him close, snuggling him against her side, wishing every moment of motherhood could be as easy as a hug.

"You sure?" he asked, pushing back to study her face. "You look funny."

She could imagine how funny she looked with her puffy eyes and blotchy cheeks. The devastation from tears stuck with her for hours. Luckily, Jack had believed her excuse of having a cold. But add to that her confusion over the day's dilemmas, and "funny" was probably a nice way to describe her ravaged appearance.

Joy pasted on a reassuring smile. "I was just wondering how you'd feel about living somewhere else."

Dark eyes going wide, he froze. "I don't want to live anywhere else." Looking around, he said, "We live *here*. My stuff is here."

She hadn't expected that immediate rejection of the idea. "We could take your stuff to a house. A bigger place." A place where she could get him a dog of his own.

"A house like Royce's?"

Pleased with his interest, she nodded. "Yes—"

He started bouncing up and down. "We could live with Royce!"

*What?* Good grief, she'd botched this horribly. "No, sweetie, that's not what I meant! I meant a house *like* his. Not...not *his* house."

The bouncing stopped. "But I like his house," Jack mulishly insisted, his brows down in confusion. "I like his yard and I *love* Chaos. If we lived with Royce, Chaos could be my dog."

"I love Chaos, too," Joy said. *And I especially love Royce.*

Oops, had she just admitted that to herself?

Yes, she loved him. If she'd had any doubts, his gentle understanding today would have settled it. Poor Royce. Loving him meant she'd opened up to him completely, to the point of sobbing against his shoulder. Even with Maris, she'd be horrified by that emotional display. With Royce, she couldn't control herself—and no longer wanted to.

She loved him more than she knew was possible. That meant she wanted to share everything with him, her difficult past and his. Together, it felt like they could deal with it all.

Jack gave one insistent bounce that jostled her. "Let's live in Royce's house and Chaos can be our dog."

"Jack—"

"If we had Royce's yard," he continued, "we could get Chaos a dog friend."

"I doubt Royce wants another dog." He wouldn't have a dog now if Chaos hadn't shown up when he did. Trying to be upbeat, Joy said, "Let's think about a different house, okay?"

Jack's chin went stubborn and his mouth pinched. "I like Maris, too. And Coop and Baxter and Ridley and Daron and Phoenix. My playground is *here*. Sugar is here."

Funny that he considered the playground his own, even when other campers brought their kids to play. Joy understood, because she felt the same. The park was home in a way few places could ever be.

She smiled at him. "Everyone here is our family and nothing would change that. We would still work here."

"You work here, Mom. Not me."

"You help a lot," she pointed out.

He crossed his arms with decisive attitude. "I don't want to move."

"What if—"

"I don't want to move," he repeated stubbornly, and his bottom lip quivered.

Well…that decided that, didn't it? She'd done enough crying today for both of them. She wouldn't have Jack going to
sleep upset.

"Then we won't move," Joy promised, giving his shoulder
a gentle squeeze. "I just wanted to see how you felt about it."

"I want to live with Royce, or I want to live here." Worried
now, he asked, "Okay?"

Only one of those choices was currently possible, so… "Got
it," Joy said, keeping her tone light. "We'll stay here." She tickled his ribs until he lost his frown and squealed, then she hugged
him tight, kissed his forehead and tucked him under the covers.
"I love you bunches and bunches, Jack."

He yawned widely, pulled up the covers and said, "Love you,
too, Mom."

Joy stayed near the door, watching him to make sure he'd
be able to sleep. When his breathing deepened and his face relaxed, she eased away. New tears stung her eyes, but they were
tears of gratitude, recognition of her blessings.

No matter what happened tomorrow, she'd deal with it.

And as Royce had said, she would always protect her son.


"So how'd it go?" Maris asked the second Joy walked into
the camp store the next morning.

"Oh no you don't. I want to hear more about you and Daron
first." As Joy peeled off her coat, she said, "I have a feeling I've
missed a lot in the past week. Time for some catch-up!"

Though Joy wore her usual makeup, her eyes were still a little puffy, evidence of her tears the night before. It broke Maris's
heart.

Maybe, she thought, it'd be easier for Joy to ease into the subject of her parents and the meeting if they chatted about other
things first. That worked for Maris, since she was nearly burst-
ing to share the wonder that was Daron.

"First order of business," Maris said. "We never let another week go by without a Summer's End club meeting."

Agreeing, Joy made a checkmark in the air. "Even if we only talk by phone."

Maris nodded. "Even if we're each getting nonstop orgasms."

"Whoa! Back her up." Making a rewind gesture with her finger, Joy asked, "You're getting nonstop orgasms?"

"I meant you."

"Oh." With a pout of disappointment, Joy said, "Yeah."

So little enthusiasm. Stifling a laugh, Maris said casually, "And me."

That earned a squeal. "You and Daron? Seriously?"

Maris couldn't hold back her grin. "Oh my God, Joy, he's a certified stud. If I'd been wearing socks, he'd have knocked them off."

Joy cheered, honestly, truly happy for her. It made Maris laugh, too. Who knew great sex made the perfect excuse for a celebration?

"I knew you were seeing him all week. Everyone knew," Joy said. "I'm surprised no one took bets on how it'd turn out. FYI, we were all rooting for you guys as a couple."

Maris wasn't sure where things would go, but she was pretty damned satisfied about it. "Halloween puts a kink in communication, with everyone being so busy."

Putting her hands on her hips, Joy said, "I can't believe you weren't here Sunday to give me a report."

Maris shrugged. "Actually, we spent Sunday in bed."

"Ah, well, then you're forgiven."

"I should have texted, but I thought I'd tell you in person yesterday, after you finished your meeting—"

"And I got that stupid flat tire." Shaking her head, Joy headed straight for the coffeepot. "I'm so glad you two are finally on the right track."

"What exactly do you consider the right track?" Following her, Maris warmed up her own cup.

After inhaling the steam from her coffee and taking a cautious sip, Joy hooked her arm through Maris's and led her to a booth. "Sex is a good start."

"Daron would agree with you there."

"Of course he would," Joy said with good humor. "And you?"

Maris grinned. "I'm loving it."

Joy asked softly, "Are you loving Daron, too?"

Why not tell her? It felt absolutely wonderful to be able to share, so Maris admitted, "Pretty much, yeah." Saying it aloud made it all too real, prompting Maris to squeeze her eyes shut and groan.

"You need to tell him," Joy said.

Admitting it to Joy was one thing, saying it to Daron would be entirely different. "Why should I do that?"

"Because once you tell him, I'm sure he'll tell you, and then you can get on with a life together."

"Listen to you." Maris sipped her coffee, a little afraid to think too much of the future. "Have you told Royce how *you* feel?"

"Well..."

Of course she hadn't. Maris could tell by the look on her face. Lifting a brow, Maris suggested, "Maybe you should follow your own advice."

"Honestly..." Joy hesitated, then sighed. "I think the timing is off. I've got all this stuff going on with my parents and I don't want to tackle too many things at once."

"I don't think you'd need to tackle Royce, but okay. Let's talk about the other first." Maris set aside her coffee. "What happened with your folks?"

Joy winced. "Are you sure you want to hear this? Wouldn't it be more fun to just talk about sex?"

No doubt. There were a lot of delicious details Maris wanted

to share. *Later.* "We'll get to that," she promised. "But how are you? I've been worried all night, so give over."

Sighing, Joy shared the whole awful story.

Wow. Maris had a hell of a time not reacting. She had to keep reminding herself that these were Joy's parents, and whatever strife they had going on right now, their relationship could change. Sounded like that's what her parents wanted.

And if they did reconcile, Maris didn't want to be on the outs with Joy for stating her mind. In the long run, it'd be for the best if Joy found some form of peace with her mother and father—as long as they treated her better.

At least this morning, Joy seemed more like herself. Seeing the tears in her eyes last night had left Maris feeling so helpless. She would have liked to go to battle for Joy, but she knew Joy well enough to know she wanted to fight the toughest battles herself.

"Were you able to sleep?" Maris asked, once Joy wound down. She knew sleep was Mother Nature's way of calming disordered thoughts and easing a troubled heart.

"It took me a little while, but I did finally doze off." Her brows tweaked down even as she smiled. "I'm a terrible crier. My head gets congested and my eyes swell horribly."

"They're a *little* puffy," Maris admitted. "But I wouldn't worry about it." God knew Joy had other, more important things to concern her. "What will you do?"

"The big question, right?" Joy shook her head. "I'm not sure, but at least today I'm not so weepy. Yesterday it all just piled up, and God, you don't know how much I hated getting all emotional." She quirked her mouth to the side and confessed, "I cried on Royce."

"He's a big boy. He can take it."

She laughed. "He was so understanding, Maris. Every time I turn around, there's something else to love about him."

"Know what I think? You should settle this stuff with Royce before you make any decisions on your parents. That way, you'll have Royce's support." He could help share the burden with her. Joy had been alone long enough.

Staring down at her coffee, Joy whispered, "It would be nice to deal with this stuff during the day, and then come home to Royce at night."

"Well, then?"

"I think he needs to make that move first, you know? I can't go to him and say, 'Hey, guess what, Jack and I want to keep you so how about we shift into a more permanent, committed relationship?'"

"That's what you want *me* to do!"

"Because it's just you, and you're a catch. Don't forget, I come with a little boy."

Maris said, "Jack is a bonus. Everyone adores him."

Gratitude put a smile on Joy's face, but then she pointed out, "There are my parents to deal with, too."

With a feigned groan, Maris said, "Look at it this way. If Royce accepts them, you'll know he loves you an awful lot."

They both laughed.

Oh, it was so nice to do this, to take problems and lessen their impact just by sharing.

Idly tracing a permanent stain on the booth top, Maris said, "Know how I realized I loved Daron?"

"Seeing him naked?"

They both fell into another fit of giggles. Maris said, "Can't deny that helped. He's pretty scrumptious. The thing is, I looked around at his house and it's everything I ever wanted. The perfect home. Cozy and clean, nicely decorated and comfortable."

Carefully, Joy said, "I know that's important to you."

True. "But as much as I love that house, I know I'd want

Daron even if he didn't have it. If tomorrow he had to sell it and live in his car, I'd still want him. Crazy, right?"

Joy reached over and took her hand. "That's *love*."

"Probably," Maris agreed, meeting Joy's gaze. "Because I'd still love you and Jack if you lived in a cardboard box."

Their smiles faded. Joy drew in a shuddering breath. "I'm so glad we're friends."

Nodding, Maris tamped down the surge of emotion. "Actually, I wouldn't let you live in a cardboard box. I'd move you and the squirt in with me."

Joy sniffled. "Stop or you'll have me crying when I swore I wouldn't do that today." She drew a slow breath, sipped her coffee and then dabbed at her eyes. With a wicked grin, she said, "Besides, you'll be living with Daron in his gorgeous house and we'll just be coming over for dinner now and then."

As if to ensure that would happen, they lifted their coffee cups in a toast. Bringing the conversation back around, Maris promised, "I'll talk to Daron soon. When will you talk to Royce?"

"If he calls…" Joy fidgeted. "Usually he does, just to say good morning. I haven't heard from him today, though."

"Huh." Doing her best to hide her frown, Maris suggested, "Maybe he got busy."

"Maybe." Joy hesitated. "I talked to Jack last night about the idea of getting a house of our own."

Maris choked on her coffee. As she struggled to catch her breath, Joy half stood and passed her a napkin. Waving her back, Maris managed to gasp, "You're moving? Leaving the park?"

Quickly, Joy said, "No. I mean, if I ever got a house, it'd be near here and I'd still keep my job. But Jack didn't want to hear about it."

"I agree with Jack!" Damn it, she and Joy had just become the best of friends. Selfish or not, no way did she want her mov-

ing. "How would we have coffee in the mornings? What would happen to the club?"

Joy laughed. "A club of two."

That made Maris scowl. "Small clubs are the best kind."

"Maris," she said softly with a touch of censure. "Maybe you don't realize what a difference this has made for me." Joy gestured to encompass the camp store and everything beyond it. "I cherish our friendship. You have to believe that. I grew up alone. My parents were always traveling and the house staff wasn't interested in listening to a kid. When I went to my parents, they gave me things. Just that. Lots of things. Having someone to talk to, someone who really listens, that means the world to me. *You* mean the world to me. Trust me when I say I'm not going anywhere."

Damn it, now Maris was on the verge of tears, and she never cried. Fighting back the emotion, she nodded in agreement. "I couldn't talk to my dad because he was usually drunk or sleeping off a drunk. If my mom knew something was bothering me, she prayed about it." Maris gave a sad smile. "She meant well, but hearing verses from the Bible isn't the same as someone just hearing me." She swallowed heavily and met Joy's gaze. "You hear me, Joy. You always have."

With a shaky smile and glistening eyes, Joy lifted her cup for another toast. "To sisters," she whispered.

"To sisters." Maris clinked her cup to hers. To keep from getting too maudlin, she asked, "So...what are you thinking?"

"That I need more time to consider everything."

"But you talked to Jack about moving. That sounds like you're leaning toward accepting your mother's offer."

"The extra money? No." Joy shook her head. "I couldn't do that. It would destroy me to be under her thumb."

Well, thank God.

"Plus that would require I move back near them. I love ev-

eryone here as if they were actual family, because in my heart they are. *You* are. Even if someday I buy a house, and it wouldn't be any time soon, I won't ever actually *leave*."

Feeling the same, Maris again lifted her cup. "To our family here at the park."

"To each of them," Joy seconded.

After sealing that vow with a drink, Maris said, "Okay, so I just thought of something." Determined now, she leaned forward. "If you don't mind me jumping in with ideas, I mean."

"Of course not. I was hoping you would," Joy admitted.

"The lure from your grandmother…it doesn't have to be all or nothing, right?"

Joy shook her head. "Basically, I just need to reconcile with them. Accept them back into my life. Be friendly."

"That goes both ways, right?"

"Yes. The attorney said Grams trusted that if I accepted the stipulation, I'd do my best to get along with them. There isn't a time limit or set of rules. My mother tacked on that part about moving back to the area. That wasn't in Grams's offer."

"So you'll give them a chance." As Maris spoke, the plan took shape. "That doesn't mean they own you."

"No, but they are determined to meet Jack."

"Sure, but you'll call the shots, not them. So invite them here to the park, on your turf. Like you said, this is home. We're your people. Make them come to you."

Joy sat back, mulling over the idea.

"Hell," Maris said, getting enthused by the idea, "bring them here, to Summer's End. We'll make sure the others join us. Safety in numbers and all that. I promise not to botch the coffee."

Intrigued, Joy paused, but then shook her head. "No. Absolutely not. I couldn't subject all of you to that drama."

"You said it yourself, we're your family," Maris argued. "Look at it this way. If anything happens that could upset Jack, one of

us can take off with him. Daron can get him outside to play with the dogs, or I can lead him back to the kitchen for cookies. It's a surefire way to introduce them, on *your* terms, where *you* control everything."

Joy put a hand to her mouth, then nodded. "It would probably be easier for Jack that way, too, instead of taking him to their house where everything is unfamiliar." She gave Maris a look. "Going back there might even intimidate me, it's been so long."

"Then it's settled." Saying it was so might help to convince Joy. "We'll do it here. You'll have fulfilled your part of the inheritance specification, and you can just stuff the money in the bank and carry on as usual until you've decided what it is you want and what is best for Jack."

Shaking her head on a small laugh, Joy said, "You make it sound so easy."

"Take out the emotion," Maris said, "and it is."

With her thoughts showing on her face, Joy frowned. "I want you to know, a little cash won't change me."

Maris hooted. "Only someone who came from money would call that windfall a 'little cash.' But yeah, I get your point. You're you, we're friends and the club is intact. So we're all set?"

Joy bit her lip, then looked around as if considering it. "This would be a good time for it. We don't have any campers."

"Just your family." Maris put a hand over her heart, making it a vow. "Your park family."

"You're sure the others wouldn't mind?"

"What part of 'family' are you not getting?" Maris took her hand, understanding her worry, her hesitation. "I have a feeling your folks will get it together—I mean, who couldn't love Jack? That kid is all personality. But you may as well hedge your bets as much as you can."

Gratitude brightened Joy's eyes and she nodded. "Yes." After squeezing Maris's hand, she got up and circled the booth, draw-

ing Maris up for a hug. "It will be absolutely perfect. Thank you—for everything."

It took some getting used to, the demonstrative affection, but Maris liked it. She squeezed Joy tight, and before she could let her go Daron opened the door and stepped in.

He almost tripped over his feet, he stalled so abruptly when he saw them. "Um..."

"Come on in," Maris told him over Joy's shoulder, opening an arm to him.

Cautiously, he edged forward—but when Joy held out an arm, too, he grinned hugely and grabbed them both up for a three-way hug. "What are we celebrating?"

Hiding her face against his shoulder, Maris said, "Well, for one thing, I've decided I love you."

A sudden silence fell before he went rigid and tried to pull back.

Neither lady let him go. For her part, Joy was laughing too hard to do anything but cling to him.

Maris asked her, "Was it unfair for me to blurt it out there like that?"

"Whatever works," Joy replied, and she hugged them both more.

Maris grinned. Having Joy near made it easier, and at least now she'd gotten it over with. No reason to dread it. It was all out in the open now.

"You should probably say something," Joy told him.

Yes, he should, Maris agreed, before she died of false expectations.

"Did she...?" Daron floundered, bent his head to Maris, and asked, "Did you...?"

"She did," Joy confirmed, snickering in glee.

Maris decided that was better than Joy's upset any day. Glad that she could lighten her mood, she leaned into Daron, lov-

ing them both, feeling so very grateful for the turn her life had taken. "I did," Maris repeated.

Daron struggled against her, then barked, "Damn it, woman, let me loose."

Both ladies released him, stepping back to stare at him, at each other, then back at Daron.

Maris swallowed heavily. He didn't sound pleased.

After tugging at his sweatshirt, Daron pulled off his hat to run his hand over his hair, exhaled a big breath and said, "Now."

Crossing her arms, prepared for anything, Maris asked, "Now what?"

"Now I can do this." He hauled her in and took her mouth in a kiss so scorching hot she forgot Joy was still there until she heard her clear her throat.

"I think this is my cue to go."

"Or," Daron said, smiling down at Maris as he kept her draped back over his arm, "you can stay and hear me tell this lady how crazy she's made me."

"I agree you're a little nuts," Maris said, her tone deadpan.

"I've been waiting on you for years." He kissed her again, quick but thorough. "Marry me?"

*Marriage?* Just like that? She glanced at Joy.

Grinning ear to ear, Joy said, "I'm going now so you two can talk, but Maris, I expect—"

"Full report later," Maris promised, before pulling Daron back into a kiss.

Marriage. Yes, she liked that idea.

Because she loved Daron.

What the hell had taken her so long to accept it?

Once the door closed behind Joy, she ended the kiss and straightened, but kept Daron close. Fingering the lapel of his coat, she asked, "You love me?"

"Have forever, but man, you're a tough nut to crack."

She punched his shoulder.

Laughing, he squeezed her close so she couldn't strike him again. "You're also gorgeous, funny, smart, sexy as hell, and yes, I love you so damn much."

Maris threw herself against him, loving the strength in his arms, the heat of his body, the way he made her feel. "How did I resist you for so long?"

"I don't know. Never could figure it out." His hand went down to her behind, fondling her. "How soon?"

Tilting back, Maris asked, "How soon what?"

"How soon can you move in?" He brushed his lips over her throat, his voice dropping to a growl. "How soon can we get married?"

When she didn't answer, he raised up to see her. "Maris? Say yes."

Her heart seemed to fill her chest, beating heavily, pumping happiness into every inch of her being. "You know, I was used to being alone. I had no plans to date, much less...everything else. But you wouldn't leave me alone."

"I couldn't," he said, his tone and expression serious. "We're meant to be together."

She believed that now. And oh, this was so much better than what she'd planned for herself. Spending the night in Daron's bed, waking to him in the morning, having dinner together, arguing and laughing—it was the stuff of dreams.

Thank God Joy had convinced her to give him a chance. "Could I just get used to loving you for a little while longer?"

"You'll get used to it a lot quicker if you're with me." He smoothed his hand down her ponytail, then cupped her face. "God, babe, after waiting so damn long, I don't want to spend another single night without you."

The last of her resistance faded away. "Same," she whispered, a little broken up over the reality of loving him so very much.

She didn't know if he wanted a big wedding or small, or what his family would think, and none of it mattered.

Whatever Daron wanted was fine, as long as he wanted her.

The rest of Tuesday came and went, Wednesday also, and Joy didn't hear from Royce. She had so many things she wanted to say to him, so many things she wanted to share, but she hesitated to seek him out.

He'd relocated to free up his life and what had she done?

She'd unloaded her problems on him, and that was so unfair. No matter how desperately she missed him, she wouldn't do it again. Neither would she put him on the spot by asking him if their relationship was over.

But oh, it was so very difficult. In a short time she'd gotten used to him being in her life, and every second of every day she felt the void.

The closest she came to caving on her resolve to leave Royce be was when Jack asked about him. Her son missed him as much as Joy did, and she didn't know what to tell him.

On Thursday, with a full tank, a phone charger and new confidence, Joy met with Ms. Wickham and her parents.

Though she did so kindly, it felt good to refuse her mother's money. She explained that she wouldn't leave the park any time soon, and if she ever did, she wouldn't relocate to the same area as her parents.

Her mother wouldn't look at her so Joy couldn't gauge her reaction, but her father was visibly disappointed.

Hoping to ease them both, she said, "I've thought about it, and if you still want to meet Jack, I can arrange that."

That announcement changed her father's expression, carving a smile into his face. "Did you hear that, Cara? We'll get to meet our grandson."

Cara sat prim and proper in her chair, her hands clasped over

her purse, her expression somehow stoic. She still wouldn't look at Joy, but her profile spoke volumes.

Was she fighting tears? Joy couldn't be sure, but it seemed so.

"Mother?" Joy asked gently.

Cara straightened and cleared her throat. "You will both come to dinner next—"

"No."

Her brows snapped down. "What do you mean? You just agreed we would meet him."

"And you may." It was strange, but instead of the familiar hurt, Joy felt a measure of…pity. What Royce had said was true: Cara was her own worst enemy. She'd let her rigid pride cost her so much.

Joy wouldn't contribute to that. She'd do her part to make things easier, but with Jack's welfare uppermost in her mind. "You're both invited to Summer's End. My friend Maris will host us."

Clearly appalled, Cara's mouth worked before she could find her voice. "You want us to *dine* there?"

Joy continued as if it wasn't a big deal for Cara Vivien and Wallace Barkley Reed to have dinner in an RV park diner. "It's one of Jack's favorite places. He'll be more at ease there." And who knew? Maybe they, too, would fall in love with the area. Joy wasn't sure how they could resist.

Ms. Wickham beamed at her. "This is excellent. A perfect solution."

"It's no such thing," her mother snapped.

"Cara," Wallace warned. He turned to Joy. "What day and time? We'll be there."

"First," Joy said, her gaze direct on her mother, "I need you both to understand that this is an assessment period."

Eyes narrowed, her mother glared. "What does that mean?"

"If either of you say anything to upset Jack, or hurt his feel-

ings in any way, I won't give you a second chance." She turned to the attorney. "And if that negates my inheritance, I'm fine with that."

"It won't," her father said, reaching out to take her hand. "All that your grandmother wanted was for you to give us a chance, and that's what you're doing."

"How do you know that?" Before now, Joy hadn't thought to wonder too much about her grandmother's motivation. She'd always loved Joy, always treated her kindly, but she hadn't interfered in family matters.

"I asked her to," Cara stated, her chin up. "And before you say I manipulated things, I'll freely admit that I did. You have stubbornly withheld our grandson and—"

"Mom," Joy said evenly, unwilling to engage in more anger, "you never asked to meet him."

"I shouldn't have to!"

Joy felt like she'd learned many things over the last six years, most of it valuable, some of it commonsense practice, but some of the lessons had been on what *not* to do. This, she decided, was one more lesson to learn.

Pride couldn't replace love. Stubbornness was downright destructive. And never, ever would she let either one keep her from those who meant the most to her.

Smiling toward Ms. Wickham, she said, "I should be going." She stood and pulled on her coat. Her father also pushed to his feet.

Her mother sat in stony silence…and then she seemed to burst. "We're not monsters."

Startled, Joy turned to her.

"We wouldn't do anything to upset our own grandson."

Realizing that she'd hurt her mother without meaning to, Joy nodded. "I only meant that he's a little boy with a child's vulnerability. He knows nothing about the reason for our…dis-

agreements. I expect you to keep it that way." She couldn't even begin to imagine how Jack would feel if he knew the truth.

When he was older, he might understand their reasoning, and that it hadn't been about him at all, not really. Their actions were because of Vaughn, and Joy's bad decisions.

But he didn't need to hear about it now.

Her mother's mouth tightened, then she gave one sharp nod.

Her father smiled. "Of course we wouldn't say anything. That's all better forgotten."

Joy knew she'd never forget, but she was willing to forgive. Going on tiptoe, she kissed her father's cheek. "I'll be in touch to let you know what day will be best."

Hugging her, he whispered in her ear, "Thank you."

Joy turned to her mother...and impulsively dropped a hand on her shoulder. "See you soon, Mom."

Cara's hand came up to cover hers, her grip firm for a heartbeat, then she nodded.

Well. That was something, right? A fragile beginning—which was better than a yawning void.

Joy felt better about things already.

Now to prepare Jack.

She got home in time to get him from school, and although it was cold, she walked with him to the playground.

Just for fun, she proved that she did, in fact, fit on the slide, even though she'd told him she was too big. Jack loved it.

Side by side on the swings, they talked about his day in school. Joy let him scamper over the jungle gym even though Royce wasn't there to catch him. She did her best, but she knew if he dropped, they'd both go down.

Later, as they walked to the apartment, Joy said, "There are some people I want you to meet."

Finding a pinecone, Jack picked it up to study it closely. "Who?"

"Actually, it's your grandmother and grandfather."

Scrunching up his nose, he looked at her. "I have those?"

Joy straightened his stocking hat to cover his red ears, letting her hand linger on his cheek. "Yes. They're my mother and father and I haven't seen them for a long time, but now we've talked and they want to meet you. What do you think of that?"

Shrugging, he turned his gaze down to his feet. "Do I have a dad, too?"

The question rocked her for a moment. Carefully, she chose her words. "You have a father, but he didn't want to stay with me."

"Did he want to stay with me?"

"Oh, honey, he's never met you or I'm sure he would have. You're pretty darned terrific."

"Will I meet him some day, too?"

Joy paused to squeeze his shoulder. "I don't know where he is now. I haven't seen him since long before you were born."

"I don't want to." He peered up at her. "Will I have to meet him, too?"

"No, you don't." Thank God. Worried, Joy asked, "Do you mind meeting your grandmother and grandfather?"

He turned the pinecone over in his hand. "How come you haven't seen them?"

Joy leaned back against a tree and stared toward the lake. How to explain something so complicated to a little boy? "We had an argument. I was stubborn, and my mother was stubborn, but I think we're making up now."

He leaned against her side, his hand catching her coat pocket to hang on as he swayed a little this way and that. "What did you argue about?"

"Silly things." She tried a smile and failed. "Dumb things." Joy crouched down to his level. "Maris invited them to the camp store. You can meet them there. What do you think?"

"Will you be there?"

"Yes." She caught his face between her hands. "I'll be right next to you. Plus everyone else will be there, too. Daron, Coop and Phoenix, Baxter and Ridley. It'll be like a party."

"With cake?"

Joy choked. "I will definitely get a cake. What kind do you want?"

"Chocolate."

"Done." Hoping it'd be that easy, Joy smiled. "I'll make sure there's a lot of icing, okay?"

He pretended a great interest in his shoes. "Will Royce be there?"

Shoot. Definitely not easy.

Joy's heart beat a little too fast. "I don't know, honey."

"Will you ask him?"

The thought of approaching Royce when he might not be interested made her mouth go dry, but for Jack, to make this introduction to his grandparents easier, she'd do it. "Of course I will."

"Promise?"

"Promise." And if Royce said no?

She couldn't imagine him doing that. He'd always been so great with Jack. No matter where their relationship now stood, she believed he cared about Jack.

Joy thought of all the time she'd wasted with her parents. With Grams. Yes, she'd wanted Royce to come to her, but did it really matter?

No, not in the larger scheme of things.

So why not tell him how she felt? Clearing the air now would make it easier if they saw each other in the future. He'd still be free to stay or go, but she wouldn't let miscommunication on her part cause her another sleepless night.

"Mom? Do you think they'll like me?"

"I think they're going to adore you."

Jack looked away. "Will I like them?"

Now that was the big question. "I hope so, but you can take your time getting to know them, and then we'll see." Joy kissed his forehead. "How about we go get dinner? You can help me make mac and cheese."

"Mac and cheese," he cheered, excited in his special little-boy way.

"Pan-fried hamburgers, too."

More cheers. Joy grinned as she watched him. She'd deliberately chosen his favorites for today.

He'd taken her news well. The only thing that could have made it better was if Royce and Chaos were joining them for dinner.

Tonight...and for the rest of their lives.

# CHAPTER SEVENTEEN

From the supply building, Royce saw Joy and Jack leaving the playground. As he'd watched them play, he'd badly wanted to join in. So had Chaos. The dog whined now as he saw them walking away.

The effort to hold back had Royce locking his teeth. God, he missed them both and it had only been a couple of days. He and Chaos had both gotten used to their company, and without it the days dragged.

"You're an idiot, dude."

Drawn from his thoughts, he turned to Daron. "Go screw yourself." Daron had been heckling him since he got to the park. Royce was starting to think it was the only reason Daron had asked for his help.

Shaking his head, Daron said, "Whatever. I'm too happy to let you bring me down with your sad-sack attitude. But," he added, "you could think about poor Chaos."

They both looked at the dog, who had just gone after Royce's laces. When he realized he was busted, he released the now-

wet, untied laces, flattened his ears and sat back, his big dark eyes apologetic.

Sighing, Royce dug a dog treat from his pocket.

"You realize you're rewarding him for doing the wrong thing."

"You said to give him something else to chew on."

Daron laughed. "It's a timing issue. You should give him something else *before* he attacks your shoes."

Royce blew out a breath. Today it seemed that everything amused Daron, and Royce knew why. He and Maris were officially engaged.

They deserved to be happy. "Why exactly did you ask for my help?"

"Good question, since all you've done is moon after Joy and Jack." Daron hefted another bag of salt and put it on a pallet.

Rolling his eyes, Royce looped Chaos's leash over the door handle and then went over to finish up for Daron. "There's not enough work here to need two grown men to do it."

"Eh, maybe. I took pity on you, though. Joy told Maris she hadn't heard from you, and Maris told me, and we're all trying to figure out why the hell you're sabotaging yourself."

Frustrated with the situation, Royce wondered what else Joy had said.

Did she miss him?

Was she excited about regaining family ties?

Royce worried for her, but he kept telling himself it would be better now because Joy was stronger, more independent. A woman to be reckoned with. She wouldn't take any shit from anyone, and she sure as hell wouldn't let anyone insult Jack.

Joy would own that situation, one hundred percent.

Daron stood in front of him, arms crossed, one brow cocked. "There you go again, wallowing in misery. What's up with you, man?"

Instead of answering that question, Royce said, "Come here. I want to show you something."

They walked out to his work truck and Royce lowered the back gate.

"What's this?" Daron asked.

"Before I moved here, I was a mobile sawmiller. I paid a driver to bring my trailer to me, along with some of my equipment. I was waiting for them to arrive and now that they have, I made something. For Maris, I mean."

Daron ran his hand over the highly polished plank of wood, then over the live edge. "This is beautiful. What do you mean it's for Maris?"

"I saw her working on the booth tops one day. They have a few stains and stuff... I thought I'd offer to replace the old tops. These would make the camp store more rustic, but they'd look great, don't you think?"

"I think you'll blow her mind." Daron bolted up into the truck bed to take another look. "This is a work of art."

Royce grinned. "My mother was an artist, but I never had the talent—except with wood." Maybe he'd shared more common ground with his mother than he'd realized. "I put two pieces together to make it wide enough. This is just a sample. I'd take measurements before doing any more, but I've missed working with my hands, so..." He'd missed Joy, too, so damn much. He'd needed a way to occupy his time and woodworking had always been a balm to his troubled thoughts.

Daron shook his head in awe. "She has ten booths. You know that, right?"

"There are more than enough trees between the drive-in property and the park to cover that. Some of the trees need to come down, anyway."

"Amazing." He met Royce's gaze with a grin. "I volunteer to

help in whatever way you need. Just let me know when you're ready."

"Great." At least he'd accomplished one good thing, then. Royce nodded. "Thanks."

"Hey, man, thank *you*. Maris is going to flip." He hopped back out of the truck and headed for the supply building. "You know how much she loves that store."

Yes, he did. "Glad I can do something to repay her." For all the coffees, the meals and her friendship.

"You know what'd really make Maris happy? For you to get your head out of your ass and go see Joy."

Yeah, it kept coming back to that. Royce took Chaos's leash and followed Daron into the building. While the dog sniffed around, Royce decided it wouldn't hurt to explain things. "You know Joy is going to make up with her parents."

"Maybe." Daron glanced at him. "So what?"

Damned if Royce knew how to articulate it. "She comes from wealth and privilege."

Suddenly Maris was there, rudely shouldering her way in around him. "What does her background matter?"

Without waiting for an answer, she grabbed Daron for a lusty smooch. "Hey, babe. Miss me?"

"Every second," Daron said.

Great. Just what Royce didn't need to see: nauseating happiness. "I should go," he said. "Let you two do—" he looked at them, all clutched together "—whatever you plan to do."

"Not until you explain," Maris said, turning to pin him in her gaze. "Joy is going through hell right now and you decide to bail? Don't you think she deserves better?"

Every muscle clenched in pain. "What do you mean, she's going through hell?" Yes, she'd been upset Monday night, but the entire day had gone wrong for her. By the end of their visit, she'd pretty much decided to reunite with her parents.

Plus he'd asked her to call him if she needed anything.

She hadn't.

"Hello," Maris said. "You met her mother. Would you be happy to deal with the Arctic Circle?"

Incredibly bothered by the idea of Joy still upset, Royce murmured, "Joy can handle her."

"Yup. My girl is badass. But she shouldn't have to do it alone."

No, she shouldn't. Tension gathered in his neck. "If she wanted my help, she'd have asked me."

"If you care," Maris shot back, "she shouldn't have to ask."

*If* he cared? Jesus, he loved her. "I didn't want to impose."

Daron choked, and gave him a pitying look.

He was starting to think he needed the pity. "All that money didn't faze her," he said defensively. Yes, Royce's own mother had made a nice living off her art, but she hadn't been wealthy. He knew nothing about a lifestyle where half a million dollars was chump change. "Know why it didn't faze her?" Maris asked, her tone sharp. "Because the money doesn't matter to her."

"Case in point," Royce barked back. "Who the hell doesn't care about that kind of cash?"

Shaking her head, Maris turned away. "You don't know half what you think you know."

"Maris," Daron said, chiding. "Let up a little. The guy's suffering, if you can't tell."

She stopped, drew a breath and nodded. "Okay, fine." She turned to Royce again. "Why. Are you. Not. *With her?*"

Instead of answering, Royce asked a question of his own. "Are you saying she turned down the inheritance?"

"Nope. But you'd already know that if you were talking to her."

Of course she hadn't. The money would go a long way toward taking care of Jack, securing his future, giving him things she couldn't give him before. Things Royce would never be able to

give either of them. "I just settled in here, Maris. If she's moving back with her family—"

"Are you for real? Acknowledging her folks and moving in with them are two very different things. Joy's happy here. She wants no part of that world."

Okay...wait. How could she take the inheritance and not be a part of it all? Confused, Royce said, "It's *her* world. She was born to it."

"So what? I came from poverty. My folks took handouts for food, hand-me-downs for clothes, and they didn't mind us being the neighborhood charity case—but you don't see me embracing it still."

That stopped Royce cold. Maris's family had been poor?

He couldn't imagine the proud, independent woman standing before him forced to live that way. He glanced at Daron and got his nod.

Shit. "I'm sorry."

"Don't be," she said with a shrug. "Made me who I am, and Daron likes me."

"I *love* you," Daron corrected. "Because, rich or poor, you're amazing."

Maris patted his cheek. "See, Daron gets it."

Yeah, he did. And they were so damn *happy.*

Wishing it could be that easy, Royce said, "This is different."

"No, it's not. Joy is the same. Her situation remains the same. You're the only one making it different."

Daron gave him another look. "She's not wrong, man."

Royce's heart suddenly pounded, his breath going shallow. As if to back them up, Chaos barked, turned a circle and stared at him. "No," he admitted. "Maris isn't wrong."

God, he'd let Joy down. He'd been so busy trying to second-guess things, assuming he couldn't fit into her rich lifestyle, he'd

really screwed up. No matter what, Joy was a beautiful person, and he loved her.

That was the only thing that mattered.

Lifting Chaos into his arms, he said, "Thanks, Maris."

"You're welcome."

Royce turned on his heel to walk away.

"Are you going to her?" Maris asked.

"Yes."

"Great. Give her my love," Maris sang after him, her tone rich with satisfaction.

Yeah, he would—right after he gave her his own.

Standing at the stove, Joy moved the hamburgers to a plate, making sure to keep Jack's away from the onions she loved. He'd helped her with the mac and cheese, and he'd chosen applesauce as an additional side dish, whereas Joy would have a salad.

They were ready to eat when the knock sounded on her door. Jack started to dart away from the table, but she said, "No, I'll get it," which at least slowed him down a little.

It might be Maris. Joy had made an extra hamburger just in case. But regardless, she didn't allow Jack to answer the door without her.

As she went to the window to peek out, he stuck close to her side.

It wasn't Maris.

Royce stood there, his expression stern. Maybe worried. He held Chaos in his arms, and at least the dog looked excited.

"Is it Royce?" Jack asked, his tone hopeful. "It's Royce, isn't it?"

Her smile felt a little sad. Jack had really missed seeing him the last few days. She'd planned to contact Royce later tonight, hoping she'd have a handle on things before Jack saw him again.

Now here he was, and she had no idea where they stood.

*"Mo-om,"* Jack complained, tugging at her shirt.

"Yes, it's Royce." She hesitated, wondering what to expect.

Jack squealed, bouncing with excitement. "Open the door, Mom!"

"All right. Hold your horses." Laughing, she opened the locks and, trying to be casual, greeted Royce. "Hi."

Jack ducked in front of her. "Royce!" He grabbed him around the legs, still bouncing, making Royce brace his feet apart or topple.

"What a welcome." Shifting the dog to one arm, Royce hefted Jack up with the other to bring him eye level. Grinning, he asked, "Did you miss me?"

"We did, didn't we, Mom?"

When Royce's dark-eyed gaze touched on her face, Joy avoided answering by stepping back. "Come on in."

"You can have dinner with us," Jack offered. "I helped cook it, didn't I, Mom?"

"Yes."

Royce hugged Jack close. "Bet it's perfect, then." Chaos was whining and wiggling, so Royce bent to lower both boy and dog to the floor.

No matter how many times they'd visited, Chaos always did an immediate inspection of the apartment. Nose to the floor, looking much like a furry vacuum cleaner, he began his excited tour.

"Jack," Joy said, "why don't you close the bedroom and bathroom doors so we don't have to worry about Chaos getting into anything?"

"Okay. C'mon, Chaos." They took off in a run together.

Normally Joy would have reminded him to come right back for dinner, but instead she looked at Royce. "Is everything okay?"

"No." He inhaled, filling his lungs, then slowly let out a breath. "I mean, I hope it is."

Joy tipped her head, confused but starting to feel as hopeful as Jack.

"Screw it." Royce brought her in close and bent his head to hers.

His lips brushed over her mouth, once, twice, opened just a little so his tongue could tease her bottom lip...and she felt herself turn to putty.

She'd missed him so very much.

"Joy?" he whispered.

She heard longing and apology in the way he said her name, and it did her in.

"I'm sorry." He feathered kisses against her cheek, over to her ear. "So damn sorry. God, I was an ass and now that I've realized it, I just..."

Hands to his chest, she looked up at him. "You just what?"

"I want to make it right."

Jack came flying back in, saw them together and slammed his brakes. "Whoa."

Chaos looked around in confusion, wondering why everyone had gone so quiet.

Flustered, Joy started to retreat, but Royce didn't let her go. "Do you mind if I talk to your mom for just a minute?"

Jack blinked at each of them in turn. "Are you going to stay for dinner?"

Royce looked to Joy, and she said, "There's enough if you're not too hungry."

"Yes," he said immediately, "I'd love to stay."

"Okay, then you can kiss her." Jack watched, making Joy snicker.

"Um..." Royce shifted. "How about you show Chaos your room again instead?"

Skeptical, Jack said, "All right. But I'll be right back."

"Don't let him chew anything," Royce called after him.

They watched boy and dog disappear down the short hall.

The second Jack's door closed, Royce framed her face in his hands. "I love you."

The declaration took her breath away.

"Who knows when he might come charging back in here," Royce explained, "and I needed you to know."

Trying to fill her lungs, Joy gasped. "I… You took me by surprise."

"It took me by surprise, too. But it's true." He pressed a firm kiss to her mouth and said again, "I love you, and I love Jack, too."

She steepled her hands over her mouth, suddenly over-whelmed. "Royce—"

"Just so you know, the money has nothing to do with it."

That made her blink. "What do you mean?"

He shook his head. "The money *does* matter. Hell, the idea of you inheriting that much spooked me. I thought it would change everything. Where you lived, *how* you lived."

That's why he'd acted so funny?

"I just meant that it's yours. Yours and Jack's. I want noth-ing to do with it."

"Never, not once, did I think the money would be a draw for you." But then, neither had she known that it would turn him away. Thinking about it now, she could see how disconcerting her cavalier attitude about a million dollars would be.

"Good." Royce cupped her shoulders in his hands. "What-ever you have going on with your parents, we'll figure it out. Maris said you had no interest in moving, but if you did, I'd fix up the house and sell it. I want you to know that. I wouldn't expect you to pass on better options—"

Laughing, a little giddy with happiness, Joy put her fingers

over his mouth. "Better options than you? Not possible." She opened her hand against his jaw. "I'm in love with you, too, Royce. But I'm not moving away from the area. This is home."

She saw the relief that stole the worry from his gaze, the way his big shoulders loosened. He crushed her close, lifting her off her feet to spin her in a circle, then setting her back again. After a big exhale, he admitted on a laugh, "I'm glad, because I like it here. I just need you to know that I could be happy anywhere, as long as I'm with you, and I'm sorry I didn't tell you that sooner."

That meant the world to her. "I was going to call you tonight, after Jack went to bed. I had it all planned, everything I'd say. Mostly that I loved you." Beneath her palm on his chest, she felt the steady thumping of his heart. "I was a little nervous about it, so thank you for telling me first."

"Maris was ready to kick my ass if I didn't." He grinned. "She and Daron—hell, everyone at the park apparently—knew I was making dumb assumptions." Royce put his forehead to hers. "I'm sorry I put us both through that."

She didn't yet know where their relationship was headed, but he loved her and that was a good start. "Before Jack returns, you should know that I turned down my mother's money. That was always a given. I'm ready to work with her, to try to have a peaceful future together, but that's as far as it goes."

He smiled. "Sounds like a generous compromise to me."

"I gave it a lot of thought." Talks with Maris had helped. "The bulk of the inheritance from my grandmother will go into a trust fund for Jack, with me as trustee so I can ensure that when he turns eighteen, he doesn't blow through it."

"No crazy fast cars?"

She grinned with him. "Exactly. He'll have options for college, trade school or an art academy if he's still into that when he's older."

"He will be," Royce said with assurance. "I'd bet on it." He

ran his hand over her hair, tucked it back and traced her lips. "I want a future with you, Joy."

Those words did more to brighten her than any amount of money ever could. Smiling, her eyes a little misty, she nodded. "I want that, too."

Jack crept in this time. "I'm getting hungry," he said as a bold hint, his gaze scrutinizing them both.

Accepting that details for their future would have to wait, Joy got another plate and served the food while Royce helped with drinks.

Thankfully, Chaos found a comfortable spot by the window and curled up to nap.

She'd gotten her very first bite in her mouth when Jack announced, "I have a grandma and grandpa."

Keeping his tone neutral, Royce replied, "I heard about that."

"Maris is going to have a party so I can meet them. Mom's getting me a cake."

"That sounds nice," Royce said.

He shrugged and glanced at Joy. Sotto voce, he asked, "Did you invite him, Mom?"

She bit back her smile. "I was going to call him tonight, but since he's here, you can invite him yourself."

Shy now, Jack muttered, "Will you come to the party?"

"Wild horses couldn't keep me away."

"Really?" Grinning, Jack said, "We'll all be there, right?"

Royce nodded. "Are you excited to meet your grandparents?"

Pushing his fork through his applesauce, his gaze on his plate, Jack said, "I'd rather have a dad." He cast a coy glance at Royce to gauge his reaction.

"Jack," Joy said softly. "I explained—"

"He's not here," Jack insisted in a burst, rushing out with, "Maybe Royce could be my dad?"

Clearly stunned, Royce dropped back in his seat, his fork suspended, his gaze locked on Jack.

Uncertain now, Jack whispered, "Would that be okay?"

Without a word, Royce nodded, swallowed heavily and then finally, *finally*, he smiled. "That would be incredible. Thank you."

Jack grinned. "For real?"

"No matter what, I'd love to be your dad."

He looked at Joy. "I'd also love to marry your mother."

Joy covered her trembling mouth. That was the most roundabout proposal she could imagine, but she loved it just the same.

Jack turned to her. "Will you, Mom?"

Smiling, Royce set aside his fork and said softly, "I love you, Joy. You love me. We both love Jack."

Jack grinned.

"Will you marry me?"

Nodding hard and laughing, Joy said, "Yes."

"Yes?" Jack asked, wanting it confirmed.

"Yes," they both repeated.

And Jack whooped so loudly he woke Chaos.

For the first time, of what Royce hoped would be many, he helped tuck Jack into bed.

"Will you be here in the morning when I wake up?" Jack asked.

"No." Royce wouldn't ask to stay the night until after he and Joy married. It was an old-fashioned idea, but Jack had enough new ideas to deal with right now. Royce didn't want to throw too much at him at one time. "I can come back over before you go to school, though."

"Okay." Jack hugged a stuffed dinosaur and turned on his side. In a hushed whisper, he asked, "When can I call you Dad?"

Unsure how to answer that, Royce deferred to Joy.

She smoothed Jack's hair. "Whenever you want to, honey."

His sleepy eyes grew heavy and he yawned. "Okay." Snuggling into his pillow, he grinned. "Good night, Mom..." He peeked one eye open. "And Dad."

Royce knew he'd never grow tired of hearing that. "Good night."

Joy took his hand and led him from the room. On the couch, she leaned against him, both of them quiet for a moment. Finally she said, "What a week it's been."

"I'm so damn sorry I made it worse."

"All in all, I think you made up for it. Jack loves you very much."

Every time he heard it, Royce liked it more. "I feel the same about him." He pulled her closer, saying, "He's such a happy kid, I'm surprised he missed having a dad."

"He didn't," Joy whispered, "until he met you."

"Then we're even. Kids are the biggest commitment of all, and I didn't think I wanted anything to do with them—until I met him."

She smiled, and pulled out her phone. "I only need a second."

Amused, Royce shook his head. "I'm not going anywhere."

Holding the phone so he could read the screen, Joy texted, Royce proposed.

A mere two seconds passed before a fist emoji appeared, along with the word YES!

"Maris?" he asked, already knowing it was.

"Yes." She put her head on his shoulder. "We share everything." She replied, Details tomorrow. Luv u & thx.

Luv u 2 & welcome!

Grinning, Joy set the phone aside. "She's with Daron. Otherwise, she'd be demanding details right now."

"They're happy."

"Very."

Royce cupped her face, turning it up for a soft kiss. *Soft*, because he would not get carried away.

They visited for another hour or so. Joy told him everything that had happened with her parents, and they made plans. Plans for tomorrow, next week and next year.

It was the start of a lifetime.

Royce thought he felt the tension more than Joy did. She presented a perfect picture of poise and serenity as she introduced Jack to her parents.

It never ceased to amaze him how she could pull it together for her son.

Music played in the background and their friends, friends that were more like family, chatted casually to each other to help make the moment less conspicuous for Jack.

Even Sugar and Chaos contributed by yapping at each other from the corner where they played.

It bothered Royce to see Jack so subdued. Since he'd known him, Jack had gotten chattier, more playful—and more affectionate. He hugged freely, sometimes even crawling into Royce's lap.

Yet today, in these circumstances, Jack had reverted to a very quiet, withdrawn little boy.

Standing protectively close, Royce put a hand on his small shoulder.

Jack looked at his mom first, then to Royce, before screwing his mouth to the side and taking a step forward.

He held out his hand, just as Royce had shown him.

Pride burned in Royce's chest. No doubt knowing exactly what he felt, Joy leaned into his side. He loved her so damn much that the urge to shelter her from this made his muscles clench.

And then tears sprang into Cara Reed's eyes.

Happy, emotional tears, Royce could tell, and that show of feeling humanized her more than anything else could have.

He and Joy shared a look of surprise.

Wallace grinned, accepting Jack's hand and then holding on gently.

Once Cara had fished out a tissue and dabbed at her eyes, she drew a steadying breath. With a smile that looked rusty, she said, "I'm your grandmother, Jack."

"I know," Jack said, sounding a little in awe. "Mom told me."

Wallace's grin widened. "Would you like to sit down and get acquainted?"

Jack glanced back at Joy again.

She said, "I'll be right here with you."

Next, Jack turned to Royce. "You, too?"

*I'd like to see someone stop me.* "You bet. We've got a booth right here." Royce gestured for Cara and Wallace to take one seat, and then Joy slid in opposite them, Jack in the middle, and Royce on the aisle side.

Sandwiched between them, Jack regained his precocious personality. Going to his knees, he studied both people. "I have Mom's ears."

At that announcement, Cara lifted her brows. "Hmm, perhaps you do." Gently, she reached out to touch his face. "Actually, you look very much like your mother when she was a little girl."

"I do?"

Wallace nodded. "You really do."

Jack scrunched his nose as he considered that. "Mom's hair is different."

"It wasn't when she was five," Cara said. "In fact, her hair stayed as light as yours until she was nine or ten. Her eyes were different, though. They were always that beautiful golden green shade. She got them from my mother."

Jack leaned closer to her, much as he had done to Royce when they'd met. "You have the same eyes."

Pleased, Cara preened. "Yes, I do. They're not as bright anymore, but oh, when I was young they were pretty."

As if she'd never heard her mother say such a thing, Joy blinked and her lips parted.

Wallace chimed in. "They're still very pretty, don't you think, Jack?"

Jack took in Cara's eyes the way only a young artist would. "They are. I could draw them if you want."

Wallace looked pleased. "Your mother said you're an artist?"

Rubbing his ear, showing a modicum of humility, Jack nodded. "Dad says I'm good, but that I'll keep getting better as long as I practice."

Gazes shot his way. Royce met them without flinching. They needed to know he was a part of Joy's life now. Never again would she have to face them alone.

Cara frowned at Joy. "I thought you said—"

"We're getting married," Joy stated. "We only recently decided and haven't set any definite plans yet."

As if to challenge any questions, Jack lounged back against Royce. "He's my dad *now*, though. Ain't that right, Mom? I don't have to wait."

"Absolutely right," Royce said.

Joy nodded with a smile.

Wallace studied them both. "Your mother and I would be happy to have a wedding for you."

Dread washed over Royce, but he manned up and stayed silent. If Joy agreed to some big fancy shindig, he'd muster through it.

"Thank you, but we'll handle it," Joy said. "We'll likely have the wedding here."

"Here?" Wallace gave a dubious glance around the camp store.

"In the lodge actually," Joy explained. "I've helped organize other weddings there." She shared a tranquil smile. "I *am* the recreation director, after all."

Cara's face had gone stiff and now remained that way.

Until Joy added, "We'd be pleased if you wanted to attend."

From that point, everything changed. He had a feeling Cara was on her best behavior for both Jack and Joy. Royce sat back and took it in, relieved for Joy because he knew a truce with her family would make her life easier.

Wallace had questions for Royce, too. It made sense that a father would be curious about his daughter's future husband. Cara's questions were a little more intrusive, and yet Joy had a way of curbing her tendencies by introducing people at the park.

When Maris joined them, Royce excused himself and let her have his seat. He stayed close—keeping vigil with Daron, who'd come with Maris.

Not that either of the ladies needed them.

They made a great team, finishing each other's sentences, playing off conversational topics, laughing at jokes no one but them understood.

Daron glanced at Royce, saying low, "Looks like we'll be sort of related."

With a meaningful glance at Cara and Wallace, Royce nodded. Voice low, he murmured, "Welcome to the family."

They both laughed, and soon everyone was there, crowded around that single booth.

Family newly reunited.

Friends who'd become family.

A future he'd never expected—that was better than anything he'd known to hope for.

★ ★ ★ ★ ★